Raven's

Justice

To Bob!
Best wishes
Roy French
July 2022

1

Also by Roy French

The Raven Series:

- Raven's Honor
- Raven's Return
- Raven's Fury
- Raven's Revenge
- Raven's Kiss
- Raven's Shadow
- Raven's Blood
- Raven's Lament

The Patrick Kelly Series:

- Whispers on the Wind
- The Black Rose

Dedication

For George

BOLLOX

Belfast, 1967

An army Land Rover crawled slowly past an intricately detailed paramilitary mural painted on a gable wall of a row of houses. The unbelievably young British squaddies were jammed inside like sardines wrapped in as much protective equipment as they could lay their hands on. All had cigarettes dangling from their lips, a welcome distraction from their endless patrol. SLR rifles lay across their laps, armed and ready, and nestled in their breast pockets were their first line of defense against a terrorist attack: their yellow card. Their rules of engagement were complex, a cruel joke foisted upon them by a committee of spineless politicians. If fired upon, they had to stop and shout a warning to whoever was firing at them and wave the yellow card before returning fire. It was the one piece of Standard Operating Procedure (SOP) steadfastly ignored by one and all.

In the mural, two masked gunmen carrying the ubiquitous terrorist special, an AK-47 — in all the murals all gunmen carried AK-47s — crouched as if on point. Between them, ornate lettering

proclaimed this was a UFF area (Ulster Freedom Fighters).
Between them, the Red Hand of Ulster, more of a fist really,
saluted the surrounding flags whose titles were undecipherable,
apart from the two obvious: the Union Jack and the Ulster flag.

Life went on despite the constant patrols and the bombs
and the shootings, the long-suffering population facing each day
with their shoulders hunched as if walking into a storm. Across the
street from the patrol, yells and whoops of excitement emanated
from three young boys who played in the nearby hills that
bordered the river. Oblivious to politics and the narrow-
mindedness of those who would not see them play together, the
three were fast friends and had been since they were able to walk.
Sean Daly, the only Roman Catholic in the group, grew up beside
David Allen and Neil Diamond. Despite their religious differences,
their families enjoyed a warm relationship, born of the trials of
hardworking families who had just enough to get by. They shared
milk, sugar, and whatever went short before the weekly payday
rolled around.

At the top of a hill, the three boys, all of ten years old,
paused for a moment to admire their handiwork. School was out
for the day, so now it was time for fun. Halfway down the slope sat
a mound of tightly packed soil that they had laboriously created as
a ramp for their bicycles. Ever the daring one, David wheeled his
bicycle to the front and threw his leg over.

"See yiz at the bottom," he yelled and launched himself
down the slope, pedalling furiously to build up a head of steam

before hitting the ramp. The others held their breath. Many of their other schemes had gone horribly wrong, resulting in painful scrapes or bruises, or worse still, landing in a patch of stinging nettles. Nettles were the absolute worst.

David hit the ramp perfectly and in a shower of dirt and debris found himself airborne, whooping as the bike flew through the air and landed several feet down the slope with a bit of a wobble. The others caught their breath as they thought he was going to lose it, but he fought it back under control and slid the bike around in a graceful arc. It had rained earlier in the day, and a huge, muddy puddle glistened just off the track at the bottom of the hill. A few more feet and David would have been in the middle of it.

"Fuckin' magic," yelled Sean, wheeling his bicycle to the edge. Climbing aboard, he too raced down the slope and into the air, screaming like a banshee. Seconds later, he too slid to a halt beside David, grinning from ear to ear.

They looked back up to the top of the hill. Neil appeared somewhat apprehensive as he faced the slope. "He's feared," David said, resting his arms across the handlebars.

"Aye, that he is."

"C'mon, Neil," David shouted. "It's as easy as anything."

"My wee sister could do it," shouted Sean, and they both laughed. Any comparison to the female species was always a huge motivator to demonstrate masculinity.

At the top, Neil wheeled his bike to the edge, climbed on, and started down the slope, his legs rising and falling like pistons.

"I knew that would get him going," Sean said. "I think he likes Martina."

Neil hit the ramp faster than either of the two, which had the result of launching his bicycle a lot higher in the air than the others. As they watched in horror, Neil started a slow spin as the front wheel came up level with his head.

"Jesus, Neil, let go!" David shouted, but it was too late.

With a great splash, Neil landed on his back in the muddy puddle with the bicycle on top of him. The others tossed their bicycles to one side and raced over to where Neil was slipping and sliding as he tried to in vain get out of the puddle. He looked a bit winded, his cheeks red with anger.

"Told you he'd make a bollox of it." Sean grinned, revealing a wide gap in the front of his face where his four front teeth used to be. "Now pay up."

David extracted a silver coin from his pocket, a whole shilling, looked at it longingly, and handed it over to Sean.

"Are you all right?" David asked, hefting the bicycle up off the ground and inspecting the tires. "Yer bike's okay."

Managing to get to his feet, Neil hurriedly looked at his saturated, muddy clothes, and did a quick inspection. Dirty was one thing, but ripped and torn resulted in an entirely different form of punishment. The others joined in. They knew the escalation process and quickly examined the back of Neil's clothes.

"Jesus, will you two leave me alone ... I hurt me arse," said Neil.

"Ach, dry your tears," said Sean.

"You'll be gerning like a wee'un in a minute!" laughed David. As he wiped off a patch of mud from the side of his pants, Neil's eyes widened at the torn seam that ran down a good part of his leg.

"Ah, Jesus, me ma'll kill me when she sees this!"

Their fun ended for the day, the boys wheeled their steeds down the street to the corner shop. Big bags of Maltesers were shared all around, courtesy of Sean's winnings. As they strolled out of the shop, trying to pull apart the packaging to get at the sweets, David heard a voice from over his shoulder.

"Okay, yiz wee shites, hand it over."

Turning, his heart sank at the sight of three of the older boys from the area peeling themselves from the wall and strolling over, their demeanour shouting that they were looking for trouble.

Skinners.

Brush cut hair, shirts, outlandishly coloured braces, baggy denim jeans, and well-polished Doc Marten boots completed the ensemble for each. David had endured his fair share of beatings from the bullies. For some reason he could never fathom, the oldest was named Murk. Murk was as mean as they came. Rumour had it that his father was a frequent guest of the local prison. Murk stopped directly in front of David and held out his hand.

David shook his head, defiant. "No way, pal, buy yer own…"

Neil and Sean stood off to David's side and slightly behind, one at each shoulder. Behind David's back, Sean looked over at Neil and shook his head. They knew what was coming, even if they did hand over the sweets.

"We're in for a hidin'," Neil said.

"Aye, that we are," Sean replied. "Wouldn't be the first one, though."

David stared at Murk, at the smirk on his face, then slid the bag of sweets into his pocket. The smirk disappeared.

"Fucking brave, aren't…" He didn't get to finish the sentence as David's fist crunched into his nose. Blood spurted. It was on. The others jumped in, fists flying, boots flying, a lot of grunting, groaning, and swearing. And then it was over.

The bullies walked away with their spoils, the three friends lying on the ground rubbing their bruises. David massaged his jaw, feeling a huge bruise rising on the side of his face. Blood streamed from Neil's nose, his eyes full of tears of fury, while Sean's left eye had started to swell.

"Well, that fuckin' hurt," Sean said.

"I got in one good punch," David said. "Did you see his face?"

9

"Yep," replied Neil. "It looks just like mine." He wiped his nose on a hanky. "Anyway, I'm away home for me tea. I'll see yous later."

"Aye, are we still going to do Oul Wright's place?" Sean asked.

"You bet, but we need to wait till it gets dark," David replied. "We don't want the oul bastard to see us."

*

Later that evening, in the back garden of a tiny house with well-lit rooms that cast palls of yellow out into the darkness, the three lads perched securely in the upper branches of an apple tree laden with fruit. Their faces were smeared with burned cork, just like real-life commandos. The raid had been planned with military precision in David's shed less than an hour ago. A long, thin plume of smoke rose from the chimney, and the smell of coal fire smoke hung heavy in the air.

They had worn their dark, heavy sweaters tucked inside their pants so that they could stuff the apples inside. David kept a close eye on the back of the house, where he could see Oul Wright moving about inside. The man, in his seventies, was an old curmudgeon who tormented the boys at every opportunity, the *latest being when he had slashed their football when they had kicked it into his garden by accident. It was time for payback.*

Sean was taking his time to pick the biggest and the best apples, while Neil was being less selective in the process. "For God's sake, Sean, will you hurry up?"

"Jesus," Sean hissed, "will you shut your face? Oul Wright will hear us, and then we'll all get it."

David, his sweater full of delicious apples, turned back to the house to keep an eye on things. It was his plan, so he needed to keep watch. The old man had come into the kitchen that looked out over the garden and was staring out into the darkness.

Neil noticed the same. "Oh shite, look, look he's staring out the window. I think he's seen us. Let's get out of here."

"Keep still, for God's sake," David hissed. "It's too dark to see anything!"

The old man walked across the kitchen with a pronounced limp and opened the back door, yellow light spilling out into the yard.

"Shite, he's coming," David said, clambering down the tree and dropping the last few feet to the ground. There was a loud thud as Sean landed beside him, a couple of apples bouncing free from his sweater. In the distance, Oul Wright made his way across the garden. He walked with a cane, which slowed him down. They were still enveloped in darkness, so he could only see shadows moving in the gloom. Then his voice cut through the night.

"Yiz wee hoors ... I'll wring your bloody necks."

As David and Sean headed for the back fence, Neil put his foot on a rotten branch. There was a loud, sickening crack as it snapped, and he plummeted out of the tree and slammed into the ground, knocking the breath out of him.

The old man was on him in a flash. "I've got you now, you wee bastard. It's a hiding for you and them others tonight, and that's a fact." On the other side of the fence, well hidden in shadows, David and Sean looked on in horror as Oul Wight raised the cane and slammed Neil viciously across the back. A loud cry pierced the night, followed by sobbing.

"Bastard," David, said under his breath. "There's no need for that." He emptied his sweater full of apples onto the ground then stomped every one under his heel. It gave him some small measure of satisfaction that he knew would be short-lived. It was going to be a hard night.

*

In the tiny living room of their council flat, John Allen, David's father, stared into the embers of the coal fire, shaking his head in disbelief. He had been unceremoniously summoned home from the local police station by his wife, which was never a good thing. Fortunately, it was a quiet night, and he was able to slip out for a few minutes. As head of the Mobile Support Unit, he was in charge of the teams of riot police who were being called out more and more frequently to handle the sectarian conflict.

At forty-five years old, he was short in stature but wiry, and tough as nails, as his opponents on the soccer field found out the hard way. At the moment, however, he struggled to keep his composure. Running his fingers through closely cropped dark hair now kissed with grey at the temples, he slid off the belt from his police uniform. Then, wrapping it around one hand, he angrily stubbed out his cigarette, sparks shooting everywhere.

Beside him, his boyhood friend Bill Ellis touched him on the shoulder. Bill had just returned home from a tour of duty overseas and wore his army uniform, his sand-coloured beret tucked into an epaulet on one shoulder. He was Uncle Bill to young David. On his breast pocket rode the winged dagger insignia of the Special Air Service regiment. Longish blonde hair fell over a hard face worn by the constant conflicts faced by his chosen career. A ragged, whitish scar ran down one cheek, and part of one ear was missing. Tough men, one and all, there was a reason they were renowned as the world's elite commandos.

He touched John on the shoulder, a conciliatory gesture. "Come on, John, they were only nicking a few apples. Do you really need to do this?"

"Listen, Bill," John replied, "that mean old bastard will raise all sorts of holy hell at the station if I don't. Besides, the lad needs to be taught a lesson."

"Well, go easy on him then. It's not like you and me didn't ever raid a fuckin' apple tree! And sometimes worse…"

John nodded, then shouted, "Come in here."

David, waiting nervously in the hallway to be summoned, had heard the exchange. Uncle Bill was always standing up for him.

As Bill walked out of the living room, he ruffled the young lad's hair. "Sorry, son, I tried," he said to a sorrowful-looking David. "In ye go."

Inside the living room, David faced the wrathful look on his father's face and took in the thick leather belt hanging from one wrist. It wouldn't be the first time he had gotten the strap, but he was wondering how many it would be. For really, really bad stuff it was always ten, and for lesser transgressions he got five. Robbing Oul Wright was probably a tenner, so he braced himself for the worst.

"You know what to do," ordered his father.

David obediently dropped his trousers and bent over the armchair, every muscle tensing at the sound of the belt arcing through the air. His father whacked him five times hard across the buttocks, each blow stinging like fire. He felt tears come but gritted his teeth, fighting them back. Take it like a man, he told himself.

After five harsh strokes, his father stood back and refastened his belt. "Let that be a lesson to you. Caught stealing, and you, a copper's son. Jesus, will you never learn?"

David gingerly pulled up his trousers. His father had turned back to the fire, and David felt saddened by the whole thing. It was not that he regretted stealing the apples. Oul Wright just let them rot on the ground anyway, but it was the fact that he had disappointed his father, the one man he looked up to. He walked slowly out of the living room into the hall to where Bill Ellis waited. The motion of his trousers chafing the welts on his buttocks brought a whole new wave of agony. He was on the verge of tears again.

Ellis stepped forward and put his hand on David's shoulder. He felt the comforting power of the man's grip radiating through his fingers. "The old bastard's standing outside, son, with your mother. Your mates are down the street waiting for you, so don't let him see you cry."

David walked out the front door and into the tiny covered porch to where Oul Wright was standing with a smug look on his face. His mother wore a stern look, but she was his mother, and pain was pain. He paused in front of Oul Wright, fighting the urge to spit on the curmudgeon's face.

"I'm sorry for stealing your apples, Mister Wright," he said, forcing out the words, every bone in his body rebelling against the apology.

"Well, that's better," Oul Wright said with a smirk. "I hope you've learned your lesson."

David nodded. Now was the time to keep his mouth shut. He made his way down the street to Sean's house then went around the back to the garage where they hung out. Inside the empty garage, fishing gear hung on the walls, and a solitary light bulb hanging on a wire illuminated the space. Two well-used bicycles leaned against the exposed bricks. Every garage had fishing gear hanging off the walls. With the Braid River in close proximity and an abundant supply of sizable rainbow trout available, most people who lived on the street could be found at their favourite spot on the riverbank at all hours of the day and night. On the floor were lined many pairs of Wellington boots of various sizes and colours. Sean and Neil waited until the door closed behind David.

"How many did ye get?" Sean asked.

"Five of the best," David replied.

Neil's face wrinkled up in sympathy. "Better than ten, I suppose," he commented.

"Did you get the dandelions?" David asked, looking for relief using the old faithful remedy.

"Aye," Sean replied, holding up a canvas bag full of yellow-topped stalks. "I got stacks of them, just in case!"

David dropped his trousers and bent over the bench in the garage. Behind him, Sean and Neil looked at one another in surprise at the huge, angry red welts layered across his buttocks. Blood was seeping to the surface on one of the larger welts. They had all been there.

Neil said, *"Jesus, that looks awful!"*

Sean glared at him.

"For God's sake, get on with it, me arse is on fire!" David exclaimed.

Sean and Neil grabbed clumps of dandelions, cutting off the bottoms with their well-honed penknives. Holding the stalks upright to allow gravity to work its magic, they waited for a moment until the milky white sap pooled at the bottom of the cuttings. When there was sufficient liquid, they gently dabbed at David's lashes with the end of the stalks to coat the area with the white milk. It was a renowned remedy, but sometimes getting it on was difficult.

Gritting his teeth, David groaned, "For God's sake, will you take it easy?"

Behind them, the garage door opened, and Sean's older brother Shamus walked in. He took in the scene, gazing at all three lads. He didn't say a word, but the expression on his face as he moved from face to face told the story. Turning on his heel, he walked out, shaking his head and muttering, "Yiz wee perverts!"

A couple of hours later, the pain now reduced to a dull throb, the whine of the firehall siren roused David from sleep, and he immediately rolled on to this back, a move he instantly regretted. He had gone to sleep lying on his side to keep pressure off the tender parts. The dandelions had done their work, but it would be several hours before he could sit comfortably again.

"Ahhh," he groaned, his buttocks on fire, and rolled back on to his side. The pitch of the siren increased, and he pictured the local firemen racing from their homes to the station to get the big pumper out on the road. The fire station was less than a mile away, and soon the clanging of the bell filled the air, increasing in volume until he realized it was coming in his direction. Climbing out of bed, he raced for the window, pulled back the curtains, and saw the glow. It took him a moment to realize that the apple tree in Oul Wright's back garden was ablaze, a raging inferno hurling plumes of smoke and sparks spiralling into the heavens. It was a windy night, the strong breeze fanning the flames. Glowing embers flew into the air like a million fireflies. Already some of the neighbours had congregated in the street to gawk at the spectacle.

As he followed the frantic activity, he saw Oul Wright. Dressed in a striped nightshirt and wearing white woollen socks, he pulled the back door open and stared in shock at the conflagration. The clanging ceased as several firemen raced around the side of his house, dragging long, flexible canvas hoses that spun off massive reels. Training their fierce stream on the blaze, they unleashed a storm of water over the tree.

Movement caught his eye. Off to one side, David stared at a dark shadow walking up the laneway behind Oul Wright's house. The figure paused and lit a cigarette, holding the lighter for a few more seconds than necessary. David could see that it was his Uncle Bill, dressed from head to toe in black. As he looked on, a *wide grin splitting his young face, the figure saluted him and vanished.*

CHAPTER 1

BRUTAL

London, present day

"Honest, Max, I don't fuckin' know where he is..." On his knees like a supplicant at mass, Roger "the Dodger" Thompson hawked up a great gob of bloody spittle and launched the projectile off to one side, careful to avoid the well-polished shoes of those around him. The motion created a searing, knife-like sensation in his side. A couple of ribs were gone, that much he knew from past experience. Every breath hurt. He was shirtless, hands bound behind his back, his once handsome features bruised and bloody from the constant beating he had endured for the past two hours. His one-time boss, Sean Dempsey, and a trusted lieutenant of Max DeLisle, had done a runner with about five million pounds of Max's funds, and Max understandably wanted it back.

The bank heist had gone down flawlessly, just as Max had predicted it would. Roger drove the getaway car and dropped Dempsey and the other robber off at the warehouse where he now knelt, his blood seeping on to the dusty concrete floor. The car had been left in the back streets of Brixton with the keys in the ignition.

It was probably gone before Roger had reached the end of the street and would most likely by now be in a thousand pieces in a chop shop. They were supposed to hook up the following day at Dempsey's flat, down in the Isle of Dogs, but when they got there, they discovered that Dempsey had fled.

Knowing well what would happen, they split up and spent the following day trying to find where he had gone, but there wasn't a whisper. In desperation, Roger had been going around Dempsey's usual haunts, the Irish shebeens in Kilburn. He was leaving one of the pubs when he ran into Max's goons and ended up blindfolded, lying on the cold, worn concrete floor of the warehouse. A trip to Max's warehouse did not bode a good outcome.

When they took the blindfold off, he almost puked when he realized the other robber hadn't been able to produce any information either. He too lay on his back on the ground, his headless corpse leaking fluids on to the ground. His head, removed with a butcher's dexterity by Max, sat upright on his ample stomach staring across the few feet directly at Roger.

Roger had made the mistake of watching a video posted on a website called ogrish.com, a place where people posted some of the most macabre images and videos he had ever seen. There were accident scenes, surgery scenes, autopsy photographs, and a miscellany of crime scene photographs all posted by categories that defied belief. And then there were the videos. Some wag down at the pub had been going on about it, calling it Jihadi porn, so Roger checked it out.

The first shaky video showed a ragtag bunch of Chechen rebels who had captured a young Russian soldier. The soldier, who appeared to be barely out of his teens, looked a bit out of it, sitting on the ground with his hands bound behind his back. One of the rebels walked over, raised his pistol, and shot the soldier in the shoulder. Roger was sure the rebel was going to execute the soldier with a bullet to the head. From his years in the London underworld, that was something he understood.

Payback.

Vengeance.

The young soldier looked a bit teary-eyed but didn't utter a sound. Not until the rebel pushed him over on his side, took out a wicked looking bowie knife and started sawing away at the soldier's throat. Roger looked on in horror as blood geysered out onto the grass, the young man's legs twitching as his life bled away. The rebel was really going at it by then, and presently the blood-splattered head came off completely. Holding it aloft, he proudly showed it off to his fellow rebels then wiped his knife on the corpse and positioned the head on the man's stomach. That image still haunted him.

Around him in a semicircle, dressed in their trademark black suits and ties, stood Max's three enforcers, all looking totally unconcerned for his plight. They looked like something out of *The*

Matrix. It was a scene they had witnessed many times. Roger, like them, knew well the punishment inflicted on those who dared to cross Max. If you were lucky, it was a quick bullet to the back of the head and then your body tossed unceremoniously into the backwaters of the Thames. But when Max wanted something, and he suspected you were holding out, then came the roughing up followed by … well, Roger didn't want to dwell on the next part. It was looking at him.

His immediate problem was trying to convince Max that he hadn't a clue where that fucker Dempsey had pissed off to, and try as he might, he couldn't come up with a simple answer. Unfortunately for him, there wasn't a single nugget of information he could provide that would prevent the obvious. His bladder threatened to give out, and he fought hard to prevent that shameful warmth. In front of him stood Max, dressed in his long black lambskin coat, a pair of bloodied black leather gloves on his hands. Under the jacket was a five-grand suit, handmade by Gieves and Hawkes, the preeminent tailor from Savile Row. As Max was fond of saying, "All the best villains get their suits made at Gieves and Hawkes."

At forty-four years of age, Max DeLisle had risen quickly through the ranks of the London mob. His reputation as a hard and brutal man was well deserved. From the early days working in his father's butcher's shop on Marylebone Street in the downtrodden, blue-collar docklands, Max was quick with his fists. School held no interest for him, and at thirteen he quit and worked for his father full-time. At the ripe age of eighteen he joined the British army, mainly to get out of London for a while. He did an eight-year stint as a sniper with the parachute regiment, firstly in the bloody conflict that was the Falklands, but most of the time was spent on the mean streets of Belfast and Londonderry. Max was in charge of one of the patrol groups during Bloody Sunday, one of the most notorious of the incidents that was to occur during the "Troubles" in Northern Ireland.

Bloody Sunday, sometimes called the Bogside Massacre, occurred in the Bogside area of Derry, during a civil rights protest in which twenty-six unarmed protesters and bystanders were shot by British paratroopers. The march had started out peacefully, but at a certain point, reports of an IRA sniper operating in the area were allegedly given to the army command centre. Shortly afterward, Brigade HQ gave the British Parachute Regiment permission to go into the Bogside and disperse the rioters. Much to Max's delight, the order to fire live rounds was given, and one young man was shot and killed when he ran down Chamberlain Street away from the advancing troops. This first fatality was among a crowd who were running away from the army, attested to by the fact he was shot in the back.

Continuing violence by British troops escalated, and eventually the order was given to mobilize the troops in an arrest operation, chasing the tail of the main group of marchers to the edge of the field by Free Derry Corner. Despite a frantic cease-fire order from the army HQ, the blood lust was up, and over a hundred rounds were fired directly into the fleeing crowds by troops. Max had personally killed five.

A tiny crescent-shaped scar sat high on his right cheekbone under one eye, a gift from an IRA sniper who was just a fraction of a second too late in pulling the trigger. The tactics Max learned during the conflicts had served him well after his discharge from the army. His opponents never saw him coming. The leather coat showed off powerfully built shoulders, toned and ripped by a brutal daily fitness regimen, a carryover from his time in the army. He wore his dark hair short. The handsome features ensured he was never lacking for female companionship — a bit of "strange," as he put it — given he was engaged to a former Miss London.

Max removed his gloves and rubbed his nose. Beside Max stood Lefty, a former boxer who ran the extortion rackets in East London and was called upon from time to time to put his pugilistic expertise to good practice. Ten years Max's senior, he could still splinter a rib with a single punch. Roger had heard his own crack like dry twigs snapping.

Max shook his head sadly. "So what do you think, Lefty? Think he's telling the truth, or is he giving us a few porky pies?" At that moment his cellphone rang, and he slipped it out of his jacket and peered at the display screen. The caller name said "Dawn."

"I gotta take this," he said. Picking up a well-honed blade from the table, he made a few slashing movements in front of Roger then stepped away from the group. Gravel and the remnants of broken bottles scrunched under his feet. Some feral creature skittered away in the dark corners. "You have a good little think while I take this," he hissed.

Flipping the phone open, he smiled and said, "Hello luv, how are things?"

"Max, Max, you've got to get down here," said a very excitable effeminate voice, but not one he was expecting. It belonged to Cyril, an interior decorator he and Dawn had again hired to renovate his latest acquisition, a stately home set in the idyllic countryside near Abridge, a few miles north of London. It had been sitting empty for a couple of years until the legalities had been settled, and when Dawn first laid eyes on it, the deal was done. For him, the fact that it was close to Stapleford private airport provided an additional incentive, as he needed to make the odd unscheduled flight over to Europe. His expanding business empire required the protocol of a face-to-face meeting with other crime bosses in the south of France, Germany, the Netherlands, and Albania. The house's previous owner, a Major James Skinner, had been blown to pieces by an IRA bomber, and it had taken some time to track down any surviving relatives to handle the transfer of the estate.

Dawn had gone out immediately and rehired Cyril, a proper "nonce" in Max's opinion, but the man certainly knew his stuff when it came to decorating. His skills were much sought after in the city, his waiting list of influential and wealthy clients a decorator's wet dream, yet when Max called all projects were put on hold until Max's country house was completed. Cyril knew what he was dealing with.

Their ten-thousand-square-foot designer loft in the docklands, overlooking the Thames, astounded anyone who had ever been invited, and they entertained a great deal. So Cyril's sexual mores were tolerated. But barely.

Max took a deep breath. "What are you doing with Dawn's phone, Cyril?"

"I don't have your number, Max, and besides you've got to get down here quickly…"

"I'm in the middle of a fucking meeting, Cyril. What's so fucking important?"

"Aah, we've found something…"

"Unless it's buried fucking treasure or a fucking body, I'm busy. Got it?"

"Yeah, Max. We took down that one wall you had asked for, to open up the kitchen. Well, there was a secret room in there, and it's chock full of documents — military stuff. Says 'Top Secret' in red letters on a lot of it, and there's pictures all over the walls."

Max paused for a moment, trying to recollect what he had heard about Major Skinner. In the papers it said he had been in charge of all intelligence operations against the paramilitary outfits on both sides of the conflict in Northern Ireland. He vaguely recalled that he had met Skinner once or twice, but it was over twenty years ago. It had been at the beginning of some joint operation with a bunch of those fucking SAS pit bulls who had uncovered a plot to blow up a police barracks. Max and his team had provided a wide perimeter while the SAS put themselves in harm's way. It was a good night in terms of body count, with twelve IRA gunmen on the plus side of the ledger. That was the only time he had crossed paths with Skinner.

However, knowing that the Provos had claimed responsibility for the bomb that killed him, Skinner had obviously pissed a lot of people right off.

Given his military background, Max knew the importance of intelligence-gathering. It was something he had carried over into his present career, and he presently had a long list of informants providing him with up-to-the-minute chatter about what was going on in his empire. He also knew the value of such things, so he recognized a perfect opportunity when it came calling. "Okay, Cyril, stay the fuck away from it, and keep Dawn out of there as well. I'll be down shortly."

He flipped the phone closed and took a moment to contemplate the gift he had possibly been handed. He knew that toward the end of the Troubles, the IRA had been heavily into drug smuggling, extortion, gambling, and every other illegal activity that could be used to supposedly finance their war chest. However, Max knew they were just lining their pockets. The higher-ups in the organization could see the writing on the wall and knew it was just a matter of time before the guns would be put away for good.

Real estate prices in Majorca had soared due to the demand from ex-Provos; the standing joke was that it was now called Costa del Provo.

Slipping the phone back in his jacket, he turned back to the group and strode over to where Roger cowered. "Please, Max," he begged, thinking his time had come. Max hunkered down in front of him and placed the tip of the blade against the inside of one nostril. A ruby red trickle of blood from his shattered nose ran down the blade.

"Listen, you fuck, and listen good. You've got two days to get me a whisper about Dempsey. If you don't, we won't be having another conversation. Got it?"

Rodger nodded weakly, trying desperately hard not to move against the sharp blade. Both eyes were almost swollen shut. Lefty was a master at his game. "I'll get you something, Max, I fucking will. The cunt double-crossed me as well. He'll be well done, I promise."

Max stood up and handed the knife to Lefty, who wrapped it up with the others. "Take care of this piece of filth," he ordered. "I've got to take a run up the country."

"Need a driver, Max?" asked one of the enforcers.

"Nah, it's a nice day for a drive in the country, so I'll see you all later down at the pub."

*

The drive took almost an hour, but the sun was shining and the Clash were on the CD player as he tore down the motorway, the roof of the Mercedes SLK350 convertible stowed away in the trunk. Smoking in the car was a bit of a no-no, and Dawn had been pestering him to give them up. *Old habits die hard*, he thought, tossing the remains of the fag away into the slipstream.

Max roared down the narrow, gravelled laneway, the heavy tires churning up clouds of dust in his wake. He slid to a halt beside the fountain, where a clichéd marble cherub stood pissing into the air, the graceful arc landing amongst the lily pads. Max loved the ancient decoration, aged with grime and worn down by the relentless assault of years of constant wind and rain. Outside the house sat three workmen, their overalls decorated with dust and plaster, sipping from flasks of tea and munching on sandwiches. Their truck stood off to one side of the driveway.

"Lads," Max said by way of greeting, and they all nodded. "Why don't you all fuck off for the day?" Taking two, fifty-pound notes from his wallet, he tossed them on the ground at their feet. "Have a drink or two on me. But be back in the morning sharpish, you hear, or you'll answer to me."

They nodded vigorously. They knew better than to cross Max.

Inside the house, he walked from room to room, eventually finding his fiancée sipping tea with the decorator in a glassed-in gazebo filled to overflowing with tropical plants. It looked like a miniature jungle. Setting down the cup, she sprang to her feet and kissed Max hard on the lips. He inhaled her scent and delighted in the feel of her skin under her thin dress.

"Hi, Max," said Cyril. Dressed outrageously as always in silk pants, a silk shirt and a cravat, Cyril was the epitome of gay. "I expect you want to see the stuff?"

Max nodded. "I sent the lads home for the day. I want to spend a bit of time with the info you found. And remember, not a fucking dicky bird to anyone!"

Cyril blanched and pulled his fingers across his lips. "Mum's the word, Max."

Cyril got up and led the way through the demolished kitchen, sashaying past the library and into the sitting room, where he pointed to a broken bookcase. Max pulled it away from the wall, surprised at how little effort it took. He realized it was hinged and stepped into a tiny room that contained a desk, a couple of filing cabinets, a desktop computer, and a black leather executive chair. A docking station for a laptop computer sat empty. A thin layer of dust coated everything, and spiders had been busy in the corners. The chair was the only piece of modern furniture. The walls of the room, floor-to-ceiling cork tiles, were mostly covered with documents and pictures, all pinned securely in place. The top drawer of the cabinet was half open, and a few manila folders, all bearing the imprint MOD (Ministry of Defence) with the words "Top Secret" across the top lay on the desk.

Max, having served in Northern Ireland, immediately recognized some of the faces in the pictures on the wall. Some were leading Irish Republican Army (IRA) gunmen, some Ulster Volunteer Force (UVF) gunmen, but all nasty pieces of work. There was even a picture of Gerry Adams and Martin McGuinness, presently key members of the new political assembly in Northern Ireland. Back in the day they would happily have dispatched their now political counterparts with a bullet. Some photos had a large black X through them, which Max interpreted as meaning only one thing.

Deceased.

A six-by-four map of Belfast, Skinner's main base of operations, was glued to the wall, beside it a map of Londonderry, the other major city, and on an adjacent wall a map of the entire province of Ulster. Across the surface of both were inserted a multitude of push pins of different colours. Max guessed these had represented ongoing operations, places of interest, or even safe houses. Tracing some of the streets with his fingers, he remembered being out on patrol in these spots and thought back to the angry faces and the open hostility of the people that he and his team had once been called in to protect.

It was an evil fucking place.

Flipping open some of the manila folders, he scanned quickly over reports of ongoing operations from several years ago, assessed their value, and then tossed them aside. It was a well-known fact that the Special Forces teams operating in the province had secreted weapons, munitions, and funds in various caches for easy access, and if they were still in existence, they could be a lucrative source of income.

With Britain's strict gun laws, the criminal element was always looking to acquire or rent weapons for various jobs, and Max held a goodly part of the supply. He rented out guns for a fee and then took a cut of the loot, so for him there was no downside. The fucking Yardies, violent, Jamaican-born gangsters, loved anything big and nasty when it came to weapons, so Max felt he was on a winner here.

Opening the cabinet, he scanned the top drawer of files, peering intently at the coding structure on the plastic tabs. The major was nothing if not meticulous about keeping things in order. Sliding the top drawer shut, he opened the middle drawer to find another complete set of documents. The bottom drawer held a similar trove.

"Fuck me," Max exclaimed aloud. "Someone put on the fucking kettle and get me a brew. I'm going to be here a while ... and see if there are any biccies." Like any good operator, Max understood the value of intelligence. That was one of the reasons he had been so successful in his current reign. He had made it a point to gather as much information on the competition as possible, as well as prominent figures in the legal establishment and the police force so that he could exploit their weaknesses. Whatever their vice, be it drugs, prostitutes, or aberrant versions of porn,

Max could satiate their cravings, all the while milking them for any nuggets of information that could be used to line his pockets.

He settled himself into the chair, which was oddly comfortable, smiling to himself as he thought of the major sitting here, plotting and scheming like Machiavelli. God only knew how many lives had been ended from this place. Placing his cellphone on the desk, he switched it to mute, not wanting any interruptions. Then, picking up the first file, he began to read.

Four hours later, he had just made it through the first drawer, sorting the files into those that warranted closer inspection and dumping those that he felt were irrelevant on to the floor. Placing his hand on the side of the china teapot, he felt it cold to the touch. It was time for another brew. He was about to yell at Cyril when he decided it might be time to have a break. Easing himself out of the chair, he stepped back out into the room and walked back through the house to the gazebo. Cyril was nowhere to be seen, but his fiancée was happily ensconced in one corner of a chaise long, her shapely legs tucked under her, flipping through a pile of magazines. She looked up and smiled.

"So, love, are you having fun?" she asked.

Max nodded. "Wouldn't exactly call it fun, but it's interesting. Where's Cyril?"

"I sent him back to the city," she replied, unfurling her toned legs. Her dress rode up, exposing well-tanned thighs, and Max felt his heart rate flutter. "We're all alone..." Her legs parted provocatively, and she licked her lips, teasing him. She knew what buttons to press. The dress rode higher, and he could see that she was not wearing panties. Stepping across to the chaise longue, he knelt down in front of her, unzipped his pants, and dropped them to the floor. She spat on her fingers and spread the slick fluids between her legs, toying with her clit as he pumped his hardening cock, just inches from her. Filling his mouth with saliva, he leaned over and dripped it onto her pussy then pressed the tip of his cock against her glistening lips. He held it there, luxuriating in the moment. Her fingers grabbed him and teasingly rubbed the head up and down, gasping with pleasure at the sensation.

His balls ached, and, unable to prolong the teasing, he grabbed her hips and thrust himself hard into her, a low growl escaping his lips as he held her there, impaled. He felt her muscles twitch inside, the sensations unbelievable. He pulled out until only the head of his cock remained inside then thrust violently into her. His hips ground against her, and she grabbed his forearms tightly, encouraging him loudly to slam into her.

"Come on, Max," she groaned, "that's it, that's it. Fuck me hard, slam that hard cock into me." He responded to her, matching her rhythm as she thrust hard against him, her face flushed and her eyes staring directly into his. Grabbing one of his hands, she took his fingers deep into her mouth and sucked furiously, moaning all the while.

Most times when they had sex, they could play together for hours, bringing each other to the sweet edge of release and then backing off. The final orgasm was usually blinding in intensity. It was one of things he loved about her; there were no inhibitions, no pretenses, and she genuinely loved to fuck. On other occasions, like now, it was pure animalistic lust. He knew he was approaching that final moment, and she knew it too. Picking up the pace, he was almost lifting her body off the chaise with each thrust, burying himself as deeply as possible. Stars danced behind his eyelids, and he roared in pleasure as he erupted inside her, feeling himself spurting over and over again until he collapsed on top of her, his heart pounding.

"Sorry, love," he whispered. "I couldn't fucking wait."

She kissed his forehead. "That's alright. Since Cyril left I've been playing with myself all afternoon. I'm one or two ahead of you."

"That's my girl." He laughed and pushed himself upright. His glistening cock slipped out of her in a gush of cum, and she squealed. "Fuck me, Max, been keeping it bottled up, have you?" Pulling her panties from under a pillow, she stanched the flow then went rushing off giggling to the washroom.

Max pulled his pants back up then headed off to the kitchen. She joined him a few minutes later, kissing him on the cheek. "So what are you up to tonight?" she asked. "Are you coming back to the city, or are you going to stay here?"

He sighed. "Were we supposed to do anything tonight?"

"No, love, we said we might see Billy K and the boys at the club, but that was all."

"Alright then, why don't you drive down to the village and get us some grub. There's a lot of stuff here I want to go through, and it'll probably take me a good part of the night. You can head back into the city after if you want, 'cos it'll be pretty boring for you. You can round up a few of the girls and amuse yourselves. I'll sleep here and come back tomorrow when I'm done with the files. That way I won't hold up little Cyril either, 'cos he's an expensive little fucker." The kettle boiled over, steam hissing from its spout, and the device clicked off.

"All right then," she said, brightening. "Curry and chips it is!"

CHAPTER 2

BELLIGERENT

Daniel Riordan clicked on the link for liveireland.com, selected the
contemporary Irish music button, and waited for a few moments
for the site to load. He would listen to the radio station for hours on
end while he worked on some problem or other, the Celtic
heartbeat his version of white noise. On occasion he would fire up
the webcam and contentedly watch pedestrians walking down the
cobblestoned streets of the Temple Bar district in Dublin, an up-
and-coming entertainment area of the city. The haunting sounds of
Simple Minds playing the Irish classic "Belfast Child" drifted from
the Bose sound system connected to his computer, and he adjusted
the volume slightly. Minimizing the screen, he opened the folder
on the desk beside him and started scanning the pertinent details.

Once the most feared paramilitary enforcer during the
Troubles in Ireland, a deadly assassin known only as the Raven, he
had fled the country on the heels of a bullet, started a new life on a
new continent, and for a while the torment of growing up in
Belfast seemed like a distant memory. Then tragedy struck when
his wife and young daughter were killed in a terrorist bombing, and
the ferocious creature that was the Raven surfaced once more to

exact vengeance. When all was said and done, he had vanished once more and created yet another new identity, far from the reach of the past.

Ever the loner, he made a friend, and when Allan Brown found himself embroiled in a frame for murder, the Raven, working in the shadows, helped his friend overcome the plot against him. In doing so, he came to the attention of a security specialist, Brian Featherstone, who ran a firm of ex-special forces commandos. This elite company undertook sensitive operations that the police could not or would not handle, since there were lines that could not be crossed. Featherstone's team had no such compunction. Sometimes their mostly well-heeled clients found themselves in a "bit of bother," as Featherstone put it, and needed it handled in a delicate manner. Featherstone and he immediately hit it off, and after coming clean about his history in Belfast, Riordan joined the firm as one of their investigators.

The only caveat was that Riordan could keep his consulting firm on the side, a place where he evaluated new and upcoming technology advances in the computer realm. His expertise and seal of approval was highly sought after by clients, so he did not want to let go of the lucrative business. However, the lure of danger and excitement provided by Featherstone's assignments proved too great to turn down, so he joined up.

In the interim, he met and married Nancy, an ER nurse who possessed a wild soul, well matched to his own spirit. Now they had twin boys to contend with in the mix. All in all, life was good, and his work with Featherstone provided an outlet for him to exercise the wild spirit.

Using a yellow highlighter, he commenced marking some of the pertinent information in the folder then paused as the first strains of Davy Spillane playing "Caoineadh Cu Chulainn" from *Riverdance* filled the air. The mournful, haunting melody spoke to him, touching his soul like the tendrils of a plant reaching for the sun in search of sustenance. The Black Rose was calling him home. He could feel it. It was a presentiment that had been building for some time but one that he had studiously ignored. In the past, the *Black Rose* was sometimes used as a codeword for Ireland, when English laws prohibited direct references to Ireland as a sovereign nation.

Unable to concentrate, he closed the folder. Opening up Facebook, he headed for the one page that he had inadvertently come across several months earlier. The page belonged to Neil, someone he had not spoken to for many years. Neil and Sean were part of the past that he had buried, the darkness that was Belfast. Yet like so many things buried and thought forgotten, they were destined to resurface again. By accident one evening he had found Neil's Facebook page. Now, he strayed once more, and there Neil was, as large as life, working as a software specialist just outside London. Facebook showed there was a forty-fifth birthday party scheduled and promoted a shout-out to all his friends to come and join him. That was new.

Rubbing weary eyes, Riordan scanned the site looking at the photographs. Neil was married with two teenaged kids — the wife was quite a stunner. There was a strange photograph of Sean and Neil together, both of them looking completely inebriated. It was good to see that they had remained friends. As the years sped by, he missed them greatly. And then he found something that took his breath away. At the bottom of the page, something that had not been present before, was a simple statement. It read, "David, if you ever come across this page, Sean and me would love to hear from you."

It was like all the stars in the universe had converged at that precise moment in time. Taking a deep breath to still his racing heartbeat, he tossed the highlighter aside and sat back. It was strange to see his old name used. He had gone from David Allen to David Spence to Daniel Riordan. At that moment, he heard a knock on his office door.

"Come on in, love," he said, and turned to see Nancy ease back into the office with a tray holding a mug of tea and a couple of digestive biscuits. These were from her special stash, the ones coated in milk chocolate that she bought at a shop on Robson Street that imported all things British. They were also strictly rationed.

"I heard the Irish music come on, so I thought you'd like a cuppa." She smiled. "This is getting to be a bit of a regular occurrence now."

"What is?" he asked, grabbing the mug of tea.

"Melancholy baby," she said. Lifting her mug, she peered over his shoulder at the screen. "I've been hearing Davy Spillane on the pipes quite a bit of late. And who's this?"

"Have a look."

He quietly pointed to one of the photographs on the screen, a warm smile caressing his features. It was Neil, filled out from the scrawny kid he remembered, and there beside him was Sean, wearing a full beard, eyes slightly glazed with the mischievous grin that warmed the hearts of many a girl in university. "That's Neil, and Sean with the beard, a couple of the lads I grew up with back in Belfast. They were just some of those things I had to leave behind when I ran, but I remember fondly the old days as a kid and all the trouble we got into. Before it all was blown to hell by that car bomb."

She nodded, leaned forward, and kissed his cheek, then put her hands affectionately on his shoulders, her fingertips rubbing gently. Easing his head from side to side, he savoured her touch as the mournful lament played on.

"Something's calling you home, love," she said, touching him lightly.

He nodded, a wave of sadness washing over him. His eyes moistened, and he closed them tightly for a moment, images of bygone days playing like a movie on the backs of his eyelids. In his heart he knew she was right, but what was there for him to go back to? Everyone close to him was dead, and there would be that long walk down the bleak cemetery path to see the worn white marble chips scattered on his parents' grave. Then there was the Old Man, Uncle Bill who had raised him, trained him in the art of killing, and then turned him loose on the terrorist organization that had been responsible for the murder of his parents. That gave rise to the myth of the Raven, the stone killer who struck fear into the heart of every IRA gunman. Countless numbers had died at his hand, and countless more attributed to him to fan the flames of fear in those who dared pick up the gun.

With the exception of one man, he had found all those responsible for the ambush that killed his parents and almost took his own life, and made them pay. Still, to this day, clear and bright was the image of the vehicle cruising past the burning wreck that was his father's car, almost torn asunder by the booby trap blast that took his father and mother's lives.

She, like most good, decent people, had rushed to provide assistance to what she thought was an accident victim. In the darkness, however, she had stumbled into the tripwire, a thin, nearly invisible piece of fishing line attached to a detonator that was in turn connected to a milk churn packed full of explosives. The milk churn, another terrorist's favourite, had been concealed in the trunk of the car that had deliberately been run into the ditch.

Half asleep in the back seat of the car, he had been somewhat sheltered from the blast, but a shard of glass from the shattered windscreen had embedded itself in his forehead. Through a bloody haze he had heard the demoniacal laughter as the terrorists' car slowed to allow them to inspect their handiwork. In those brief moments he had glimpsed a hand bearing a tattoo he would never forget. Seared into his consciousness, at work he would be absentmindedly doodling on a sheet of paper during a meeting, and there it would be, the tiny parachute nestled between two wings — insignia of the British parachute regiment. In the aftermath, no one believed him. They thought it was all a figment of his imagination. No self-respecting IRA terrorist would have such an insignia. No, they all put it down to the trauma of the explosion, and even the Old Man took the story with a grain of salt. He had never felt so hopeless.

He shook his head to cast the images aside, and Nancy's arms slipped around his neck as she nuzzled his ear. Her rich scent filled his nostrils. Reading the screen in front of him, she kissed his cheek. "A birthday party? And I see they haven't forgotten you."

"Yeah," he replied, "it's Neil's birthday, and they're hosting a party at some country inn."

"Sounds like a good time," she commented.

He laughed. "If I know those two, then it surely will."

"I meant for a reunion."

"Oh."

She punched him playfully on the shoulder. "Why don't you just call and say hello, and then you can make whatever arrangements you need. God knows you need a break after these last few months. Just go. I'll look after the boys while you're gone."

Riordan smiled, rolled his chair back, and pulled her onto his lap. "Oooh, I'm likin' this," she said, her lips melting against his, her tongue teasing as she wiggled into a comfortable position. It was several moments before they broke the embrace. "I'll have some of that later," she grinned, stroking the bulge in his jeans. "But first, it seems like you've got a call to make!"

Picking up the mug of tea, he took a long swig, munching happily on a digestive biscuit, his mood lightened by the prospect of seeing his old friends again. Nancy had even put a smear of butter on the biscuit, which was a special treat. Picking up the phone, he checked his watch. It showed a few minutes after 11:00 p.m., so he did the math. The time difference was eight hours, so he figured it would be just after 7:00 a.m. in Belfast. *No time like the present*, he thought. Throwing caution to the wind, he dialled the number.

It rang several times, each ring causing a tiny bubble of apprehension in his gut. Always vigilant, his training forced him to go through a set of mental gyrations that the team used before every operation. It was all about "what ifs?" But he reminded himself that this wasn't an operation; it was a meeting of old friends. Nevertheless, as the seconds ticked on, the questions popped into his head. *What if this is a mistake? What if they've turned out to be complete assholes? What happens if someone recognizes me?*

Then there was a click, and a groggy voice answered. "Sean Daly speaking."

His voice left him, as if he had been struck dumb. Words would not come.

"Hello, is anyone there? Hello?"

"Sean," he croaked.

For a moment there was silence, and the silence grew. He heard Sean's breath on the other end of the line, and he imagined Sean would be listening hard too. His heart thumped in his chest.

"David?" The voice was hesitant, but Sean would likely recognize the hisses and squeaks of an international call and perhaps had put two and two together.

Riordan's eyes misted. He could simply hang up and forget about it, dismiss the idea as wishful thinking. But he didn't.

"Yeah, Sean, it's me." He cleared his throat.

"Fuck me," came the voice, clearer now. "Howareye?"

Riordan grinned. "A lot better now, pal. It's good to hear your voice."

"You too," came the reply, full of excitement. "Did you see the note on Neil's Facebook page? I made him put it there. Oh fuck, Neil'll be beside himself when I call. You are coming for the party, aren't you?"

"My wife's making me go," Riordan replied. "She can't stand listening to Davy Spillane one more day. She say's I've gotta go home."

"Is that yer man with the pipes? *Riverdance*?"

"One and the same."

"Jesus, David, and you wi' a wife and all. We've a lot of catching up to do. So when are you coming?"

Riordan explained that it had all just happened in the last few minutes, but that he would make arrangements as soon as possible and then pass them on. Daly offered to meet him at Heathrow and then spend the night in London with Neil — a boys' night was how it was described. Riordan could only imagine the debauchery. Plans made, he promised to ring back shortly and then hung up. Treating himself to another digestive, he signed on to the British Airways website, checked the flight schedules, and booked himself a ticket in business class. *Might as well be comfortable*, he thought.

CHAPTER 3

HOUNDS

Belfast, 1979

It was the last time.

He was forced to stop once at a police checkpoint on the way home, a momentary distraction from the scene playing over and over in his mind, another in an endless loop of torment. Ahead, two Land Rovers parked across the narrow street at opposing angles, creating a chicane that could not be traversed at speed. Close to them stood angry, uniformed men, throwing hard looks ably backed up by suppressed rage. Some focused on him, some focused on the streets and houses beyond. They knew what lay in wait in the dark.

He calmly endured the cursory question-and-answer session. They were more concerned about protecting their own skins than hassling a student. Two of their own had been murdered the night before, so everyone was on edge. Even the constable who examined his driver's license and identification looked him in the face for scarcely a second. Wary eyes roved over oncoming traffic and the burned-out shells of nearby houses. Headlights reflected off the slick, wet roads, the constant downpour deadening any sounds that would alert the patrol of a possible ambush. Death lurked in those dark windows. They knew it, and he knew it and he could see the fear. The bloodied head of a pimple attested to the age of the constable; he could be no more than seventeen or eighteen. Riordan wondered if he was having doubts about his chosen profession. It was one thing to feel righteous indignation at the terrorists who ruled by fear and intimidation, and the accompanying bravado led many a young man to the recruiting offices. However, the realities of the job arrived with the force of a speeding locomotive, and walking the streets with an Armalite rifle, a pistol, and a flak jacket were a sobering wakeup call to that initial indignation.

"On yer way," said the policeman in the thick, guttural accent, and nodded to the others to let him past. He drove on through the dark streets, winding through a maze of houses until he arrived at the Old Man's place, and parked outside the wrought iron fence. A burned-out wreck of a car half-blocked the end of the street. Despite several attempts by the local council to have it removed, the barrier remained. Eyesore or not, it provided an effective means of controlling traffic in and out of the street.

He let himself into the house. The instant he opened the front door, the sweetish aroma of Old Lurk tobacco caressed his nostrils. He hung up his jacket on a set of brass hooks that lined the wall and walked down the narrow hallway to the living room. The news was on the television. Walking into the living room, he saw that Arthur Cupples, a friend of the Old Man's and a former soldier, had dropped by for a visit. The perpetual cigarette glowed in Arthur's hand.

"Arthur," he said, settling himself into a worn armchair at one side of the coal fire that blazed merrily in the hearth. Atop the fireplace a host of tiny brass ornaments gleamed. In one corner sat a tiny colour television with the volume turned up. Off to one side sat Bill Ellis, commonly known as the Old Man, smoking his pipe, one of several lined neatly up on the fireplace. He grinned and held up a newspaper for David to see the prominent headline that read: "Raven Strikes Fear Into Heartland."

Arthur Cupples took a drag of his cigarette and picked up a Waterford tumbler holding a generous two fingers of whisky. He took a sip, grimaced a little, and smiled. Arthur liked his whisky.

They all turned as the news reporter said, "We have breaking news from our correspondent in North Belfast. Over to you, Martin."

A reporter appeared on the screen, standing at the end of a blocked-off street, police and army vehicles in the background and an ambulance standing by. Their rotating lights flashed furiously in the darkness. Soldiers crouched by their vehicles, their weapons aimed up at the rooftops. Death often came from above. Neighbours and curious onlookers stood shoulder to shoulder against the barrier, watching the parade of security people stride purposefully in and out of the house.

The reporter said, "Two men were shot and killed earlier tonight in North Belfast. Although we do not have a positive identification, a source informed us that the men were suspected of being members of the ultraviolent Sons of Erin Brigade. Several weapons and bomb making materials have been discovered on the premises. No one has yet claimed responsibility for the killings, which police believe to be due to infighting within the paramilitary organization."

"So, lad," said the Old Man, "I see you got them? Any luck with the tattoo?"

David opened the hollowed out textbook and removed a pistol from the inside. Ejecting the magazine, he began loading it with fresh rounds. He shook his head. "Aye, I got them ... but it wasn't him," he replied.

"Everything go alright, lad?" the Old Man said, his brow furrowing. "You don't look so well."

"No, everything went well. I took them by surprise." He forced another round into the clip.

The Old Man smiled and said, "That's great, lad. You're making quite the name for yourself." He tossed the newspaper into David's lap. David picked it and looked at the headline, scanned the first few lines of the article, and set it aside.

"As long as nobody knows my identity, apart from you two, I don't care," he said, setting the clip down beside the pistol and staring into the flames.

"Leave it there, lad," the Old Man said. "I'll clean it for you later. Arthur and I have a few things to discuss, so be off with ye. I'll get breakfast ready for you in the mornin', and I'll run you over to the college. There's some business I need to attend to out in Carrickfergus."

David nodded, said goodnight to Arthur, and headed upstairs.

His room at the back of the house was cramped but comfortable. A newly created trapdoor afforded access to the attic, where an intricate catwalk of planks provided a path to the adjoining house, where a man-sized hole had been knocked through the bricks. That led to another catwalk, and from there to another, and so on all the way down the terraced street. In case of an emergency, several escape options were available. Closing the door behind him, he sat down on his bed. The springs groaned.

An electric guitar sat in one corner, plugged into a compact, scuffed amplifier that he had picked up in Smithfield market. On the bedside table sat two framed black-and-white photographs: one of his mum and dad on their wedding day, the other of the three lads with their arms around one another, hamming it up for the camera. Picking up the photograph of the three pals, he ran his fingers over glass, thinking back to those carefree times before his life had disintegrated. He looked around the room as if through the eyes of a stranger, seeing it for the first time. It had all the trappings of youth, but in reality, he had left that long behind the first time he had taken a life.

He was caught in a downward spiral of violence, with no end even possible to contemplate. There would not be a good end to all of this. If the path of destruction continued, he was bound to make a mistake at some point. Either the authorities would catch him, or worse still, the IRA. The latter would take their time with him, and he had seen their results first-hand. He and the Old Man had visited the morgue on occasion to see one of their own who had been lifted.

Living for the past few months with that fear riding on his shoulder like an old friend, every time he left the house the anxiety level increased exponentially. There were often nights when all he did was stare at the ceiling, intrigued by the strange shadows cast on the walls by the odd car passing through the area. He would drift off in the wee hours and then wake exhausted. Occasionally there would be the muffled crump of a bomb exploding in the distance and the tormented wail of ambulances heading toward the scene. Or muted gunfire.

The Belfast symphony.

There was not a lot to miss or say goodbye to in the little room. He set down the photograph, a decision made. This was not going to be easy. He walked slowly back down the stairs, quietly entered the living room, and sat down. Conversation stilled. He gazed into the fire for a moment, his thoughts of faraway places. Both men stared at him, waiting. The Old Man spoke first.

"What's up, lad? I can see you've got something on your mind. Is there something you're not telling me about tonight?"

53

His heart pounded in his chest. "I can't do this anymore, Uncle Bill. I've had enough of the killing. I've got to get away."

The Old Man's face hardened. "This isn't the boy scouts, you know…"

David nodded. "I know, I know."

"This is the old 'once in, never out,' remember? If you go, then I have to set the hounds on you. Besides, you'll never find that last murdering scumbag if you run away." The room was silent for a moment. The Old Man went to say something else, but Arthur Cupples laid a hand on his shoulder. No one spoke for a few awkward moments.

David said, "You do what you have to..."

The Old Man looked away. "You've got twenty-four hours..."

David smiled — a reprieve of sorts. "Thanks, Uncle Bill."

Arthur Cupples nodded toward the door, as if in agreement, and downed the last of his whisky. Picking up his cap, he said, "I better be on my way, Bill. We've got a boatload of stuff coming in tonight from Liverpool, so I want to make sure the lads don't fuck it up." Then to David, "As for you lad, I don't expect I'll be seeing you again, so mind how ye go!" He got up, shook hands with David, and left. The Old Man was deep in thought. David got up and took a tentative step forward but saw the muscles tense in his uncle's back.

Perhaps not, he thought, and went out.

CHAPTER 4

CUSHENDALL

Sean Daly, enjoying a rare sunny day, drove slowly along the road cut into the side of the former glacier valley. Today's meeting had him heading for the tiny fishing village of Cushendall, situated in on the North Antrim coast. He passed by Oisín's Grave, just off the main road and a place believed to be the burial place of Oísín, the renowned Celtic warrior poet. It was bright enough to require him to wear sunglasses, and for the first time in a long while he had the top down on his Porsche. Having a convertible in Ireland really didn't make sense. There was a good reason the grass was so green. Narrow in places and framed with a barbed wire fence that had seen better days, the road overlooked the steep drop to the valley floor. Flocks of sheep, their backs covered in multiple hues from dye packs, grazed along the ridges, seemingly oblivious to the steep drop.

Tiny tufts of fleece clung to the barbs in the wire, fluttering in the breeze. Farmers attached differing dye packs to the stomachs of their rams so that they would know which sheep had been mated. Those with many splotches of colours had the best chance of producing lambs. Unknowing tourists, on seeing these for the first time, often thought that the province had a severe problem with vandalism.

Coming out of a tight hairpin bend, he cursed loudly and slammed on his brakes. Ahead, the road was completely blocked by a farmer herding his sheep directly toward him. He recalled seeing a farm by the side of the road about a mile back. The farmers around here were a hardy bunch, surviving from selling their flocks to massive supermarket chains and the fleece to spinners. In the wintertime the roads were virtually impassable. The farms in recent years had gotten electricity, but water was still usually pumped from a spring or a well. Heating came from massive fireplaces stoked with dried peat cut from the surrounding bogs.

At the back of the flock, the farmer and his faithful dogs drove the flock onward, the dogs obediently following their master's commands — a series of sharp shouts and whistles. Realizing that progress was going to be somewhat inhibited, Sean activated the car phone and pressed a few digits. When it rang and was answered, he said, "May I speak to Mister Scullion, please?"

The receptionist informed him that Scullion was tied up in a meeting. Smiling, he told her he would be slightly delayed. Then, looking at the scene ahead of him, he said, "There's a traffic jam." Shutting down the call, Daly got out of the car in time to see some spring lambs amble up. As the bleating throng pressed around him, he glanced down at a tiny black lamb at his feet. Stooping down, he picked it up and cradled it gently in his arms. He stroked its back. Having been raised on a farm, for him it was a comforting feeling and hearkened back to simpler times.

Sighing, he exhaled. "You and me, mate, both fuckin' black sheep..."

Just over two hours later, following a successful meeting that consummated months of negotiations for a new housing development, Daly went for a walk through the village. He stopped and leaned on a well-worn railing. Running all the way along the top of the ocean wall, it overlooked the beach and the waves of Red Bay. To his left, the River Dall meandered through the local golf course to the sea. He had played there many times, losing many pricey balls in the murmuring waters that traversed the first five holes. After that, the river disappeared for a while and then reappeared at the last two holes, making any wayward shot almost sure to find a watery grave. The distant rains ceased for a moment, the sun poking through to provide a spectacular view across the Sea of Moyle to the Mull of Kintyre on the Scottish coast, some twenty miles away.

I should be happy, he thought.

Waves pounded the rocks. The wind blew hard in his face, driving whitecaps, the famous "white horses" of song, into the shore. A few brave souls ventured onto the beach, beachcombers perhaps, searching for treasure amongst the detritus swept up by the tide. All the worries of the world were etched on his face as he stared off into the horizon. Shaking his head sadly, he turned up his collar and walked back across the street to his car.

The drive back to Belfast passed quickly. It was growing dark by the time he pulled into the side of the street beside a fish-and-chip shop, above which a sign proclaimed, "THE COD FATHER." The chippy was widely renowned for having the best fish supper in the city. Sean got out of his car, made sure it was securely locked, then pressed the access key once for good measure. The alarm chirped. Leaning against the windowsills of a bombed-out house, several tough-looking youths ate chips out of newspapers, their fingers gleaming with grease. They grunted in acknowledgement of his presence, and he smiled back. He knew better than to diss them. All wore the standard "tough" uniform: jean jacket, baggy jeans, and well-polished Doc Martens. Studded belts and chains seemed to be the fashion accessory of the day.

When he opened the door, an old-fashioned striker overhead rattled a bell. The air inside felt heavy, saturated from the heavy odour of frying oil — there were no healthy, light vegetable oils used here. Behind the counter stood the owner. Peter, an overweight, middle-aged man, grinned when he saw Daly. Ornate tattoos decorated both arms, and a dark growth of buzzed hair covered a head that had come out the worst of boxing matches long ago. Peter had been an amateur middleweight, attested to by the posters curling on the wall of the chippy. The accumulation of scar tissue around his eyes, paired with a huge gold earring in one ear, made him look like a modern-day pirate.

Leaning both meaty arms on the well-polished. stainless-steel counter, he said, "Howareye, Sean? The usual?"

Daly thought for a moment but then nodded. "Aye, Peter, and put some extra chips in there."

Peter took two pieces of fresh cod from the fridge, dragged them through a bowl of flour, dipped them in batter, and dropped them into the fryer. He then took a scoop of freshly cut potato chips and dropped them into the other fryer, hissing and spitting droplets of oils. Everything was fresh with Peter. Fast-food joints had spread up across the city, but Peter's loyal following could not be tempted. There were no microwaves or heat lamps for Peter. He was old school.

The meaty arms returned to the counter. "So what's the craic? Where's the Ginger Whinger and the Aga Khan this evening?"

Daly smiled. His close friends would never be known by anything other than their nicknames. "They're both busy," he replied. "But anyway, I'm away over to London for my mate Neil's birthday party this weekend. I'm taking the eight o'clock ferry over to Stranraer in the morning."

Peter looked askance and worried a piece of fish out of his side teeth with a toothpick. "Have you ever gone on the car ferry before, Sean?"

Daly shook his head. "No, but I want to take the car for gettin' around."

Peter nodded thoughtfully. "Jesus, you're a brave man, what with all that bad weather coming in. You'll be bokin' like a whoor..."

Daly's stomach gave a little lurch, but he remembered the packet of Gravol he had purchased just in case the crossing got a bit rocky. "It's alright, Peter, I got some anti-seasick pills at the shop."

Peter laughed. "Aye, they work just great. Anyway, I'll put some extra grease on the chips for ye, so they won't hurt too much when they come back up later!"

Daly paid for his order then carried the package across to his car. The thugs had vanished, but he made sure to have a good look around before climbing in. They wouldn't steal the Porsche — it possessed too high a profile and would be easily noticed — but they would associate the car with money and might be tempted to go for his wallet. He finished off the fish and chips while listening to the radio, washing them down with a chilled bottle of Lucozade. He uttered a huge belch then rubbed his belly, grimacing when he saw his shirt starting to buckle between buttons. *Maybe I should cut back on the chips*, he thought. Somebody at work the other day had referred to him as "Sean Buddah," so his little pot was getting recognized.

He checked his mobile, saw there were no messages, then started the car and set off. Following one quick stop at his flat to pick up his case, it took just under thirty minutes to reach the outskirts of Ballymena. He took the bypass, slipped off the motorway at the Broughshane roundabout, and made his way through the familiar streets to his former abode. There were two cars in the driveway. Pulling in behind them, he took a deep breath, cut the ignition, and got out. The curtains in the living room were drawn across, just a thin sliver of light showing in the centre where they met. Peering inside, he saw his ex-wife, Jean, and his two daughters, Leanne and Lindsay, watching television.

Here we go, he thought, jabbing the doorbell. He heard a door open and close inside the house, and then the front door was dragged open. His ex-wife, Jean, stood there, her face like thunder. She dabbed at her eyes with a handkerchief.

Not a good sign.

"Come in," she spat. "Go in the kitchen. You and me need to have a serious talk."

Daly shook his head and headed down the corridor to the kitchen. Inside, he said, "Not now, Jean, I need to get their stuff and get home. We have to be up early in the morning, so I don't have a lot of time. Can we do this when we get back? I need to get their suitcases."

"The girls aren't going with you," she said.

Daly frowned. "They were this morning… So what happened?"

She extracted a bottle of prescription medication from the pocket of her jeans and waved them in his face. "They don't like to leave me on my own 'cos there's no knowing what I might do if I really get depressed…"

Anger surged within him. She was back at her old tricks again. "But you're not... Ah fuck, Jean, you're not pulling this shite again. I'm sick of you using the kids to get at me! It's not fair…"

Taking the air of a wounded martyr, she put the pills away. "Fair, you say ... and what about me? Your place is here with me and with the girls."

Daly sighed, shaking his head. "Jesus, Jean, it's been over two years ... I wasn't happy, and you knew it. Now you're just trying to turn the girls against me."

Colour rose in her cheeks, and her voice rose as it always did at this point. "So what if I am? If it's the only thing that makes you see sense, then that's what I'll do."

Daly tried the conciliatory route, knowing that arguing would lead nowhere good. "Come on, Jean," he said. "Where are their bags? You know they were looking forward to the trip…"

She screamed at him, "There's no way they'll be going with you tonight. I'll make sure of that!"

As soon as she finished, the kitchen door opened, and Leanne and Lindsay came into the kitchen. At seventeen and twenty-one respectively, they had inherited their looks from his side of the family. Tall, blonde, and willowy, they were both destined to break a lot of hearts. Immediately, Jean's demeanour changed and she started crying, burying her face in her hands. The girls put their arms around her to comfort her.

They looked at him, their faces etched with pain. Leanne shook her head sadly. It was not the first time they had been in such a position. She said, "Ach, Daddy, we can't leave Mum like this. You better go on without us!"

Lindsay nodded. "That's right, Daddy. We'll see you when you get back."

Daly fought to keep his anger in check. There was no point in stoking the fire. Between gritted teeth he said, "All right, girls, I'm sorry you can't come. I'll call you when I get back on Monday night."

Biting back the anger, he sighed and went out to his car. Jabbing angrily at the ignition button, he was about to reverse out on to the street when he saw his daughters come out the front door. He touched the window button, and it slid down silently. They walked over to the window and leaned in. "We are really sorry about this. Tell Neil we said hello and we'll see him soon." Both girls kissed him on the cheek.

"I'll do that," Daly replied.

Looking behind them, he saw Jean standing in the doorway, a knowing smirk on her face. When the girls turned around, it was gone, the sorrowful mask firmly back in place. Daly slid the power window up, backed out onto the street, and drove off, seething like a pot on the stove with a potent mix of anger and disappointment. She was certainly a master manipulator, and knowing how much he loved his daughters, she constantly used them as a weapon to get her own way. He had lost count of the number of times that little Shakespearean tragedy had been played, under various guises. The pills, however, were taking it to a new level.

*

He slept fitfully, woke up tired, and managed to have a quick shower before heading down to the docks to catch the car ferry. It was raining, and dark clouds buffeted the horizon. Whitecaps on the bay made him anxious, yet he decided to acknowledge the hunger pangs and get something to eat. Driving up to the massive Stena Lines Explorer, he was amazed to see how many cars and big eighteen-wheel transport lorries were in line ahead of him. Across the bay, he watched the planes take off and land. His preferred mode of transport was the British Midland shuttle out of the George Best Belfast City airport, which got him to Heathrow in just over an hour. From there, he could be in downtown London in less than thirty minutes. For business meetings, it was the most practical means of transport. But this time, wanting to have the car and a few days with his girls, he had chosen the ferry. He joined a line, directed by a sorry-looking youth in all-weather gear, stopped the car, and leaned back to listen to the radio. The wait was short-lived, and the many parallel streams of traffic were soon starting to move. Finally, it was time for him to board, and he followed his lane into the maw of the ship, parked the car, and made his way upstairs to the café.

He grabbed a newspaper and found himself a seat at the counter. The place was fairly empty. As the ferry horn sounded, he felt the gentle motion of the ship. A heavily made-up waitress, looking to be in her fifties, walked up to him. Brown hair gleamed from a fresh coat of hairspray, giving the impression of hard shell. The uniform with the shipping line's logo was stretched taut over a significant bosom, a good couple of inches of cleavage on show. Gold rings adorning just about every finger flashed as she took a pen from behind her ear, folded a new page in her notebook, and masticated her gum a couple of times. All that was missing from the cliché was the cigarette with an inch of ash.

"What can I get for you, love?" she asked.

Daly scanned the menu on the wall and decided to pass on the Ulster fry. "A cup of tea, please, and a ham sandwich." She jotted down a note, replaced the pen behind her ear, slipped the notebook into her apron, and disappeared into the kitchen. A moment later she returned with a tray holding a stainless-steel teapot, a stainless steel milk jug, and a cup and saucer. A teabag string trailed down the side of the teapot. Daly gave it a couple of minutes to steep then poured a cup and added a splash of milk. By the time he had finished, the waitress was back with a freshly made ham sandwich on a plate. Daly took a bite of the sandwich and a sip of the tea. The ship rocked gently.

"This isn't as bad as I thought it would be!" he commented.

"What, the tea or the sandwich?" asked the waitress with indignant look.

Realizing his mistake, Daly grinned. "No, no, love! The ferry's not rocking as much as I thought it would. It's my first time, you see."

The waitress laughed. "That's pretty obvious. We're not out of the shaggin' harbour yet!"

Daly felt stupid as he turned to see the buildings in the distance, unmoving. The ferry was still rocking gently at berth. Looking out past him, the waitress said, "It's pretty rough out there in the channel today, love. If this is your first time, it's a pretty fair bet that you're only renting that sandwich."

Irish humour at its best.

Daly took another sorrowful look at the last remaining bite of the sandwich and set it back on the plate. "Lovely, just fuckin' lovely," he muttered. He finished the tea, ordered another, and when it came he moved to one of the outer tables, where he had a clear view of the coast. The ship, now free of its moorings, surged out against the tide, the motion now becoming very apparent to Daly's stomach. He finished the newspaper as the coast slipped away, and they were out into the channel. It was stuffy in the café, and that, coupled with the motion of the ship, left Daly feeling slightly nauseous. He swallowed a couple more Gravol tablets, thinking that it might be an appropriate time to exceed the maximum dose, and decided to get some fresh air.

Opening the ferry door was a challenge in itself due to the weight of the door and the buffeting it was receiving from the wind. He managed to force it open and stepped out onto the deck, glad of the feel of the wind on his face. Dark clouds still spotted the sky, and far off to the north he could see rain coming down in sheets. Making his way to the viewing deck, he held tightly to the railing and peered ahead to where the coast of Scotland was coming into view. It was great to have a fixed point to focus on, as he was feeling decidedly unwell. Taking great gulps of air, he managed to quell the nausea for a few moments, but the unrelenting rolling of the ship brought him to that inescapable point of no return.

Hanging over the railing as far as he could, he emptied the contents of his stomach over the side, retching and retching until there was nothing left but dry heaves. In the burst of spray, he noticed the shiny blue Gravol tablets that hadn't had time to dissolve. "Fat lot of good they were," he cursed. Looking at his watch, he noticed that they had been under way for less than thirty minutes — only another ninety minutes to go. "Sweet Jesus," he muttered as the first droplets of rain landed on his face. Wiping away strings of drool with the back of his hand, he debated going inside to the washroom. A massive lurch of the ship produced yet another round of dry heaves, and he decided to cling to the outside rail.

Just a minute or two, he thought. I'll go in when it gets really heavy.

CHAPTER 5

DOBERMAN

Just outside of Reading, a large town located a few miles west of London, Neil Diamond drove slowly along the past the ivy-encrusted walls of the estate, heart racing at the prospect of yet another illicit entry into his lover's home. It was a typical British country home, built of granite and arrayed all around with beautifully kept gardens, each a riot of colour. Large orange goldfish swam languidly in the numerous ponds linking the gardens, and several fruit trees were coming into blossom. The pear tree was particularly productive, and Neil had sampled more than a few delicious pears over the past year.

At the back of the house, the former stables had been converted into several garages, each housing a high-end automobile, the pride and joy of his lover's husband. The only addition to the original house was an oversized swimming pool surrounded by a patio of interlocking stones. Majestic, ancient oak trees guarded the pool, their gnarled branches casting a protective shade. Garden parties at the house were virtually nonstop during the summer months, since Brian, the husband, loved to show off his newly found riches. He ran the local Rover dealership and owned two more in neighbouring counties, handling mostly high-end Jaguars and Range Rovers. He knew his well-heeled clientele intimately, and from what Neil had seen at the parties, some more intimately than others.

Pulling into a laneway adjacent to the estate, Neil stopped the car and got out. Hoisting a backpack on to his shoulders, he quickly scaled the wall and made his way across the back area to the house. The oak trees provided good cover for his surreptitious entry. The road was lightly travelled and the home far from nosy neighbours, so he was relatively sure he would be unnoticed.

An ancient, ivy encrusted trellis provided access to a balcony on the second floor of the home, the French doors open to air the room inside. At forty-five years old, Neil kept himself in great shape, every other day working with weights at the gym, a game of soccer on a Sunday afternoon with the lads, and the odd game of squash during the week. It all helped to maintain a lean physique, despite the occasional debauchery at the pub after their soccer games. Pints and meat pies didn't exactly constitute a healthy diet, but he knew where to draw the line. The merest hint of an excess pound or two and his wife, Fiona, would be all over him.

Pausing for a moment to catch his breath, he swung his leg over the balcony. In front of him lay an opulent master bedroom. A massive, four-poster bed resplendent with a canopy rested against the far wall. A vast array of pillows sat against the headboard.

With the doors open, the occupants would have a magnificent view of the open countryside — the lord looking out over his manor. A triple-paned, mirrored dresser sat off to the side of the bed. It was an antique; Neil had been with her when she picked it out during one of their many outings to London.

Crossing to the dresser, Neil slid open the top drawer to reveal many pairs of panties, some utilitarian, but others of silk and lace. Positioned at one side of the drawer sat a pair of red silk, high-cut bikini panties. Neil remembered them fondly. He picked up the red panties, ran his fingers over the smooth silk, and then rubbed them against his face, inhaling the scent. The smell triggered an explosion of erotic vignettes.

Opening the backpack, he took out a bottle of perfume, wrapped it in the panties, and placed them carefully back into the drawer. As he slid the drawer closed, he sensed rather than heard movement outside in the corridor. Turning his head slowly to one side, his heart skipped a beat when he saw the Doberman standing stock-still, teeth bared in the far doorway of the bedroom. It was a surreal moment, and his brain struggled to comprehend the image. Lynn had not mentioned getting a dog, but then again, this didn't look like a pet. For a moment he froze, virtually paralyzed by fear. Then, looking over beyond the open French doors to the branches of the oak tree, he judged the distance and closed his eyes in a silent prayer.

The Doberman still didn't make a sound, even though its teeth were bared. It was like watching a movie of an angry

72

Doberman with the mute button on. At once he sprinted for the balcony, leapt up on to the balustrade and pushed himself off like some swashbuckling hero. It was only a few feet to the tree, and he grabbed hold of one of the closest branches just as he heard the snicking of paws behind him on the balcony. The branch sprang up and down for a moment like a diving board then sank down a little bit and then broke off completely. Fortunately, he didn't have too far to fall, and the spongy ground cushioned the impact somewhat. Stunned, he lay on the ground, the branch lying on top of him. Above him, the Doberman's head appeared, slavering over the balcony. It glared at him. Neil laughed and gave it the finger.

"Beat you, you bastard…"

The Doberman raged silently for a moment then disappeared from view.

"Uh-oh," he exclaimed and tossed the branch to one side. Sprinting across the front lawn, he had just made it to the wall as the Doberman came racing out of the house after him. The silent approach totally freaked him out. Grasping the thick tendrils of ivy, he was up and over the wall in seconds.

"What a rush," he exclaimed. "I won't be doing that again for while."

CHAPTER 6

SAMURAI

Riordan swivelled his neck from side to side, feeling his neck muscles crunch. It was an unpleasant sound, almost like tearing apart two pieces of Velcro. The stewardess had just cleared away his tray. Grabbing the minuscule travel kit the airline provided, he headed for the washroom. At six foot four, there was not a lot of leeway for him in the enclosed area. There was a good reason he had not joined the "mile high club." It took virtually all of his strength to squeeze some shaving cream out of the tiny tube, and he checked carefully to make sure it wasn't toothpaste. It wouldn't have been the first time he had made that mistake. There was barely enough to cover his face, but he managed to shave without nicking his skin, again a major feat. After brushing his teeth, he patted down his hair as best he could then dumped the kit into the garbage. There would be time for a shower later.

The heavy, pulsating throb of the engines altered, and the pilot came on the intercom to inform the passengers that they would be landing in just under thirty minutes. If he cared to look out the left side of the plane, he would have a magnificent view of the River Thames. Then the message was repeated in French. He strapped himself back in, slid up the window cover, and peered out. Sure enough, the sky was clear, and he could easily make out the Thames as it curved like a black eel through massive housing developments. Long, flat barges dotted the river, some commercial, others houseboats where people lived year-round. With the price of real estate in London, it was little wonder people lived on boats. He had read somewhere recently about a new fad called micro lofts, where residents could acquire a 240 square foot apartment. To him that was a large toilet.

The plane banked steeply out over London Bridge, the pitch of the engines increased, and then the pilot turned toward the outskirts of the city, heading for Heathrow airport. In his youth, he had visited London several times and was still amazed at the size of the airport. He had been told that it was the world's busiest airport for international travel, so it was no wonder that over sixty-nine million passengers passed through the facility each year. Seventy thousand staff worked at the facility, making it the UK's largest single-site employer. Featherstone had a memory for such statistics and would quote them at the drop of a hat.

Given all that, it was no wonder they had the finest in security technology, especially facial recognition software from the myriad cameras located at strategic points throughout all the terminals. It was impossible not to end up on one of the video screens. Featherstone had outlined some of their security precautions over a coffee at Starbucks the day before. He had described the Samurai CCTV system, a next-generation device able to autonomously identify and track individuals that acted suspiciously in crowded public spaces. "That would be you!" Featherstone quipped. The system used algorithms to profile behaviour of individuals walking around in public, and it identified "typical" behaviour to single out the suspicious passengers.

To improve the tracking of an individual at an airport, the system had the ability to learn the routes people are likely to take — straight from the entrance to check-in, say. It could even follow a target as they moved in a crowd, using the characteristic shape of the person, their luggage, and the people they were walking with, to follow them as they walked between different camera views.

Samurai was designed to issue alerts when it detected behaviour that differed from the norm and adjusted its reasoning based on feedback. So an operator might reassure the system that the person with a mop appearing to loiter in a busy thoroughfare was not a threat. When another person with a mop exhibited similar behaviour, it remembered that it was not a situation that needed flagging.

Riordan was a bit concerned but had no good reason to feel such a way. He had never been arrested or fingerprinted but was still apprehensive about returning home. He didn't want to exhibit any sort of suspicious behaviour that would draw him to the attention of those monitoring the screens. Featherstone had laughed off his concerns. "Just don't keep touching your willy," was his only advice.

The landing was flawless, and he was soon grabbing his backpack and walking the gauntlet through a chorus of "have a nice day" from the flight attendants. Once inside the terminal, he followed the signs to immigration, joining throngs of other weary travellers as they were funnelled along the seemingly endless corridors to their destination. The cavernous immigration hall was filled to overflowing, lines of frazzled passengers snaking back and forth until they reached the ultimate confrontation with the agent on duty. The air was thick and stuffy from the massed throngs, flushed angry faces betraying the lack of air-conditioning. People fanned themselves with anything that came to hand. Fortunately for him, business class afforded the luxury of a special lane that fast-tracked him through to a much shorter line.

The immigration agent was a young woman, her cheeks flushed from wearing the heavy woollen uniform. He smiled, managed not to stammer as he answered her questions, and avoided staring up at the surveillance camera in the ceiling. Apparently she didn't feel he was a threat; she handed back his well-stamped passport and welcomed him through with a smile. He followed the signs to the baggage hall, where once again he waited by the stationary carousel, looked over by the watchful eye of patrolling police, armed to the teeth with Heckler and Koch MP5 submachine pistols. The weapons did little to settle his unease.

At last a siren blared, the light flashed, warning passengers that the conveyor was about to move, and the huge oval shunted into action. Bags spilled out, the first few with the special priority tags allocated to executive class passengers. His was the third out, and he grabbed it and wheeled it out through the green line at customs, eyes looking straight ahead as he passed by the mirrored windows. He gave a sigh of relief when the doors to the arrivals area opened and shut behind him.

He was safe.

Outside, eager faces lined the metal barriers surrounding the area, waiting to meet friends or acquaintances. Some held flowers, some stuffed toys. As usual, off to one side stood a phalanx of limo drivers, all holding placards with their fares' names scrawled in ink.

His eyes scanned the crowd and lit upon his old friend, excitedly waving his hand in the air. He could hardly believe that after all these years Sean had barely changed. Perhaps a few more pounds. The wispy ginger beard was showing flecks of grey, but he would have recognized him anywhere. As he made it round the end of the barrier, butterflies in his stomach, Sean stood waiting there with a wide grin. They shook hands, and Riordan felt himself grinning like a madman. Sean moved first, a bit hesitantly, but they embraced each other with the warmth of long-time friends reunited.

"Welcome home, mate," Sean said, the thick Belfast accent that Riordan remembered now replaced by a softer, gentler tone. "Been a long, long time."

"Aye, that it has, that it has... Now, where's the nearest bar?"

Sean grinned. "I see you haven't changed much. I thought we'd head into the city and book into the hotel first. Then we can go on the razzle!"

Riordan nodded. "That's great. After eight hours, I need a shower, a shit, and a pint."

"Oh, brilliant," Sean groaned. "You really haven't changed a bit. C'mon, we'll take the Tube into Leicester square — the hotel is not far from there."

"Fuck that," Riordan replied. "If the Tube is anything like I'm used to, in this weather it'll be stinking hot, and I've had my quota of sticky, sweaty bodies today already."

"All right then," Sean replied. "A taxi it is!"

*

Riordan checked into the hotel, promising to meet Sean in the bar in about thirty minutes. The drive in from Heathrow, bumper-to-bumper with other cars, gave them time to catch up and provide the synopsis of past lives, like strangers meeting at a high-school reunion. Riordan, wary as ever, gave a sanitized version of his past but described in glowing detail his new wife and two young sons,

Michael and David. Like every proud father, he carried the dog-eared photographs in his wallet that he could share.

Standing under the steaming hot trickle of water that passed for a shower in London, he now understood why the Brits loved to take baths. At least there was some chance that you might actually get wet. After towelling himself off, he pulled on a clean set of clothes and headed down to the bar feeling somewhat refreshed. Sean sat over in a quiet corner of the hotel bar, looking intently at the flat-screen monitor on the wall. There was a soccer game under way, and Riordan remembered that Sean was a huge Manchester United fan. A half-empty pint of Guinness sat in front of him beside a half-eaten bowl of peanuts. A full pint, perfectly poured and almost settled, sat on the other side.

Riordan heaved himself into a surprisingly comfortable armchair and wiped a finger down the side of the glass. Smiling at Sean, he said, "Jesus, I can't wait. It's been a long time since I've had a good pint of this stuff."

Hefting the pint, he clinked it with Sean, then took a long, slow swig. It was the perfect temperature, full of malty flavour that somehow could not be replicated across the ocean. Across the table, Sean couldn't restrain himself any longer. Riordan knew he had been full of questions on the ride in on the taxi but had had time to contemplate their conversation.

"So, how long is it since you've been home?" he asked.

"Something like twenty odd years," Riordan replied.

Sean grinned. "Well, here's to your first trip back home. I was just thinking about that the other night after you called. All those years ago ... you seemed to leave in a mighty great hurry."

Riordan shrugged. Time to deflect the conversation. "To be perfectly honest, I didn't have much choice at the time. But enough about me ... how are things with Jean? I saw on your Facebook page that you got married. Nice daughters, by the way."

Sean looked crestfallen. "My life's a fucking mess! I'm separated at the moment, so I'm going to write a book and call it 'Sean's ashes.' That's how good things are."

Riordan nodded. "I noticed the girls weren't here, but I didn't want to say anything. You said they were coming with you."

Sean nodded. "Yeah, they were really looking forward to meeting you. All they've seen is photographs. They've met Neil a few times, but right now they're at home. Jean knows how to manipulate them and openly admits it to me. She's upped the ante, and now she's talking about taking pills."

Riordan sipped his pint, shook his head sadly, and said nothing. Sean obviously had things he wanted to get off his chest, and the head of steam was building.

Sean spat out the last few words. "She's gone fucking mad!"

Riordan shrugged. "Have you thought about your local priest?"

Sean snorted in disgust. "There's no way she'll talk to a priest about this!"

Riordan smiled. "I wasn't thinking of talking to her. I was thinking more along the lines of a flamin' exorcism."

Sean gagged on his pint then exploded in laughter. "Jesus, you could always get a rise out of me, and Neil too. I needed a good laugh." He leaned over the side of his chair and picked up a plastic carrier bag that had the logo of W.H. Smith, the largest bookseller chain in Britain, on the side.

Sean said, "Speaking of books, I picked this up for you while I was waiting around at the airport. I remembered how much you loved to read, and this is a good one about the Troubles. It's been on the bestseller lists over here for a few weeks now."

Riordan took the proffered bag. "Thanks, mate, it's still one of the things I love to do. I've always got books on the go, so I'll look forward to reading it." Reaching inside, he slid out the hardcover, the bag slipping away like a theatre curtain to reveal the title, *The RAVEN: Myth or Reality?*

Riordan's stomach churned. He shivered, a completely physiological reaction that he could not control. He tried desperately hard to keep his emotions in check. His mouth ran dry, and for a moment he could not formulate any kind of response. Trying to be as nonchalant as possible, he scanned the cover then turned it over to review the back jacket. "Have you read this?" he asked.

82

"Nah," Sean replied. "I just skimmed through it. As you often said, I only read books with the words 'hot' and 'throbbing' in the title. I know a few people who have read this one, and they say it's shite. It's done by a former 'investigative' reporter from the *Belfast Telegraph*, but the guy's just trying to make a fast buck. Ever since the success of that movie, *Fifty Dead Men Walking*, about Martin McGartland, everybody and their brother are trying to write books about the Troubles."

"Were there any theories about the Raven?" Riordan asked, his heart hammering like a sprinter erupting from the blocks. "I know he was on the go when we were growing up in Belfast, but everyone thought he was just something the paramilitaries made up to scare people. Like the bogeyman for adults!" Riordan sipped at his pint, but his appetite had vanished.

Sean shook his head. "The author doesn't name anyone, but he interviewed a lot of police and former terrorists who swear up and down that the Raven was a real person. Mind you, any bad guys that met him didn't live to tell any tales. There are unsubstantiated rumours that he tied up a SAS commando in an observation post one night, went and whacked the IRA gunman that the commando was watching, and then returned and set the commando free. That would take balls."

Riordan swallowed hard. He remembered that night vividly.

"Anyway, read it when you get a moment and let me know what you think. We better finish these pints and get over to King's

Cross station. Neil's due in shortly. His car was in the shop for some special part, so he's having it brought over to the hotel."

"How's he doing?" Riordan asked. "He looks pretty happy in the pictures on Facebook."

"Well," Sean replied. "Do you want the long or short version?"

"Give me the highlights," Riordan replied. "It has been twenty years!"

"Let me tell you about Lynn."

"I thought he was married to Fiona."

"Exactly."

"So he's not happy."

Sean nodded. "I never understood why he married Fiona in the first place. She's an absolute ball-breaker, and I should know. At one of their fancy soirees, he met Lynn, who's also in an unhappy marriage. The two of them fell hard for one another, so misery really does love company. I guess they're just trying to work things out at the moment."

Riordan understood. He saw people around him at work in similar circumstances who were incredibly unhappy but too enmeshed financially to leave. "I hope things work out for him. Life's too short to stay in an unhappy marriage."

Sean laughed. "The unfortunate thing is he's still in it, but to compensate he's gone a wee bit over the top."

"That doesn't sound like Neil. He was always the conservative one — even at university he wouldn't touch a joint."

"Not anymore, pal. He thinks he's James Bond, fucking double-o-seven. He's taking to breaking into Lynn's house when she's not around and hiding bottles of her favourite perfume in her panties. And then the creepy bit..."

"...it gets creepier?" Riordan exclaimed.

"Oh yeah, by a long shot. Every time they have sex, he keeps the 'tissues' in a box as souvenirs."

Riordan shook his head. He had heard of some peculiar fetishes, had even witnessed a few in his line of work, but this was certainly something new. It was without question going to be an eventful reunion.

*

After the train pulled slowly into the station and shuddered to a halt, numerous passengers filed out past Riordan and Sean, who stood waiting patiently at the barrier. The platform was devoid of chairs, garbage bins, or any form of receptacle where a bomb could be concealed. The authorities in London were on high alert for a new wave of attacks from radical Islamic elements, and so any possible hiding place for devices had been removed. The public address system crackled out constant warnings to passengers not to leave their luggage unattended. Anything sitting in the open without an owner would be treated as a suspect device. To complement the warning, a heavy police presence blanketed the area. It was just like the good old days in Belfast.

Riordan mentioned the same to Sean, who laughed and nodded. "I'm always careful over here these days. I'd be awfully fucking embarrassed if I managed to survive thirty years in Belfast only to get blown up in a train station in London."

Riordan looked at the thinning crowd. "Are you sure he's on this train?"

Sean shrugged in reply. "He said this was his train. But if I know Neil, he'll probably be in the washroom with some bird!"

Riordan pointed. "No, there he is." At the far end of the platform, Neil helped a tall, dark-haired woman lift her luggage down out of the train. "You were right, he's found a bit of skirt."

They watched as Neil carried the woman's bag down the platform and out the gate. In front of them, she gave him a peck on the cheek and her business card then walked away. All three men admired the shapely figure.

Sean said, "I'll say one thing for you, you bastard ... you certainly have taste."

Neil placed a hand on his heart. "'Tis a shame my heart is taken..."

Sean hugged Neil. "Yeah, right! And if Angela finds out, she'll take your heart right out through your chest."

Based on that exchange, Riordan suspected there were more stories to come. Neil looked Riordan up and down. "Now there's a sight for sore eyes." The two men embraced warmly.

Sean said, "Okay, pint time! I thought we'd have dinner at the Indian up behind Leicester Square, and then we can go on the razzle."

*

Throngs of people milled around Leicester Square as taxis and London buses emptied tourists and locals alike onto the street. Riordan felt the energy in the air, similar to those times he had visited Times Square in New York. A constant flow of humanity bubbled up out of the Tube station. There were lots of Goths and punk rockers with strangely coloured hair, young people sitting on the benches, and young couples strolling hand in hand. The tourists were obvious: cameras, street maps, and fanny packs always visible.

Sean, followed by the others, jostled their way through the crowds to one of the back streets off the square that was lined with restaurants offering every type of cuisine imaginable. The Indian restaurant seemed to be the most in demand. Riordan recalled reading somewhere that currently the most popular fast food in Britain was chicken tikka masala. They found a table in the window, and once seated, Sean ordered wine while they perused the menus. After a few minutes they decided to have the Maharajah special, an array of dishes for five people, but since they were all hungry, they felt certain they could finish it all.

When the wine arrived, they waited until Sean had sampled it, nodded his approval, and their glassed were filled. Then they raised their glasses for a toast.

Sean lifted his glass and said, "Good friends." The three clinked glasses as the waiter delivered their appetizers to the table on a trolley, arrayed with many ornate, hammered copper bowls.

Sean said, "The lamb vindy is great here. Really opens your sinuses."

Riordan's stomach growled at the enticing aromas. "Smells good."

Riordan tentatively tasted the lamb then coughed loudly as fire raced through his sinus cavities. The Indian food he got at home had the level of heat toned down greatly compared to this lava. This was off-the-scale hot. "Jeez, this stuff is like fire," he groaned. "My nose is running like at tap."

"Wait until it hits yer arse," Sean commented.

Neil looked across the table. "I've got some tissues here if you like."

Riordan, trying to keep the look of horror from his face, replied, "Thanks for the offer, but I'd rather use my sleeve."

"What?"

Sean exploded in a fit of laughter. Neil eventually realized what had happened and glared cross the table at Sean. "You told him, you bollox, didn't you?"

Sean replied, "I thought it was funny... A little strange, but funny!"

Following supper, Sean led them to a nearby club, where Riordan had his hand stamped by a bouncer at the door. It was a long time since he had been decorated in such a fashion. Once past the entrance, dance music pulsed from a massive array of speakers, especially a muddy bass. He felt the impact of the bass deep in his chest. They grabbed a table in one corner, mercifully out of the direct barrage from the speakers. A waitress appeared as if by magic. They could always tell who were the well-heeled patrons, where they had the best chance of getting a good tip. As if to reinforce that thought, Riordan was surprised when Sean took a fifty-pound note from his wallet and handed it to the waitress.

"That's for you, love, your tip for the night, so just make sure our glasses are never empty. It'll be Guinness all around."

The waitress, who brass name tag said, "Sandy," squealed with delight, the bill vanished, and she went off immediately to get the first round of pints. Sean scanned the female patrons in the club like an alligator surveying antelope at a watering hole. "Some nice dollies here tonight," he commented. "Might get a leg over."

After several rounds of pints, where they caught up as much as possible, Riordan had had enough. The Guinness proved to be much too filling, especially on top of the huge meal, so he ordered some shots. To have a little fun with them, he ordered Black Sambuca and placed the glasses in a row on the table. Beside the glasses lay a matchbook bearing the club's imprint. "Time to separate the men from the boys, lads," he said. Featherstone would be so proud. It was the big man that had switched him on to the trick.

Neil looked warily at the matches. "Now, explain this to me again."

Riordan nodded. "It's simple. You have to light the thing and drink it in a single pour while it's still on fire."

"Isn't that a wee bit dangerous?" Neil asked.

"Oh shut up, you weenie," Riordan hissed. "This is a trick for real men."

Riordan struck a match, touched the flame to the surface of each shot glass, and a light blue flame immediately caressed the surface of the liquid. Sean and Neil picked up their glasses, careful not to spill the liquid, watching Riordan intently. He poured the liquid into his mouth, as did Sean, savouring the pungent flavour of licorice. However, Neil gagged, and the liquor splashed over the front of his shirt in a sheet of flame. Riordan immediately tossed the remnants of a pint of beer over Neil to put it out, but not before it had created several scorch marks and a few holes in the white cotton. Poking a finger through the holes, Neil laughed. "Jesus Christ, look at my good shirt. Angela will kill me."

Sean nudged Riordan in the side then leaned in to whisper in a conspiratorial manner. "Do you see that bird over there, sitting at the end of the bar?"

Riordan followed Sean's direction and gazed at the woman sitting alone at the end of the bar, sipping on a martini. The dress was constructed from some sort of shimmering material looked like it had been spray-painted on her body. "The one with the red dress?"

Sean nodded. "Aye, that one ... she's been giving me the eye."

Riordan laughed. "And I suppose you know what she wants?"

Sean grinned. "I'll go get the next round in and have a wee word. You never know..."

He got up from the table, just slightly unsteady, and headed to the bar. There was an open spot beside the woman in the red dress, so Sean eased himself in, and presently Riordan watched him strike up a conversation. At one point the woman threw her head back, laughing uproariously at something Sean had said.

"There's not enough O's in smooth for that one," Riordan commented.

Neil, having managed to cool himself down, agreed. "It's about time he had some fun," he said, sipping his pint. "These last few months have been hell for him."

"So I gather," Riordan replied gently. "For you as well."

A few moments later Sean returned to the table, beaming from ear to ear, carrying a serving tray from the bar. On the tray sat three full pints, accompanied by a blue martini. Sean said, "I'm on a sure thing there, boys. Her name's Nigella, like the woman on the telly. I'm going to have a quick drink with her, but I didn't want you two to get lonely."

Neil grinned. "Maybe she bites like the woman on the telly as well. Anyway, let us know what's happening later ... just in case."

Sean replied, "Yes, Mammy. Jesus, I've got to piss like a racehorse." Then he disappeared off in the direction of the washroom. When he left, Riordan took two blue tablets out of his pocket, set them on the table, then took a large coin and crushed the tablets into a powder. Satisfied it was fine enough for his purposes, he scooped the powder into his hand and then dropped it into Sean's drink, stirring it around with his finger.

Neil looked appalled. "What are you doing? What is that stuff?"

"Relax," Riordan replied. "A mate of mine gave me some Viagra. He said one always does the trick, but I thought Sean might appreciate two."

"Oh, fuck, he's not going to like this ... or maybe ..." He lifted his pint and clicked glasses with Riordan. "Doesn't seem like twenty odd years since we were pulling pranks on each other. Sean is the fucking devil when it comes to practical jokes. I should know, 'cos I've been on the butt end of more than a few."

"Well then." Riordan grinned. "Let's say payback's a bitch!"

When Sean returned from the washroom, he took the proffered drink from Riordan, quaffed about a quarter of it, and then carried the martini over to bar. The lady in the red dress smiled as he sat down beside her and handed her the drink. They clinked glasses.

"Perhaps we should finish our drinks up at the other end of the bar," Riordan said. "That way we can keep an eye on him." They made their way across the club to the opposite end of the bar, sliding onto seats facing Sean and the lady in the red dress, who were deep in conversation.

Neil said, "He's getting on like a house on fire, and she can certainly handle her drink. That martini disappeared in short order."

At the other end of the bar, as Riordan watched Sean signal the barman, the lady in red was sipping Sean's beer. "Uh-oh, she just quaffed about half of his drink."

"But it doesn't have any effect on women though, does it?" Neil asked.

Riordan shrugged. "I'm fucked if I know. Anyway, enough about our lad here. Tell me about your life, 'cos all I know is what

I've seen on Facebook over the past few months. Sean tells me things are a bit rocky with Fiona."

Neil nodded sombrely. "My circumstances with Fiona are pretty rough at the moment. I had a difficult time with the business for a few years, a lot of ups and downs — mostly downs, but she was always riding me. She comes from money and wanted the best of everything. Unfortunately, that came at a price, and consequently I got in way over my head in debt. The house, the kids, the private schools, the ski vacations — it's never-ending."

"Think you can make it work?"

Neil shook his head. "Nah. I don't even want to bother any more."

"Why don't you just leave?"

"The aforementioned: money, the kids, her father..."

"What's her father got to do with it?

"Plenty," Neil replied vehemently. "Daddy is one of the top divorce lawyers in the city. After he's through with me I'll be living in a shoebox and eating Spam."

"Luxury," Riordan replied in his best Month Pythonesque accent. "But take my advice, mate, don't let things drag on. The kids will be better off in the long run. If you and Fiona aren't getting along, the kids can sense it."

Neil nodded, a distant look in his eyes. "Maybe you're right..."

The pressure on Riordan's bladder became too much to bear. He eased himself up out of the seat. "Anyway, I have to go and drain the lizard." In the middle of the bar, two hard-looking cases were glaring at Riordan. He had noticed them the moment they arrived about twenty minutes earlier. They had seemed a little out of place to him and were giving off a strange vibe that he recognized immediately. Both were drinking heavily, their voices loud and angry. Judging by their body language, he knew they were spoiling for a fight. Other patrons gave them a wide berth. One hard case had a shaved head and wore a faded denim jacket, while the other wore a black leather bomber and had long dark hair, pulled back in a Steven Seagal-style ponytail. Both wore black leather brogues, well-polished, steel-toed and great for cracking ribs.

Riordan finished taking a leak, thankful for the release, and zipped himself up. Behind him, the door opened and shut. The automatic faucet clicked on, and a sheet of water glided down the back of the urinal, stirring up the remnants of the sanitizers at the bottom of the bowl. Some wise wag had written on the wall, 'Please do not eat the mints at the bottom of the bowl.' Riordan laughed, stepped back, and turned to see the hard case in the black leather bomber standing in front of him.

Inwardly, Riordan cursed.

The guy was trouble.

Riordan tried to go around him, but the hard case stepped into his way, blocking his path. Just like the movies. The reek of booze came off the guy in waves, and when he spoke, the stench of stale tobacco almost made Riordan gag.

"I heard your accent out there in the bar," he stated. "I hate fuckin' Yanks!"

Riordan nodded. "Actually, I'm Irish..."

The thug laughed. His teeth had not fared well under a steady diet of nicotine. "Well 'actually,' I hate fuckin' Micks even more..." Riordan heard a click, and a switchblade glinted in the thug's hand. Riordan shook his head. There was no getting away from this.

Riordan, his voice hard, said, "So you're an equal-opportunity bigot, are you ... put the knife away before you hurt somebody!"

"Fuck you, pal..." The thug lunged at Riordan, who stepped inside the thrust, grasped the knife hand, and removed the knife easily. It was a simple matter of mechanics and leverage. Hefting the knife, he hurled it into the doorframe. He then drove the edge of his knuckles into the man's throat, propelling him back against the washroom door. Both hands instinctively went to his throat, and choking noises gurgled from his mouth as he gasped for breath. Riordan walked over and removed the knife, then slammed his head into the man's nose.

Cartilage cracked loudly.

A Belfast kiss. The thug dropped like a stone, unconscious. Riordan bent over the man, grasped the ponytail, and hacked it off.

Souvenir in hand, Riordan straightened, pushed open the door, and walked back into the bar. He made his way over to where the thug's partner was sipping his beer. Smiling, he dropped the severed ponytail into the man's pint. Then, leaning over, he said, "You better go and check on your little friend, and if I set eyes on you two again tonight, I'll fucking well gut you!" The man's eyes widened, and he had enough smarts to know he was outclassed. His mate was the tougher of the two.

Riordan made his way back over to the bar and sat down.

"What was that about?" Neil asked.

Riordan shrugged. "A little misunderstanding, that's all."

In front of them, the barman, who wore a shiny brass badge that proclaimed his name was Tony, dried the glasses that had just come steaming from the dishwasher. Riordan figured he was in his early twenties and spent a good portion of every day in the gym, judging from the way the black silk shirt outlined his tattooed biceps. An unspoken warning for troublemakers. A dusting of dark stubble covered his head, and several hooped earrings decorated each earlobe. All in all, a tough piece of work. Neil nodded toward Sean.

"So what should we do? Do you think we should leave him?"

Riordan shook his head. "I've no idea..." Bad Company came on the stereo; the strains of "Feel Like Making Love" blasted out of the speakers. "Oh no, there he goes." On the dance floor,

Sean and the lady were wrapped around each other, their bodies swaying in time to the music.

"Jesus, she looks like she's going to ride him," Neil commented. "She's grabbing his arse hard enough."

Riordan laughed. "She's in for a surprise if she grabs his other parts. The Viagra will have kicked in by now."

The barman stopped polishing glasses and leaned across the bar. "Was that your mate at the end of the bar just then?"

Riordan nodded. "Yeah, why do you ask?"

The barman laughed. "Nigella's in here most Fridays and Saturdays and pretty harmless. Likes to dance. But her real name is Nigel ... she/he's a tranny!"

Riordan was taken aback for a moment, then he too burst out laughing. "Dear Lord, it doesn't get any better than this. Anyway, I'll be back in a minute. This fucking beer's going through me like there's no tomorrow. Once you start pissing, you can't stop." In reality, he wanted to ensure the thugs had disappeared.

Riordan smiled when he returned to his seat. The two hard cases had vanished, and back out on the dance floor, Sean was still dancing with the woman in red, snogging furiously during a slow song. His eyes were closed, a dreamy expression on his face. Suddenly his eyes popped open with a look of sheer terror. A few heated words were exchanged, and Sean strode back to the bar, sliding on to a barstool beside them. His face, flushed, wore a very annoyed look.

"A pint of Guinness, please," he snorted.

"Everything okay, Sean?" Riordan asked, barely able to keep his face straight.

Sean nodded toward the dance floor. "God, she was a handful. We're not on the floor two minutes, and I'm getting the old tonsillectomy. Mind you, no complaints from me. Then I spring this boner that would cut glass, and about a minute later she's got a boner to match. I tell you, that was a fucking Kodak moment and a half."

The barman set a pint on front of Sean. "That'll be five pounds, please."

Riordan laughed. "Here, I'll pay for it. It was worth it to see the look on your face."

The three men clinked glasses.

*

About an hour and several drinks later, Riordan heard a bell ring out. It had been a long time since he had heard a barman ring the time bell to alert patrons to the fact that the bar was closing. It was one of his favourite lines from the "Sultans of Swing," Dire Straits' breakout hit of the seventies and one of his all-time favourite songs. For years it had made his iTunes playlist for top fifty songs, as well as his top fifty guitar solos. There was a mad rush to the bar to get last call in, but Riordan had had enough and was content to get back to the hotel. Sean and Neil decided to have a wee one for the road, and their barely-able-to-focus eyes foreshadowed the sad tale of the next morning. Featherstone's comments about the older you get, the more tragic hangovers become echoed in his brain. The old rule about jet lag was to try to stay to local time, but Riordan's body was providing subtle clues that it was almost out of gas.

Outside, the welcome cool night air was refreshing to his face. London pubs didn't have air conditioning, and the place had grown stifling as the evening drew on. All three bore the sweat-stained armpits to prove it. There had been a rain shower at some point during the evening, the streetlights reflecting off slick, glistening cobblestones. The scene, combined with the antique decorative lights designed to look like Victorian gas lamps, made it feel like they were stepping back in time.

Cobblestoned streets were always a romantic foil for poets and lovers, but for three men with a skinful of drink, they proved a treacherous hazard. Twice on the way down the street, Neil, who was always the clumsy one, almost took a header into a parked car. This was much to the amusement of Sean, who was still having problems with his equipment. He halted periodically to make adjustments.

They turned into a darkened street off the main drag, and Riordan frowned as he looked at the street name mounted on a gable wall. He possessed an uncanny sense of direction, and this most definitely was not the way they had come. However, Sean and Neil seemed completely at ease, so he let them take the lead. Sean had discovered an empty beer can at the side of the road and was dribbling it like a soccer ball down the middle of the road. Neil ran alongside, and Riordan grinned. It was like being transported back in time to his childhood, when anything that rolled could be used as a substitute for a soccer ball.

"... and Beckham takes the ball and streaks down the right wing. Miller is in the centre waiting for the cross," Sean yelled, kicking the can down the street ahead of himself. Across the street, Neil was waving his arms wildly, "I'm open, I'm open..."

Sean kicked the can high into the air; it flew over Neil's head, continued a few feet and bounced off a car windscreen. "Oh fuck," he groaned, seeing figures inside the car. As Riordan looked over, the electric window of the car slid down, and the hard case from the bar stuck his head out with a wide smirk. The state of his teeth gave credence to the old jokes about the quality of British dentistry.

"Shit," Riordan whispered.

Sean and Neil turned to look just as four car doors swung open at the same time, almost as if choreographed. The hard case with the leather bomber got out, along with his mate from the bar and two others, equally mean-looking thugs.

Riordan recognized the type.

Bullies.

Instead of taking a beating like a man, the guy had gone for reinforcements. Riordan took a deep breath. Looking behind him, as well intentioned as they might have been, Neil and Sean did not appear the types who had been in a good scrap for years. This bunch looked like soccer hooligans, well accustomed to talking with their fists and their feet.

The hard case from the bar rubbed the back of his head, where Riordan had shorn off the ponytail, pointed at him, and said, "We've got some unfinished business here, mate!"

Perhaps it was muscle memory, perhaps it was just reflex, but Riordan felt a flush of warmth flow through him as Sean and Neil moved to flank him, just as they did when they were kids.

The man facing Riordan threw back his head and laughed again, but it was forced laughter. Riordan had made him look bad, and now he had to try to save face. Never taking his eyes off Riordan for a moment, over his shoulder he said, "Oh look, just like Charlie's Angels..."

The other thugs laughed.

The laughter died midstream when Riordan said, "I thought you had enough..."

The hard case spat on the ground. "Jumped me when I wasn't looking, didn't you? Now we'll see..."

One of the others spat on the ground and said, "Yeah, Mo, give it him."

From behind him, Riordan heard Sean whisper, "We're in for a hiding!"

Neil replied, "Aye, that we are..."

The fog cleared from his brain as the adrenaline kicked in. Riordan stepped forward until he was just a couple of feet away from the thug named Mo. The guy's name was likely Morris, which was why he shortened it to Mo. Riordan had gone to school with a couple of guys named Morris, and that was the first thing to go. If you were tough enough, Morris became Mo overnight; otherwise it became Doris. And nicknames like that stuck for years.

He said, "Do you..." then, after rubbing his chin with his right hand, slapped the left side of the man's neck with the back of his hand, a quick, powerful flick, and stepped back. The lightning-fast blow landed perfectly. The man's eyes bulged out, and he tried to speak but could not. Riordan saw the fear in his eyes as the man realized he was completely paralyzed. Drool trickled from the side of his mouth, and strange moans emerged from his mouth. The others stared at their friend, and then at Riordan, as if unsure of what to do.

Riordan gave them hard eyes, then made a show of looking at his watch. "If you don't get him to a hospital within the next ten minutes, he's dead! It's your choice."

They looked stunned for a moment then grabbed their friend and dragged him off to their car. One of the man's shoes fell off, caught by the sharp cobblestones. Riordan picked it up and hurled it at the car. "You've lost your shoe, Cinderella," he roared. The gang had a bit of trouble manoeuvring their friend into the back seat, but they eventually managed, and the car roared off down the street, its tires spinning on the slick road trying to gain purchase.

Turning to the others, Riordan said, "We better go, lads, and quickly."

"Wow, now that was amazing," Neil said. "Will he really die?"

Riordan shook his head. "Nope. That was a called a carotid slap ... sends a little shock wave into your brain that paralyzes you for about two minutes. Looks scary, but he'll be fine, and then he'll be really pissed off. So we better scarper!"

Sean laughed, slapped Riordan on the back, and the three ran off down the street.

Back at the hotel, they congregated in chairs in Riordan's room. Jackets were off, tossed randomly on the floor. The blackened singe marks on Neil's white shirt stood out vividly in the bright light of the room. A few chest hairs had also been singed, the skin underneath a dull shade of red. It hadn't looked quite so bad in the bar's dim lighting. Neil wore the shirt proudly, like a badge of honour.

Riordan extracted a large bottle of Black Bush from his suitcase, set it on the table, and grabbed three glasses from the sideboard.

Sean grinned. "Ah, good man yerself. 'Tis mother's milk."

Sean tore off the seal, uncorked the bottle, and poured a couple of fingers worth into the three glasses. The three clinked their glasses and swallowed the first shot. Riordan felt the familiar burn and inhaled deeply. It was going to be a longer night than he planned. Fortunately for him, the lads were too far gone to ask too many awkward questions. There would be more tomorrow, in the clear light of day.

Riordan refilled the glasses and said, "Speaking of Bushmills, let me tell you about a contract I did a while ago in San Diego."

Sean gave a dramatic flourish. "The stage is yours..."

"Anyway, I was working in one of the company's divisions in San Diego. So I flew down there on a Sunday, worked like a dog all day Monday, and I was sitting in my office about seven o'clock on the Monday night, exhausted and starving. I was dying for a drink, so I asked one of the tech guys, a real cool black dude called Michael, where I could find some Black Bush! Jesus, I thought he was going to kill me! When I asked him if he liked the taste, that was a whole different discussion until we sorted out the confusion."

Sean and Neil laughed heartily. Riordan poured them another shot, and then another. They laughed, drank, toasted, and told stories until they could go no further. As the hours passed, the innate wariness that he had nurtured over the years receded like waves on the beach at low tide. These were good, decent people, and with every story the years peeled away until it was like they were children again. Then, like marathon runners crossing the finish line, they collapsed.

*

Riordan cracked open one eye and immediately pressed his fingers hard against his temples in a futile attempt to reduce the throbbing. The inside of his mouth felt like it was full of cotton, his lips were parched. Even his eyes were crusty. Trying hard to focus on the coffee table across the room, he saw the empty Black Bush bottle. He heard snoring, and turning over, peered across to the other double bed in the room. Sean, still fast asleep, was running his tongue across dry lips. Riordan stared at where his four front teeth were missing. They had been knocked out when Sean was about nine and had gone over the handlebars of his bicycle, using his face to break the fall. They had called him VD, for Vampire Daly, for the longest time.

There was no sign of Neil. Perhaps he had managed to make it back to his room. Pulling back the sheets, Riordan eased himself upright, not at all surprised to see he was still fully clothed. He stumbled across the room to the bathroom. Inside he found Neil, lying in a twisted heap beside the toilet. Neil had obviously been making calls on the big white telephone. Riordan breathed through his mouth as the stench hit his nostrils. The urgency of the situation kicked in, and Riordan unzipped his fly and let loose a long, blissful stream into the toilet. There were audible, loud cracks as he rotated his neck to get the kinks out.

When he finished, he was just about to flush the toilet when the light glinted off something. He peered into the bowl. Floating just under the surface of the noxious stew was a dental plate holding four teeth. "Oh fuck, no! No!" he muttered under his breath. Screwing up his face in revulsion, he knelt down and put his hand into the toilet bowl to retrieve the plate. Then he flushed the toilet. Neil did not stir. Having recovered the teeth, he went over to the sink, rinsed them under the tap as best he could, and then poured a generous helping of mouthwash over them.

After rousing the two groggy lads, he issued them forth to their respective rooms. Riordan swallowed a handful of Tylenol, jumped in the shower, and once again cursed the little stream of water that fell out of the shower head. What he wouldn't give for a real shower. He washed up as best he could, then pulled on a fresh T-shirt and jeans and headed downstairs to the restaurant. By then the headache had receded somewhat. He had a fierce hunger, and after ordering a pot of coffee from a waiter who could barely speak

English, decided on the "full English" breakfast. It would never be as good as an "Ulster fry," but when in Rome…

The coffee, predictably, was awful, and barely hot enough, but there were faint traces of caffeine present. Several cups managed to dull his cravings. He made a mental a note to find a Starbucks later in the morning. Like his hometown, they seemed to have sprung up here on just about every street corner. As he waited, he checked his BlackBerry for messages. There was a quick text message from Nancy, curious about how things had gone. He responded that it had been a good night and that he would call later.

He knew there was an eight-hour time difference, did the mental arithmetic to arrive at the conclusion that it would be 3:00 a.m. local time, and decided not to call. Not that she would mind, but he knew how precious sleep was for her after the arduous shifts in the ER. Following the last round of staff and budget cuts at the hospital, the weary staff that remained were being forced to work longer and longer hours. He knew how dedicated she was, as were all the other ER nurses, and staff nurses, the "everyday angels" who treated their patients regardless of cuts. It was a fitting sobriquet.

The breakfast arrived, and surprisingly the plate was hot enough to remove fingerprints. The sausages still sizzled, the over-easy eggs looked cooked to perfection, the toast was thick and sopping with butter. The only questionable item was the black pudding. He tucked in with relish and was almost halfway through the plate of food when Neil and Sean sat down beside him. Both men looked very much the worse for wear.

"Want some coffee?" he asked.

Sean sucked furiously on his teeth as if tasting something strange. Looking at them both, he asked, "Was I drinking crème de menthe last night?"

Riordan shrugged innocently. "Who knows? There wasn't too much that we didn't drink."

Neil groaned. "Let's grab something quick and be on our way. I think I'm supposed to be attending some function this afternoon, but I forgot to plug in my phone last night, and it's out of power."

After checking out, Sean and Neil retrieved their matching Porsche Carreras from the underground parking. Riordan nodded appreciatively when Sean pulled up to the foyer. "You must be doing all right," he commented.

Sean grinned. "Midlife fucking crisis, I think."

It took a while to get out of the rat's nest of streets that was downtown London, but they soon hit the motorway and headed southwest. Traffic was light, and Sean hovered just above the speed limit with Neil following close behind. The radio played quietly in the background. Lady Gaga was singing "Poker Face."

Riordan said, "Oh, my poor head. You'd think we'd know better by this age." The headache had returned with a fury, the Tylenol barely making a dent. He took another handful.

Sean nodded. "Ach, life is for livin', so they say. Mind you, I don't feel very much alive just at the minute. I'm not what you'd call 'open casket-worthy.'"

Riordan agreed. "You're right, you know. People often ask me about the difference between Irish and North American cultures. I tell them if a guy comes to work in the morning, hair unkempt, clothes the same as yesterday, unshaven, and generally rumpled in North America, coworkers would take one look and say 'Jesus, you look awful!' An Irish person would say, and this is the fundamental difference, 'Ach, it must have been one hell of a night!'"

Sean laughed. "Now, isn't that the truth!" Leaning on one side, he let go a long, noisy fart.

Riordan groaned, trying hard not to breathe as he slid down the window. "Oh jeez, awww Sean, for God's sake! You could at least have warned me."

"Oh, hell, it's worse than I thought," Sean commented, sniffing. "It's that bloody curry returning for vengeance. Call Neil ... I've got to find a bog."

Following a quick pit stop at a motorway service station — Sean referred to it as a "choke and puke" — he dialled Neil on the car phone. When he answered, Sean said, "We were just wondering about the plans for your party this evening. What time are things supposed to start?"

"If you had bothered to read it, you bollox, the invites said 9:00 p.m.," Neil replied, "so any time around then is fine. I'm going out for dinner with Fiona and her parents first, so we'll probably be there around eight thirty. Fiona likes to make sure things are in order."

Across the car, Sean mimicked shoving two fingers down his throat.

Riordan nodded. "That's grand. Sean and I can have dinner at the Inn."

Sean looked across the car at Riordan and winked. "Is Lynn coming, by any chance?"

"Yes, of course," came the indignant reply. "And unfortunately, her husband as well."

Riordan said, "Isn't that cutting it a little close to the bone, Neil? Alcohol is a great one for loosening tongues..."

Neil replied, "Don't worry, lads, everything will be cool."

Sean laughed. "Why does that not give me any comfort whatsoever?"

Riordan shook his head as Sean broke the connection. He was astounded at how quickly the bonds of friendship had reformed and how comfortable he was in the company of these two men, old friends that he hadn't seen or spoken to for over twenty years. It felt like slipping into an old sweater. There was an innate sense of trust, and he was never one to trust another person lightly.

They took the exit for Reading, passed through the bustling university town and headed toward the outskirts, speeding along hedge-covered, narrow roads. Neil had taken the lead, and presently they turned off the main road, passed through a pair of ancient red-brick pillars, and onto a gravelled, cedar-lined driveway. They followed a graceful arc and pulled up in front of Neil's house, a large, old, country Victorian the walls of which were completely hidden behind a dense coat of ivy. The ancient, gnarled branches of ivy looked like veins under the greenery. As he got out, Riordan admired the building. Gravel crunched under his feet. The windows appeared to his eye to be leaded glass originals. A massive, well-polished brass knocker in the shape of a lion's head mounted in the centre of the stout wooden door announced visitors.

Riordan said, "Jeez, talk about the Lord of the Manor. This must've cost a pretty penny."

Sean stood beside him, gazing across the expansive, manicured gardens. "That's Neil for you, always living beyond his means. He..."

The front door flew open, banging hard against the interior wall. Framed in the doorway, Neil's wife, Fiona, a petite blonde woman dressed in a one-piece navy dress adorned by an eye-catching set of pearls, glared at her husband. Riordan took in the wide eyes, the flared nostrils, and the colour rising in her cheeks. Not a happy camper. Then, seeing Riordan and Sean, she got it under control. The smile didn't entirely look genuine.

"Sean, nice to see you again, and late as always," she commented. "And you must be David."

Sean smiled, ignoring the barb directed at him.

"That would be me," Riordan replied, stepped forward, and shook her hand. "A pleasure to meet you." Her grip was firm, her skin cool.

Turning back to Neil, she asked impatiently, "Are you all coming in?"

Sean replied, "No, thanks, we're just taking some stuff down the inn for Neil, and we've got to check in." Neil disappeared into the house, followed by Fiona, and Riordan listened to his footsteps retreating on the hardwood floor. Loud, angry voices echoed up the corridor. Smiling, Riordan and Sean exchanged sympathetic glances.

Riordan said, "That sounds familiar..."

Sean, "You don't know the half of it! Maybe we should just get out of here."

Riordan heard Fiona say, "Daddy will be extremely annoyed. I promised him we'd be there to hear him speak." Then her voice seemed to go up an octave. "And what the hell happened to your shirt? Is that a burn? How the fuck did you burn your shirt?"

The place lapsed into silence, and Neil returned to the front door carrying a couple of boxes. Riordan recognized the world-weary look on his face.

He said, "Sorry, lads, apparently I am supposed to attend some function this afternoon, and I'm late and hung over. I'll catch up with you later!"

Sean put his hand on his friend's shoulder. "Everything all right, mate?"

Neil shook his head sadly. "Far from it, far from it..."

*

Rodger the Dodger rubbed eyes weary from lack of sleep. He poured himself another cup of black tea from the stainless-steel teapot sitting on the scarred wooden table of the cafe. Nestled in the back streets of the Isle of Dogs, the mouth-watering aroma of bacon fat and frying sausages permeated the greasy spoon. It was not exactly a haven for the health conscious. Even the bread was fried. This was a place for working men, local laborers and dock rats who made their living off the strength of their backs.

Normally his stomach would be growling at the enticing fare, but his appetite was nonexistent at the moment. His mind kept flashing back to the image of the headless corpse lying on the floor of DeLisle's warehouse.

The cafe was empty, the lunchtime crowd having passed on, and he needed a moment to think. He liked to come to this little place because it was one of the few establishments remaining that used real tea instead of those fucking poncy teabags, the resulting brew so strong you could almost stand a teaspoon upright.

The swelling in his left eye had almost subsided. His vision, alarmingly, remained blurry, leading him to wonder if there was more permanent damage. A lancing pain flashed across his side each time he moved, leaving him almost breathless. He had examined the results of the beating in the washroom mirror. One side of his chest sported a mottled green and purple and black shade, his skin hot to the touch. Yet there was no time to get medical help, not while Dempsey was still on the run. Max DeLisle's deadline was rapidly approaching.

He reeked; the rank odour of sweat and fear rose in ripples off his unwashed body. He itched. Worst of all, he looked like a fucking Irish pikey every time he saw his reflection in a mirror. The last three days had been spent scouring the city, looking for some trace of Dempsey, but the search had been futile. It would have been easier to find the Holy Grail than track down the Irish cunt. It was like he had vanished into the proverbial thin air. There were rumours, all unsubstantiated, that Dempsey had once been a member of the INLA, an ultraviolent splinter group of the IRA, and if he had survived for all these years with the Brits on his tail, then he knew how to elude DeLisle's people. And he was not the only one looking for Dempsey. Apparently, the bastard owed a lot of people and had skipped out on his debts.

The prevailing opinion was that Dempsey had fucked off back to Ireland, and when people discovered that he had crossed

Max DeLisle, there was a general consensus that disappearing was probably the wisest move. All of which provided little comfort for Roger. Max DeLisle didn't issue idle threats, and once more the image of the decapitated head staring at him caused the bile in his stomach to churn. He topped the mug up with a splash of milk, stirred it, and was staring into the liquid when the door to the cafe opened and Billy K walked in. Roger's immediate physiological response was to take flight, but as he rose, two of Billy's boys came in through the kitchen, effectively blocking his path. He was trapped.

Billy K grabbed a mug off the counter, sat down across the table from Roger, and poured himself a cup. Roger's leg trembled uncontrollably under the table. He placed a hand on it in an attempt to keep it still. Billy didn't say a word, allowing the tension to build. He added a splash of milk, stirred the tea, and took a sip. He nodded appreciatively then placed the mug back on the table.

"They always make a great cuppa here," he said.

Roger nodded. Words were not forthcoming. Billy was wearing his soccer shirt, the new blue Chelsea strip, over a pair of jeans and Doc Martens. The shirt was stretched tightly over a heavily muscled frame. Billy was Max DeLisle's "muscle" in more ways than one. A heavy gold link chain encircled his thick neck. Roger vaguely remembered there was a Chelsea home game today, but it would have started already, which meant that Billy, a fanatical Chelsea supporter, was missing the game. Not a good sign.

Roger grew more agitated. The Saint Vitus dance escalated under the table.

Leaning back in the chair, Billy opened his hands, palms up, in a gesture that spoke volumes. He sniffed the air. "Fuck me, Dodger, you smell like a right cunt, so I'll be brief. What have you got for me?"

Roger shook his head sadly. He knew his life hung in the balance, and that particular scale was tipping in the wrong direction. "I've been everywhere, Billy, that's the God's honest truth, and nobody's seen the cunt. I even went to some of those fucking shithole Irish pubs in Kilburn where he used to drink. They all say the same fucking thing — he's done a runner. Most of them think he's legged it over to Ireland, and if that's the case we'll never find him. You know what these fucking micks are like."

Billy nodded. "Yep, that's the word me and the boys have been getting as well." Picking up the mug, he took another swig. "But Max is not going to be happy about that, and you know how Max gets."

The image of the severed head again flashed into Roger's mind, and he absentmindedly touched his throat. "I'm sorry, Billy. I did everything I fucking could to find the cunt." Billy's goons had come up behind him, one on each side, and his insides turned to water. One of them, and he couldn't remember which one, had a reputation for using a pearl-handled straight razor. Roger had seen the end result. The long, thin blade could open you up like gutting a fish. Both of them were wearing too much aftershave. "Please, Billy."

Billy sat motionless, as if pondering something. Roger knew all it would take would be a nod of his head, and it was lights out. "Okay, Roger. You've been a good earner up to now, so it'd be a shame to waste those talents. I'll tell you what, you fuck off to Blackpool for a couple of weeks until things have quietened down, and then you come back. I'll deal with Max. So you owe me." Billy rubbed his thumb and forefinger together in that age-old gesture.

Roger almost cried with relief. "Thanks, Billy, you fucking won't regret this. Honest."

Billy K nodded. "Make sure I don't. Okay, lads, let's go and catch the second half of the match."

One of the thugs slapped Roger so hard on the back of his head that his eyes watered. Billy strolled out the front door, followed by the pair. The one wearing a black leather jacket pulled out a straight razor. When he popped the blade, gleaming, well-stropped steel carved the air.

"Next time, Dodger, next time..."

*

As they drove through the scenic, winding country roads, Sean at the wheel, Riordan fidgeted with the plastic bag containing the book about the Raven. He had thought about the hows and wheres and whens, but there was never a good time to break the news, so he decided to plow straight ahead. Sometimes there was no better option than to just let go. But trusting people did not come easy. He had learned, however, from painful experience with Nancy that it was far better to share than play his cards close to the vest. It had not been an easy transition for him, and more than a few furious silences had been created because of it.

Riordan said, "Sean, there's something I need to tell you, to explain about all these years I haven't been in touch, but you need to promise not to tell a soul."

Sean smiled. "From your lips to God's ears, pal. You forget, we've been mates since we were kids. Despite the long separation, I'm glad you're back in our lives. You are back, aren't you?"

Riordan smiled and nodded, touched by the words. It was heart-warming and reassuring, and he knew the words came from the heart. "You got that right. But this stuff all happened when we were at university, when we were young and foolish. Full of piss and vinegar, thought we knew everything — thought we were invincible. That book you gave me yesterday..."

Sean grinned, "...about the dreaded Raven, supposedly the most fearsome enforcer for the Protestant paramilitaries. I thought you'd enjoy it."

119

Riordan grimaced and sighed. "Sean, the reason it shook me so badly…" Sean turned his head slightly, a frown crossing his face.

"Go on, you've got my attention."

Riordan exhaled a long breath. "Let's just say it'll be interesting to read my alleged biography!"

Sean's eyes widened, and the car almost swerved off the road. "You ... the Raven ... but he, you..."

Riordan looked over at his friend. "Look, Sean, I couldn't tell you at the time. It was too dangerous. I never professed to being a saint, but all those people that got offed deserved it. It started with the guys who killed my parents. I got most of them, but there was this one guy — I never caught up with him."

He paused for a moment to let it sink in. He could only imagine the questions starting to race through Sean's mind. "My uncle, the Old Man, had access to intelligence reports, so he knew who the suspects were. He trained me to go after them. Then the guys at Army Intelligence started doing stuff and blaming it on the Raven, and pretty soon the legend grew. There came a point where I couldn't take it anymore, so my only choice was to run far, far away."

Sean nodded. He puffed out his cheeks and exhaled slowly. "Oh boy, I don't know where to start, or even what to ask. It'll take a wee while to digest all of this. And what do we tell Neil?"

Riordan shrugged. "All in good time. Neil's got a lot on his plate right now. And thanks for listening to me. It's been a heavy burden to carry all these years."

"I can only imagine," Sean replied.

Sean lapsed into a silent contemplation, which gave Riordan pause to reflect if he had done the right thing. Yet he felt okay placing his cards on the table. If they were to re-establish their friendship, something he desperately wanted, he had to be honest about his past. Nothing built on a foundation of lies would last.

They continued down the road in silence for a while, and Riordan was relived to see the sign for the inn appear, just outside the town of High Wycombe. "We can talk more about it later, Sean, since there's an awful lot of water under that particular bridge."

Sean nodded. They turned off the main road and into a narrow roadway that ran across a humpbacked bridge. A shallow, fast-flowing river passed under the bridge and disappeared behind the inn. "Wonder if there's any fish in there?" Riordan asked, and Sean laughed aloud. The tension Riordan felt dissipated immediately.

"Jasus, it's like you never left. You were always looking into rivers and asking that same question. Do you still fish a lot?"

"Oh yeah, that's the one link to my father that I always remember. Over the moat catching trout, with him smoking up a storm, or down to the pier at Glenarm, sitting in the car with the heater on and the rods hanging out the window. Not to mention the fish supper on the way home. My mother..." He paused, choking up for a moment. "Ma used to make us these incredible egg and onion sandwiches on a pan loaf and ship us off with a big flask of tea. Man, oh man, nothing tasted so good. I can't wait until my boys are old enough to take them fishing."

Sean bypassed the sparsely used parking lot. The cars parked there — Mercedes, Jaguars, and Range Rovers — provided an indication of the affluence of patrons of the establishment. He pulled up to the front of the inn, switched off the ignition, and popped the trunk. Taking their bags, they went inside and checked in, informing the receptionist that they were attending the birthday party. Fiona's father had arranged a special rate for guests. At the elevator, Riordan turned to his friend. "Listen, Sean, is Hereford far from here?"

"Nah, it's about a couple of hours up the motorway. Why?"

"No particular reason. But would you mind if I borrowed the car for a couple of hours? There's a couple of errands I need to run, and I to have wrap Neil's present as well. But I promise to look after it."

Sean tossed him the keys. "No problem, mate, just remember we drive on the other side of the road! If you've got the address, plug it into the GPS and away ye go. Give me a call when you get back, or come and look for me in the bar. There might be some talent in there."

Riordan laughed. "Oh, you'll have to go a long way to beat last night, pal."

"Fuck you!"

*

The Porsche handled like a dream. Riordan cruised up the motorway at just over the speed limit, getting off at the exit for Hereford, former home of Stirling Lines Barracks, the training camp for the elite Special Air Service regiment. Encircling the town sat the hills of the Brecon Beacons National Park, dark and brooding. Just like his mood. Rain was on the way. Following the stilted voice of the GPS lady, he drove through the bustling little town, past the railway station, and pulled up outside a small yet dignified church. Solidly built from Ashlar sandstone and a dark Welsh slate roof and topped by a brooch-spire with an iron weathercock, St. Martin's was the final resting place of many SAS soldiers.

Getting out of the car, he turned up his collar against the strong winds and the oncoming rain and opened the front gate. The massive church door had recently received a fresh coat of red paint. Walking down the driveway of the church and over to the regimental clock, he scanned the brass plate for his uncle's name, putting his finger reverently on the name Bill Ellis. The gale tugged at his collar, old ghosts propelling his hesitant feet forward. Then he turned and walked through the cemetery, checking the tops of the gravestones one by one until he found the marble headstone with the name engraved in gold letters. It sat atop the famed regimental crest, the winger dagger. He had come to know that the blade was in fact a representation of Excalibur, wreathed in flames, but the "winged dagger" had been made famous in the media, and the name stuck.

Resting his hand on the cold marble, Riordan swallowed hard, blinking hard as his eyes began to water. Tears streamed down his face as he stood in a silent reverie. *You gave your life for me*, he thought, *so that I could have a chance at a new one*. He had never forgotten that moment. Several years ago, at the edge of a cliff, the Old Man had switched guns with him and sent him on his way. The Old Man knew there was only one way to allow his adopted son to escape, and that was to take a bullet for him. The wind whispered amongst the headstones as Riordan knelt down and ran his fingers gently across the engraved letters.

The Old Man had taken him under his wing after the death of his parents. While he diligently studied at school during the day, training of a more arcane nature occurred after hours. The Old Man, a former SAS commando, as well as several others, had taught him martial arts skills, knife fighting, explosives, and marksmanship. The goal was to provide him with the tools necessary to hunt down the terrorists responsible for detonating the booby-trap that killed his parents.

He was astonished at the amount of intelligence the Old Man had access to and even more surprised when the Old Man divulged that virtually all of the terrorists in the province were known to the authorities. There were a few, he disclosed, whose identities were buried so deep that it was impossible to track them. Wild cards, he called them. The problem for the authorities was catching any of the terrorists in the act. Riordan had no such rules to follow. It was the Old Man who had christened him Raven, and the attacks attributed to the name struck fear in every back alley shebeen, every drinking club, every reach of the province. No one who encountered the Raven lived to tell the tale, the only lingering trace of his presence being two gleaming brass shell casings and the two shattered eyes of his victims.

After a few moments of silent reverie, he walked back to the car and drove off, raindrops spattering against the ragtop. Behind him, a well-concealed CCTV camera transmitted the images of Riordan via satellite to an intelligence server hosted at the new SAS base.

*

Back at the inn, Riordan parked and ran across the carpark as raindrops started bouncing off his jacket. Another spring day in England. As expected, Sean was in the bar, a half-empty pint in front of him. A half-eaten bowl of peanuts sat beside the pint. His attention was totally focused on a flat screen-TV on the wall, showing one of the Premier League soccer games. Riordan slid on to a bar stool beside him, ordered a couple of pints, and handed Sean the keys.

"Thanks for ride," he said. "How's the game?"

"Fucking Spurs are losing again," came the disgusted reply.

"Got money on it?" Riordan asked, remembering that Sean had been a bit of a gambler. But he came by that honestly. Sean's mother, the venerable Mrs. Daly, had hosted a family poker night up until the week before she died. She had the gift and fleeced everyone. He received a nod of the head in reply. The whistle blew for full time, and Sean switched off the TV, turning his attention to the beer.

"We should go and check out the party room," Sean suggested. Taking their pints, they crossed the lobby and into a large ballroom, decked out with streamers and balloons of every shape and size. On a stage at one end of the room an Irish folk group were tuning up their guitars, preparing for the festivities.

"These are some friends of Neil's," Sean offered. "They're called Black Rose, and I've heard them a few times. They'll get the place on its feet, all right. So what about you? I know you were mad for the guitar at university. Do you still play?"

Riordan shook his head. "One of those things that went by the wayside, I'm afraid. Still, I keep thinking about taking it up again." The band launched into a rousing rendition of "Whisky in the Jar," and Sean sang along, out of key as Riordan remembered. He had always maintained that Sean couldn't carry a tune in a bucket, and it was gratifying to see that the years hadn't mellowed his friend's irrepressible efforts to try to sing.

They took their seats back at the bar, and just as Sean was ordering another couple of pints, his phone chirped.

"Sean here," he said, taking out his wallet and passing a couple of banknotes to the barman. For a moment, he looked puzzled, then he frowned. "You'd like to suck what? Where did you get this number, you fucking perv?"

Riordan tried desperately to keep a straight face as Sean angrily stabbed the "end call" button. In the washroom of the nightclub the previous evening, Riordan had added Sean's cell number to a long list that had been scrawled on the tiled wall. "Who was that?" he asked.

"Some bastard says he wants to suck my dick."

"Wouldn't have been your friend from last night, would it?"

"No fuckin' way, pal, I don't give out this number to anyone."

In the reception room, waitresses floated like wraiths through the crowds, carrying trays of elegant hors d'oeuvres. Riordan saw Neil and Fiona in the corner, deep in conversation with another couple. Neil did not look happy in the slightest. "Oh look," Sean said, "horses' ovaries!" He grabbed a couple of skewers of shrimp and chewed away happily.

Then Riordan noticed Neil's face brighten, like the sun appearing out from behind a cloud. He turned to see another couple walk into the reception area. The woman wore a stunning silver minidress that looked like it had been spray-painted on a well-toned body. Her blonde hair, pinned up with a silver clasp, revealed a slender neck. Diamond studs adorned her earlobes. Heads turned and the crowd parted like the Red Sea as they headed in the direction of Neil and Fiona.

Sean said, "There's Lynn and Brian. We better go and say hello."

As Sean headed over to greet them, Riordan took a hard look at Lynn's husband.

Riordan commented. "So that's Lynn. She's absolutely gorgeous ... I might have known. The husband, however, does look like a hard case. Ex-military type for sure — I'd know them a mile away. Running to seed a bit, though." The beginnings of a beer belly protruded over Brian's tightly cinched belt.

"That she is, mate. I've met her a few times and been an alibi more times than I care to remember. You're spot-on about the husband as well. He's a proper cunt!"

Neil made the introductions, and as Riordan had expected, Brian tried the "I'll crush your hand to show you how strong I am" approach. He got more than he bargained for but didn't let on. Riordan knew that not many people had a stronger grip than his own. Following some polite chit-chat, Riordan wandered off and found a comfy chair to watch the goings on. He was an ardent observer of people, and it was interesting to see the social rankings that exposed themselves as people arrived. For some it was like pledging fealty to the Lord of the Manor. Fiona's father was the one they made a beeline for before greeting his daughter. As Riordan expected, the pile of presents took over one corner of the room, and shortly after ten, when the room was filled to capacity, Fiona took to the stage to announce that Neil was going to unwrap his gifts.

Neil, a little glassy eyed from all the alcohol, dutifully began opening the presents handed to him by Fiona. She sat beside him, helping him sort through the enormous pile. After he had gone through a few, Riordan carried a large, well-wrapped box to the table and set it on the pile. He then went back to stand beside Sean.

Sean looked over with a strange expression on his face. "What the hell did you buy him?"

Riordan grinned. "It's not the gift, you know, it's all about the wrapping. I had to wait until he got here."

Neil held up a silver hip flask with his initials engraved on the side, grabbed his glass, and raised a toast to Sean.

"Thanks, mate," he offered. "This is great! Fiona, why don't you open that one that David brought?"

Riordan's stomach roiled. He shook his head slowly at Neil, but his head was turned away. "Oh fuck, this is not going to be good," he muttered. Neil's wife tore off the wrapping to reveal a cardboard legal box with a hinged lid. She smiled over at Riordan.

She said, "Must be very valuable if you had to wrap it in a legal box, David."

Sean leaned over and whispered in Riordan's ear. "Tell me that's not what I think it is..."

Riordan nodded. "Yep ... I needed a big box, and there was one in Neil's car..."

The conversation between Fiona and Riordan eventually sank in, and a stunned look crossed Neil's face. He turned pale as the blood drained from his cheeks.

Fiona commented, "Must be very delicate to be hidden in all these tissues."

Beside him, Riordan heard Sean say, "Fuck, I can't look..."

Fiona rummaged through the tissues and pulled out a piece of Inuit soapstone carving. Sean was making gagging sounds behind Riordan's back.

"Well, isn't that impressive," Fiona said, holding it for the crowd to see. She set the box aside, much to Neil's relief, and continued the distribution.

Riordan grinned and lifted his glass in a toast to Neil, who responded by shooting him dark looks. He could only imagine what he was muttering under his breath. Anxious to get out of the line of fire, Riordan headed over to the bar and found himself standing beside Brian.

Brian said, "Yank, by the sounds of you. Neil never said anything about having a friend in the States. I'm pretty good with accents, but I can't place yours. So what part are you from?"

Riordan said, "I'm from Vancouver, in British Columbia. You know, where they had the Winter Olympics. It's part of Canada." He was about to say more, but Lynn walked back into the hall and across to them. Before Riordan had a chance to speak, her husband frowned at her.

Brian said, "What were you doing out there?" Riordan was surprised at the demanding tone.

Lynn glanced at Riordan, and her face reddened in embarrassment. "Just calling my mum — I was supposed to call her earlier. Anyway, my drink's empty."

Brian responded, "There's plenty over at the bar. Help yourself and get me another Scotch while you're at it. And get one for David here, his looks a bit low."

"Fine," she responded curtly. "Hold my purse."

Brian drained the remainder of his whisky then peered into the top of Lynn's purse. Riordan noticed the cellphone nestled there. He looked on incredulously as Brian lifted it out, thought for a moment, then pressed the redial button and the hands-free.

Riordan heard a cellphone begin to ring, about six feet away. Neil, whose back was turned to Brian, discreetly took out his cellphone. Riordan put two and two together about the same time as Brian. From the speaker on Lynn's phone, Riordan heard Neil's voice say, "Hello, love, miss me already?"

Brian strode over, his face dark with rage, tapped Neil on the shoulder, and held up the phone. He yelled, "Hello you too, you little fuck. I knew something was up." Grabbing Neil by the shirt he shouted, "You're fucking her, aren't you?"

Riordan watched as Lynn rushed across the room, totally shocked by the scene in front of her. She grabbed Brian by the arm, but he shrugged her off effortlessly. Bravely, she tried again, but the attempt was futile. Brian was just too strong. She stumbled but managed to keep her balance.

"Please, Brian," she pleaded, "let him go! Please..."

Instead of releasing Neil, Brian head-butted him hard in the face, smashing his nose. Neil cried out, and his hands instinctively cupped his face. Blood streamed in torrents out of his nostrils and down over his shirt. Several others who were closer to the altercation attempted to drag Brian away from Neil, but the bloodlust was up, and he shook them off like swatting flies. Lining up like a rugby fly half, he kicked Neil hard in the balls. Neil collapsed to the floor in agony, crawling into a fetal position, hands cradling his bruised testicles. Brian towered over him for a moment, panting heavily, then grabbed Lynn viciously by the arm and dragged her out of the room.

Riordan stepped back through the crowd and slipped out the French windows that opened on to a darkened terrace. He watched Brian drag Lynn out through the lobby, his fingers digging deeply into her arm as he hustled her over to their car, a Jaguar XJ6 convertible. It was parked at an angle across two spots. Lynn, in tears, sobbed loudly, and went over on her ankle because of the high heels.

Brian shouted, "Get into the car, bitch." When she resisted, he gave her a violent backhand across the face, splitting her lip. Shaking her head, she looked at the blood on her hand.

Riordan recognized the defiant posture in her body as she spat at Brian. "You bastard, that's the fucking last time. We're done!"

Good for you, Riordan thought. He was just about to step into a pool of light to provide assistance when Brian pulled out a gun and pressed it so hard between Lynn's eyes that she was bent backward across the car. Riordan recognized the Glock 19 right away. Effectively a reduced-size Glock 17, it was a compact weapon designed primarily for military and law enforcement and used a magazine with a standard capacity of fifteen rounds.

Riordan stared at the strange scar on the back of Brian's hand that flexed when he grasped the pistol.

Brian hissed. "If you ever pull a stunt like that again, I'll fuckin' top you and bury your body where nobody will ever find you. That's a promise. Now get in the fucking car." The fight went out of her at that point, and Riordan watched helplessly as she meekly opened the door and climbed in.

As the Jaguar screeched out of the parking lot, gravel pinging off the neighbouring cars, Riordan lit up the cigar that Neil had given him and took a long draft. It was a Cuban, Romeo y Julietta. No expense had been spared for the party. Riordan enjoyed the occasional cigar, the scent of tobacco instantly triggering memories of his father sitting beside the riverbank, fishing rod in hand, staring intently at the tip as he waited for the elusive trout to strike.

As the dense smoke swirled around him, he smiled at the memory, took another long drag, and then ground it out against the brick wall. He slid it back in the aluminum tube; it would be a treat to savour later with a nice glass of whisky.

Returning to the reception, he found the place in chaos. The lights were up, and people were either standing around, too embarrassed to move, or grabbing their coats to leave. The party was over, in more ways than one. Off to one side, Neil stood silently, holding a blood-soaked handkerchief to his nose. Great splotches of red stained his white shirt. Sean stood beside him, shaking his head. Off on the other side of the room, he saw Fiona deep in discussion with her father, and Riordan could tell from the body language that it was not a pleasant conversation. Her father looked like a spring wound too tight and kept clenching and unclenching his fists. Points of red stood out on her cheeks. Her eyes flashed as she spat the words at her father, who kept staring at Neil like a ravenous pit bull staring at a T-bone. Riordan was too far away to hear the exchange. He could only imagine.

Turning on her heel, she made a beeline for Neil just as Riordan crossed to the small group. Hands on hips, she spat, "You better book a room here for tonight. Then you can come tomorrow and pack your bags. You and I are finished!" She went to move away but wheeled around and slapped Neil viciously across the face with the back of her hand. Then she stormed out of the room.

Neil eyes watered, and he hissed, "Not the fucking nose again!"

Sean touched his friend gently on the shoulder. "You can stay with me tonight, pal. You know, sometimes these things are for the best. At least it's out in the open."

Neil shook his head. "That's a strange way to look at things."

Sean's grip tightened. "Listen, I could never figure out why you married her anyway, because she was always a miserable cunt. It's no surprise to me you looked elsewhere."

Riordan was about to add his thoughts about the encounter in the parking lot but decided it would be best to wait until morning. He could hardly wait to tell Nancy about the drama.

CHAPTER 7

BLISS

Riordan awoke from a blissful sleep feeling totally refreshed, the uncomfortable jetlag having passed. He was now on London time. Stretching languidly, he rolled out of bed. Padding across to the open window, wrapped in a towel, he inhaled deeply the fresh country air, savouring the view of the lush green fields and the river. It hearkened back to better times, balm for his soul. Forgoing a shave, he took a quick shower, dressed in a t-shirt and jeans, and headed down to the dining room, his mouth watering in anticipation of a hearty breakfast. Apart from a few meagre morsels the previous evening, he had not eaten. And to cap it all, the inn's rooms were not furnished with the dreaded minibar, although that probably saved him a small fortune.

He walked along the corridor to Sean's room. Just before he reached it, a red-haired lady he recognized from the party opened the door, smiled at him, and headed for the elevator. She held a pair of high-heeled black pumps hooked in her fingers. Riordan smiled back at her and rapped on the door. He heard a voice say, "Forget something," and the door opened. Riordan pushed his way into the room, eyed the bottle of champagne, the two glasses, and then the unruffled bed.

Smiling, he asked, "Shag her on the floor, did you?"

Sean looked indignant. "No, if you must know, we spent most of the night talking, and we fell asleep on the couch. She's a real sweetheart. Now, enough about me. How's Neil?"

Riordan shrugged. "Fucked if I know. Last I heard he was going to shack up with you, but I see that didn't happen."

"Nah," Sean replied. "He decided to get his own room, so I stayed in the bar for a last call and met Kathleen."

"And one thing led to another? I didn't picture you as the cuddly type, especially after your performance on the dance floor."

"You're not going to let that one go, are you?" Sean said.

"Not for a while," Riordan replied.

Sean grinned, that mischievous grin that Riordan remembered so well. "Neil's probably sleeping it off. I saw him carrying one of those big bottles of champagne off to his room. However, if you ask me, he's probably relieved that he doesn't have to go sneaking around anymore."

Riordan nodded. Sometimes it was better to rip the Band-Aid off the cut.

Scratching his tousled hair, Sean said, "Perhaps Lynn and him can try to make something together now that everyone knows about them. I know he's crazy about her."

At this Riordan sighed. From what he had witnessed last night, it was unlikely that Lynn's husband would simply back down and let his wife go off with another man. Lynn was a glamorous trophy, a prize to trot out in front of people. No, there would certainly be more trouble. The man was a bully, a wife-beater, and he had a gun.

"That I wouldn't be too sure about," Riordan said. "Anyway, why don't you call Neil and let's all have breakfast — order me a good Ulster fry or some semblance thereof. I'll be down in a minute, and I'll tell you both what I saw last night in the parking lot."

Sean peered at Riordan's arm then reached out and tentatively touched Riordan's shoulder. "Is that…"

Riordan nodded. "Yep, it's a tattoo. When the colours were mixed, it produced a ridge around the banner of the insignia. It's called hypertrophic scarring, so apparently I'm allergic to red ink." Riordan pulled back the sleeve to reveal the banner, shaded in blue and outlined with a raised black and red ridge. Inside were the words, "Who Dares Wins."

Sean looked at it for a moment, looked into Riordan's eyes for a heartbeat, and then headed off to the shower. The motto of the Special Air Service was renowned all over the world. Riordan knew there were more questions coming.

*

Riordan's stomach grumbled noisily as the waiter placed a full carafe of coffee on the table. He helped himself then offered the pot to the others, but they politely declined. Tea was their thing. The quality was actually quite decent, so the first cup disappeared in rapid fashion. A few minutes later the waiter arrived with their meals, warning them all about not touching the plates. Riordan got stuck in, savouring the farm eggs and the local bacon. The taste was incredible, a far cry from the factory-farmed produce he was accustomed to buying. The others must have been equally hungry, because there was silence at the table for a few minutes, punctuated only by the clicking of knives against plates. Riordan refilled his coffee several times during the meal, annoyed again at the petite cups that had been provided. "It's like having coffee with Barbie," he commented but realized the others did not understand the analogy. "Barbie, Barbie dolls, kids' tea sets…" he expounded.

"Yeah, right," Sean commented, wiping a smear of brown sauce off his cheek. "So what's the story about last night in the parking lot?"

Sean took two slices of toast, patiently buttered both, then smeared a thick helping of strawberry jam on top. Riordan shook his head. "I think that's what killed Elvis."

"I didn't know Elvis liked strawberry jam," Sean commented.

Riordan finished chewing a piece of sausage. "I was out in the car park last night for a breath of air when I saw Brian and Lynn leave. He slapped her around a bit and then threatened to kill her. I'd say she got a bit more when they got home."

"What the fuck?" Neil exploded. "And you stood there and watched? I'd have lamped the bastard."

Riordan nodded. "Me too, but I have an aversion to lead."

Neil looked puzzled. "Lead? He had a gun?"

"Yep, a Glock 17, military version, if I'm not mistaken. Mind you, it was quite dark."

Sean shivered. "Jesus, it's a good thing I didn't jump him when he nutted Neil at the party."

"He's got a bad temper," Neil said quietly, a sorrowful look on his face. "Lynn hinted as much. He's ex-military — did a lot of tours of Northern Ireland with the paras, and you know their reputation as a bunch of hard men. Apparently was investigated for supposedly selling weapons on the side to the Sons of Erin. He surely has a lot of money that's hard to account for. His father was a brickie, his mother a cashier at Woolworths, so he came from humble beginnings. They all lived in a council flat in St. Margaret's, just outside Richmond, but today he owns a couple of high-end dealerships."

Riordan shivered at the mention of the Sons of Erin, and he swallowed hard. Sean glared at Neil, but Riordan caught the look.

"Shit, I'm sorry," Neil said. "That was the bunch that killed your parents."

"It's okay," Riordan responded, but it was far from okay. His mind went down that rathole, as it had done so many years ago. The one guy from that night he had never been able to find. What if Brian had sold the weapons or the explosives that had been used to kill his parents? No one believed him about the para regiment tattoo he had seen, and to be honest, the more he thought about it, the more ludicrous it sounded to him as well. Sighing in frustration, he dismissed the idea, like he had done innumerable times before over the years, as just another flight of fancy. It would be too big a coincidence.

Most of the Sons, an ultraviolent splinter group of the Provisional IRA, had been identified by the Old Man, and Riordan had dispatched them with ruthless efficiency. Yet there was always the one elusive figure, the man in the car. Over the years, he wondered if his mind really had been playing tricks on him, the image produced by concussion. The thought of a para collaborating with terrorists was simply preposterous. He felt nauseous, bile rising in his throat like mercury on hot day. Setting down his cutlery, he wiped his chin and tossed the napkin on the table.

"Where's the washroom in this place?" he asked. Sean pointed off to one corner. "The 'bathroom' is over there..."

Riordan went into the washroom, grateful that it was empty, strode over to one of the sinks, and turned on the cold water. The cracked mirror reflected his face like a mosaic. Even in the cracked fragments he could see the anger simmering just below the surface. Splashing his face with cold water, he grasped the side of the sink and breathed deeply, fighting back the nausea. As he stared in the mirror, he recalled the strange scar on the back of Brian's hand. Maybe he had a tattoo removed?

Exhaling several times, and then filling his lungs with deep, cleansing breaths, he hissed, "Let it go, pal ... let it go! Now you're fucking well imagining things." Turning off the tap, he ran his fingers through his hair and then headed back to the table. Sean and Neil had apparently been having a heated discussion. Neil's face was the colour of a stop sign.

"So what can I do?" Neil said defensively. "There's no way I can take that bastard on myself! He's got a gun."

Riordan nodded. "I think I know a way we can get our own back on him."

Sean grinned. "Oh yeah, well, count me in. I'm yer man!"

Looking about the room that was now starting to fill up with guests, Riordan said, "Not here. Finish your breakfast, and then we'll have a chat up in your room." To Sean, "I think there's a couple of bits of toast you missed!"

Minutes later, seated around a small table in Riordan's room, he explained his plan to two incredulous faces. Neil rubbed his face in his hands. "What do you mean, shoot him?" he asked, a shocked look on his face.

Riordan shrugged. "A typical punishment shooting, a warning. Just a flesh wound through the arse, like I said. From what you've told us, we can pretend we're from the lads over beyond, and he sold us some duff gear. I know from all the reports I've read, there are still dissident factions trying to restart the conflict. And dissidents need weapons!"

"Fuck me, I sell software. That's insane! How..."

Riordan put up his hand to halt the tirade. "If we do it tonight at his house, there will be a lot of witnesses. You said this is his regular poker night."

"Yes, it is. But he's got a gun, and we don't."

Riordan said, "I'll get us guns as well. He's hardly likely to have his gun nearby when his friends are around. He'll feel safe in his own home."

Sean smiled. "This feels like a scene from *Snatch*. All vee need is zee Germains!"

"But what if we get caught?" Neil asked.

"We go to jail," Sean replied. "But wouldn't it be worth it just to get your own back on that bastard? David and me here would be okay, but you're so pretty, you'd be passed around like a pack of cheap cigarettes."

Neil glared at him, ruminating. Eventually he relented. "Okay, what do we do?"

*

After outlining his plan and giving them each a few tasks to keep them occupied, Riordan decided to take a walk down to the river. They had gone off, excited, like they were ten years old again, preparing for the raid on Oul Wright's apple tree. He had noticed a sign by the front desk indicating that fishing equipment was available for hire, or a ghillie could be booked for a couple of hours to take guests on a tour of the best fishing spots. Depending on how the day progressed, he might actually have time. He loved to fish, it being one of the outdoors activities that kept him firmly anchored to his childhood.

The beautifully manicured gardens gave way to thickets of weeds and clutches of birch trees by the river, providing shady pools where trout loved to hide. Taking out the cigar from the previous evening, he lit it up, sucking furiously on the wet tobacco. A few puffs, and it was well lit, and he leaned against a tree and revelled in the silence. Sunbeams penetrated the gloom like tangible entities, and tiny birds flitted from tree to tree. The river, its surface dark and glassy, flowed past silently, not a blemish on its surface.

This was his equivalent of church, his sanctuary, where peace lay wrapped around him like a blanket. It was always the way when he found himself alone by a river or by the shore. The hypnotic motion and sounds caressed his soul, bearing him back to the times before the Troubles, the times of innocence. Closing his eyes, he stepped forward into a ray of light, savouring the warmth of the sun on his face. He stilled his breathing, lowering his heart rate, and melded into the moment.

He had just taken six or seven deep cleansing breaths, feeling his body relax, when suddenly his eyes popped open, his senses ranging out in all directions. He was not alone. Pausing, his senses intensified, and it was almost as if he could feel the air being pushed in his direction as someone or something moved toward him. The motion was deliberate, not by error, the feeling indicating that someone was trying very hard to come up on him unnoticed. It wouldn't be Sean, for he already knew of his identity, and Neil was off to the nearest shops. He flexed his wrist, and the ceramic blade slipped into his palm. He always carried the knives when he travelled, especially the ceramic variety. They were completely undetectable by airport scanners. Heartened somewhat that he had a weapon, he waited until the person was almost directly behind him then whirled around, the blade up and ready.

As he completed the arc, he saw a tall figure, a man in his late sixties or early seventies, dressed in a tweed jacket with leather elbow patches, elegant black pants, and black brogues. A white shirt lay open at the top button, and under the collar he wore a cravat. A blackthorn walking sticking topped by a decorative brass handle protruded from under his elbow. The impression was that of a country gentleman out for a stroll. Yet there was no mistaking the hardness in the eyes.

"Hello, lad," said Arthur Cupples, "fancy meeting you here. I see you haven't lost the touch."

Riordan could barely speak; he was so surprised. Here was the Old Man's dearest friend, and one of his personal mentors in hand-to-hand combat. Riordan had no illusions about what Cupples could do with the cane should he have the opportunity. However, of more pressing concern was what he was doing here.

"Arthur," he said. "Aren't you looking well." It seemed the right thing to say at the moment.

Cupples laughed. "Relax, son, I just want to talk, that's all. I knew you had managed to escape all those years ago. The Old Man told me before he left that he would do whatever it took to keep you safe, and he was true to his word, even though it meant giving up his own life. I miss the old fucker every day."

Riordan's eyes misted over, and he swallowed hard. "You and me both. Well, talk then, Arthur."

"Not here, lad, let's have a cup of tea or maybe something a wee bit stronger. And put that knife away before I make you!"

Riordan laughed. "As bold as ever still, Arthur…"

Walking back across the gardens, Riordan noticed a slight limp in Arthur's gait. Curiosity got the better of him, so he spoke up.

"Ach, that," came the nonchalant reply. "Fucking arthritis! Doctor says I need a hip replacement, but at my age, why the fuck bother. I try to avoid hospitals 'cos all you do is get sick when you go in."

"Isn't that the truth." Riordan laughed. "My wife's a nurse, so she looks after me at home."

Riordan walked up to the patio, made his way across to a shaded table, and sat down. A few guests were scattered around, mostly in the sunny spots, drinking tea and reading newspapers. Riordan recognized one or two people from the evening before and could only imagine the conversations. These hoity-toity folks loved nothing better than a good scandal, and the phones in the place must have been burning all morning. Cupples eased himself into a chair, took out a packet of cigarettes, and lit up. Riordan realized his cigar was lying somewhere by the riverbank.

"I went to his grave yesterday, Arthur, to pay my respects. I expect it was you who brought him home."

Cupples nodded. "Took a bit of doing, given the circumstances, but the regiment did the right thing. He's buried with his comrades."

"That's what he would have wanted," Riordan said quietly. "So you did the right thing. But what alarm did I trip?"

Cupples smiled. "There's a CCTV camera hidden at the church, 'cos you'd never believe the people who show up there from time to time. The boffins at headquarters have incredibly powerful facial recognition software, and also stuff that can age a person and do a match on a computer projection of what that person might look like ten or twenty years older. I put you into that system a long time ago and imagine my surprise when I got a call yesterday, about ten minutes after you left."

"Call? Why would … anyone…" Riordan's mind spun with possibilities.

Cupples smiled and nodded. "Yep, you've got it. Got a bit of a job with MI6, the Brit version of Homeland Security, you might say. Gives me access to lots of stuff. We got the car license plate, tracked it to Sean Daly, checked credit cards, receipts, etc., etc., the whole trail of breadcrumbs scattered through cyberspace, and the latest transaction was here. So I thought I'd take a wee drive in the country."

"Neat stuff," Riordan commented. He had read about such advances and been lectured on some of the technology that was close to magic. He could only imagine the finger-wagging that would come when he told Featherstone the story. "I came over for a birthday party, if you can believe it, and there was a bit of drama last night, involving an ex-para."

"Oh yeah?" Cupples ears pricked up. "I understand the draw of family and friendship. It's always there, swirling away like a whirlpool, and once you get pulled in, there's no easy way out. One of the reasons that so many people in the witness protection program get whacked is because they cannot leave their old life behind them. No matter how many dire warnings we give them, someone always decides to make contact with an old mate, or an old girlfriend, and the next thing they know there's a knock on the door, and Bob used to be your Uncle."

Riordan said, "I know you still have contacts back in Belfast, Arthur, you always did. I need to find out about a guy called Brian Thompson. Ex-military, ex-para, owns a fancy Mercedes dealership in Reading. Been investigated for selling weapons to the Son of Erin ... and I need the current codeword for tipping off the police."

Cupples's face hardened. The knuckles gripping the walking stick whitened. "Do you think this guy is the one you missed? But what happened to the sleeping dogs?"

Riordan said, "They refuse to lie down, Arthur, so just find out. This guy has scar tissue on the back of his hand where a tattoo used to be. It might have been removed by a laser, but I couldn't be sure, or I could simply be barking up the proverbial wrong tree."

Cupples nodded skeptically. "The old para tattoo? And you need this when?" When Riordan smiled, Cupples just shook his head. "You always had good instincts, so I'll humour you this time."

"I'll get the drinks in," Riordan offered, when the waitress appeared. "It must be noon somewhere in the Empire!" Cupples got up out of his chair, surprisingly spritely for a man of his age, and headed into the pub, the lighted cigarette dangling from his lips. It seemed to Riordan that the man almost had a spring in his step, the limp almost forgotten, but he knew from experience that the prospect of action did that to people. Old soldiers never died.

Riordan was enjoying his drink and the view when Cupples returned, holding some notes scribbled on the back of the cigarette packet. Easing himself back into the chair, he took a sip of his whisky, squinted at his notes, and then said, "He was a member of the parachute regiment at the time your parents were killed. Then he was seconded to the 14th Intel group and did a lot of surveillance work. After Bloody Sunday, he and his mates had the regimental crest for the paras tattooed on the back of their hands, a badge of honour, you might say. Got an honourable discharge after the Falklands and went into business for himself, buying into a Mercedes dealership. No indication of where the money came from to fund the business, but at one point MI5 suspected he was dealing weapons. They did carry out an investigation, but the informants disappeared, so it went cold."

Riordan took it all in then finished his drink and slammed the glass on the table. As he stood to leave, Cupples looked at him. Riordan knew the look from eyes as clear and bright as he remembered.

"Do you think this could be him, David?" Cupples asked, "or should I call you Daniel? Is it time for the Raven to return?"

Riordan shook his head. "It may well be him, but that's all behind me now. This Brian has got something coming to him, that's for sure. But the queen's pardon is retroactive only from the Good Friday agreement, so I'm not going to whack him, if indeed he was the man who killed my parents. He's got fucking immunity too, and it would be impossible to convict him now, as I killed every other possible participant in that attack. But there are other ways to punish people, Arthur. Wouldn't be the first time I've pointed it out, but, as the song goes, 'I never knew there were worse things than dying!'"

Cupples grinned. "That's what I need to hear, lad. Now, there's a couple of things I need to tell you about the past." Sliding his hand inside his jacket, he extracted a large brown envelope and tossed it on the table. Riordan picked it up, feeling its bulk and examining the handwriting on the top. He recognized the Old Man's scrawl right away.

"What's this?" he asked.

"Fucked if I know, but I imagine it's his last will and testament. He got me to sign a copy as witness the night before he left to meet up with you. He really minded his investments, some of which have done very well for me as well."

Riordan ripped open the envelope and unfolded the stiff, handwritten pages. Instantly, an image of the Old Man sitting at the kitchen table popped into his mind. He often watched him sit there, a mug of tea off to one side, writing copious notes using a Parker fountain pen that was never far from his hand. The Old Man possessed an innate distrust of technology and was quite happy to write stuff down and then toss the papers into the fire.

He scanned the words then peered inside the envelope to see yet another smaller white envelope, a heavy red wax seal on the flap. "He liked to use Barclay's bank in London," Cupples commented. "Everything is held there."

Riordan nodded and put the documents away. He would read it all later. "You said there were a couple of things, Arthur?"

"Yep," Cupples replied. "After you left, the Troubles intensified, and the Raven's activities continued unabated for about another year or so."

Riordan shrugged. "I've do idea about that. After I moved, I deliberately tried to avoid listening to what was going on over there. It was all too raw."

"It was something he wanted me to tell you, if you ever showed up again. There were two more like you, lad, but neither of them came close to you in terms of ability. The first one, Alastair Robinson, got caught in an ambush one night after killing two INLA guys. We managed to sanitize that situation. The other incarnation of the Raven was called Gordon Catterson, and he's off somewhere in Iraq at the moment working for Blackwatch, a private defense contractor for the US military."

"I've heard of them," he replied. "They have a great reputation for hiring only the best ex-special forces people."

Riordan was hardly surprised by the revelation, knowing the Old Man to be a master strategist who sought to exploit any or all weaknesses of his opponents. He could have taught Sun Tzu a thing or two about warfare.

Cupples stood, and Riordan took the outstretched hand and shook it warmly. "Well, good luck, Daniel, with whatever you decide to do," Cupples said. "The codeword is 'Medusa,' should you need to find me again. Mind how ye go!"

*

Later that afternoon, Sean followed Riordan's instructions as they drove along a narrow country road just outside Reading, near the famous university. Between the road map he had printed off from Google and marked up with a pen, and the occasional furrowed brow from trying to recall landmarks, they had made good progress. The problem they faced was that Riordan had created the arms cache in an empty field over twenty years ago. Who knew what might have happened in the intervening years? It might have been paved over, or worse still, been turned into a housing estate.

Sean kept scanning the road ahead, looking for the landmarks that Riordan had mentioned. He looked like a kid on a school outing. "I didn't want to bring it up in front of Neil, but do tell me about this arms cache business. What's that all about?"

Riordan shrugged. "I'm sorry, Sean, there were many times back then when I wanted to talk to you about all this, but the less you knew the better — potential witness and all that! But I figure that after twenty years I could put it behind me."

Sean nodded. "So we're going to find a twenty-year-old arms cache."

Riordan winced at the mention of twenty years. At the time he had taken great pains to prepare the cache, but under normal circumstances, a weapons cache would be used within a few months or a couple of years of being created. This one had lain dormant for years, and so the quality of the equipment inside would be suspect. However, he needed a weapon, and he wasn't quite ready to ask Cupples for help with weapons. Gun laws in Britain were amongst the strictest in the world. Possession of an illegal firearm meant a mandatory stint in jail.

Riordan said, "This is one I buried." A sign flashed past and he put a finger on the map. "Here it is ... I knew it was near an old farmhouse, about twenty miles north of Reading. I did it the weekend we had that exchange project with Reading University."

Sean looked surprised. "I remember that. I got off with that bird from Cambridge House. Sandy, her name was..."

Riordan laughed. "That's right. You were busy dippin' yer wick, so you weren't concerned about what I was up to. That gave me time to slip away and establish the cache. Now, let's hope they haven't built a housing estate on top of it."

Sean shook his head. "Any other deep dark secrets?"

"Yep," Riordan replied, "I'm addicted to *Coronation Street*. Every Sunday morning just like Pavlov's fucking dog."

Sean's face fell. "Ach, David, *Coronation Street* ... I'm not sure we can be friends any more."

Riordan pointed to the farmhouse that was coming up on their right. "Look, there it is. Drive past the farmhouse gate for exactly one mile. The cache was in a drain that was newly built in the middle of the field. There's a ladder down into the drain."

"Right," Sean said, a note of skepticism creeping into his voice. "This is starting to sound like *Indiana Jones*." He looked at the odometer, drove exactly one mile, and pulled to the side of the road. "Let's go," he said.

Riordan paused.

"What?" Sean asked.

"Are you sure about this?" Riordan asked. "I don't mind taking the risk."

"Fuck that for a lark," Sean scowled. "This is great craic!"

Riordan carefully climbed the fence, taking care not to get caught on the rusting barbs. Sean followed, and they walked across the field, making their way carefully around the piles of cow manure. Flies buzzed around the steaming piles. Riordan realized they were freshly made. There was no sign of any cows. Perhaps it was milking time. At the centre of the field, Sean excitedly pointed to a rusty manhole cover.

"Fuck me," he exclaimed. "This really is like something out of a movie."

While Sean looked on, Riordan slipped his fingers into the rusting slits, braced himself, and heaved. The ancient hinges creaked and groaned, but it moved, brown flakes falling to the ground. Letting the cover fall back on the grass, Riordan peered inside. Cobwebs saturated the narrow tunnel, which was a good sign. No one had been down there for a long time. Grasping the top of the narrow ladder, Riordan tugged hard, trying to move it but it held firm. Another good sign. Easing himself over the edge, he climbed down slowly, hand over hand, brushing away the thick mass of cobwebs as he descended. Above him, Sean peered over the side.

"I'll wait here," Sean said. Riordan grinned. Apparently bravado only went so far, or perhaps he didn't like spiders.

About halfway down, he stopped. If he remembered correctly, the cache was just opposite the tenth rung on the ladder. He scraped away a piece of the wall, letting it fall with a splash into the sewer below. Behind the narrow facade, embedded in the wall, sat a large, dusty satchel.

"I've got it," he said, peering upward. There was no reply. He felt vibrations on the ground, tiny tremors surging through his fingers as they gripped the metal rungs, and he paused for a moment. "Sean, what's that noise?"

Hearing no response, Riordan clambered back up the ladder, pushed the heavy black satchel out of the drain, and stuck his head through the opening. In front of him, he saw Sean running across the field, away from the fence they had climbed over. From his gait, Sean obviously hadn't been exercising much.

Turning around at the top of the drain, Riordan saw the reason for the vibrations he had felt. About a hundred yards away, standing in a opening between a clump of shrubs, a massive black bull stood snorting and pawing the ground. Sean's red Manchester United jersey had obviously caught its attention.

"Son of a bitch," he hissed. Climbing out of the drain, he grabbed the satchel and started after Sean. It was a lot heavier than he remembered, but it had been many years, and he kept glancing over his shoulder, the weight a constant handicap. The bull cantered across the field toward him, great streams of snot exploding from its nostrils. In his mind he made a mental note to thank Featherstone for all the wind sprints and training runs the big man had made him do, not to mention their weekly squash games. Toward the end of the field he caught up with a red-faced Sean, who was labouring heavily. A large brick wall covered in greenish, slippery moss faced them. He didn't remember the wall from before.

Riordan said, "I see you're as fit as ever."

Sean gasped, his face flushed. "Fuck, we'll never make it." He jammed his fingers into his side, his face contorted as a stitch shook him. "Shite, I've got a cramp."

Riordan laughed. "Oh, that's not a problem. I can beat you to the wall, and as long as I make it first, the bull will be content to play with you."

Sean looked afraid. Riordan said, "I'm only kidding, take deep breaths and just keep running. I think we'll make it, but we've got to jump the wall. There's no choice in the matter. Besides, it's not that high."

Riordan tried to sound optimistic, but the bull was closing behind the two men. The menacing grunting was coming closer. Toward the centre of the wall sat a galvanized metal tank full of water. Almost in synch, the two men jumped on to the tank and launched themselves over the wall. What they hadn't accounted for was the drop on the other side. It was about fifteen feet lower than the field and contained the farm's supply of fresh manure, so they had a soft landing. Above them, the bull snorted wildly at the other side of the wall.

Riordan lay back, soaked and winded, sinking slowly into the manure. "Oh yes, I can see the headlines now. One of the most feared enforcers in the history of Belfast was arrested in a pile of cow shite. Come on, let's get the hell out of here."

When they got back to the car, Riordan tossed the satchel in the trunk and then went to get into the passenger seat. Sean said, "Wait a minute. You're not getting in my new car with all that cow shite on your clothes."

Riordan glared at him. "Oh yeah. Do you have a plan?"

Sean pulled off his Manchester United jersey, uncovering a pale, sparsely haired chest, and then removed his trousers to reveal a pair of leopard-skin thong underwear. Riordan rubbed his face in his hands, not a good move, as the pungent reek of manure hit his nostrils.

Riordan shook his head. "No, no friggin' way! What if we get in an accident?"

"For fuck's sake," groaned Sean. "Hurry up before someone comes along and sees us."

Riordan sighed, stripped to his underwear, black, utilitarian boxers, and tossed his clothes into the trunk. "Okay, leopard boy, just concentrate on the driving now. An accident would be all I need to round out the day! Now, have you seen my sunglasses? That albino body of yours in fucking blinding me."

Back at the inn, Sean parked the car beside the fire exit. Both men grabbed their dirty clothes and ran up the back stairs to their rooms. Riordan said, "You've got twenty minutes, then get Neil and bring him in here."

Inside his room, Riordan jammed the dirty clothes into the laundry bag, tied the knot several times, then headed straight for the shower. It took some time to cleanse the reek from his body, and his hair required rinsing several times until he was certain it was clean. After donning a fresh set of clothes, he dumped the contents of the satchel on the bed then commenced unwrapping the sealed packages.

A few minutes later, a knock came to the door, and he peered out to see Sean and Neil waiting in the corridor. He ushered them quickly into the room then directed them to sit at the round table located at one end of the room. Their eyes widened at the set of pistols displayed on the table. Riordan unwrapped the boxes of ammo, checked the quality of the shells, and field-stripped the pistols in a flash.

Sean and Neil looked on in amazement, their mouths falling open. Then, just like kids, they started. "Can I touch them?" asked Neil.

Riordan nodded. "They're all empty, and still well oiled, but I'll have to clean them. The basic rule is always assume the gun is loaded, and never point it at anything you're not prepared to shoot. So for the next while, remember these two words: ACTS/PROVE. Here's the quick lesson: assume every firearm is loaded, control the muzzle direction at all times, trigger finger must be kept off the trigger, see that the firearm is unloaded. Did you get that?"

The two men nodded.

"Good. The next part is also critical. So, we have the word PROVE: point the gun in the safest direction, remove all cartridges, observe the chamber, verify the feeding path, examine the bore."

"These look as if they are brand new," Sean commented.

"They were, twenty odd years ago," Riordan said. "These are Beretta twenty-two calibre models and work really well with suppressors. The Mossad are big fans of Beretta. However, these particular weapons have never been fired."

Neil picked up a package that Riordan had just laid on the table, examining it closely. "What's this orange stuff? It looks like plasticine." Grease-like stains covered the brownish wrapping paper, and Neil examined the tips of his fingers.

Riordan grinned. "It's called Semtex — one of Czechoslovakia's finest exports. That lot would probably destroy this inn."

Sean and Neil looked horrified, and Neil gently set the package back on the table. "It's okay," Riordan said. "It's completely inert until you insert a detonator." He finished unwrapping the last of the packages then sat down beside the two stunned friends.

Looking at Neil, he asked, "Did you get the balaclavas?"

Neil nodded, took a plastic bag off the floor, and emptied the contents on to the table. Riordan peered at the three balaclavas, one red, one blue, and one green, and shook his head. "What the fuck is this?"

"*This* is all I could get," Neil replied indignantly.

"You do realize we're supposed to be terrorists," Riordan said.

Never lost for words, Sean laughed and grabbed the red balaclava. He pulled it quickly over his head and his eyes danced with merriment. "We could be the gay liberation front."

Riordan shook his head. "You've certainly got the underwear to go with that statement, thong boy. Okay, okay, we'll have to improvise, so we'll deal with it later. Now, Neil, I want you to describe the house in detail, and then I want you to take a piece of paper and draw the layout for me. Given the number of times you've broken into it, you should know it like the back of your hand. I need to know the location of all the entrances and exits. For us to pull this off, Sean and I need to be able to move about that house like you do."

"Do we get to see the pantie drawer?" Sean laughed.

Neil shook his head.

*

Five hours later, dressed all in black, Sean and Neil sat in a rented car just up the road from Lynn's house. Riordan crouched down beside the open driver's window. Inside, Neil fidgeted with the black stocking mask that Riordan had given him to wear. He had been up for the adventure at the beginning, but as the day wore on he seemed to pull back, the reality of the situation causing him to question his actions. Sean, on the other hand, was raring to go.

163

Riordan said, "You two wait here. I need to do a few things first, and then I'll come back for you and we'll pay the game a visit. You're still all right about this?"

Both men nodded, and Riordan turned and slipped off into the darkness. He found a portion of the wall where the ivy was sufficiently thick to hold his weight, gave it a few tentative tugs, then scaled the wall quickly. After examining the base of the interior wall, he dropped silently down on the other side. Twisting an ankle at this point would make him feel very foolish. Lights blazed from every room on the bottom floor of the house, but the upper floor was mostly in darkness, the only light on the second floor emanating from a corner room. According to Neil's orientation, this would be the master bedroom.

A dark shadow slipped into the dappled moonlight and headed toward him. Riordan was ready. It was not the first time he had faced these surgically altered guard-dogs, yet it was somewhat surreal to see the large animal bearing down on him. Not a sound emanated from its severed vocal chords. It was like watching a movie with the volume turned down. Riordan went down on one knee and gave a low whistle, which halted the dog in its tracks. When it paused, confused, he shot it twice in the head, the small-calibre silenced weapon making no more than a low cough.

Moving down the wall, keeping to the shadows, Riordan smiled when he saw the exotic cars lined up outside the garages. There was no reason for them to be out other than for Brian to show them off to his friends. Taking off his backpack, he headed for the rear entrance of the garage.

The task took about ten minutes, and then Riordan retraced his steps back out to the road. Sneaking up on Neil's car, he pulled on his stocking mask and rapped hard on the side window. Neil and Sean jumped in fright. Riordan rolled up his balaclava and laughed at the two.

Riordan said, "Jeez, you'd make a great pair of terrorists. Did one of you squeal like a girl?"

Neil and Sean got out of the car, their faces flushed.

"That was Sean," Neil said. Sean looked sheepish.

Riordan said, "Okay guys, get the masks on — it's showtime."

They followed the route Riordan had taken earlier and crept across the garden, keeping to the shadows, Riordan in the lead. He had concealed the dog's body behind some shrubs so that it would not startle them. Inside the house, in the room designated as the library, five men sat around a large poker table, all smoking cigars. A window was open, and the night air was filled with the heady aroma of tobacco. Riordan inhaled the sweet scent, recognizing the familiar tang of a good Cuban cigar. Blurred voices carried to his ear. There was an occasional burst of raucous laughter.

Cards and poker chips lay scattered in a pile on the felt covered table. A sumptuous buffet spread was laid out on a sideboard, and it looked like they had made some inroads into the food. Large crystal tumblers sat beside each man, and a half-empty bottle of Johnny Walker Blue sat off to one side of the table. According to Neil's information, these were the five regulars at the poker game hosted by Brian. The local police chief was one of the five, the three other "business types," but Neil was unable to shed any more light on their background other than the fact that they had known each other for years. One of the men had served in Northern Ireland at the same time as Brian, although Neil was unsure if it was in the same regiment.

That was the one Riordan would identify quickly and keep a close eye on. Ex-military personnel could pose a threat, although Brian was not exactly a sterling example of keeping in shape. He had somewhat gone to seed, that much was apparent from Riordan's close-up perspective the evening before, the face starting to take on that jowly look, puffy from good food and too much booze. But he still a possessed that mean streak, evidenced by the violent head butt Neil had received and his subsequent actions in the car park.

Riordan crept around to the kitchen door, and when the others were beside him he reached out and grasped the handle. He had picked the lock earlier and left it open. His finger had just grasped the handle when Neil touched his shoulder.

"Guys, I'm not sure about this," he whispered. "I'm having second thoughts."

"Great fucking time to bring it up," Sean hissed.

Riordan sighed and stepped back, flattening himself against the wall. "It's your call, pal, but you girls need to go back to the car, and I've got to undo all the stuff I've put in place. I can't leave it."

"Jesus Christ," Sean muttered, "we've got this far. The cunt beat the shit out of her, and you're just going to walk away?"

Neil was quiet for a moment then replied, "Yes, you're right. He needs to be taught a lesson."

"Are you fucking sure?" Riordan asked. "I don't need another fucking crisis of faith when we go in there. We go in hard, and we stay hard. Now get the guns out and follow me."

Riordan eased the door open, walked quietly down the corridor, and into the library, followed by Sean and Neil, weapons up and ready.

Riordan said, in a heavy Belfast accent, "Good evening, gents, having a quiet game, are we? I hope you're not losing any of that money we gave you, Brian."

All heads swivelled toward them, but Brian didn't seem intimidated in the slightest. He spat, "Who the fuck are you? What do you want?"

Riordan waved the gun casually in his direction, his eyes scanning the men at the table. The police chief he identified right away — the man was still wearing his regulation white shirt with the epaulettes showing his rank, as if he had come straight from work. The two men to his left looked frightened by the display of weapons, but it was the man sitting to the right of Brian that gave Riordan concern. He tossed his cards on the table and stared at the intruders, seemingly amused by the episode. He wore a blue Lacoste golf shirt, tight enough to accentuate the powerful physique. Under other circumstances Riordan would have shot him, thus removing a potential threat and intimidating the others.

Riordan said, "Dear Lord, now Brian, is that any way to treat your business partners? It seems that some of the last shipments you sent contained some faulty stuff."

Brian looked about him, not so sure of himself now. The others stared at him. "What? I have no idea what he's talking about."

Riordan shook his head. "Now, now Brian, one or two of the pieces just happened to have wee transmitters concealed in the detonators. It's a good thing we dismantled the rest and checked them out. We lost one good lad, so I'm here to make amends."

Riordan tossed several pairs of plasticuffs on the table. He had already configured them in the standard police figure-eight layout. "You know what these are. Put them on your mates here, and then put them on yourself. I suggest you don't fuck around." Brian did as he was told, then sat back down and pulled the cuffs tightly around his wrists, tightening the clasps with his teeth. Riordan checked the bindings on each of the men, then nodded to Sean, who stepped forward with a roll of duct tape, tore off a strip, and wrapped it across the mouths of each the poker players, with the exception of Brian. They were mostly compliant, with the exception of the hard case, who glared at Riordan.

Brian said, "I don't know who you are, but you're a fuckin' dead man."

Riordan laughed. "I can't honestly say that's the first time I've heard that, but I'm still here, big man. I'm not someone you can push around, pal. Not like your lovely wife."

Brian's eyes narrowed. "What?"

Riordan said, "I was watching you in the car park last night when you beat the shite out of her. Then you threatened to kill her and bury the body."

The others at the table turned to face Brian. This obviously was news to them.

Riordan said, "So it's a bit of a secret, is it? I think we should get her down here. I wouldn't want her to call the police on us." Turning to Neil, he said, "Keep your gun on them — anyone moves, don't fuckin' hesitate!" He pointed at Brian. "Put a bullet in him first."

Neil moved across the room, stood behind Brian, and jammed his pistol into the back of his head. Riordan left the room and ran upstairs. Making his way down the corridor, he slipped silently into the master bedroom. There he found Lynn, sitting in front of a mirror wearing a white nightie and dabbing at the bruises on her face with a cotton bud. Her bottom lip was cut and swollen, and she winced when she touched the fresh wound.

There were old and new patterns of fist-sized bruises on her pale arms, especially near her shoulders, and a reddish, fresh cigar burn near the tip of one breast, encroaching on the edge of her aureole. The burn was dark and angry but could be concealed by a bra. Brian knew what he was doing. All the prior signs of abuse could be covered by a dress, but he had lost it completely last night and split her lip. She sobbed quietly. Riordan despised bullies, those that preyed on the weak as a means to boost their own flagging self-esteem with their words and their fists.

A dark rage grabbed him as he walked across the room, into her vision, the pistol up.

"Don't move, don't say a word," he hissed. Turning to face him, she looked defiant, unafraid, and her words chilled him to the soul.

"Did Brian send you to finish his dirty work?"

Riordan shook his head. "No, love, Brian crossed some people over in Belfast, so it's time for him to pay the piper. Put these on and come downstairs with me." He tossed a pair of plasticuffs on to the dressing table. She fumbled with them for a moment, then put on the cuffs and stood up, embarrassed by the cuts and bruises.

"Can I at least put on a dressing gown?"

Riordan shook his head. "No, it's important that the people downstairs see you like this."

Riordan led her gently by the arm back down the stairs and into the library. All heads turned toward her. The men stared in horror at the bruises on her face and arms, and her eyes filled with tears. She hung her head in shame as Riordan pulled out a chair for her to sit on.

Riordan pointed his gun at Brian and said, "Stand up and drop your trousers — you do it or I do it."

All the while, Neil had been staring in disbelief at Lynn at the bruises on her arms, the burns marks, and the battered lip. The gun wavered away from Brian for a brief moment, and in that split second, Brian saw his chance. He ripped the gun from Neil's hands, shoved him backward, and held it steady in both hands, the barrel pointing directly at Riordan. A triumphant grin covered his face as he sneered, "Got you, you cunt."

Riordan's gun pointed toward the floor.

Brian looked quickly at Sean. "Drop your gun, you bastard. Drop it, or I'll top your mate right now."

Sean immediately let the gun tumble to the floor.

"Now you too, you mouthy bastard," he spat at Riordan.

Riordan shook his head. "And then what — are you going to kill us all? After all, they are witnesses to the conversation we just had."

"Don't worry about them. You just drop your fucking gun."

Riordan stared at Brian. He knew the type. Brian was getting more and more wound up by the moment, at the

171

anticipation of violence. Some ex-soldiers were like that; they lived for the thrill of battle, real or contrived. Riordan grinned. "My father always said you can't drown a man that was meant for hanging."

Riordan raised his pistol.

Across the room, Brian squeezed the trigger. There came a resounding "click." He frowned, then pulled the trigger several times with no effect.

Riordan laughed. "Oops, it would appear to be empty. You have to understand, Brian, we're kinda short on bullets these days. Now, I asked you to drop your laundry! And I guarantee you, this one is loaded." He fired one shot, nicking Brian's earlobe. Brian cried out, dropped the gun, and grasped his ear. Blood trickled through his fingers.

Riordan motioned toward his pants with the barrel. Brian undid his belt, his movements hampered by the plasticuffs, dropped his trousers, and then pulled his underwear, a leopard-skin thong, down to his knees. Having served in Belfast, he probably knew of the various types of punishment shootings, and getting shot in the arse was probably the lightest form. The notorious "six-pack" — elbows, knees, and ankles — was reserved for more serious transgressions, never mind the "Black and Decker job."

Riordan looked at the underwear, then over at Sean. "Must have been a sale." Riordan walked over, pressed the suppressor of the gun against the fleshy, right side of Brian's buttocks, and squeezed the trigger.

Brian gasped as the pain hit and dropped to his knees, cursing. "Bastard, bastard," he cried, "I'll fucking kill you."

Riordan jammed the hot end of the suppressor against Brian's temple. "You won't be sitting down for a wee while, will you, boyo?"

Brian grasped the back of the chair and started to pull himself up, favouring his right leg. A small trickle of blood streamed from the wound. As he did so, his hands rested on the rail at the back of the chair, his face turned in profile to Riordan. In that instant, Riordan's mind flashed back to the car cruising past the carnage when his parents were killed, the image transposed on what he saw before him. The profile, the hand, and the scar where the tattoo had once been drove him to the realization that Brian really was the man in the car, the one he had searched for years to find but had been unable to locate.

Now it made sense. He had been looking in all the wrong places. Never in his wildest imagination would he have thought that a British soldier would have collaborated with terrorists. That would explain the money. All the years spent in the futile search for this man flashed through his mind like scenes from a movie played in reverse. For a second, he was back in the car, a frightened boy, bloodied and scared, listening to the gurgling, watery noises emanating from his father in the front seat. He felt unsteady on his feet, as if the floor beneath him was falling away.

173

With trembling fingers, he raised the gun again to the back of Brian's head and held it there for a heartbeat, his blood rising. He looked at the faces in the room, his recently reacquainted friends, and saw the looks of horror on their faces. They sensed that something had changed. Taking a deep breath, he realized that it was not the time or the place, then moved the gun away.

Swallowing hard, he said, "Now, everybody out on the patio. It's time for the fireworks show."

Riordan pushed the poker players out onto the patio, where they had a clear view of the five luxury cars parked outside. Riordan was not a huge car fan, but he recognized the models. The red Maserati, black Aston Martin Vanquish, blue Bentley V8 Continental, red Ferrari Diablo, and yellow Lamborghini Countach presented an enviable and expensive montage. Through Neil he had learned that Brian always put the cars out on display when he had guests. Brian shuffled out like a penguin, trousers at his knees. One by one, Riordan forced them to their knees on the patio. When it came to the hard case, the man shrugged him off and refused.

"Your choice, pal," Riordan growled and dealt him a hard kick behind the knees. He collapsed beside the others. Satisfied his audience was ready, he pressed the first detonator, and the first car exploded, a roiling, greasy fireball from the gas tank spinning into the air. A thousand gleaming diamonds of glass rose toward the sky, twinkling like stars in the glow. He then pushed the next three buttons, and one at a time, the next three cars detonated. Brian's eyes glistened with tears.

When he pushed the last button, nothing happened. He pushed and pushed the button, but Brian's prized possession, the Lamborghini Countach, was still intact.

"Fuck!" Riordan exclaimed.

Brian shook his head sadly, but his wife had a look of grim satisfaction on her face. "You thought more of them than you did of me. Serves you right, you bastard..."

Riordan tossed the faulty detonator on the ground in disgust then ground it under his heel. "Piece of junk. You sold us a bag of shit, just like before. It's no wonder some of the council wanted to top you, me included, but since we have a ceasefire, the others thought a warning was best. Okay, lets go." He swatted Brian across the face with his gun, hearing a satisfying crack as a tooth shattered.

Grasping Neil firmly by the arm before he did anything stupid, he quickly retraced their steps to the wall.

*

Back in the car, Sean was ecstatic about getting their own back. After the initial rush, however, Neil was more subdued. "I hated having to leave her there with that fucking animal."

"I know," Riordan replied, "but people had to witness the violence. When it's a dirty little secret, no one can do anything.

175

But it's all going to end in tears now, especially for Brian. The chief of police cannot turn a blind eye to what he just witnessed, not if he wants to keep his job. He'll turn on Brian like a cornered rat. Besides, there will be more witnesses soon."

Ahead of them, a fire engine and two police cars came screaming down the road toward the house, lights flashing, and moments later two dark-coloured cars passed them at high speed.

Riordan grinned. "That'll be the guys from the antiterrorist team. I called them too, using the current codeword. They'll take the place apart and find the SEMTEX and the spare detonators hidden in the garage. The guys from the newspapers should be there as well shortly. It's going to be quite a party."

*

At the back of the house, Brian gathered up his trousers, limped down the steps to the back garden, and made his way to the garage. Glass crunched under his feet. In the distance came the low wail of sirens, but they were far to late. In front of him, the four cars were all ablaze, virtually nothing left but scorched metal carcasses. However, his treasured Lamborghini stood off to one side, miraculously still intact. He needed to move it away from the conflagration.

Brian grimaced. "My beauty is still safe." As he crossed the grass, he felt something catch his leg and looked down to see a piece of monofilament fishing line. He had time to blink, realize it was a tripwire, and then raised his face to the line of cars.

"Noooooo, nooooo," he cried just as the Lamborghini exploded into pieces, the blast hurling him backward across the lawn.

In the car, Riordan grinned as he heard another loud blast in the distance. Looking in the rear-view mirror, he saw the swirling orange and black fireball rising above the house.

"What was that?" Neil asked.

Riordan smiled. "That was the Lamborghini blowing up. I rigged it with a tripwire and put in a wee bit extra SEMTEX."

Sean clapped his hands together. "Brilliant, just fucking brilliant."

*

Lying face down on the freshly mowed grass where he had been kicked, Max DeLisle raged under the duct tape. Recognizing the futility of the action, he nevertheless strained against the plasticuffs until they dug deeply into his skin. He felt warm blood on his hands. That stupid cunt Brian had dragged him into some sort of sectarian conflict with a bunch of fucking Micks. How stupid could Brian be, in this day and age, to be selling weapons to the IRA? Or even one of the insane splinter groups.

All because of that greedy little shit Brian, now he, one of the most feared gang bosses in London, would have to deal with the ignominy of the event being played out on TV and that fucking YouTube and Facebook and every other social media platform. There were enough villains out there who wanted a part of him, and what had transpired tonight showed there was a chink in his armour. Part of him wanted to get the three intruders alone in his warehouse and have a bit of sport with his knives, but he knew it would be a futile endeavour. They would be well on their way back to that shithole they called home and would disappear into the warren of safe houses in and around Belfast.

Besides, he knew better than to go up against the IRA, or the Real IRA, or whatever the fuck they were calling themselves nowadays. For every one he whacked, there was another to take his place. Ireland was full of redundant terrorists whose services were for sale on the world market. Even that cunt Dempsey, rumoured to be a former terrorist, had managed to disappear without a trace. But Max wasn't giving up on him — there was simply too much money at stake. That was a criminal enterprise, nothing to do with politics, so Dempsey was fair game.

CHAPTER 8

THERMITE

It was shortly after midnight when Max returned to his home in the docklands. After parking in the underground, he took the elevator to the penthouse, stabbing angrily at the buttons with barely restrained fury. The fucking coppers had given him a hard time until he told them to fuck off and called his lawyer. They had backed off at that point and let him go, but then he had to face the phalanx of reporters who had lined up outside the walls of the estate. It seemed like everybody and their fucking brother had showed up. Fucking camera flashes were going off against his windscreen, and television cameramen crowded around his car as he tried to ease out through the throng, everyone jostling to get footage as guests left the estate. Now he understood why movie stars hated the paparazzi.

On the drive home he called and brought Billy K up to speed on what had happened and put the pressure on again to find Dempsey. His wrists burned where the ambulance attendants had coated the abrasions from the plasticuffs with some sort of antiseptic cream.

Inside his penthouse he found Billy K and Ravinder Singh, better known as Rav the Raver. Singh, in his early twenties, had been born and raised in the East End of London and despite his young age was an electronics genius. Spread around the surface of the elegant glass designer dining table lay a variety of instruments and tools, encircling a brushed aluminum attaché case that Max had discovered in the major's house. There were no locks, just an electronic keypad, so he had called on Rav's services. He had a sense that there was something valuable in the case.

Tossing his jacket on the chair, he poured himself a couple of fingers of Scotch from a crystal decanter, offered Billy K a refill — Billy was never shy about helping himself — and sat down at the table.

"Okay, Rav, what's the fucking story, mate?"

Rav scratched his head, the movement causing a wave of heady aftershave to reach Max's nostrils. "This is one of those Ministry of Defense specials that have an antitheft device inside. If you try to tamper with the seal, it gets triggered, or if you type in the incorrect password five time, it gets triggered. There's a small incendiary charge — probably thermite — built into the lining that will destroy the contents. They use these for highly classified documents."

"Fuck me," exclaimed Max, pushing away from the table.

Rav laughed. "Relax, it's not big enough to do any damage other than to the contents."

"That's good to know," snorted Max, downing the whisky. "I've had enough fucking excitement for one night."

"Did you happen to find a burn bag with these?" Rav asked.

"Burn bag?"

"Yeah, it's an insulated bag that spooks use to destroy sensitive documents once they have been read. It's called a burn bag for obvious reasons, but sometimes they use acid to destroy the docs. That way they can never be reconstituted."

Max shook his head but was certainly intrigued now. He had gone through most of the files from the major's house, and it was certainly a treasure trove of intel. But this case, tucked away under a pile of folders, warranted a much closer check. It was, like most intelligence affairs that he had dealt with in Ulster, peeling away the layers of an onion, stripping lies and illusions away one at a time until you reached the truth. If you ever got to the truth.

Rav gingerly pried off the face of the keypad, which contained a four by four matrix of squares, and attached some alligator clips leading to a device that presented a mirror image of the keypad. That device was connected to the USB port on a tiny netbook, and once the wires were set securely, Rav typed a few commands on the screen, and instantly the screen filled with an array of numbers that flowed past so quickly, Max could barely make them out. As Max watched, one of the squares on Rav's blank keypad lit up and presented a digital number "1" in the square.

"It's not enough to know which squares have to be pressed, but you have to have the correct sequence as well," Rav explained. "We were lucky with the first one, but the rest should take about twenty minutes."

Rav was smart enough not to ask questions, and he was paid a handsome retainer to do just that. During the day he worked as an engineer in the advanced electronics department of Raytheon Defense systems, but at night, like most twenty-somethings, he frequented the clubs in and around the East End. It was in the Palm Beach casino, one of Max's clubs, that he had first come to the attention of Billy K. Rav was consistently winning high amounts of cash at the blackjack table, more than the casino's statistical norms would suggest, so he was put under intense scrutiny each time he came to visit. With the help of micro cameras and a couple of high-priced call girls, Billy K managed to discover that Rav had invented a way to count cards. That, combined with a thorough background check, provided enough evidence to bring Rav into Max's office late one evening for a "chat."

When Max showed Rav a couple of high-resolution colour photographs of former card sharks who had been kneecapped, he broke down, promising to pay the money back. He had done it for the challenge and also to get money for the "dollies" in the club who had expensive tastes in champagne. Bottles of Cristal didn't come cheap. As with most modern criminal enterprises, there was always a need for electronics specialists, so Rav was made an offer he could not refuse. Most banking institutions, secure warehouses, and high-end private homes utilized complex electronics in their alarm systems, and so far Rav had been undefeated in cracking their defenses. He had exceeded all expectations.

Max looked over to see that three of the buttons had lit up. "How many more?" he asked impatiently.

"Dunno," Rav said. "It's up to the user to set the number of codes. There are sixteen keys, so conceivably you could use them all, but then you have to remember all sixteen and also the correct sequence. How many digits do you have on any of your bank PIN numbers?"

Max thought for a moment, then replied, "Four." Although for his offshore stuff, he used much more complex passwords, but he wasn't about to share that info with Rav.

Rav nodded. "That's about the same for most people. It's more about ease of access and the ability to memorize digits. The average person can remember seven digits, so that's why phone numbers are seven digits long. Secure passwords on computers are supposed to be eight or nine characters, with a mix of upper and lower case as well as numbers, but nobody ever follows those rules. Take our BlackBerry android devices at the firm, for example. We implemented a security policy at the BES servers that says you have to have an eight-character password. I'd hazard a guess that about fifty percent or more of the folks in the office have a password that is QWERTYUI, the top row of the BlackBerry."

"Okay, Rav," groaned Max, "thanks for the fucking lesson. I'm so bored I could fucking top myself right now."

Billy K laughed and patted Rav on the shoulder. "Once a nerd, always a nerd!"

After a couple of minutes, a tiny alarm sounded from the netbook, and the green river of digits on the screen ceased flowing. Rav peered at the screen for a moment then looked over at the box that had six squares illuminated. "We're done," he said.

"Okay then," Max ordered, "you open the fucking thing."

Max and Billy K prudently stepped well back, just in case Rav was mistaken. They were both accomplished at creating booby traps and knew that often there was a secondary trigger employed, tripped when the first was deactivated. It was an old terrorist trick.

Rav gently pressed the digits of the case in the same order as they had lit up, and the latches on the case popped open. Then he slowly raised the lid and stepped away from the case. He knew better than to see what was inside.

"Go have a drink, Rav," Max ordered, leaning over and staring at the thick folder lying inside. It, too, had the MOD Top Secret logo emblazoned across the front, and he gingerly lifted it out, ever mindful of the incendiary device built into the lining. A thick rubber band encircled the file to keep the contents from spilling out. *Whatever it contained it must be important*, he thought. In the hundreds he had gone through, it was the only file that had been subjected to such a level of security. Maybe this one had bank codes or secret accounts over and above the ones he had discovered already. He almost drooled at the prospect.

Flipping the cover open, the first thing he saw was a black-and-white surveillance photo, dated only a couple of years ago. It appeared to be taken near a harbour, since there were boats in the background, mountains, and lots of tall buildings. The man in the photo was about six four or five, by Max's estimation, and had short, dark, curly hair. He wore a pair of jeans and a golf shirt, and there didn't appear to be much flab on his body. It was a profile shot, slight grainy, as if taken with a telephoto lens. Lifting it up, he found another underneath, this one much clearer, a shot of the man's face staring almost directly into the camera. There were slight creases at the eyes, as if the man laughed a lot, and there was a wry smile on his face, as if he had just heard something amusing. It was a hard face, though, the piercing eyes almost looking directly into Max's soul.

Max shivered.

Billy K commented, "Hard-looking fucker, that is." The ice cubes in his glass clinked as he took a long swig. Max nodded.

Max flipped the photos over, searching for details, but there were no clues as to the location. Putting them to one side, he opened the manila folder and scanned quickly the contents of the first page.

185

"Well, fuck me sideways, Billy," Max exclaimed. "Hard cunt wouldn't be half of it. This is mister Daniel fucking Riordan, Billy. Better known as the Raven!"

Billy K picked up the photograph. "This is the guy the book's about, the one that's in all the shops at the minute. It didn't uncover his identity, though. There was a pretty high body count, as I recall from what I read in the papers. There's talk of a movie as well, and they mentioned Liam Neeson's name as a possible lead."

"And then some," Max said. "Now I know why the case was protected. There's still a huge fucking bounty on this guy's head. Peace process be damned, there's a long list of people who'd want to get their hands on this guy." Tossing the pages to one side, he leaned back in his chair, a wide grin splitting his face.

"Oh, fuck," Billy K exclaimed. "I know that look."

Max smiled and took a long sip of his whisky. "You know the old saying, Billy, 'Set a thief to catch a thief?' Well, I'm going to do one better..."

"Dempsey..." Billy K laughed, realizing what his boss was alluding to. "Fucking brilliant, Max."

"Yep, our new friend here is going to find that cunt Dempsey for me. Who better?" Looking at his watch, he saw that it was a few minutes after 2:00 a.m. "How many hours do you think Vancouver is behind us, Billy?" Max asked.

"I know Toronto is five hours behind us, 'cos my cousin lives there, and I think he said that British Columbia is three hours behind them, west coast time. So that would make it eight in total."

"Good, that puts them about 6:00 p.m. local time. He'll just be sitting down to supper with his lovely wife, Nancy. Mind you, this stuff's two years old, so who knows what might have happened. It's worthy of a call, though. Give Rav some dough and tell him to fuck off before we start, Billy. Actually, I'm feeling generous. Give him a lot of dough!"

After a very grateful Rav had packed up his gear and disappeared, Max set a portable phone on the table, pressed the hands-free button, and dialled the number that he had found in the file. It rang for a few moments, then it was picked up.

A breathless voice said, "Nancy here," and in the background Max could hear the excited shrieks of children.

"Good evening, Nancy, my name is Max DeLisle. I'd like to speak to Daniel, please," he said in his politest British accent.

There was a moment's hesitation then she replied, "I'm afraid he's not here at the moment. Can I get a number and have him call you?"

"That would be great, Nancy. It's a London number, and I'll be here beside the phone for the next hour or so. This is an emergency, so please get him to call immediately."

"I'll see what I can do," she replied, her tone wary but still friendly. "But I can't guarantee anything. Can I tell him what's it's about?"

"It's a private matter, relating to the Ministry of Defense. He will recognize the name Major James Skinner. That should give him sufficient incentive to call."

Max winked at Billy K, broke the connection, and poured himself another Scotch. He could hardly believe his good fortune. "The fucking stars are aligned, Billy," he commented, and the two men clinked glasses.

*

Riordan lay back in the armchair in his room, feet up on the coffee table, a cold Corona in one hand and the cable changer in the other, flipping through channels on the TV. The inn had satellite television, but like back home, there really wasn't much worth watching. Every other channel seemed to be broadcasting a soccer match, many of them from the European leagues. The announcers there were a study in contrast to the usual reserved British announcers. The adrenaline rush from the evening's activities had started to wane, and he was finally starting to feel tired. He popped a couple of melatonin tablets and washed them down with a mouthful of beer. *Every little bit helps*, he thought and switched off the TV.

He undressed, leaving his clothes piled on the floor, and climbed between the fresh sheets. Nancy was forever giving him grief about building a nest by the side of the bed. The daily newspaper lay on the night table, and he was about to pick it up when his BlackBerry vibrated a couple of times and then rang. Picking it off the table, he saw it was Nancy calling.

Smiling, he pressed the answer key and said, "Hello, love, this is a pleasant surprise." There was a momentary pause. "Nancy?" The smile vanished like flicking a switch.

"Hi, love," she said, but her voice was full of concern.

He was immediately on edge and rolled to the edge of the bed. He could tell just from those two words, by the tone, the inflection, that something was wrong. This was not good news. Nancy said, "I just had a call from someone called Max DeLisle, in London. He said he wants you to call him and that he'll be by the phone for the next hour. Here's the number."

"Hold on a moment," he said, looking for a pen and a piece of paper. After finding utensils in the drawer of the night table, he scribbled the number on a pad beside the bed. "Never heard of him," Riordan replied, wracking his brain to recall the name or some connection to the name. "Did he say anything else or what it was about?"

"He mentioned the name, Major James Skinner." Riordan shivered, and a cold chill enveloped his being. He shook his head sadly, and his stomach churned like a parachutist in freefall. Skinner had been blown to pieces after threatening Riordan and his family. During their final phone call, Riordan had given him one last chance to back off, but after seeing there was no compromise, he had sent a coded signal to the major's cellphone to detonate a small charge of C4 explosive. The blame went to a variety of terrorist organizations who were only too eager to accept responsibility, even though they had nothing to do with the act. It simply raised their cache.

And now the ghost of Skinner was back.

"Does that mean anything, Daniel?"

He swallowed hard, trying to keep his voice steady. "Yeah, I know the name. Listen love, I better make this call and see what's up. It's after two here, so I'll call you later when I get more details. Love you."

"Don't you fucking dare hang up on me," she exploded. "I want to know what's going on. Are we in trouble?"

Taking a deep breath, he said quietly, "I honestly don't know, love. And you should know I can't discuss it further on an open line. Let me find out what this guy wants, and then we'll discuss it. Okay?"

"Fine." Curt. Abrupt.

He shook his head and broke the connection quickly.

Rather than let his imagination conjure up all sort of possibilities regarding the circumstances, he decided to face this one, like all others, face on. Picking up the hotel phone, he selected an outside line then started keying the digits he had written on the paper. Just as he was about to enter the last digit, he paused and set the phone back on its cradle. There was an eight-hour time difference between Vancouver and London, and since the caller thought Riordan was still in Vancouver, that might give him some sort of advantage. Advantage over what he hadn't a clue, but he'd take what he could get, especially since he was in unknown territory.

Powering up his laptop, he attached a couple of tools that Featherstone's tech team had provided and plugged one end into the bottom of his BlackBerry. The software enabled him to record any call that he made or received, and for incoming calls it could display the stress level in a person's voice. It was useful at times to be able to dissect the various frequencies during a call and to screen out voices and raise background noises. Sometimes, analysis of background noises — a siren, a bell, a train rumbling past — could provide clues about a caller's location. Picking up his BlackBerry, he dialled the number and waited.

"Max DeLisle here," came a voice. The recording started.

"I understand you want to speak to me," Riordan replied.

"Fuck me, if it isn't the famous Raven?" came the reply. Riordan understood, in a moment of absolute clarity, that his world as he knew it teetered on a knife edge. This man obviously wanted something, otherwise the link between himself and Skinner would have been all over the newspapers. He waited.

"Lost for words, are you my son?" came the thick Cockney accent.

"Just waiting for you to get to the point," Riordan said.

"Okay, mate, here's the fucking point." The stress analyzer's bars climbed. "My name's Max DeLisle. I was with the paras over in that shithole you once called home, but now I run a big part of London, if you get my drift. Your dear friend Major Skinner kept very detailed records at his house, records which are now in my possession. I'm looking at photographs of you and your pretty little wife even as we speak." DeLisle didn't mention the children, which meant Skinner's info was old.

"I'm still waiting for your point," Riordan interrupted, breathing evenly to keep his heart rate in check. The pressure on that particular dyke, however, was enormous. The bars on the stress analyzer climbed again. Max had a short fuse.

"Here's my fucking point. One of my crew, another Irish cunt named Dempsey, stiffed me on a bank job and fucked off with about five million quid. He's supposedly ex-IRA or some such, and my boys can't find him. I want you to find him for me and get me back my money. Is that to the point enough?"

"I knew we'd get there sooner or later," Riordan said calmly. "Is there an 'or else' coming, or should I just make it up?"

"Smart cunt, aren't you," DeLisle hissed. "Leaking this stuff to the newspapers would be the least of your worries. There are a lot of terrorists on both sides of the Troubles who would like to get their hands on you. Peace process or not, we're talking about Cookstown sausages..."

Riordan took a deep breath. The Cookstown reference was one that had been making the rounds for a long time. Some thought it to be one of those urban legends, and even though there was no way to verify the story, he believed that some of the IRA terrorists he had come across were more than capable of taking such action to give birth to the legend. It related to two young undercover British soldiers who allegedly had been captured while out on patrol. Apparently, they had been tortured extensively, and then their naked bodies had been thrown into a sausage machine. Once the story came to light, it had been a PR nightmare for the company. Cookstown "family" sausages, as recommended by the beloved George Best, took on a much more macabre connotation.

"Okay, I'll see what I can do to find him," Riordan replied evenly, knowing that he needed to buy some time to see where the chess pieces were placed. Right now he was very much at a disadvantage. "How do you want to handle this?"

"Get on the next flight to London, call me with the itinerary, and I'll have one of my lads pick you up at the airport. He can provide you with all the background details, and then I'll give you about a week to find Dempsey and get my money. When the money is transferred, you can shoot the fucker, knife the fucker, or even club the fucker to death, and then I will send you all the files that I have in my possession. And you can go on living your comfortable little lives..."

"Not much of a deal," Riordan replied.

"It is a bit one-sided." DeLisle laughed. "But those are the kind I like."

"I'll be in touch," Riordan replied. "Oh, there is just one more thing."

"Oh, and that would be?"

"If this goes pear-shaped, and you expose my family, the first person to die will be you. And I promise it won't be quick."

"Don't you fucking threaten me you cunt, I'll fucking see..." Riordan hung up as the stress level indicator slid into the red zone on the screen. It had been a bit childish on his part, but he always had had a low tolerance for bullies of any shape or form. Based on the device readings, DeLisle was probably throwing things at the moment. Which, unknown to him, was probably the least of his worries. He had threatened Riordan's family, and in Riordan's world, regardless of the outcome of the search for Dempsey, that came with a mandatory death sentence. What DeLisle simply failed to comprehend was that Riordan didn't make threats.

He waited for a moment then called up Featherstone's number. Featherstone owned the security and investigations firm that he worked for, and though technically his employer, the men were close friends.

"Featherstone here."

"I'm in trouble," Riordan said.

"There's a surprise. Tell me," Featherstone replied.

So he did.

He slept fitfully and woke at nine, completely exhausted and entwined in the damp sheets. He had tossed and turned during the night, never really getting the refreshing REM sleep that his body craved. Several times he had fought his way awake after feeling trapped in a black pit, his arms and legs nonresponsive. Sweat dripped from every pore when he woke each time, breathless and weak. And then he would drift off only to wake later, panting and soaked. These were the dreams that had come to him in Belfast during his last days there, dark wraiths that tormented his soul and robbed him of precious sleep.

Logically, he realized this was his body's stress reaction to the phone call, the threat of exposure that had dangled over his head like the sword of Damocles, but on an emotional level he felt fear.

Not for himself.

No, he had made his peace many years ago, and death was no longer something to be feared. The fear was for his family. They were an innocent party to all of this and at worst would be considered collateral damage by those seeking revenge on the Raven.

There had been a quick call to reassure Nancy that all was okay and that he needed a few days to deal with a small problem that had arisen. She knew better than to ask over the phone but realized he would explain things when he could. Feather would already have placed a surveillance team in the area to cast a watchful eye over Nancy and the kids, so he was not concerned on that score.

Featherstone employed only the best ex-special forces and intelligence agents available, each member being put through a rigorous acceptance and probationary period before coming on board. Much more of the company's revenue was now coming from investigative work rather than strong-arm stuff, but the two skill sets complemented each other well. His family would be well protected, or there would be hell to pay. Featherstone didn't believe in half-measures. During their call, he had committed some of his resources to be in London to provide ground support or whatever logistical support Riordan required. The team looked after their own.

Rolling his feet to the floor, he stood up, feeling slightly light-headed, and headed for the shower. He stood under the miserable shower for several minutes, wishing he were back under his own high-powered, luxuriant, rain-forest heads. It refreshed him somewhat, but after climbing out and towelling himself off, the dark funk returned with a fury.

After deciding to forego shaving again, he pulled on a clean shirt and his jeans and went downstairs to get some food and a lot of coffee. The dining room was empty, the weekenders having moved on. His hearty breakfast order was soon sitting on the table. The kindly waitress left the coffee pot, since the petite cups were for him a form of aerobic exercise. He got stuck into the bacon and eggs with gusto and felt a bit more human with some food inside him. His mind raced, as it always did when faced with a complex problem, various scenarios unfolding all at the same time like moving multiple pieces on a chessboard. It was like writing a screenplay in his mind.

He had once watched a TV program that showed interviews with famous screenwriters, and one of things that had stuck with him was a comment one of them had made about his "process." The writer had said that "we play the 'what if' game when we're creating a script." It was mental mechanism Riordan used frequently when planning an operation. The base scenario would be created, and then the "what if?" conversation would begin. Right now, the "what if?" process had already begun. He was always careful to put Mister Murphy in the deliberations, as he always came calling at some point during the event and not in a good way. His favourite law, which always seemed to apply, went something like "Success can be insured only by devising a defense against failure of the contingency plan."

What if he didn't find Dempsey? What if DeLisle revealed his identify to the newspapers or the terrorist factions who would dearly love to know the identity of the Raven? And for each of these questions he needed an answer, and for that answer a strategy to cope with the consequences. It wasn't like he had not thought of this day, but as the years went by and the fragile peace process in Northern Ireland eventually took root, he felt the possibility of his identity being revealed becoming more and more remote. After all, it had been a closely guarded secret, only known by a select few. And with that came complacency, and now he was scrambling, caught blindsided by an event he had hoped would never happen. His entire existence, one that he had worked so hard to create and live a life of normalcy, sat balanced on the knife-edge of the outcome of the next few days.

He knew well that people like Max DeLisle, thugs that exploited people's weaknesses, would never let him off the hook, even if he did succeed in finding Dempsey. So he had to plan for the first task, and then the second of dealing with DeLisle. He refilled his coffee and was patting his stomach when Sean slipped into the chair beside him.

"Whataboutye pal?" Sean grinned. "You're sitting there with a face like a wet Tuesday."

Riordan laughed, in spite of himself, and shook his head. His spirits lifted like the sun poking out of storm clouds.

"That's better," Sean replied. Freshly showered and dressed in jeans and an Irish rugby shirt, he looked ready for the day. "What's the craic?"

The waitress appeared, and Sean peered over at Riordan's ketchup-stained plate. "I'll have whatever he had, love, and a pot of tea." The waitress, a pretty, young thing barely out of her teens, giggled and headed off to the kitchen. Sean watched her go, admiring the swing of her hips.

"If I was only a few years younger," he commented.

"Fuck me," exclaimed Riordan. "Do you ever stop?"

Sean looked offended. "And why would I?"

"No reason, I suppose," Riordan conceded.

"Exactly. So why the long face?"

Riordan sighed, took a sip of coffee. "There's a guy called Max DeLisle here in London who wants to see me. He called my house last night, and Nancy forwarded his number to me, so we had a few words in the wee hours. He knows who I am and is threatening to expose me to the newspapers and worse, if I don't do a job for him." Riordan didn't want to go into the circumstances of how he found out.

Sean scratched his head. "Oh, is that all?"

His tea arrived, and Sean poured himself a cup, added some milk and a lot of sugar, then sat back in his chair, folding his arms across his chest. "So, how can I help?"

Riordan smiled, amused and yet comforted by his friend's willingness to provide assistance. The years and miles had fallen away like the sun burning off the early morning mist on a river, and they were boys again, shoulder to shoulder against the world.

199

"I've got to think this through and get some more information. DeLisle thinks I'm in Vancouver at the moment, so I have today to set things in motion, and then I'll show up at the airport tomorrow morning."

"That's grand," Sean replied. "I've got the week off, so I can drive you anywhere you need."

"Thanks, mate," Riordan replied. "I've got to make a few phone calls, and then we need to check out. We'll need to get a room in London under your name and then head down there before lunch. You wouldn't by any chance have brought an iPad with you? I need to jump on the Internet, and there's no connection here at the hotel."

"Nope, I left all that stuff at home," Sean replied. "And there's not much of a signal out this way anyway. You'd be better off to wait until we get to London."

"Fair enough," Riordan replied. "Then book us into a hotel that has Wi-Fi, a network, or at least a business centre."

Sean was quiet for a moment. "What's the job, if you don't mind me asking?"

Riordan paused for a moment, wondering how much to share. He decided to keep some of the information back, since the prospect of him having to off Dempsey was something Sean might not be able to handle. Not to mention DeLisle.

"One of DeLisle's thugs did a runner with the proceeds from a bank job, and DeLisle wants it back."

"And where do you come in?"

"DeLisle wants me to find the guy."

Sean looked puzzled. "You haven't been around for years, so how does he expect you to find him?"

"He's ex-IRA, or ex-Real IRA, or one of the factions. I think DeLisle believes he may have gone to ground over in Ireland, and that's where I unfortunately come in. I used to hunt these guys, and DeLisle thinks I can do it again."

"It's been a long time," Sean said. "A long fucking time, and the landscape has changed dramatically, especially in and around Belfast. As for Dublin, I think half of Eastern Europe is over there right now."

"Yeah, I know," Riordan replied, "but I don't have much of a choice at the moment. DeLisle is holding all the cards. You remember, just like your mother!"

They chatted aimlessly for a few minutes, then Riordan left just as the waitress delivered Sean's breakfast, after agreeing to meet in thirty minutes in the lobby.

*

Back in his room, he packed quickly then took a seat by the window. Outside his window the gardens bloomed, full of life and vibrant colours, and beyond the pristine, manicured shapes, the river meandered across open fields, sunlight sparkling upon its surface. Sliding open the window, he was struck by the silence and tranquillity. Perhaps it was the calm before the storm. Taking out his BlackBerry, he picked up the business card from the coffee table and peered at it for a moment, gnawing in indecision at the corner of his lip. A tiny grin split his face as he recalled Featherstone reciting the Marine Corps "tongue in cheek" rules for a firefight, the top three being particularly resonant at the moment: always bring a gun to a gunfight; always bring lots of guns; bring lots of friends who have guns.

He dialled the number then slid the card back into his wallet. It rang a couple of times, then a voice answered. "Didn't think I'd be hearin' from you again, lad," said Cupples in his guttural Belfast accent.

"That goes for me as well," Riordan replied. "But I'm in a bit of a bind right now, and you might be part of the collateral damage."

"You have got my undivided attention, as they say," Cupples replied in a light-hearted manner, but Riordan could hear the underlying tension in his voice. He knew what was at stake. Riordan spent the next few minutes outlining the call from DeLisle and the task that he had been forced to undertake. Cupples quickly understood the implications, given his connection with the Old Man and Riordan.

"Okay, lad," he said when Riordan had finished. "Give me a few hours to check into this. I've heard of DeLisle; he's a notorious mob boss here in the city, ex-military from what I understand, so I'll get what I can for you. As for this Dempsey character, if he was one of the old-school IRA villains, there should be a file on him as well. I can email you stuff as I get it. When you get into the city this afternoon, come by my office and we can discuss this further. I'm based in Thames House, in Millbank, near the Lambeth bridge. It's the MI5 headquarters, right beside the Northern Ireland office."

Well, that's just priceless, Riordan thought. One of the most hunted enforcers during the Troubles, waltzing into MI5. Featherstone was going to love this one. Riordan wrote down the address, and when Cupples hung up, entered it into his cellphone. Talk about friends with guns...

*

They checked out of the inn, and after Riordan settled himself in the car, he quickly checked his BlackBerry to see if there were any messages from Cupples.

"Expecting something important?" Sean asked. "That's about the fifth time you've checked that thing in the last half hour."

"Yep," Riordan replied, sliding it back into his jacket. No messages had come through from either Featherstone or Cupples. "I'm hoping for reinforcements."

"Grand," Sean replied, sliding the car into gear and roaring out along the curving driveway. "I booked us into 51 Buckingham Gate, a really nice upscale place in the city. It's on Victoria Street, not too far from the palace, in case you need to see the queen, and it's fairly central to everything. As well, it has a great business centre and I've stayed there and hosted meetings there many times over the past few years."

Riordan took out his BlackBerry, keyed in the address, and sent it off to Featherstone. Depending on timing and what Featherstone had planned, it would be good to have everyone in close proximity.

Sean switched on the CD player, and Riordan grinned at the raunchy twelve-bar blues emanating from the speakers, his foot tapping along to the beat. "Thought you might like to hear the boys," Sean said, pulling a CD case out of the side pocket of the car.

Riordan touched the cover of the remastered greatest hits of Status Quo, one of his favourite bands while growing up in Belfast. The music press often dissed them as three-chord wonders, but there was no mistaking their appeal. They had never reached the heights of popularity of the Stones or the Faces, but they toured constantly and still had a massive following everywhere except North America. Riordan and Sean were part of the "denim army," as Quo fans were known, their heroes wearing only denims and t-shirts, a stark contrast with the glam rock outfits of the seventies. Neil, of course, had pursued that path, and the photographic evidence was tragic.

"Do me a favour, mate," he said, "put on 'Caroline' and crank it."

Sean complied, and the meaty, pounding chords blasted out of the speakers as they roared down the motorway toward London. For a few precious minutes, Riordan lost himself in the music. Letting it wash over him like a furious tide, he closed his eyes and relived the joy again of his very first concert, seeing his heroes live in action at the Apollo Theatre in Dublin.

When the song ended, Sean eased back on the volume. "That was quite the night," he commented, and Riordan nodded, smiling. "I saw them about a year ago, over in Manchester, and man, they rocked the place. They did 'Caroline' that night as well, their opening number, and the fucking place went wild.

"Do you miss playing?"

Riordan shook his head. He had put the guitar away many years ago, one of the many habits that had been left by the wayside. "Nah, I keep meaning to take it up again, but between work and the boys, I don't have a lot of time. Still, the thought's what counts."

"Aye, it is."

They drove in silence after that, Sean respectfully allowing Riordan to quietly contemplate what would transpire over the next few days.

*

True to Sean's word, the hotel was magnificent, and after checking in and dropping off his luggage, Riordan headed to the business center to jump on the Internet. He checked his home email address and his work email, just in case there were connection problems with the new Android BlackBerry. The BES servers, even with all their special levels of encryption, were notoriously flakey, so much so that Featherstone kept threatening to head into the computer room with an AK-47. His were not idle threats. He had, on occasion, handed a cellphone to one of the techs with a smoking hole in the center of its screen, put there by a 9-millimeter round.

A few moments after he logged on, the device vibrated, and a message appeared simultaneously on the computer screen. It was from Featherstone, letting him know the times of the flights and what time they would be arriving at Heathrow. Tosser and possibly Jean-Marc, two ferocious ex-specops warriors, would accompany him, depending on availability.

A quick search on Max DeLisle produced numerous hits, and he scanned the headings, looking for any tidbit of information he could use. Cupples would have access to much more detailed data, but Riordan wanted to have a broad brush of the man. There were vague references to connections in the London underworld, but mostly it was fluff about attendance at charity events, Wimbledon, and the grand soirees that made London famous. Most of it was text-based, especially the newspaper columns, but the article in *Hello* magazine had a photo attached, a blurry group setting and then a close-up of Max and his fiancée.

Riordan inhaled sharply and expelled a long breath as he stared at the face of the man he had confronted the previous evening.

"Small fucking world," he hissed and sent the image to the printer. He logged off, picked up the sheet, and went into the lobby. Sean was already seated, a white tablet lying on the table in front of him. He grinned and passed the iPad over to Riordan.

"Picked this up for you. It's already fully charged, so you can use it while you're moving about. I set up the GPS, just in case, 'cos this is a fuck of a place to get lost. So, let's eat. The curry here is great."

"Jeez, thanks, pal," Riordan said, genuinely taken aback by his friend's generosity.

As the day was warm, they decided to have lunch in the courtyard, which turned out to be an opulent tiled patio, resplendent with linen-covered tables surrounding an ornate fountain. Canvas umbrellas provided shelter from the rain, a necessity in London. Off to both sides were beautifully manicured gardens, overflowing with flowers of every shape, size, and colour. Small green-leafed trees afforded some shade. Tiny birds flittered in the trees, swooping down to steal errant morsels, bold enough to land directly on the tables.

"Pretty impressive," Riordan commented. "You must be doing all right if you stay here a lot."

Sean grinned. "Business is good, and this is a write-off, so enjoy. It's a shame that things transpired the way they did. For four nights a week here they transform the back of the hotel into an outdoor opera house. It's quite the evening."

"Opera?" Riordan commented.

"Aye, I'm a cultured culchee," he replied, referring to the Irish colloquialism for farmer.

The liveried butler led them to a secluded table and then disappeared. Their waiter arrived a few moments later, and Sean ordered a curry and a pint, raising one eye when Riordan ordered the same meal and a pint of water. When the waiter had gone, Sean looked over. "Bit early for you?"

"Nah," Riordan replied. "I might have to kill somebody later, and I need a steady hand."

Sean blanched. After a few awkward seconds, Riordan exploded in laughter. Sean relaxed and smiled. "Good one, pal, you really got me there." *If only you knew*, Riordan thought.

"I need to keep a clear head for the next few days," Riordan replied, "but if I have to find this Dempsey, I imagine I'll have to hit few bars as well, and that'll require a drink or two." Anyone drinking water in an Irish pub stood out like the proverbial sore thumb.

The food, when it arrived, was incredibly flavourful and the presentation flawless. Riordan made a mental note to put this one into his list of favourites, as he was still a little in awe of the place, a tiny, sheltered oasis in the heart of London. He finished the remainder of his naan bread, wiping the plate clean with the remnants. Then, while Sean quietly sipped at another pint, he used Google maps to provide directions to Thames House. It was about five minutes by cab, but he wanted to stretch his legs, get some fresh air, and mentally prepare himself for what lay ahead.

After leaving Sean, he asked the concierge for the fastest route to Lambeth Bridge and tried hard not to smile as the man listed off the names of streets like Horseferry Road, Artillery Road, and Greycoat Place, thinking they sounded like something out of Middle Earth. Being a huge fan of the *Lord of the Rings* trilogy, he was looking forward to reading the books to the boys. The iPad proved invaluable as he walked along the busy, tree-lined streets, making his way slowly toward the Thames. It was a sunny day, quite a rarity in London, and he enjoyed the feel of the sun on his face. When he reached the bridge, instead of turning down the street to Thames House, he crossed the road and paused for a moment to take in the sounds of the river.

As a boy he had loved the sound of the water, be it the river across from his house or the angry surf pounding on the rocks at the shore, and here he was, standing on the bridge of one of the most famous rivers in the world. The river was still widely used for commerce, and small, brightly coloured freighters glided gently past under the bridge. On the far bank were moored numerous pleasure craft for taking sightseers on a historic journey up and down the Thames. There were joggers everywhere, which surprised him, pounding along the embankment, old-school iPods or iPhones strapped neatly inside Velcro pouches attached to their biceps. Despite its serene appearance, the waters were murky, the surface rippled by a dangerous undertow.

The British government was in a constant state of vigilance on the river. Since so many important government and state buildings were located either on or close to the Thames, there was a real possibility of a terrorist attack from a boat. London also possessed the highest per capita number of CCTV cameras in the world, so Riordan scanned the area, looking for these eavesdropping devices. They weren't hard to spot, and the very fact that they were highly visible also made them a deterrent for most domestic terrorists, the exception being Islamic extremists, of course, who were all on a one-way journey into the arms of a significant number of virgins.

His reverie concluded, he crossed the road again, dodging cars at the roundabout and made his way along to Thames House. The massive curved archway leading to the interior of the building gave him the willies, putting him in mind of one of Her Majesty's prisons. On each side of the arch, gazing sternly down at him, were sculptures of St. George and Britannia, guarding the entrance. It looked like the place had recently received a significant makeover, since the blocks looked clean and grime-free, unlike their counterparts in other areas of the city. The place appeared deserted, and he felt more than a little apprehensive approaching the entrance. A pair of CCTV cameras on either side would already have taken his picture, uploaded it to their specialized facial recognition software, and checked to see if he was on any watch lists, no-fly lists, or any type of security database. Any alert would provoke an immediate armed response. The Brits took their security seriously.

Hesitantly, he reached out and turned the door handle, pushed the door open, and walked into the cavernous reception area. His heart hammered in his chest. *This is how Daniel must have felt strolling calmly into the lion's den*, he thought. A perky receptionist whose badge proclaimed her to be Madge smiled sweetly when he informed her he was expected by Arthur Cupples. She made a quick call, keyed a few details into her computer, a printer whirred, and a few moments later she presented him with a visitor's badge.

"Make sure to wear that visibly at all times," she instructed in a very posh accent. "You have to go through a security check next, just like at the airport. Someone will be down to fetch you in a couple of minutes, so please have a seat." She pointed to a set of black leather chairs arrayed around a glass-topped coffee table, the surface of which was littered with glossy magazines. It was amazing to see how many people, when left alone for a period of time, would pick up a magazine and flip through its pages. There was a goodly assortment of topics that might pique the interest of a visitor.

Given this was MI6, the magazines would be a good source for fingerprints. As he moved over to take a seat, he wondered if she was armed. The Brits had extremely restrictive gun laws, both for citizens and its own police force, but given the security profile of this building, he imagined that weapons were readily accessible. This building and the sister building, which housed MI6, the other security service, would be high on any terrorist hit list of targets.

He recalled a conversation many years before in Belfast with an old family friend who was head of the Special Patrol Group of the Royal Ulster Constabulary (RUC). The man's office was at the top of a six-storey building. With typical RUC humour he announced that, "if we get attacked by terrorists, they'll be awful tired by the time they climb those six flight of stairs to get to me." Riordan couldn't remember exactly why he had been visiting the man, but it was the next part of the conversation that stayed with him. The "Cat," as he was known to his men, pointed to a piece of waste ground about half a mile away. "We captured a new type of rocket launcher the other day and carried out a few tests on it. It's a bit scary, but that's the only place where they could launch it from to actually do any damage. So we try to keep a close eye on it!"

For the rest of the conversation, Riordan's eyes strayed back to that piece of waste ground time and time again, wondering what it felt like to always be a target for some nutter with a gun or a bomb, or in this case, a rocket launcher.

Moments later the interior doors opened and a young man, probably in his early twenties, strode out. He made a beeline for Riordan, who stood to meet him. "Mister Riordan," he said, extending his hand. "I'm Danny Lock, Mister Cupples's assistant." The Belfast accent was there, but slightly softened. The man's grip was firm, and Riordan shook it.

"That's me," he replied.

"Let's get through security first," he said, heading back toward the doors. Lock swiped his pass card on a flat pad, the door clicked open, and he passed through. The doors were several inches thick, probably blast-proof, Riordan realized as he followed. Inside, several hard-faced men and women manned a security area, similar to the airport scanners. He was thoroughly patted down by hand to the extent that he was going to offer the man a ten-pound tip, but they seemed a humourless lot, so he let it go. Next came the hand scanner, and then he had to walk through the detector. All was well, so he replaced his wallet, smartphone, and iPad and followed Lock up two flights of stairs to another set of doors, also activated by security card.

"Make sure you keep your badge in sight at all times," Lock said, repeating the mantra from downstairs.

Riordan, never a big fan of rules, was now curious. "What happens if I don't?"

Lock grinned. "Believe me, mate, you don't want to know."

They passed through into a narrow corridor lined with paintings and prints, to Riordan's eye a rather eclectic mix of traditional and modern art. The traditional tended toward military scenes, mostly sea battles. Lock tore off down the corridor at a fast pace, as if he had somewhere else to be. There were many doors set into the corridor but no indication of what lay beyond, a further level of security should there be a breach. At the end of the corridor they came to a T-junction, which again had many doors leading off in both directions. Lock turned right and walked all the way to the end, where an enormous window looked out over the river. The image shimmered slightly as Riordan peered through, realizing that the glass appeared to be over an inch thick, and he shivered slightly, remembering the conversation in Belfast about the rocket launcher.

"This is Arthur's office," Lock offered, opening the door and stepping inside. There was a small desk in the room, on top of which sat a wide-screen monitor hooked up to a laptop. Several filing cabinets, new looking, lined one wall, and a couple of leather chairs sat just inside the doorway. The small desk guarded another door. Lock took a seat and nodded toward the door.

"Go on in. I'll see you out when you're done."

Riordan knocked on the door, turned the handle, and pushed it open. The room was obviously at the corner of the building and provided stunning views of the river and the city on two sides. Cupples sat behind a large, glass-topped desk, arrayed with a variety of advanced technology. The high ceilings gave the room an airy feel — Riordan liked high ceilings — and the two solid walls held a massive white board and a full map of London, respectively. There was barely a space on the white board, and Riordan recognized Cupples' neat printing. Multihued push-pins made the map look like a pin cushion. A small table in one corner was flanked by two chairs, and Cupples eased out from behind his desk, picked up a folder, and made his way over. Dressed in a white shirt and a cravat, he looked every bit the English gentleman.

"Have a seat, lad," he said, "and I'll bring you up to date on what I've got. Fancy a cuppa?" And away went the picture of the English gentleman, and they were back in the Old Man's living room in Belfast, huddled around the fireplace, mugs of hot tea in their hands and an open packet of jaffa cakes lying on the stool. Riordan grinned. *You can take man out of Belfast*, he thought, *but you can never take Belfast out of the man.*

"I'd love one," he replied.

"Danny," Cupples roared, and the young man stuck his head in the door. "Can you get us some tea?"

"Aye, boss," came the reply.

215

Opening the file, Cupples pulled on a pair of reading glasses and said, "So here's what I've found out about this guy Dempsey. Joined the IRA as a volunteer at the ripe old age of sixteen and was one of the select few who were sent for training in Libya."

Riordan nodded. Muammar al-Ghaddafi, a huge contributor to the IRA, had provided both money and weapons. He remembered stories about Army Intelligence tracking guys who had disappeared for a few months at a time and then returned, deeply tanned from their time in the Libyan desert. They might as well have walked around with signs around their necks proclaiming, "I'm a terrorist!"

Cupples continued, "He came back a master sniper, but he also received training in a variety of demolition techniques, not to mention tactics. What we in anti-terrorist circles call 'not your all around common or garden variety' terrorist. What set him apart was his willingness to put all these skills to use as often as possible. He wanted more and bigger targets, delightfully called 'spectaculars,' and when the IRA refused some of his more outrageous plans, he joined the Real IRA, the ultraviolent splinter group who did not possess the same reservations. According to the files, he's probably killed or been involved in the killing of about thirty or forty people."

Cupples paused for a moment, flipped the page, and scanned it quickly. "Says here he got caught with a Barrett sniper rifle, just after two squaddies were offed with a single shot. An

216

SAS team got lucky and caught him before he could get rid of the rifle. Spent three years in Long Kesh and then was released as part of the Good Friday agreement. There's not a lot of work in Ireland these days for a master terrorist, so, like many of his compatriots, he moved into organized crime. He made the move to London and started working for Max DeLisle, who put his talents to good use."

The door opened, and Lock backed in carrying a tray holding a pot of tea, with two strings hanging down one side, two mugs, a carton of milk, and a bowl of sugar. A brand new packet of digestive biscuits lay unopened. Lock set the tray on the table and left.

"I'll be mother," Cupples said, checking the consistency of the tea before pouring. Riordan opened the carton of milk and added a splash to his mug.

"Only the best china for visitors, Arthur?"

Cupples snorted. "With all the fucking cutbacks around here, you're lucky to get milk!" He tore open the packet of biscuits, spilled a few on to the tray, and then took a sip of tea and munched happily on the digestive, crumbs scattering everywhere. Riordan waited patiently for the ritual to finish.

When the biscuit was gone, Cupples picked up the second file. "Now this one is where the trouble starts. Max DeLisle. Underworld boss, controls a good part of London's criminal activity: gambling, prostitution, porn, drugs, human trafficking. There's not much he doesn't do, but what he does best is rob

217

banks. At least his teams do, based on superb intel, excellent planning, and execution. The latter, as you might have guessed, is down to our dear friend Mister Sean Dempsey. The latest haul was in the order of five million pounds, but word on the street confirms that Dempsey scarpered with the loot. That's why DeLisle wants him found. One of the other members of the gang was discovered floating in the Thames, minus his head. That'll give you a sense of what DeLisle is all about. A thoroughly nasty piece of work."

Riordan gnawed on a digestive. "Does Dempsey have a criminal record here in London — known associates, that kind of thing? Strikes me that he'd be pulled in for questioning about the robberies, especially some of the previous jobs."

"The file is pretty sparse. Dempsey's a gambler. He plays in high-end poker games — wins some, loses some. Likes the ponies as well. He's well connected, so he always has an alibi and used to frequent DeLisle's restaurant called the Gun. I've got all the addresses for you, as well as DeLisle's place, and I can email them to you. What are you thinking?"

Riordan shrugged. "I don't have a whole lot of options at the moment, so I've got to start looking for Dempsey. Any help you can provide in that regard would be great, and this is a great start. If he's ex-IRA, he'll likely have hung out in Kilburn, so that's where I'll head later. All I can do is try to annoy enough people to get someone's attention and take it from there.

"Be careful in Kilburn," Cupples warned. "It's a pretty closed community over there — wall of silence and the like. They don't take kindly to strangers, so if I were you, I'd get tooled up in some shape or form. Dempsey's not the only ex-IRA member who has relocated to London. Have you access to gear in London?"

Riordan shook his head. There was no point in letting Cupples know about the storage lockers in Paddington Station, the keys to which were secreted in the back of his desk at home. They were for dire emergencies. If Riordan and his family ever had to go on the run from city to city, at least he would have access to identification papers, cash, and a variety of other supplies.

Cupples tossed a key across the table. Made from shiny brass, it had the number 207 stamped into the top. "You'll find what you need in there. It's unmarked and untraceable, and there are a couple of boxes of ammunition, plus assorted other devices. The locker is in Waterloo Station, near the Eurostar platform, just in case you need a quick getaway to Europe, and I suggest you retrieve the bag of tricks before you go exploring. And, lastly, write down your email address for me before you go so I can forward this stuff to you." Cupples handed him a notepad and a pen, a fancy Gold Cross ballpoint with the royal crest engraved on the side.

"Nice pen," Riordan said, scribbling his address.

"Keep it," Cupples replied. "Think of it as a souvenir of London. You can catch a taxi outside the reception — they come along fairly frequently. Other than that, stay in touch and let me know if there's anything else I can do. This is strictly off the books, so I'm limited to how much I can do before alarms start going off."

Riordan finished his tea, sampled another digestive, and then stood up. "Thanks, Arthur. Thanks for everything." He held out his hand. The grip in return was firm.

Cupples grinned. "Mind how ye go lad, and please, keep the body count to a minimum."

"As ever," Riordan replied just as Danny Lock appeared in the doorway.

*

Later, back at the hotel, Riordan opened the zippered leather bag he had retrieved from the station locker and dumped the contents out onto his bed. In a plastic carrying case, he found a brand new Berretta .40 calibre handgun and a threaded sound suppressor. The serial number had been ground off, but it looked as if it had come straight from the factory. A Ziploc bag contained several pairs of surgical gloves, and he pulled on a pair, stripped the gun quickly, impressed that it was well maintained, and then quickly loaded two of the empty magazines. Forensics being what they were these days, fingerprints could be lifted from spent cartridges or even from live rounds. Jamming the last few rounds into a spring-loaded magazine required a fair amount of thumb pressure, as many criminals had discovered, and not in a good way.

There were two disposable cellphones in the pile, and he powered them up. The address book in both was completely blank, as were the call lists. He slipped the phones into his jacket pocket. There were also two matte black folding knives, tactical folders made by SOG, a company whose products Featherstone's team used extensively. These were two from the new line containing a new mechanism called SOG Assisted Technology (SAT). Riordan liked the knives, and one had come in handy recently since the mechanism was designed to propel the blade open once the user initiated the one-handed opening action. The last items on the comforter brought a smile to his face. Four flash-bang grenades, capable of disorienting an entire room with blinding flashes and ear-splitting percussion, each with two-second fuses. These were standard fare for all tactical units. He slipped one into his pocket and replaced the others in the bag.

Pulling out his cellphone, he saw that it was almost 6:00 p.m., so he put in a quick call to Nancy. She usually took a break at around 10:00 a.m., but since she was an emergency nurse, scheduled break times were highly fluid depending on circumstances. The phone rang a couple of times and he heard her voice say, "Daniel?"

He swallowed hard. "Yes, love, it's me."

"Thank God, I was starting to get worried."

"Things are well in hand here, but as I mentioned there's been a bit of a complication. The guy who called the house the other night has some documents that show my history from Belfast all the way to the present, or at least to the point where you and I got together. He's threatening to release all the material to the press, or worse." He paused for a moment to let the implication sink in.

"I see," she replied, her voice terse, those two words twisting his stomach into knots. The moment was filled with the transatlantic crackle from the cell, an ever-expanding silence growing between them.

"I'm sorry, love," was the best he could offer. Being thousands of miles away, what he really wanted to do was wrap her in his arms, kiss her, and tell her everything would be okay. Skin to win was how she often put it, and at that particular moment it was all he could do to stay calm and focused. Part of him just wanted to get on a plane, go home, pack up his family and move, but that meant a new identity, massive upheaval, and the trauma of leaving friends behind. It was not out of the realm of possibility and could certainly be accomplished, but this being the Internet age, everyone with a fucking camera and all too eager to mind everybody else's business, establishing a new identity would bring its own set of complications.

No, the right thing to do was to see this through and try to prevent DeLisle from releasing the documents. He had no illusions about what that would mean — there would be a trail of bodies somewhere. People like DeLisle didn't just let you off the hook. Once that barb was set, they had you forever, and could play you whatever way they wished. That was how evil bastards like DeLisle operated.

"When will you know if we are in danger?" Nancy asked.

"I've got a week to find someone for DeLisle," Riordan replied. "After that, I don't know. I have an old friend helping me out at the moment, and he has a vested interest in making this all go away, so at least I'm not flying solo. Feather is also sending some of the boys over to help out. In a few days, hopefully this will just be a bad memory and we can get back to our lives." He heard himself say the words, but they were more for Nancy's benefit than his own. He had a bad feeling about this and, try as he might, he couldn't shake it.

"I've got to get back to work," she said, her voice cold. This was taking its toll already. "Call me when you can." The connection broken, he stared at the phone, his heart heavy.

Fucking Max DeLisle.

Riordan shook his head sadly, wondering if he would ever find peace. He truly knew what people meant when they said they were haunted by their past; victims of abuse, be it physical or sexual, or young soldiers barely equipped to deal with the horrors of war, or simply regular folks who brushed against the darkness. Life for them was never the same.

The cellphone vibrated in his hand — an incoming call. He looked at the screen and saw it was Nancy calling back. He clicked the receive button.

"Sweetheart," she said, "I'm sorry about that. It's just so ... unfair."

"I know, love. I know."

"I was being selfish. I can only imagine what you're dealing with right now, so you don't need more shit from me. So go and do what you do best and come home safe to me. And please, try not to get any more holes in your body. I think the surgeons here have got a pool going about when they're going to see you again."

Riordan grinned, the dark mood lifting. "Thanks, love. I'll be home soon, and I'll call when I can. If you can't reach me, call Feather, as he'll be pretty much up to date with what's going on."

"Love you," she said.

The connection was terminated, but he felt heartened by the call. He put everything away inside the bag and locked it in the wall safe that the hotel provided. He slipped the Beretta into his leather jacket and put a full magazine into the other pocket. The Beretta held fourteen rounds plus one in the spout, so it was more of a precaution than anything, since he rarely needed more than one or two bullets. However, this was unknown territory for him, and the extra firepower might come in handy.

Checking the time, he saw he had a couple of hours free before he was to meet Sean, so having gone through every preparation that he could think of, he sprawled out on the bed and indulged in his favourite pastime: the movie channel. When he and Nancy had the opportunity to get away for a weekend, or even for a one-night stay in a hotel, there was nothing they liked better than ordering room service, a couple of bottles of fine wine, and then movie after movie. After a shag, of course.

His glance caught the adult selection, and he grinned like a naughty schoolboy but passed by and went to the new releases. Movies in the UK were always behind those released in North America, but the home-grown stuff, Irish and British independents, took a long time to cross the pond. These were some of his favourites. As it turned out, there were five or six that he hadn't seen, so he selected one, grabbed a packet of very expensive nuts from the minibar, along with a Perrier and settled down to watch.

The room phone woke him up. He cursed under his breath, having missed almost the entire movie. Rubbing his eyes, he saw it was almost a quarter to eight, and he had promised to meet Sean at seven thirty. He had slept for three hours. He grabbed the phone, said hello, and smiled when he heard Sean's voice, his words slightly slurred.

"David, wherethefuckareye?"

"Sorry, Sean," he said, rolling his feet to the floor. "I fell asleep."

"Grand. Well, I'm downstairs in the restaurant, and there's a bottle of wine here with your name on it."

"Alright, mate," he replied. "Pour me a glass. I'll be there in a minute."

The wine was waiting for him when he arrived at the table, and Sean just was handing the menus back to their waiter. The unique shape of the bottle, like something invented by Picasso, showed it was a Fiole du Pape Châteauneuf-du-Pape. Riordan knew the one-of-a-kind bottle shape was created in 1952 by Pere Anselme, the vintner, in collaboration with local master glass craftsmen.

"I took the liberty of ordering a bunch of stuff for us, as I'm so hungry I could eat a small pony. We've got some onion bhaji coming as appetizers."

Sean's eyes were a bit glassy, so Riordan presumed the afternoon had been spent in the pub. Voicing that opinion produced vigorous nodding in response.

"Aye, I was. Walked the fucking streets of Kilburn, I did, looking for yer man."

Riordan froze. "What?" His head turned from side to side, scanning the faces in the room, terrified that Sean might have picked up a tail. Fortunately, nothing and no one seemed out of place.

"I thought I'd see if I could find yer man, Dempsey," came the response.

Riordan shook his head, "Fuck me, Sean, these are very bad guys, and believe me, you don't want to get involved."

"Do you think I came up the Bann in a bubble?" came the caustic reply. "I've lived over there since you left, so I know a thing or two. My nephew Martin, and even wee Gerry, come over to London all the time for the football, and afterwards they head off to Kilburn. I've been out with them after the match, so I know the place pretty well, and a few of the bartenders know me. I fit in over there, but you'd stick out a mile, unless you're with me. Ye see, I talk like one of the natives!"

There was no denying that point, so Riordan didn't bother. "Fair enough. So did you find out anything?"

There was a gleam in Sean eyes. "Aye, I did." He took a long sip of wine, deliberately drawing out the suspense. "Wid ye like to know?" His accent thickened.

"Alright, alright, you made your point," Riordan replied. He raised his glass in a toast, and Sean clinked his against it.

"May ye die in Ireland?" he said.

"Almost did," Riordan replied, and drained the glass. "Several times..."

"So, after much walking and drinking, I found out that Dempsey hangs out in a couple of pubs over there in Kilburn. One's called Powers Bar — has sessions most nights — the other is called the Old Bell. That's as much as I got. I'll leave the rest up to you."

"Thanks, mate," Riordan replied. "You've saved me a lot of time, and maybe now I've got a chance to get out ahead of this thing. DeLisle and crew think I'm arriving tomorrow, so that allows me time to check out these places tonight."

"I need to eat something before we go," Sean said. "I did have quite a few already."

"No kidding." Riordan laughed. "But no, tonight I go on my own. I don't want anyone to see us together, 'cos if things go sideways, I know how to handle myself. These are nasty people, and the last thing I need is to for you to get hurt, or worse." He patted his jacket pocket.

"Oh, it's like that," Sean said, his face serious.

Riordan nodded. "These people play for keeps, Sean. From what I've been told, DeLisle has been involved either directly or indirectly in as many as twenty gangland murders, most of them his competition. Do you remember the Shankill Butchers?"

Sean swallowed hard and nodded.

In the late seventies, a group of UVF members, known as the "Shankill Butchers," abducted, tortured, and killed and number of Catholics. A gang of the UVF men worked in a meat-packing plant, so they put their skills to good use on their victims, their grisly handiwork terrifying the people of Belfast. They were eventually captured, but some were released early as part of the Good Friday agreement. Upon his release, their leader, who was in the process of creating another gang, was assassinated outside his home by two IRA gunmen.

"Max DeLisle would put the Butchers to shame," Riordan said quietly. "You helped me immensely by that foolhardy stunt this afternoon, so let's have a nice meal, and then you can retire to the bar to find a nice dolly, and I'll be on my way. That's the extent of the danger I need to find you in tonight."

"Not another fuckin' word about trannies!" Sean growled.

*

About an hour later, with Sean safely ensconced at the ornate bar, a brandy snifter at his hand and a direct view of some elegantly dressed ladies at the other end, Riordan headed outside. A round of drinks had already been sent to the "ladies," and Sean was fancying his chances with the redhead. A liveried bellman hailed a taxi, and Riordan climbed inside, asked the driver to take him to Kilburn High Road, and settled back. The driver made a brave attempt to draw him into conversation, but Riordan remained quiet, and he lapsed into a sullen silence. The streets were busy, the traffic slow. At the last moment he had decided to leave the gun in his room. In a crowded pub, with patrons jostling one another, it was hard to conceal a weapon. Instead, the brace of knives pressing against his ribs provided a constant reminder of what was to come.

The cabbie cut through Hyde Park, the first time Riordan had ever been there, and he was surprised to see the Serpentine, the large lake that cut the park in two. He was familiar with the famous Speakers' Corner of the park, where various and sundry individuals took to their soapbox on weekends. At the other end of the park the cabbie headed west, and a few minutes later Riordan began to see Celtic script appear in shop windows and advertisements.

This was Kilburn, home to the largest Irish population of any area of London, and a fiercely tight-knit community that protected its own with a strict code of silence. The place was often referred to as "County Kilburn" or "Little Eire," after the Irish Republic. In a previous life Riordan had come hunting here, his target an IRA gunman who had accidentally killed a schoolgirl. The little girl had the misfortune to be following behind an army foot patrol on her way home from school. The gunman had sprayed the soldiers with bullets, not caring who else got in the way. This particular schoolgirl happened to be the niece of a close friend of the Old Man. Once the target had been identified, Riordan went after him. The gunman had been sent out of Belfast to hide until the furor died down — gunmen were too scarce a resource to waste. Thanks to an informer, the Old Man had managed to track him down in Kilburn. His body was found floating in the Thames, both eyes shot out.

Riordan asked the cabbie to stop outside the Old Bell, and he paid the man, giving him generous tip, and climbed out into the street. Kilburn High Road bustled with traffic and pedestrians, and Riordan spent a few moments getting his bearings. He had already viewed the place on Google Street View, so he knew the Tube station, part of the Bakerloo Line, and the train station were nearby should he need to get away quickly.

He walked briskly down the street. There was a dingy amusement arcade just to the left of the bar, beside it a bookie's and then the entrance to the Tube station. A few young, hard cases, dressed in thug-chic denims, Doc Martens, and leather jackets, loitering outside the arcade, gave him the eye as he passed. Riordan ignored them and picked up a few subway tickets as a precaution then strolled back to the bar.

The Old Bell, with its red brick facade, looked relatively well kept, with six or seven hanging baskets overflowing with brightly coloured flowers lining the narrow overhang. Several patrons hung around outside the front door, cigarettes in hand. Above the worn Old Bell sign, an equally worn red banner announced a beer garden to the rear of the building.

Riordan took a deep breath, nodded to the smokers, and pushed in through the doors.

A sign on the wall proclaimed, "Free Wi-Fi," which to Riordan was a bit strange, but then the UK was much more advanced than Canada when it came to Internet use, as was most of the civilized world. He was accustomed to free Wi-Fi at Starbucks and other coffee shops, but that was about it. Having it in a pub somewhat made sense, as most Brits used the pub as their meeting place. He made a mental note to have a chat with the owner of the Flying Beaver, his local pub, when he got home.

The place was packed, the conversations lively. Trying to compete with the din, and failing, was piped-in contemporary Irish music. A series of half-filled pints of Guinness lined the bar, waiting for the head to settle before the barman finished the pour. This was a local, evident by the looks he received as he pushed his way to the bar. People checked him out. He knew because he did the same when strange faces turned up in his local.

The barman, a lad in his twenties who worked out hard and wanted everyone to see it, appeared in front of him. He wore a black t-shirt with a Guinness sign that proclaimed, "Don't be afraid of the Dark." His arms, heavy with muscle, were decorated with ornate Celtic knotwork patterns that would have taken hours to complete. His head was buzzed, a thin black stubble covering it, and a heavy gold earring drooped in one ear. It seemed to be the standard "look" for a barman these days. There was a bit of scar tissue under his eyes — a boxer of sorts — and he had fists like ham hocks. Riordan imagined that the Old Bell didn't have much trouble in the way of bar fights.

"What can I get yous?" the barman asked, the heavy Dublin accent pronounced.

"Those pints look mighty fine," Riordan replied, easing himself on to the bar stool. "I'll have one of them."

The barman nodded, grabbed one from the end, and filled it up slowly, scraped some of the head off with a knife, and then finished topping it up. Behind him, bottles of whisky, both blends and single malts, lined the glass shelves, Bushmills, Jameson, and Paddy being the favoured tipples. The barman placed the pint in front of Riordan.

"Will you have one yourself?" Riordan offered. He was rewarded with a shake of the head and a gruff, "no thanks, maybe later." Riordan handed him a tenner and let the change remain on the bar.

"So tell me," he said, just as the barman turned to move away. "Which pub has the best pint, here or Powers?"

"No competition, pal, we've got the best pint here. Those arseholes don't clean their pipes properly, so it tastes different..."

Riordan grinned at the barman's response. It was the same as he had heard in pubs the world over. Quality of the Guinness was a bellwether for any Irish pub, and for the most part, they took ferocious pride in their product, so there was always some means of castigating the other pub's quality. Riordan sipped the pint and savoured the taste. It was surely better than any pint he had tasted in North America.

"Now that's a fine pint," he commented, and the barman nodded. "Mind you, the fellow I'm supposed to meet spends half his time here and half his time in Powers, and I've never heard him complain. However, I've also seen his taste in women, and if that's anything to go by, he probably isn't fit to be commenting about pints. But the cunt is good at cards and took me for a couple of grand a few weeks ago. I'm just back in town, and I'm looking for him, but he hasn't surfaced yet, and he's not answering his cell."

Riordan shut up at that point, having laid the foundation for further interaction. To bring Dempsey's name up at this point would set off too many alarms, especially if he was a patron, as Sean had already determined. "Ach, maybe he'll show," said the barman. "We get a lot of cunts in here. It's early yet, and we don't get really busy for about another hour or so." The barman walked away down the bar, and Riordan sipped his pint. An older man, white-haired, wearing a beaten brown leather jacket, eased on to the barstool beside Riordan. Ancient ink tattoos of anchors were visible on the backs of both gnarled hands, hands that had obviously seen hard labour, probably at sea. There was a brownish stain in the upper corner of the beard, either from a pipe or cigarettes.

"A pint and a Paddy, Michael," he ordered when the barman showed up.

"Grand pint, isn't it," he said, staring straight ahead.

Riordan nodded. "It is, that it is," he said.

"That's a bit of a strange accent," the old man commented. Turning to face Riordan, his green eyes were bright and clear, his gaze piercing, despite his obvious age. "You sound like a Yank for a minute, then you sound like Belfast, and then there's a hint of Dublin. Get around, do you?"

Warning bells gently tinkled in Riordan's head. "I've worked all over," he replied, "and really don't call anywhere home."

"And what sort of work would ye do?" the man asked. It was a typical conversation that two strangers would have in a bar anywhere else in the world, but this was Kilburn, and this was not casual conversation. The barman placed a pint in front of his interrogator and then free-poured a healthy shot of whisky into a glass.

"Freelance consulting, mostly in technology," Riordan replied. The best cover was one that had some semblance of truth, and Riordan could talk about technology until the cows came home. The old man nodded. He took a swig of the Guinness then licked the creamy head from his moustache.

"And you're here to pay a debt?"

As expected, the barman had been asked about the stranger. Keeping up the act, Riordan snorted. "Fucking Dempsey. Took me for two grand that I couldn't afford to lose, so I had to find the money." He dragged an envelope out of the inside of his jacket, fanned the high denomination notes inside, and laid it on the bar. "Somebody told me he hangs out here or over at Powers, so I'd thought I'd find him already, but he's not answering his cell. I'll

235

give him a couple of hours, and if he doesn't show then I'll head over to Powers."

The old man nodded. "Hope you find your friend," he said, throwing back the shot of Paddy then picking up his pint and disappearing off into a booth in darkened corner of the pub. There were two or three others in the booth, judging by the number of glasses, but it was impossible to make out any faces. Riordan breathed a sigh of relief. So far, so good. The bait had been set, and the old man had unwittingly acknowledged that this was one of Dempsey's hangouts. When Riordan had said the name Dempsey, the old man's eyes had widened, ever so slightly, a microexpression, but it was enough to betray him.

Microexpressions are those momentary, involuntary facial expressions that people unconsciously display when they are hiding an emotion. They occur so quickly, usually in fractions of a second, that only those trained to watch for such events can notice them. They are typically caused by involuntary movements in facial muscles, triggered by an emotion response. All of Featherstone's team had been trained by an ex-FBI investigator to recognize these tells during an interrogation. As the investigator told them, the movements are not necessarily proof that someone is lying, but the response shows the subject is having some type of emotional response to the question. Which in turn leads the investigator down a specific path of further probing questions. Riordan had used the technique many times.

The old man didn't say "Dempsey who?" or ask for a first name. He knew Dempsey, knew he was a gambler, so the comment about Riordan owing him money from a poker game rang true. Riordan mentally thanked Arthur Cupples for the intel. It was Dempsey's penchant for gambling that had been identified as a possible area of weakness to exploit, so Riordan had taken the chance with the bundle of money as a cover story.

He ordered a shot of the sixteen-year-old Bushmills single malt, nursed it for a while, then waited until the barman's back was turned and emptied the remains into the drain. Under normal circumstances, that would be an act of sacrilege for his beloved Bushmills, but these were difficult times, the waste forgiven. He ordered another and did the same, stacking one glass on top of another as he finished. To anyone watching, he was slowly getting hammered.

People came and went. He looked at faces in the bar mirror, hoping that Dempsey might show. This would certainly be a safe area for him to lie low. A couple of guys came in carrying guitar cases, and there was much backslapping and talk of a session. Several rounds of pints were sent in their direction to get them well lubricated for the gig. A few patrons sat beside him for a while, there was small talk about soccer and the weather, and then they moved on. After a couple of hours, the stack of shot glasses had reached six high, so he closed his tab and eased himself off the barstool, somewhat unsteadily for the benefit of those around him.

"I'm away to Powers to see if the cunt is there," he announced to the barman, patting the pocket of his jacket. "He doesn't deserve this money." Tossing a tenner on the bar, he saluted the barman and wove his way through the patrons, now lined three deep at the bar.

He lurched out into the street, elbowing his way through the midst of a throng of smokers huddled around the entrance, and took a deep breath of air. Then he turned right and set off down the street. He knew from his research that Powers was just about half a mile away, situated between a hairdressers and an Italian restaurant. Traffic was heavy on the street, and all the establishments, from cafes to bars to restaurants, were filled to overflowing with locals. Traditional Irish music was the currency of the night, flowing out of open windows and doors, and signs and hoardings decorated with ornate Celtic script showed the area's pride in its Celtic roots. Riordan loved traditional Irish music, the uilleann pipes raising the hackles on his neck every time he heard them played. These pipes possessed a different harmonic structure than other pipes, producing a sweeter, quieter sound. Riordan didn't particularly like Scottish bagpipes. To him, the definition of a gentleman was someone who knows how to play the bagpipes but doesn't. But from the first time he had listened to Davey Spillane playing the haunting lament from *Riverdance,* he had been hooked.

It was not always that way. Having been raised in the British school system, his entire frame of reference had been

British history, British battles — a seemingly endless litany of dates that had to be remembered by rote — and for the most part, British music. It was not until he had gone to university and from there to the south of Ireland that he had been exposed to the rich Irish culture of music and literature. He had absorbed it like a sponge and developed a voracious appetite for Irish music, both traditional and contemporary. When there was an open mike night at the local pub, Featherstone often requested him to provide a rendition of "Dirty Old Town," one of Feather's personal favourites.

He checked the address for Powers bar on his cellphone as he progressed down the street, and in the distance he could see the massive trestle bridge across the high road leading to Brondesbury railway station. It was the only darkened area off the main street, so if someone was going to intercept him, that was where it would likely happen. Using Street View, he had noted a tiny alleyway running off the main street beside the bridge, probably a good site for a late hours "knee trembler" when the pubs closed. He had paused several times along the way, peering into shop windows, but had not noticed a tail. But then again, this was Kilburn, and there were eyes and ears everywhere. So good was the Kilburn grapevine that during the Troubles, IRA volunteers on the run could roam these streets without fear of being arrested. Mind you, he had made a couple of trips to Kilburn at the Old Man's behest, and a few of those "volunteers" disappeared never to be seen or heard from again.

He was right.

There were two of them, and they had gotten ahead of him. As he approached the pool of darkness at the side of the bridge, one of the men stepped out of the shadows, blocking his path. Out of the corner of his eye he could just about make out the silhouette of the other. They were both of medium build, with the rounded shoulders of bodybuilders — muscle, not brains. The thug in front of him wore a loose-fitting leather jacket with deep pockets, denim jeans, and a pair of flashy trainers. One hand, his right, was deep in the pocket as if clutching something. There was no way to tell the age of the man in the shadows, but the blocker was in his late twenties or early thirties, hard around the eyes, no stranger to violence. He had longish dark hair and a couple of day's worth of trendy stubble. He wore a diamond stud in one ear.

"We hear you're looking for Sean Dempsey," the blocker said in a heavy Northern Irish accent. "We'd like to have a wee word with ye." He gestured with the hand that was deep in his pocket, an implied threat, wanting Riordan to move into the alley.

"That's my business," Riordan replied, slurring his words, swaying slightly, playing up the appearance of intoxication.

"Sean's a mate of ours, and he didn't mention anything about ye. Now fucking move."

The blocker stepped forward, and Riordan felt the hard edge of a pistol jammed into his ribs. He allowed himself to be manhandled deep into the alleyway, keeping his back to the wall as the two men braced him.

"So who the fuck are ye?" the second thug asked. "And we won't ask ye twice." The blocker had removed his hands from his jacket, and they were now by his side, his fingers twitching. Riordan made the assumption they were both armed, but as yet they didn't perceive him as a threat. They were itching to use him as a punching bag. It was always easy to beat up a drunk. They didn't fight back.

"My name's..." he whispered, and both men unconsciously leaned in to hear him better. It never failed. Riordan lashed out with his foot, putting all of his two hundred and forty pounds of muscle into the swing, kicking the blocker hard in the balls. His toe made hard contact, and he was rewarded with a gratifying expulsion of breath like air escaping a tire. The kick actually lifted the blocker a couple of inches in the air, and then he collapsed in a heap, a high-pitched whine escaping his lips.

The other thug immediately dug in his pocket for his weapon, a bad mistake since it cost him a second or two. Riordan didn't hesitate and punched him hard in the throat, feeling something crack under his knuckles. The thug dropped like a stone, fingers grasping at his throat. Four seconds had elapsed. He kicked the man hard in the temple, just enough to render him unconscious, and then turned to the blocker, who was lying in a fetal position, both hands cradling his ruined testicles. The blocker coughed once, then vomited violently onto the pathway.

241

The fight had gone out of him. Riordan took the pistol out of the man's jacket. It was a snub-nosed .38 calibre revolver, better known as a Saturday Night Special. Nice for close-up work. He pocketed the gun then went over and tied the unconscious thug's hands and feet with plasticuffs. Satisfied the man was immobile, he searched him quickly, finding yet another gun in his pocket. The thug would have to explain the presence of a weapon to whoever found him. British guns laws, being extremely restrictive, would mean jail time if he could not provide a reasonable explanation for the weapon.

Riordan rolled the blocker to a sitting position against the brick wall then grasped his shoulder. "Breathe deeply, five or six times," he ordered. The blocker did as he was told but held tightly to his balls as if they were his most prized possession.

"You've fucking broke something, ye bastard," the man hissed.

"And what were you planning to do to me?" Riordan asked. The blocker lapsed into stony silence.

"Get up," Riordan ordered, dragging the man to his feet. "And if you try anything, you'll get a worse smack."

The blocker did as he was told but could barely straighten up, as if he had severe back problems. Riordan knew the feeling well. In the weekly sparring sessions with Featherstone and the team, where they were drilled in hand-to-hand combat, someone was always getting smacked in the bollocks. As the instructor, a humourless former marine, told them, the testicles were one of the weakest points on the male body, so many of the strikes were directed there as a means to disable an opponent quickly. Many an evening Riordan had spent with a bag of frozen peas on his scrotum, much to Nancy's amusement. "You know, there are other forms of contraception," she mocked.

"Do you live around here?" Riordan asked.

The blocker nodded.

"Far?"

A shake of the head.

"Walking distance?"

A nod.

"Address?"

"Five Netherwood Street."

"Let go of your balls and put your hands in the jacket then," Riordan said, wrapping one arm around the man's shoulder and setting off down the street, two drunks helping each other home, a familiar scene on a week night. The blocker smelled like he hadn't bathed in about a week, noxious fumes reeking from his skin. "Just in case you get any ideas," Riordan said, "I don't like guns, but I have a knife, and if you do something stupid, I'll gut you like a fish."

CHAPTER 9

TUESDAY

The blocker lived in a ground floor flat, just steps from the high street. When they reached the front door, the man rustled in his pocket for a set of keys, selected one, and opened the door. Every movement caused him pain. Riordan could see it reflected in his face, even though he tried desperately hard not to show it. A tough guy no longer.

"What's your name?" Riordan asked.

"Shane Jordan," came the gruff reply.

"Okay, Shane, lead the way," Riordan ordered.

The front door opened directly into a spacious open plan living/dining room, with a kitchen off to the left of the dining room. The place was decently furnished and surprisingly tidy. A plasma screen was mounted on one wall, with a set of high-end, Bose surround-sound speakers flanking the screen. Several remotes lay on a coffee table placed in front of a black leather sofa. A dark mahogany dining table, with four sturdy wooden chairs, stood in the dining room. The table was set with two place settings, two wine glasses, and a centrepiece with some sort of greenery draped across the table, a female touch. What looked like an expensive, abstract oil painting hung on the wall of the dining room. On the sideboard sat several photos of Jordan posing with a soccer team, all arms crossed and macho, lined up behind a huge silver cup. Picking up the photo, Riordan asked, "Soccer player, are you? What position?"

"Striker," came the response.

"I used to play centre half," Riordan commented. "But that was a long time ago."

Riordan guided Jordan over to the dining table, dragged out a chair, and forced him on to it. There was no fight left in the man, every movement causing a tight grimace. Riordan pulled his arms behind the chair and secured them with a set of plasticuffs. He then fastened both ankles to the legs of the chair, again with a set of plasticuffs. He extracted the blocker's wallet and examined each piece of information carefully.

"So, you are Shane Jordan?" Riordan asked.

The blocker nodded.

"Belfast?" Another nod.

"You and I are going to have a wee chat," Riordan said, "as I need some information, and I need it quickly."

"Fuck you," Jordan spat. "I'm no fucking tout."

"I understand your point of view entirely," Riordan said, opening the barrel of the revolver and emptying the six shiny brass shells into his hand. "However, the way I see it, you have at best five chances to tell me what I need to know. At worst, you have one!" The posture deflated somewhat, the bravado weakening, and Jordan licked his lips. He was nervous. His eyes never wavered from the shiny brass shells in Riordan's hand. Riordan pulled out one of the other chairs and sat down directly across from Jordan.

Riordan pocketed five of the shells. He then took out his folding knife, flipped it open with a one-handed flourish, and commenced etching a cross deep into the tip of the bullet. "Where I come from, this is called a dum-dum bullet," he offered, blowing away the tiny copper fragments and inspecting his handiwork. "When it hits something solid, like a bone for example, it shatters completely like a miniature grenade. The amount of damage it causes to a human body is a thing of beauty."

Jordan blanched. "I don't care if you kill me or not," he growled. "I'm not sayin' a fucking word. I'm no fucking tout."

"You did mention that already," Riordan said. "Do ye know that famous folk song called 'Waltzing Matilda,' the famous antiwar ballad?" Riordan asked, now reverting to the guttural tones of the Belfast streets. A puzzled look came across Jordan's face, and he nodded.

"What about it?"

Riordan dropped the shell into the chamber, clicked it back into place, and then spun the cylinder. "As well as being a dum-dum, these are magnum rounds," he said, pointing the barrel directly at Jordan's kneecap. "And, as the song goes, 'I never knew there were worse things than dying.' The bullet will blow your leg clean off, and you'll be going about like a gimp for the rest of your days — no more Sunday soccer for you. And the mates, well, they'll have sympathy for a while, but then they'll be calling you things like peg-leg, or Blackbeard the pirate, all behind your back. And those prosthetic legs, they just itch the stump something awful, and to be honest, women just don't like guys with stumps."

Jordan's eyes darted from side to side, feverishly looking for a way out. A nervous tic tugged at the corner of his lip.

"Last chance, pal," Riordan said, cocking the hammer. The harsh, metallic click echoed in the small room. He stared hard at Jordan until the man moved his eyes away.

"Where's Dempsey?"

"I don't know," Jordan replied.

Again, no denial about knowing Dempsey. Riordan jammed the barrel hard into Jordan's knee for effect then pulled the trigger. The hammer clicked down on an empty chamber. Jordan took a couple of staccato breaths, almost as if he was going into shock. Blood drained from his face, and an acrid odour touched Riordan nostrils. He had pissed himself. A darkening stain spread across the front of Jordan's jeans, and he hung his head in shame.

"I haven't got all night," Riordan hissed, cocking the hammer again. The barrel slowly turned, lining up another possible bullet. "Where's Dempsey?"

"I don't fucking know," he spat, his eyes misting. Riordan stared hard at him. Pissing yourself with fright would be a difficult thing to explain to his mates, never mind the man who had sent him. It was one of those things that people would always remember — the time Jordan lost his bottle. Riordan kept up the pressure. He realized that Jordan was telling the truth, and maybe he didn't know where Dempsey was — if Dempsey had any regard for his friends, then he would have made sure they had no prior knowledge of his plans. Being ex-IRA, he knew well how to interrogate people and knew, as Riordan did, that everyone talked. Sometimes it took minutes, sometimes hours, and even days, but ultimately everyone cracked.

"I don't believe you," Riordan said and jammed the pistol into Jordan's kneecap again.

"Please, please, I'm telling the truth," Jordan almost wailed.

"Not good enough," Riordan replied, and squeezed the trigger slowly. Jordan's eyes watched his finger tighten.

The dam broke, and the words spilled out of Jordan in a torrent. Anything to ward off a bullet. "Look, mate, I don't where the fuck he is — he didn't say a word to me, I swear to ye, but I know someone who might."

"Lying bastard," Riordan spat, jamming the pistol harshly into Jordan's kneecap.

"No, no, please. Let me explain."

"Talk," Riordan replied, "and this better be good."

"He was seeing this bird, he was, name of Elva. She's a barmaid over at All-Bar-One, on Chiswick High Road, near the police station. He kept it pretty quiet, but they were datin' for most of a year — getting pretty serious they were, and all. I don't think anybody else knows about them, so if anyone knows where he is, it would be her."

Riordan nodded and eased back the hammer.

Beads of sweat tricked down Jordan's face. "Why are you looking for him?"

"It's simple," Riordan replied. "Dempsey crossed Max DeLisle. Max wants Dempsey."

"Alive or dead?"

"Preferably alive," Riordan replied. "But knowing DeLisle, as soon as he gets what he needs, I don't imagine Dempsey will stay that way for long."

"Fuck!" Jordan exclaimed. "I've heard of DeLisle, but I didn't know Dempsey was involved with him. Word is DeLisle likes cutting on people."

Riordan slipped Jordan's wallet into his jacket. Taking out his old faithful standby, he tore a strip off the roll and then pulled the piece of duct tape tightly across Jordan's mouth. "I'm going to check out what you told me. If it's legit, I'll call the bar and tell them to send someone over to let you go. If you're lying, I'll give the wallet to Max's boys, and his enforcer, a nice chap by the name of Billy K, will be over to see you."

He took a cab back to the hotel, went straight to his room, and used the iPad to locate the All-Bar-One to get some background on the place. It appeared to be a lively establishment, more of a wine bar than a pub, which was a bit problematic. A single guy alone at a pub was an accepted norm, but a single guy sitting alone in a wine bar would draw attention. Picking up the phone, he called Sean's room, half expecting the call to go to voice mail.

"Sean here," came the reply.

"Hi, Sean, I just got back from Kilburn and..."

"So how did it go? Did you get what you needed? Was there any aggro? What..."

"Fuck me, Sean," he replied, shaking his head, "could you just calm down a bit and I'll tell you?"

Sean cut him off. "I'll meet you downstairs in the bar. I want to hear all about this."

The phone went dead, and Riordan sighed. He stretched out on the bed for a few minutes, the adrenaline slowly working its way out of his system and leaving fatigue in its wake. Crawling onto the floor, he assumed the position, raised his body off the floor on his toes and elbows, and held a plank for two minutes. His stomach muscles vibrated from the effort, and he collapsed face-first into the soft pile carpet, glad of the momentary respite. He counted off a thirty-second break then repeated the move three more times. His trainer would have been proud. By the time he had finished, his energy level had risen substantially, the fog of sleep lifting. To further invigorate himself, he polished off a couple of cans of Red Bull from the minibar.

Downstairs, Sean had found himself a cosy spot at the bar, swirling an amber liquid around in a substantial balloon snifter, inhaling the fumes as his hands warmed the drink. "Benedictine and brandy," he proclaimed. "Does that ring any bells with you?"

Riordan grinned. "That night at the bar, I thought you had poured it for me..."

"Too right," Sean replied. "I was looking forward to that particular drink, and you scarfed it!"

"Have you heard of a pub called All-Bar-One, over in Chiswick?"

"I know the place," Sean offered. "A mate of mine used to go out with a bird that lived near there, in one of the terraced houses, and I've met him at the place a few times for a drink or two. It's a grand spot, lots of nice birds, and they have a good wine list. The grub's not bad either, and the waitresses are something to see." Sean sipped the brandy, smacking his lips.

"Very classy." Riordan snorted.

"So why do you want to know? Are we going there?"

"Yep. Dempsey was going out with one of the waitresses from the bar. They kept it on the quiet, so I need to have a word with her. How long will it take us to get to Chiswick?"

Sean shrugged. "I take it Dempsey was a no-show?"

Riordan nodded, deciding not to share the details of his encounter. Some things were better left unsaid, and besides, given the set of villains he had encountered, the less Sean knew the better. Sean swirled the drink some more. "As for getting there, at this time of night we'd be better off taking the Tube. You get off at the Turnham Green stop, and it's just about half a mile's walk from there. About thirty-five minutes or so, I'd say."

"Well then, throw that down your neck and let's go," Riordan ordered.

*

The Tube was jammed with bodies, forcing them to stand for a good part of their journey. They rode in silence, staring across the battered trail cars as they rocked their way out of London and into the suburbs. The thronged passengers represented the diverse cultures of London; seemingly every skin colour under the sun was represented, dressed in traditional garb, many of the women wearing brightly coloured saris, some dressed like Westerners. There was the usual gaggle of posturing youths, white iPhone wires dangling from their heavily pierced ears. The Tube flashed past row after row of red-bricked, terraced houses, all leaking coal smoke into the night air.

It was just like home, Riordan thought as he watched the endless miles of graffiti-tagged walls, some of contemporary music or street scenes, but many menacingly proclaiming the beginning and end of gang turf. It seemed that no major city in the world was immune to gang violence, and in London, with skyrocketing unemployment rates, disenfranchised youth were turning more and more to street gangs as a means of adventure.

He had read a recent article in the *Times*, one of the many newspapers to which Featherstone subscribed, that the Metropolitan Police estimated there were almost two hundred street gangs in London, fashioning themselves after their ultraviolent counterparts in US cities like Los Angeles or New York. Their names were slightly more stylish than the Bloods and Crips, names like the Mozart Bloods or the Monarch Park Goons, but they were no less violent.

They got off at Turnham Green station and discovered, much to Sean's chagrin, that the escalator was broken. "Everything's breaking down these days," he grumbled, "including me!" They climbed the long, steep stairway to the street, where they had to pause for a moment to allow Sean to catch his breath.

"No fucking smartass comments from you," Sean warned, resting his hands on his knees and breathing deeply. His face was flushed a deep red, and tiny beads of perspiration pebbled his brow. Riordan was barely breathing hard. "Alright, let's go," Sean said after a few moments, and they walked along the street until they came to Chiswick High Road. It was a wide street, and traffic was surprisingly heavy for the time of night. Both sides of the street were lined with shops of every shape and size, selling everything from flowers to fish to speciality cheese. Interspersed between these sat numerous restaurants, still busy even at the late hour.

It reminded Riordan of Burrard Street in Vancouver, where the mega chains and big box stores, barbarians at the gate, had been held at bay. It gave him that small-town feel, each place unique in its own right, each visit an adventure. Sean pointed off to the right, and they crossed the road onto a broad pedestrian terrace that had recently been landscaped with ornate paving stones and deep-set concrete planters overflowing with flowers. It was unusual to see so many ancient trees scattered along the walkway.

The bar was located on the ground floor of what appeared to be an old Victorian building, with worn, coffered windows and high spires. An ornate clock tower with massive clock faces on all four sides showed the time to the entire community. Baskets of ivy lined the front of the building, their tendrils draped over the awnings above each entrance to the bar. A few wooden tables and shiny aluminum chairs littered the area outside the bar, half-empty pint glasses and wine glasses sitting atop, their patrons flushed from good cheer.

Riordan followed Sean inside, and a pretty waitress led them to a table against one wall that faced the bar. At the back wall of the bar stood shelves of wine bottles, all back lit. A few token beer taps were stationed along the bar, but this was a wine bar, judging from the number of opened bottles on the tables.

"My name's Siobhan, and I'll be looking after you this evening. Are you going to be having a meal this evening?" the waitress asked, "'cos our kitchen will be closing shortly."

Riordan picked up a hint of an Irish accent, the sing-song traces from her roots in the west of Ireland. It was faint but unmistakable. Sean licked his lips. "We'll just have some appetizers, love," he said. "And to make it easy, we'll have whatever you recommend. So what're your favourites?"

"We've got small plates, like a tapas menu, and you can have five for twenty-four pounds or seven for thirty-three pounds, depending on how hungry you are. I love the calamari, and the tiger prawns, and the meatballs are always good..."

"I'm always hungry, darlin'," Sean replied, "so we'll start with the five, and maybe get some more."

Riordan shook his head. It seemed that there wasn't a woman alive that Sean would not hit on, and the waitress was certainly appreciating the attention. He tuned the banal conversation out and turned his attention to the rest of the room. There was a high percentage of women in the place, of all ages, compared to the number of guys. It was well lit and had a very open feel, as opposed to the more claustrophobic nature of a pub. Which would probably account for the women. It also gave the impression of being more upscale. Perhaps it was the clothing or the jewellery, or the general appearance, but that was the vibe he was getting. The waitresses, all dressed alike in tasteful skirts and matching tops, flitted about between the tables, balancing bottles of wine and glasses atop their trays. There was one exit at the rear of the bar, near the washrooms. It was always important to know where the exits were located.

Their waitress arrived back a few minutes later, carrying a bottle of wine and two glasses. She presented the bottle to Sean, who nodded approvingly, and then she started to open the bottle. It was a bottle of Guigal Côte-Rôtie, Riordan's all time favourite red wine, and he grinned at Sean. "I see you've been paying attention," he commented. The waitress was impressed as well. It was probably one of the most expensive bottles in the bar. Which meant it came with a good tip.

The waitress looked over. "Are you visiting?" she asked upon hearing his accent.

Riordan nodded. "Here for a reunion with old friends," he replied.

She extracted the cork flawlessly, again receiving high praise from Sean, and then poured a taste into his glass. Sean went through the ritual and then sampled the wine. He nodded appreciatively and set his glass back down. "Like an angel crying on your tongue," he commented.

"And a poetic soul as well." She laughed.

"Oh, he's a poet all right," Riordan said.

"Can I offer you a glass, Siobhan?" Sean asked with a gleam in his eye.

"I'm not allowed to drink with the customers," she replied. "But if you think it might be corked..."

Sean nodded gravely. "Wouldn't be wanting to send it back now, would we?" She picked up Riordan's glass, poured a small amount, and sniffed the bouquet. Then she swirled it vigorously to aerate the wine and took a mouthful. She swallowed, ever so slowly, her eyes closed as she savoured the wine. It was a sensual movement, not lost on either of the men.

"I love good wine," she said, "and this is spectacular. But I can't afford bottles like this on my budget. Let me get you a fresh glass."

Riordan shook his head. "That one's fine, love. Just pour me a glass."

She did so, then filled Sean's glass and went off to place their food orders. "Fuck me," Sean exclaimed, "Did you see the expression on her face? That almost gave me a boner."

Riordan looked at his friend. "Pal, I have the feeling there's not a lot of things that don't give you a boner!"

Sean laughed, and they clinked glasses. "Ach, isn't that the truth."

The first couple of plates of food arrived shortly, and Sean scornfully looked at the tasty morsels. "Jesus, she wasn't kidding about small plates. These wouldn't feed a wee child!"

Riordan burst out laughing at Sean's indignance, and for a moment the seriousness of his situation vanished, and he was lost in the moment, enjoying the camaraderie of an old friend. Sean helped himself to the wine, and by the time the next set of plates arrived, the bottle had all but disappeared.

"Will you be having another?" she asked, and Sean nodded.

When she arrived back with the new bottle, Sean, somewhat glassy eyed by now, insisted on having fresh glasses. When they came, he winked at Riordan and said, "Have you been working here long? I haven't seen you here before."

"About five months now," she replied. "Time goes awful quick."

"Aye," Sean replied. "That it does. I was in here a couple of months ago with a mate of mine, and I got chatting with a girl called Elva. She went to university in Belfast with my nephew Gerry, and she wanted his address. I lent her my good fountain pen, and by the time I got back home to Lisburn I realized she hadn't given it back. It's a Mont Blanc, you see, and worth a small fortune, otherwise I wouldn't be bothered."

"I've heard of them," she replied. "As for Elva, she doesn't work here anymore, at least that's what I heard. She just didn't show up for work one day, and nobody's heard from her since. The boss was pretty pissed off about it."

Sean laughed. "She's probably found out how much my good pen was worth and absconded with it."

"Are they that expensive?" she asked.

Sean reached in his jacket and took out a pen, which he laid on the table. "This is its twin. It's a Marlene Dietrich special edition fountain pen. Eighteen-carat gold nib, mother of pearl inlay, and a sapphire embedded in the platinum rings. They were a present, and this one is worth about five grand."

"Holy mother," she exclaimed, picking it up. "It's beautiful. No wonder you want it back."

"Look," Sean said in a conspiratorial manner. "Is there any way you could get me a phone number or an address? I think she said she lived in a flat around here somewhere, but I can't remember if she told me the address or not, and she's not in the phone book."

"Yeah, she wouldn't be listed. We all just use our mobiles — less expensive than having two phones. Let me see what I can do for you." She handed the pen back to Sean, who slipped it back in his jacket.

"Thanks, love," Sean said, and as she walked away, he winked at Riordan. "See, I could be a private detective any day."

Out of the corner of his eye Riordan watched the waitress go behind the bar and speak to one of the barmen, a bald-headed

259

behemoth with broad shoulders and a tight-fitting golf-shirt that strained to contain his tattooed biceps. As she pointed over toward their table, the guy was scowling and grasped her shoulder in a meaty paw as if to emphasize what he was telling her. Then he brushed past her and came out into the bar area.

"Does all that charm you just used work on guys?" Riordan asked.

"Never tried," Sean replied.

"Well, here's your chance," Riordan said just as the barman reached their table.

"I hear you gents are looking for Elva," the barman said tersely, putting two ham hocks of fists on the table and leaning over between them. "Would you mind stepping out the back so we can have a quiet word?"

Sean got to his feet, rather unsteadily, and the barman took him by the arm and guided him through the tables over to the rear exit. Riordan followed them out the back door onto a darkened patio that was frequented by smokers. A young couple, halfway through their cigarettes, turned to see the three men come through the door.

"Fuck off," the barman said without preamble, and they hastily stubbed out the cigarettes and went inside.

The barman shook Sean by the arm. "So what's all this about Elva and a missing fucking pen?"

"Look, I was here a couple of weeks ago, with my mate, and she borrowed my pen to write down Gerry's address — she went to university with my nephew. We got chatting and she forgot to give it back. I've called a couple of times, and she wasn't here, so I was over here on business and decided to drop by to see her. It's an expensive fountain pen, and I want the fucking thing back."

"Look, pal, we don't give out information about our employees, and I don't like people coming around here asking for them. Elva, the cunt, just fucked off and left me in the lurch, no notice, no nothing. So, finish your drinks, pay your bill, and fuck off."

"All right, all right," Sean said, angrily shaking his arm loose.

Let it go, Sean, Riordan thought. *Let it go.*

The barman turned to Riordan. He was a couple of inches taller than Riordan, about six-six and a good thirty or forty pounds heavier, most of it muscle. There wouldn't be many punters who would take him on, which gave him that aura of menace. And also, the ability to push around barmaids.

"If I ever see you two around here again, I'll give you a fucking slap!" He jabbed his two meaty index fingers hard into Riordan's chest, as if to emphasize his point. Riordan grabbed both fingers and levered them back in a heartbeat, hearing the satisfying crunch as both fingers snapped. "Fucking cocksucker," the barman bellowed in pain, "you broke my fucking fingers."

"You assaulted me, pal," Riordan said and kicked him hard in the balls. The fight went out of the man, and he dropped to his knees, a keening wail escaping his lips. "You're a fucking bully, and I hate bullies." Riordan punched him hard in the temple, and the barman grunted and fell over.

"Remind me never to cross you," Sean said, rubbing his arm. "That was like putting my arm in a vise."

"Let's pay the bill and get out of here," Riordan said. "You have no idea how stupid these Neanderthals can be, especially in groups."

Inside, the waitress looked surprised when they returned to their table. "Just get us our bill, love," Sean said, knocking back his glass of wine.

She returned a few moments later with the bill, folded in two inside a leather case, and handed it to Riordan.

"I'm sorry about all that," she said contritely. "He has all the staff information, and I thought it would be okay to ask."

"No worries, love," Riordan replied, giving her a quick wink. "He's having a wee nap outside." He took out his wallet, opened the bill. Below the total was a hastily scribbled phone number and an address. Riordan smiled, put the bill away in his wallet, gave her a massive tip, and then they left.

Outside, Sean said, "See, I told you I was a good detective."

Riordan patted him on the shoulder. "That you are, pal, that you are." Taking out his cellphone, he keyed in the address and asked for directions from their current GPS location. The network was slow, but he laughed when the results came back.

"What's up?" Sean asked.

"She lives about three hundred yards from here. Let's go."

They made their way along the darkened terrace until they reached number 27. It was a massive structure, four storeys tall, with worn concrete steps leading up to the front door. Off to the side, a wrought iron gate blocked the entrance to the basement apartment. The upper floors were sheathed in darkness, but light spilled through curtains in the basement. Flickering shadows showed someone was moving inside. "The waitress didn't say anything about a roommate," Sean offered.

"You wait here," Riordan said. "And if anyone but me comes out of there, you lamp them!"

Sean grinned. "No worries, pal. I'm good at lamping!"

"Yeah, I noticed," Riordan replied, his voice full of sarcasm.

Riordan eased the gate open and crept carefully down the steps. The door looked pretty substantial, a requirement for basement flats, and he moved over to the side of the window and peered inside. Large brown boxes were piled to one side of the room, and a young man, probably in his mid twenties, was assembling more.

Someone's packing up, Riordan thought.

He stepped back to the door and pressed a lighted button barely attached to the door jamb. He heard a two-tone chime from inside, and a moment later the door opened. The tenant was lean and wiry, had a brush cut, with a couple of earrings in one ear, and wore an oversized New York Giants baseball shirt, denim jeans, and a brand new pair of hightops. He looked Riordan up and down. "Can I help you?" he asked.

"Mind if I have a word inside? It's getting cold out here?" Riordan replied.

The tenant moved aside, and Riordan stepped into the apartment. It was fairly small, all open plan, with a bed over in one corner, a tiny kitchen with a stove, and a small fridge off to one side and a bathroom on the other. On the wall of the kitchen hung a notice board made from old wine corks, and a bunch of business cards had been pinned to it, along with some flyers.

There was another door at the side of the kitchen, probably leading out to a back yard. Two heavy security chains secured the door, and there were heavy-duty security bars on the inside of the windows. A worn sofa sat in the middle of the room, facing a small television, and an expensive Samsung sound system sat atop a pair of shelves. There were a few paperbacks and one or two framed photographs on the shelves. Riordan had the sense that this was a transient space, not a permanent home.

The door slammed behind him, and the tenant went back over to his boxes, picked up an industrial box cutter with a Day-Glo yellow handle and resumed his construction efforts.

"I'm looking for Elva," Riordan said.

"Aren't we all, mate," came the response in a heavy Cockney accent. "She fucked off without paying her rent, so now I've got to box up all this fucking stuff and take it to the dump."

"You're her landlord?" Riordan was skeptical.

"Nah, mate, I work for the estate agent that manages these flats. I get all the shit jobs."

"Mind if I take a look around?" Riordan asked.

"Only if you pay me a month's rent," came the response, "otherwise you can fuck off."

Riordan sighed. The guy flicked the box cutter blade all the way out of its yellow handle and folded his arms, as if daring Riordan to make a move. He had obviously seen the posture on TV. Shaking his head wearily, Riordan took out his wallet, flicked through the bills, extracted a one hundred-pound note, and held it up for the guy to see. "I only need to be here for about ten minutes, so I figure a hundred should cover it. I'd say that was a pretty good deal, since the estate agent will never see any money that I give you."

"Fuck off, mate," the guy spat, unfurling his arms.

Riordan remained calm. "Let me explain the facts of life to you," he said quietly, but there was no mistaking the menace in his voice. "You've got a box cutter in your hand. In my line of work that's considered a weapon. The fact that it's in your hand makes you a threat, and I've been rather well trained to neutralize threats in a semi-permanent or permanent manner. So perhaps you could put it down and just take the money?"

The guy's face flushed red, and the blade cutter sliced the air in front of him. "You don't look so fucking tough, mate, so get out of here before I fucking well cut you."

Riordan took a pair of black leather gloves from his jacket, pulled them on, and flexed his fingers. Then he dragged the tactical folding knife from his pocket, flicked it open, and threw it hard, underhand, across the seven feet separating him and the would-be hard case. The heavy knife embedded itself to the hilt in the meaty part of the guy's thigh. His eyes widened in shock, moments before the pain hit, and he dropped the box cutter and leaned over and grasped his leg. Riordan took a couple of steps and kicked him in the side of the head, just enough to render him unconscious. He dropped to the floor. Riordan dragged the knife out then grabbed a roll of Scotch tape and wrapped it around the guy's leg several times to contain the bleeding.

Then he methodically went around the flat, looking for any evidence of where Elva might have gone. Based on what he knew so far, he was pretty sure that she was with Dempsey, so that now provided him with two routes of investigation instead of one. Heartened by this knowledge, he flipped through each of the paperbacks, shaking the pages in case there might be something concealed there. He tossed the pillows from the sofa onto the floor and looked under the bed, which had been made neatly made up. In the closet he found a few dresses, wrapped in plastic from the drycleaners, and several pairs of high-heeled shoes. In a dresser were t-shirts and sweaters, but the top drawer, the pantie and bra drawer, according to Nancy, was completely empty. She had left in a hurry. There were a few boxes of staples: rice, pasta, baked beans, and bread in the kitchen cupboards. A half-empty bottle of Chardonnay rested in the fridge door, along with a carton of milk. There were some cold cuts, already turning a nasty shade of green, a couple of furry, ready-to-serve pasta dishes, a tub of margarine, and a large tub of yogurt, which almost filled the small fridge. On the counter sat a bottle of Bushmills whiskey and an unopened bottle of rum. There were about four fingers of whisky missing from the Bushmills bottle, and in the sink sat two glasses.

Riordan stared at them for a moment.

A farewell toast, perhaps.

He peered at the wine-cork noticeboard. It was a fairly ornate construction, definitely not a home job, inlaid with painted, hand-carved wooden designs. The artist's signature, Ron Pace, had been wood-burned on to the frame. Pinned to the corks were flyers for Chinese food carry outs, pizza joints, and a couple of promotional posters for coming attractions at the pub. A handful of business cards were pinned neatly in one corner: taxi services, doctor, dentist, a local plumber, and the estate agent's card. Several postcards, all overlapping, lined the bottom, and he started taking them off one by one and reading the messages. They all seemed to be in the same vein: having a great time, wish you were here, lots of hot guys, and all from Torremolinos, Spain. He had just gone through the first three when there was an urgent rapping at the door. He stepped over and cracked the door open to see Sean's face.

"C'mon, there's a two-man police foot patrol coming down the street. One of the neighbours here just told me that there have been a lot of break-ins, and they're doing a door-to door to check up on everyone." Sean's eyes flickered past Riordan to the pair of feet lying on the floor.

"Is he..."

"Unconscious," Riordan replied, switching off the lights and pushing out through the door. "Let's go. I've seen all I need here."

*

Sean wanted to hail a cab, but Riordan refused, instead walking at a brisk pace back to the Tube station. Sean moaned all the way and was virtually out of breath by the time they reached the platform. "Why the fuck do we have to take the Tube?" he asked, his breathing ragged.

"Safety in numbers, pal," Riordan replied. "It's called tradecraft, or the art of being a spy. You'd be surprised how fast these supposed hard cases will call the police when they get their asses kicked. If he does and attempts to lay charges, the first thing the cops will do is check with local taxi firms to see if they picked up a couple of guys matching our description. Cabbies would sell their own mothers, in my experience, so the cops could track us back to the hotel, and then things get tricky. Does that explain it enough for you?"

"Sorry, mate, I wasn't thinking," Sean replied, chastened.

"That's alright," Riordan replied cheerfully, "think of it as a free lesson in espionage."

The rocking motion of the Tube, combined with the amount of alcohol Sean had consumed, found him fast asleep on Riordan's shoulder in a matter of minutes. Riordan thought it was funny until Sean started to drool. He eased him away gently until Sean's body's momentum tilted him against the window. His head bobbled back and forth like one of those little toys dogs that people kept in the back window of their car, and Riordan grinned. It reminded him of another night, many years ago, when Sean, Neil and himself had been out at a party at Leighmohr House, a fitting name considering the amount of shagging that went on in the car park. Sean, having just broken up with his girlfriend, was drowning his sorrows by consuming as many pints as humanly possible. Neil, resplendent in his new leather jacket, was chasing skirt and had just returned to check on Sean's status.

Sean's claim to fame in those days was that no matter how much booze he drank, he never threw up, or "boked" in the local parlance. He was leaning on Neil's shoulder at the particular moment he decided that tonight was the night to break his rule and heaved his guts up over Neil's brand new jacket. Afterward he claimed it was the scent of the cheap leather that had set him off. Riordan moved slightly away from Sean, just in case.

When they approached their stop at St. James's Park, Riordan shook him awake. Sean blinked wildly for a few moments, licked his lips like a dehydrated dog, shook his head, and said, "Fuck me, I needed a nap. Time for a nightcap."

"Fucking incorrigible," Riordan muttered and followed Sean out into the brightly lit yet deserted station. The doors slammed shut and the silver train roared off into the night, its metal wheels grinding against the rails. For a moment the station was completely silent, a strange sensation given the hustle and bustle in the streets above. "It's like one of those apocalypse movies," Riordan commented. "All we need now is a few zombies..."

"Aye," Sean replied. "Just wait until closing time ... there'll be more than a few zombies around here, and more than a few bums trying to cadge a bit of change from the drunks. Good thing about the hotel, though, as long as we sit in the bar, they have to serve us."

"Fuck me, Sean," Riordan exclaimed, "make sure you don't sign the organ donor card at the back of your driver's license. I wouldn't want anyone to be getting that liver."

Sean laughed heartily. "Good one, mate. I'll have to remember that line."

*

Back at the hotel, he reluctantly joined Sean in the bar but refused to drink, instead ordering a cappuccino. He had a couple of calls to make and desperately needed to have a clear head in the morning. Sean appreciated the company, but almost as soon as they were settled, a couple of harried ladies in their mid to late thirties came in carrying shopping bags from some of the flagship stores in the downtown core and took a seat at the bar. From their accents they were obviously tourists, and well-heeled, based on the number of shopping bags. Riordan figured them from one of the Midwestern states.

Several glances were exchanged, and Sean rubbed his hands in glee. "Well, if you're not up to it, I'll have a shot. Been a while since I had a threesome."

Riordan drained the last of the coffee and stood up, patting his friend on the shoulder, and leaned down in a conspiratorial manner. "Maybe you should check for an Adam's apple this time," he offered.

"Cunt," came the reply.

"He's all yours, ladies," Riordan said as he strode past the two women. One of them pouted a little, which Riordan took as a compliment, and then raised her glass to Sean.

"Fox in a henhouse," Riordan muttered, stabbing the elevator button with his thumb. Back in his room, he tossed his jacket on the chair, picked up the hotel phone, and dialled a number.

"That was quick," came the response from Cupples. "I see you've been creating a bit of mayhem out in the west end. It would appear the police are holding two miscreants under the Prevention of Terrorism Act, so they'll be incommunicado for a few days. Weapons were found at both scenes, but, and here's the big surprise, both of them are refusing to talk. Now tell me, what have you found out?"

Riordan didn't ask where the intel came from. Cupples had resources that specialized in surveillance, and only a very experienced operator could pick up on them. He had obviously been followed all the way to Kilburn. "Dempsey has dropped off the grid, so I think he's out of the country. Could be back in Ireland, or God only know where. He'll go somewhere he feels safe, so that's why Ireland is a possibility. Or if he did any freelance work for the IRA, maybe in Colombia or even in Spain, he might run there."

"That makes sense," Cupples replied. "There's nothing in his jacket to indicate freelance work, but that doesn't mean he wasn't contracted out. We had a few of the 'lads' show up in

Colombia last year, posing as tourists, but they were there to provide training to the FARC guerrillas. Nothing to do with sympathy for their cause, just a lot of money changed hands."

"There's one other thing," Riordan replied. "He's got a girlfriend with him. They've been hot and heavy for the past year, but he's kept it pretty quiet, well below the radar. Her name's Elva McCormick, and she worked over at All-Bar-One, in Chiswick. Her place has been emptied, and from what I've seen, she went in a hurry."

"That's interesting. I'll check her out for you and see if we have anything on her. In the meantime, get some sleep, and I'll be in touch in the morning."

"Sounds like a plan," Riordan replied, feeling a wave of exhaustion flow over him. He would sleep well tonight.

CHAPTER 10

BENEDICT

Unfortunately, sleep proved to be an elusive mistress. Riordan spent the night tossing and turning again, barely drifting off to sleep before starting awake, pursued by shadowy figures dressed in black and wearing black balaclavas, eyes glinting like cold fire, their clutching hands always just out of reach. He finally gave up trying, rolled out of bed at 4:00 a.m., and spent an hour on the floor performing hard physical exercises, pumping oxygen into his muscles as a breathless reporter from Sky News filled him in on the status of world events. He ordered breakfast from room service, then jumped in the shower, relishing the pounding hot jets as the heat soaked into his tired muscles. He decided not to shave; overnight flights left little time for such things. He had dressed before the knock came to the door. He had to play the part of a weary traveller.

He felt a little guilty about ordering the eggs Benedict — Nancy was always threatening him about his eating habits — but after the hour of calisthenics, he mentally balanced the scale. As he ate, he scanned the copy of the *Times* that had been delivered with the breakfast, enjoying the articles, the acerbic British wit, and the elegant prose. It was a momentary yet welcome distraction.

He had ordered a taxi for seven thirty to get him to the airport so that he would be on time for the arriving flight. No warning email alerts about any potential delays had arrived on his cellphone, so he made the assumption the flight would be on time, but he fired up the iPad anyway and logged on to the British Airways website to verify the flight details. It too showed the flight was on time.

Featherstone was relentless about mastering the 7 P's of tradecraft — prior perfect planning prevents piss poor performance — so no operational detail, no matter how trivial, went unchecked at least twice. He would check again when he arrived at the airport.

Reluctantly, he left the weapons in the room safe, including the knives. There was no way he could explain them away if Max DeLisle's crew decided to search him, and he figured that was exactly what would happen. DeLisle had a massive ego, and Riordan had given him the proverbial "Harvey Smith," so there would come some point during the morning where DeLisle would make an appearance to put him in his place, so to speak. He was about to leave when the phone rang.

"Hey, mate," came a groggy voice. Sean sounded slightly the worse for wear.

"Howareye?" Riordan replied, a wide grin splitting his face.

275

"My willy hurts."

"In a good way?"

"Bejasus, them two women were fucking wild. They're both recently divorced and came to London to see the sights and to have a wee bit of fun. Honest to God, I felt like a wee dog's chew toy the way they were going at me. Still, I gave as good as I got. Anyway, enough about me. What's the craic for the day?"

"I'm just away out to the airport to pretend I'm arriving, and then I'll play it by ear after that. I've no idea when I'll be in touch again, so hang tight. If you've got to go home, leave me a message but make sure my room stays booked."

"Go home, are you kidding? I haven't had this much fun in years. Besides, there's not much to go home to." Riordan heard the note of melancholy in his friend's voice.

"Fair enough. I'll speak to you soon."

"Mind how ye go, mate."

As soon as he hung up the phone, Riordan grabbed his cellphone and deleted his call history, contacts, and all prior emails. They were all safely backed up on the office server. It was unlikely that they would check his cellphone, but it was a prudent thing to do. Grabbing his bag, he went downstairs and was directed by the concierge to a waiting limousine. When he questioned the limo, he was told that guests of the hotel were provided with a complimentary limo shuttle service to the airport. So, no taxi for him.

The British Airways flight arrived exactly on time, and Riordan waited until the first passengers appeared in the arrivals area before merging slowly with them, following the burgeoning flow of humanity toward the baggage area. In the throng he set eyes on Featherstone, and then Tosser, and Jean-Marc, two stalwart members of the team and both seasoned warriors. Tosser was tall, lanky, and a former SAS commando possessing a Pancho Villa moustache that he combed on a regular basis, mostly to remove bits of food. Tosser would eat all day long and was forever asking "Done with that?" when they went out for supper and someone set down their knife and fork with some food left on their plate. Riordan suggested that perhaps Tosser had a tapeworm that ate half of his dinner, which amused Featherstone greatly.

Jean-Marc, the diminutive Frenchman and former member of the GIGN, the antiterrorist team, sauntered through the airport, his chic wraparound sunglasses perched atop his brush-cut head. Nancy was very fond of Jean-Marc because he had almost died while protecting her during a previous mission that had gone sideways. The epitome of Gallic charm, he was never in want of female companionship, despite the ever-present Gauloises cigarettes.

They ignored Riordan completely, but he knew they would be watching his every move. And there would be some more of Featherstone's contacts waiting outside, all ready to form a protective ring around Riordan. It felt heart-warming that they were here for him, and some of the worry diminished.

Some...

He passed along a narrow corridor with endless pictures of tourist London, with websites and phones and text forms of communication displayed vividly, each vendor competing for the lucrative tourist dollar or Euro or rupee. The ads for cellular phones, which he had not noticed before, distracted him momentarily, since the rates they advertised were a fraction of what he paid at home. He cursed his local provider for the staggering monthly bills. Nancy loved her iPhone, but being a nurse it had to endure a fair amount of abuse, and consequently every few months a new, replacement device was required. And with it came a further extension of his extortionate rates plans. That monthly invoice was like waving a red flag in front of a bull.

At the bottom of the escalator leading to the baggage area stood several limo drivers, resplendent in formal livery, caps askew, holding placards with their fare's name scribbled in black marker. The one exception was a well-built, balding man in his early thirties, wearing a Chelsea soccer jersey, jeans, and a brand-new pair of Nike trainers. Several gold chains adorned his neck, and a huge in-your-face watch adorned his wrist. It looked like a Sebring to Riordan. The other drivers were giving him a wide berth.

The soccer guy was holding a card that had the name Daniel Riordan written across it and was carefully scrutinizing the faces of everyone coming down the elevator. When he looked in Riordan's direction, he grinned and pointed. Obviously, he had

278

seen the surveillance photos, which made Riordan wonder how many others had seen them as well. This was not good.

Riordan walked over to the guy. There was a strong waft of aftershave. "Are you the taxi driver?"

"Don't be a cunt, mate," came the terse reply. "Max sent me to get you. The car's waiting outside, so we'd better get a move on. You don't have a lot of time."

Riordan followed him out through the throng of people waiting for the famous black London taxis, and immediately a black Humvee pulled away from the curb where it had been idling and stopped beside them. Riordan shook his head at the sight.

"I'm Billy K, by the way," the soccer guy said, opening the rear passenger door. Riordan climbed in and slid across, and Billy K followed. The interior of the vehicle had that new car scent and was immaculately groomed.

The driver glanced at him in the rear-view mirror then looked away and pulled out into the stream of traffic.

"So you're him," Billy K said, looking Riordan up and down.

The aftershave was really intense in the small space. Riordan rolled down a window to let some air in. It was raining lightly, and overcast, another beautiful day in the city. Tiny droplets of rain touched his face.

"Yep, I'm him," Riordan answered. "And what's your part in all of this?"

Billy K's chest almost puffed out a little, but his posture definitely changed. "I'm Max's number two, or 2IC, as he likes to call me."

"2IC?"

"It's military. Means second in command."

Riordan nodded. "So, you know where all the bodies are buried."

Billy K grinned and slipped a brown envelope from the pouch on back seat in front of him. "Max asked me to bring you up to speed on Dempsey. Here's a photo of the cunt and his last known address. My boys haven't been able to turn up a whisper, so you've got your work cut out for you. Maybe some of those Irish cunts you know can point you in the right direction."

Riordan was about to ask Billy K to be more specific about the Irish cunts but thought that sarcasm would be lost on him. Instead, he slipped the photo out of the envelope and stared at it for a while. It was a full head shot, like that of an actor, but a little grainy, as if it had been cropped and blown up from a bigger picture. Dempsey had dark, wavy hair and thin, sallow features, almost rat-like. He was grinning in the picture, revealing a tiny gap between his two front teeth. He was allegedly in his late thirties but looked much older. But that's what living in a war zone did for you. It put years on, especially around the face.

Riordan took out his cellphone, held up the photo, and used his camera to record the image. It was much more up to date than the one Cupples had shared and better quality. People were more likely to offer information about someone they could look at discreetly on a small screen rather than a huge photograph. He then turned it over and keyed the address into his contact list.

"Any chance of a phone number?" he asked.

"No point, it's been turned off."

"Have you tried to get a copy of his phone bill?" Riordan asked.

"Never thought of that," came the reply. Billy K took out his iPhone, ran his finger across the screen, and pulled up a number. "Here it is."

Riordan entered the number into the contact list as well, saved the entry, and put away the phone. "Anything else you can tell me?"

Billy K shrugged. "He was always a bit of a loner. Loved the drink, but then again, what fuckin' Mick doesn't, and he spent a lot of time over in Kilburn. They don't like outsiders much over there — fuckin' Irish code of silence and all that shite — so my boys didn't get too far. And his place is empty, cleared it out, he did."

"How long ago was this?" Riordan asked, wondering what sort of a head start Dempsey would have had. From the sounds of it this hadn't been a last-minute decision and obviously had been well thought out.

"The blag happened two weeks ago, and Dempsey was supposed to show up with the money a few days later. When Max didn't hear a dicky, he sent me to find him, and that's when we discovered he'd done a runner. Left the other two guys in the lurch as well. They haven't a clue where he went either."

"How do you know?"

"Max asked them." Billy K grinned and made a slashing motion across his throat. "They would have grassed up their mothers when Max was done. They're out looking for him as well, at least one of them is..."

Riordan filled in the blanks.

Billy K's cellphone blasted out a reggae beat, and he pressed the receive button and held it to his ear. "Yeah, Max, he's sitting right here." Billy K nodded a few times and replied with a "'yep" now and again, as if responding to questions. He finished with a "see you there," which was what Riordan was expecting.

"We've got you a room at the Gun," Billy K offered. "It's a pub that Max owns, and we use as a meeting place. Good grub as well."

"Suits me," Riordan replied. "I don't expect to be there much. Dempsey's probably out of the country by now, as well as the money, so what am I supposed to use for cash?"

"Fucked if I know," came the response. "You'll have to ask Max about that."

"Thought you were number 2," Riordan answered. "You don't know much, do you?"

Billy K's face darkened, and Riordan saw a smirk cross the driver's face. Billy K saw it as well, and he slapped the driver across the back of the head. "What the fuck are you laughing at?" he snarled. "Mind your fucking business. And you, mate," he growled, turning to face Riordan, "less of the fucking lip, or you'll get a slap."

"Yeah, right," Riordan replied. Then he remembered reading about the one word that had been voted as the most likely to piss people off. "Whatever..."

Billy K looked like he was going to have a fit. Clenching his fists, he looked like he was trying to crush his cellphone. Riordan saw his jaws grinding under his skin and knew he was a fraction away from getting into it. It was a tiny nugget of information to be filed away and used later. Billy had significant control issues. Riordan defused the situation.

"Sorry about that. I'm just tired from a long fucking flight, sitting beside some bastard that reeked of curry and was jabbering on to his mate in Urdu the whole way."

Billy K nodded. "Know what you mean, mate. Fucking ragheads."

Riordan had pegged him right. Billy K was a racist as well.

Riordan stared out the window of the Humvee, and the remainder of the journey was spent in silence. It had started to rain heavily, raindrops splattering noisily on the roof of the vehicle, but they were virtually drowned out by the heavy bass beat from the speakers. The driver was listening to BBC Radio One, his fingers beating time on the steering wheel, and the electro pop music sounded to Riordan like the music from a German porn movie: loud and irritating. At least it was better than conversing with Billy K, who had eased back into his seat and was playing a game on his cellphone in between texting someone. He seemed to be uncomfortable, and after a while leaned forward, extracted the pistol from the small of his back, and eased it under his thigh. It was a Glock 22 with an extended clip.

Billy thought he was a gangsta.

Eventually they turned off the carriageway and headed for the docks. Massive cranes lined the banks and across the way sat the O2 Arena, a white, domed structure punctuated with spear like protuberances, giving it the appearance of an oversized World War Two mine. Riordan didn't have much of an appreciation for architecture, but to him it looked weird. The Humvee pulled into a narrow, cobblestoned one-way street that was so tiny it looked like they would have trouble getting through. The driver stopped outside the pub, a neatly painted structure with trim finished in black. Billy K slid the pistol back into his jeans, got out, walked around the vehicle, and held the door open for Riordan.

Riordan grabbed his bag, stepped out, and followed Billy K into the pub. Behind them the Humvee took off. At a long, polished mahogany bar, Billy K turned and said, "You wait here.

I'll be back in a moment." The room, elegantly appointed with linen-covered tables, wine glasses, and silver service, was about a quarter full, the patrons, mostly business types given their expensive outfits, feasting on what appeared to be a sumptuous breakfast. The mouth-watering aroma of bacon teased his nostrils. The front of the pub provided an excellent view of the Thames, long, narrow barges chugging slowly along against the strong current.

Riordan sat down at the bar and ordered a coffee from a less-than-impressed barman. To pass the time he picked up the bar menu, scanning the notes about the bar's origin. The pub took its name from the gun that was fired to celebrate the opening of the West India Docks in 1802, and apparently, in the late 18th century, Lord Horatio Nelson used it for secret trysts with Lady Emma Hamilton. A few years ago it had burned to the ground and had been restored by the new owner, presumably Max DeLisle, which explained the fresh-looking facade and the large oil painting of the Battle of Trafalgar that hung on one wall.

The barman delivered a plate of chips to the patron sitting a couple of seats down, and despite his large breakfast, Riordan's stomach rumbled at the scent. The menu itself was impressive, one of the new breed of restaurants of British chefs had coined "gastropubs," regular pubs that were now offering upscale fare. Items such as potted Morecambe Bay brown shrimps with toasted sourdough, or oysters from the Wright Brothers of Borough Market, in a red-wine shallot vinegar, were a far cry from the curry and chips of traditional pubs. Under different circumstances he would have enjoyed such a place.

He was in the process of scanning the wine list, extensive by most pub standards, consisting mainly of French reds that were on his own list of personal favourites, when Billy K reappeared, snatched the menu, and tossed it on the bar.

"Let's go," he ordered. "We've got a couple of snugs back here." The barman glanced over, and his eyes caught Riordan's for just a moment. The look said it all. The barman had obviously been party to other such meetings, and given Billy K's posture, he understood that it was not a social event. The barman himself, dressed neatly in a white, starched shirt, and black pants, stood about six feet, no shrinking violet, but he was wary of Billy K.

Riordan grinned, tossed a five-pound note on the bar, picked up his bag, and followed Billy to a private "snug" at the back of the pub. The snug, also sometimes called the smoke room, was typically a small, very private room with access to the bar that had a frosted glass external window, set above head height. A higher price was paid for beer in the snug, and in these rooms, nobody could look in and see who was drinking. He knew that the Crown Bar in Belfast was renowned for its ornate snugs and also for the fact that some of the most heinous atrocities of the Troubles had been planned in those tiny rooms.

Originally, the snug was for patrons who preferred not to be seen in the public bar. Ladies would often enjoy a private drink in the snug in a time when it was frowned upon for them to be in a pub. The local police officer would nip in for a quiet pint, the parish priest for his evening whisky, and lovers would use the snug for their rendezvous.

Fuck only knows what's going to happen today, Riordan thought, and just as that thought crossed his mind, Jean-Marc walked into the pub and headed for the bar. They collided, Jean-Marc apologizing profusely in French, but Riordan motioned that he was okay. Jean-Marc let him pass, took a seat at the bar, and ordered a glass of wine.

Billy K opened the door to the snug, and inside Riordan saw Max DeLisle. The same angry face as he had seen at the poker game glared at him, and a manila folder with the words "MOD Top Secret" lay on the table in front of him. DeLisle wore a black sports shirt with the Lacoste emblem on the chest, open at the neck, and Riordan could see a tiny gold chain nestled in a field of dark chest hair. An elegant china service consisting of a teapot, two cups, and saucers, and a milk jug and matching sugar bowl sat on a silver server.

"Have a seat," DeLisle said, lifting the teapot and pouring a cup of tea. "Fancy a cuppa?"

Riordan nodded and sat down at the narrow oval table, setting his bag on the ground and pressing the tiny, adhesive transmitter that Jean-Marc had passed to him to the underside of the table. As DeLisle poured, a heavy gold chain, propelled by gravity, slid from under his cuff and tinkled off the side of the teapot. Riordan could also see the heavily bandaged wrists.

287

"Nice bandages. Did your boyfriend put the handcuffs on a little tight?" Riordan asked.

DeLisle looked him up and down, an incredulous look on his face, then turned his head to look at Billy K. "Got a real smart mouth, this one," he commented.

Billy K nodded. "Did the same to me, Max." Riordan noticed that Billy K hadn't been asked to sit down, nor was there an extra cup. Then again, Billy K standing was certainly an intimidating sight. The two certainly had honed their act. It was an old trick often used by police officers while interrogating suspects. The "good cop" would sit close by and empathize while the "bad cop" towered over the suspect in a menacing manner. Given their chosen profession, DeLisle and Billy K would be well acquainted with the technique.

"I'd put it down to jet lag," Riordan said. "So, let's cut to the chase. I find Dempsey for you, get the money back, and you give me back this file. That about right?"

DeLisle sipped the tea. "That's about right."

"I expect he's out of the country," Riordan said, adding some milk to his tea and stirring it with a silver spoon. "Maybe Ireland, maybe somewhere else. Do you have any idea what he did before he came to work for you, other than being an IRA gunman?"

"Nope," DeLisle replied. "Said he'd been overseas, and he came highly recommended by one of his now deceased comrades."

"Not exactly a great deal to go on," Riordan said.

"Them's the cards." DeLisle laughed. He had excellent teeth, but they were all veneers. "Besides, I know you're motivated to find him. This, however, is one of seven files Major Skinner had about you, and just so you know I'm serious, you can take this one and read it. That way you'll know I'm not bluffing. A kind of good faith payment, you might say."

"Okay then," Riordan said. "Logistics. I need money, and a fair amount of it for getting around, the odd bribe, and God only knows what else. And I need some way to contact you directly, should it be necessary."

DeLisle shook his head. "You deal with Billy here. Anything you need or want he will supply. When you find Dempsey, pass the word to Billy, and all the details about the cash and how I get it back. We likely won't be seeing each other again, Mister Riordan, so for your sake I hope you find Dempsey. We wouldn't want the world to be knowing your little secret, would we now?"

"I'll need a gun, a knife, and about thirty grand for a start," Riordan said, looking at Billy K. Then, taking out a pen and a piece of paper, he wrote out an account number, a country code, and a transit number. "If I need more cash, wire it to that account."

DeLisle nodded, and Billy disappeared. He came back a few minutes later carrying a small duffel bag that he handed to

Riordan. "There's a room in the back you can use," DeLisle offered, but Riordan shook his head.

"Thanks, but no thanks," he said. "I'll make my own arrangements. Besides, I'll only be here for a day or two at the most." He picked up the duffel bag, slipped it into his carryall, drained the remainder of his tea, and left the snug, passing Jean-Marc on the way out.

*

Behind him, Billy K took a seat and rapped on the glass window that sealed the snug from the bar. The window slid open and Billy ordered a pint of bitter and a Johnny Walker Red.

"Want one, Max?" he asked.

"Sure, Billy, why not. I'll be having my five mil back in a few days, so I think a quick pint is in order."

"And what do we do about Riordan when he gets us the money?"

DeLisle shrugged. "It'd be great to keep him on a short leash, but he's too smart for that. When he finds Dempsey for us, then we'll off him. He's the only remaining link from Dempsey to me, and he knows about the bank job. So we can't have that, can we Billy, can we?" The drinks arrived, and they clinked glasses.

*

Outside the bar, Riordan hailed a taxi and instructed the driver to take him to the Crowne Plaza Hotel. It was about a ten-minute walk from where he was staying, but there was no point in letting DeLisle know about his accommodations. After about ten minutes, his cellphone rang and he picked it up.

"Riordan here," said.

"Hi Daniel, it's Feather," came the welcome response. "We heard it all, and then some. Where are you headed? Back to the hotel?"

"Yep."

"See you there."

The cabbie dropped him off at the entrance to Crowne Plaza. Riordan paid the cabbie and watched him drive away. He was barely out of the semicircular driveway before Riordan saw him putting his cellphone to his ear, presumably reporting back to Billy K and Max. Riordan walked in through the lobby and made his way through a rabbit warren of corridors out to Seaforth Place, then headed down to Buckingham Gate and from there back to his own hotel. He had scoped out a route the previous evening and knew he could easily give a tail the slip in the huge hotel.

He headed directly to the bar and found Featherstone sitting in a corner reading the newspaper, a pot of tea sitting in front of him. Riordan fell into the chair beside him, set his bag on the floor, and even before he had time to speak, a waiter was standing beside them. Riordan ordered a large coffee and some pastries.

"Thought you might like a treat, Feather," he offered.

"Partners in crime, you mean." Featherstone's fiancée was always trying to get him to eat healthy foods and get him to stay away from donuts and candy and Bounty bars, his favourite. However, for a man who possessed the metabolism of a Grand National winner, Featherstone could pretty much eat what he pleased.

"How are you doing, Daniel?" Featherstone asked.

"About as well as can be expected," Riordan replied. There was a dark anger building in him, like stoking a fire to be used to temper steel. He knew the symptoms. Now all he had to do was harness the rage and direct it. "I'd like to tear DeLisle's throat out, and before this is all over I may just do that. But I've got to find Dempsey."

"You weren't followed from the pub," Featherstone offered.

"How do you know?" Riordan asked and then felt stupid for asking.

"'Cos we followed you, and you didn't have another tail."

"What happened after I left?"

"Pretty much what you expect from this bunch. Drink drink, blah blah blah, get our money, blah blah blah, kill him, blah blah blah, drink drink."

"You have such a way with words, Feather," Riordan said. The coffee arrived, along with the assortment of fancy pastries. Featherstone scrutinized them for a moment, looking as if he would like to take a bite out of each.

"You first, Daniel," he offered.

They bit into their delectable treats and then settled back.

Featherstone said, "Bring me up to speed on what you've got so far. Jean-Marc will be back shortly, and Tosser's lurking about somewhere. There are a few extra set of eyes I've got that you haven't met as yet — lads from over here — so they'll stay in the wings. This is your show, pal, so tell us how you want to run it."

Riordan sipped his coffee and related the events of the previous evening, detailing each piece of information he had found. Featherstone was very detail-oriented, no tidbit too small for him. Riordan outlined the meeting with Cupples, which produced a raised eyebrow, and then the final outing of the night over in Chiswick. He was in the midst of telling Feather about the search of the flat when something tugged at his senses, like the first hit of a trout on a fishing line. There was something he was missing, or had seen that was important, and he instantly replayed the entire event in his mind, almost in slow motion.

Featherstone, to his credit, recognized the behaviour and stayed silent. Riordan recalled the conversation with the agent, then the struggle, then the search of the place. The books...

From his side there was a flurry of activity, and Sean stumbled into view, one arm twisted halfway up his back, held there firmly by Tosser. Featherstone was just about to spring when Riordan said, "Hold it."

"Found this cunt spying on you," Tosser said proudly, releasing Sean's arm but standing within easy reach.

"This is my mate, Sean," Riordan said, standing. "Sean, this is Tosser and Feather, the folks I was telling you about."

"Oops," Tosser said. "Sorry about that."

"Come and sit down," Riordan said.

Sean rubbed his arm, trying to get some sensation back into the muscles. "My fuckin' arm's gone numb," he complained.

"It's just pressure points," Riordan replied. "You'll be okay in a minute or two."

"Good job I don't need to take a piss," Sean joked.

Riordan sighed. The moment was gone, like a shadow passing across the moon, and with it that tenuous link to some trivial piece of information, but it felt like a piece of a puzzle he had missed.

"No good?" Featherstone asked.

"Nah." Riordan shook his head. "After I started the search of the place, and it wasn't very big to begin with, there was something I glossed over. You know, one of those things your brain registers at the time, but you don't realize its significance until much later, or until it's too late to make a difference. I had to rush out of the place as Sean saw a foot patrol coming our way, so it may have been something I glimpsed as I was leaving."

"Sean was with you?"

"Keeping dick," Sean replied, and Featherstone laughed.

"Fuck me," he exclaimed, "it's been a few years since I heard that expression. Not since my time over in the North have I heard that one. We used to call the little fuckheads who kept watch at street corners 'dickers,' so I guess that's where it comes from."

"Never gave it much thought," Sean replied. "But then again, Belfast folk have a language all of their own, never mind the accent. I often get strange looks when I come over here for business meetings and use one of those colourful expressions that I grew up with. I still struggle with cigarettes, and my ex was always berating me for not being politically correct when I called them fags."

"Too fookin' right," growled Tosser. "Speaking of which, I'm going outside for a fag."

Riordan shook his head. "Anyway, I need you and the boys to keep an eye on DeLisle and see if there's any way you can get those files back. He gave me one set but claims there are seven more, so he'll probably have them stored someplace safe. I'll leave that in your hands." His cellphone vibrated and then rang. It was a private number, so he pressed the answer button.

"Daniel, it's Arthur Cupples. I haven't been able to dig up much on this Elva person, so I'll need some more time, but I have got you a meeting with one of the ex-IRA commanders from South Armagh. This guy used to be Dempsey's commander, so he might be able to provide some insight."

Riordan felt a chill. Despite the peace process, these IRA types had long memories and held a grudge even worse than Italians. He was well aware that there was a high-priced contract out on the Raven and that it had never been lifted. "Suits me fine, Arthur. When do I meet him?"

"You me *we*, son, I'm coming too. This old devil owes me a favour or two, so I'll make the intro. We're meeting him at the Knightsbridge Hotel bar, just off O'Connell Street, at five tonight."

"Dublin! What the fuck..."

"Relax, son. I've got a plane on standby at the City airport. Meet me there at two o'clock, and we'll head over to Dublin. I'll email you the plane's tail number, and when you get there go directly to the private entrance. You shouldn't need it but bring your passport, and make sure you leave all your 'toys' back at the hotel. If we need stuff, I can arrange for it when we get to Dublin. It should only take you about twenty minutes to get to the airport from where you are."

Cupples signed off. "Looks like I'm off to Dublin," Riordan said. "I've got a meet with an ex-IRA commander."

"Strange bedfellows," Featherstone commented and bit into another pastry. Flakes of pastry sprinkled his shirt like a miniature dust storm.

"Fuck," Riordan exclaimed. "Cupples must have a tail on me, 'cos he knows where I'm staying."

"Wouldn't surprise me," Featherstone replied. "If Cupples is MI5, they've got some of the best surveillance guys in the world. Even my team would be hard-pressed to spot them."

"I suppose so," Riordan reluctantly admitted. But he didn't feel comfortable with the fact that there were more and more eyes being brought to bear on the situation. More bodies brought more questions, and these types of operators were taught to think and perform under their best discretion in the field. He had a sense that events were slipping out of his grasp, and consequently the blissful life he had created for his family was now in jeopardy. The thought of going on the run again filled him with dread. In this day and age, with the pervasiveness of any form of social media, it was almost impossible to remain anonymous once you were illuminated by the public spotlight.

Looking over at Sean, he said, "Why don't you come along with me? It's been a while since I've been in Dublin, and if we need to make a side trip to the North, you know your way around better than me."

"Sounds good to me," Sean replied, rubbing his arm.

Riordan was going to head to his room but thought better of it. Handing his backpack to Featherstone, he said. "My stuff is in there, plus a few toys from DeLisle, and the first sample of the file. Look after it for me."

Then, looking at the time on his cellphone, he got up and Sean followed suit. "Let's go."

*

The taxi dropped them outside the terminal, and they were through the reception area for private charters and into a security clearance area in minutes. Riordan was amazed at the place. It hadn't been in existence during his time in Northern Ireland, all air traffic at that time being directed through the insanity that was Heathrow Airport, one of the world's busiest and most congested international hubs. To be checking in merely minutes after stepping out of the taxi was an incredible luxury.

As Cupples had promised, the tail number arrived in an email. They were politely but carefully frisked at the security area and then directed to a small waiting area where Riordan could see a Gulfstream jet sitting outside the tall glass windows. Everyone they encountered was polite, pleasant, and efficient, a far cry from what he was accustomed to seeing in local airports. At a few minutes before two o'clock, a black Jaguar XJS rolled to a stop in one of the parking spots outside the terminal. A liveried driver got out, walked around the car, and opened the back door. Cupples got out, leaning heavily on his cane, and walked across the few feet to the terminal.

"He's aged a bit," Sean commented. "I remember him sitting in your house eating fish and chips and downing a lager. Come to think of it, that was all I ever saw him do."

Cupples walked through the sliding doors and made his way over. He wore a tweed jacket with black leather elbow patches over a heavy Arran sweater, looking every bit like a visiting professor. He looked Sean up and down and then stared at Riordan, as if waiting for an explanation.

"This is Sean Daly," Riordan said. "He..."

Cupples cut him off. "I know who he is; he was over at the house often enough. What I want to know is what he's doing here? I'm not running a fucking charter airline."

Riordan didn't react. Despite the veneer of sophistication, Cupples was still very much the hard case. He replied, "Sean helped me out over the past few days, and he can help me get around if I have to get about Dublin or even head north."

"Nice to see you again too, Arthur." Sean beamed.

Cupples pondered this for a moment, then sighed and nodded toward the plane. "The lads are just about done the preflight, so I'll let them know there's one more on the manifest. We still have to do the customs thing in Dublin, but that's a formality."

He limped off toward the door, and Riordan and Sean followed him out on to the tarmac and across to the plane. The plane was furnished for executive travel, with wide leather seats and plenty of legroom. Sean whistled at the sight. "Now this is the way to go," he commented.

In front of them, a steward pressed a button, and the automatic door slid into place. He then manually closed the lock. After checking all was secure, he paused by Cupples's seat. "We'll be taking off in a few minutes, and when we get airborne I'll bring around some drinks. The flying time today will be just over an hour."

After taking off, Cupples, in the seat in front of them, opened up a laptop and proceeded to scan a bunch of websites, as well as read email. Over his shoulder he said, "I've managed to get a hit on Elva McCormick. She's originally from Dun Laoghaire. Her parents owned a pub there called McKenna's that they bought from the original owner called Arthur McKenna. It's on George's Place, down near the harbour, and apparently is run by her brother Frank. The brother has had a few run-ins with the law but nothing serious. The father appears to be deceased now, but the mother is still alive. Elva has done a lot of travelling and has spent a fair amount of time in Greece, Spain, and most recently, France. Looks like she lived in Marseille for more than two years." Cupples went silent as he absorbed the information before him. Riordan knew well what he was thinking. In Cupples's hand, a blue fountain pen travelled miles through his fingers, and from time to time he would pause, underline a passage in the document, and the journey would resume.

The Basque separatist group called ETA was based in Spain. The Greek separatist group known as November 17 focused most of its attacks on Athens. Finally, Marseille was a notorious haven for gun traffickers, drug traffickers, and any form of lowlife that operated on the wrong side of the law. Cupples would be wondering if he had found a wild card, a terrorist sleeper who had managed to stay under the radar. Given her affiliation with Dempsey, it was not too far of a stretch.

Riordan heard the chatter of fingers flying over a keypad and imagined that Cupples was sending out some form of alert. That was how it went sometimes during investigations. A seemingly innocuous piece of information would completely change the direction and dynamics of the thought process, and often a series of independent assignments would be created to follow the thread. Unravelling the thread would lead to a much bigger reward in terms of intelligence-gathering. Sometimes a robbery was just a robbery, and sometimes it was a cover for something more sinister, such as funding for another operation to procure weapons or other ordnance. And the five million that Dempsey had taken would buy a lot of weapons.

Beside him, Sean busied himself reading the newspapers, poring over the soccer results and then the racing programs from

301

Lansdowne Road. Judging from the look on his face and the constant muttering, he had climbed aboard a significant losing streak.

The steward brought a pot of tea for Cupples, then another for Sean. Riordan went for the coffee, which was surprisingly good, given how much airline coffee he had tasted. Freshly made ham and cheese sandwiches were also on offer, so they had a quick snack. Riordan found himself famished, then realized he had skipped lunch, so helped himself to another round. Sean did the same.

Shortly after that the engine note changed, and Riordan felt the jet begin its descent as it crossed the Irish coast and raced toward fields of brilliant green. They encountered a bit of turbulence as they crossed the coast, but that was nothing unusual given the howling winds that blew in off the Irish Sea and buffeted everything in sight. Just below, Riordan scanned the fairways of the famed Portmarnock golf course, amazed at the number and size of the bunkers. The place from the air looked like a war zone that had been bombed to hell. They made an incredibly smooth landing, and the jet taxied to a private hangar off in a secluded corner of the airport.

A Green Range Rover awaited them, and when the steward opened the plane's door, a driver got out and approached Cupples at the bottom of the steps. The driver, solidly built, with neatly trimmed dark hair, greeted Cupples like a long-lost friend. The hard, hawk-like eyes looked Riordan up and down then gave Sean a cursory glance. Cupples made no move to introduce them, so Riordan took his cue and climbed into the back seat of the Rover. Sean climbed in the other. The exterior of the car, especially around the wheel wells, was coated with fresh mud, and the interior reeked of wet dog, so the guy was obviously some sort of landowner.

"So Arthur," the man said, dragging out the "a" as he started the engine, "another surprise visit to the Rose... Where do you need to go?" The accent was definitely British, and upper-class British at that, so Riordan couldn't place it. The guy was former military, of that he was certain, and he knew that there were many Brits who had taken up residence in Dublin and the surrounding countryside just before the real-estate boom hit.

"We've got rooms at the Temple Bar Hotel in case we need them, so drop us down there. I have a meeting set for five o'clock, so depending on how that goes we'll either be heading to the hotel or somewhere else. If I need you I'll call, so why don't you hang about at the hotel across the Liffey."

"Will do, Arthur," came the reply. "I see you've brought your own muscle, so you won't be needing backup."

"This should be a quiet visit, but you never know with this crowd," Cupples said.

"Isn't that the truth."

Riordan felt decidedly uncomfortable at this last exchange. He wasn't accustomed to playing nice with the IRA, official, or ex-

, or whatever mantle of respectability they were currently flaunting. Any terrorist he had come across was dispatched with extreme prejudice, a fact of life with which Cupples was well acquainted. Cupples had even helped select some of the targets and had provided the intelligence and support materials to carry out the job.

The roads were busy as they headed into the downtown core, many of the stores with signs saying "Mówił polski" indicating that polish was spoken. It was a sobering reflection of the changing demographics of Dublin since the staggering upswing in the Irish economy, better known as the Celtic Tiger. Most of the influx, as much as 10% of the population, had arrived from Poland and the Baltic states as young people came to seek their fortune. For most it was a turnaround in the fortunes of the once-beleaguered county, and for once, the country's prime exports were not her young. Between the late 1980s and the early nineties, Ireland was transformed from one of the poorest countries in Western Europe to one of the wealthiest. Disposable income soared to record levels, enabling a huge rise in consumer spending. And then the bubble burst.

Like any major city, rush hour clogged the main arteries, and they crawled down Parnell Street and onto O'Connell Street. The first thing that Riordan noticed was the enormous steel spire protruding skyward from the middle of the street. "So that's the needle," he commented. "I had read about it, but it's quite something in real life."

The driver nodded. "It's the world's large art installation, called the Monument of Light, and it's about four hundred feet high. It caused a lot of controversy at the time, because they cleared away a lot of the old trees so people could see it, they implemented pedestrian walkways, and they forced the shopkeepers on both sides to upgrade their old ratty signage. Certainly cleaned up the street."

As they passed the spire, milling tourists of every variety were taking photographs of the art, and Riordan had to admit it was impressive. The driver stopped on O'Connell Bridge to let them off. The pub was on Bachelor's Walk, which was a one-way street, one of many in Dublin that confused the hell out of tourists who foolishly rented cars. Not that people rented cars much anymore. The rental cars were prime targets for alcohol-fuelled joyriders who stole anything that moved, and consequently, insurance rates skyrocketed.

When they got out of the vehicle, Riordan took Sean by the elbow and steered him over to the side of the bridge. He needed a quiet word, out of earshot of Cupples. A wooden deck had been constructed out over the Liffey to allow tourists to get a good view of the river. Brand new blue square canvas patio umbrellas sheltered shiny aluminum chairs and tables situated along the tiny platform, and a small café provided coffee and sandwiches.

"Look, mate," Riordan said, pointing to the cafe, "go and grab a coffee, and we'll pick you up on the way back. It shouldn't take too long, but I don't want you near any part of this. These are bad people, and you don't want to get on their radar for any reason."

"But…"

"Sean, this is my world," Riordan said gently, seeing the concern in his friend's eyes. "Featherstone, whom you met, is very fond of quoting Nietzsche. 'When you look long enough into the abyss, the abyss also looks back at you.' I don't want these people looking at you or your family."

Sean nodded. "But I'm muscle…"

Riordan grinned and patted his friend's shoulder. "That you are, that you are."

Returning to Cupples, he said, "Okay Arthur, let's go."

*

Cupples walked along the quay, stepped up to the black-painted wooden façade of the Knightsbridge Bar, and pushed his way inside, his limp pronounced, and Riordan followed. Inside the enormous oak-panelled room filled with stained glass, a sea of low-slung wooden tables was filled with the rowdy banter of patrons enjoying one of Dublin's best-loved pubs. The entire room was bathed in a honey glow emanating from iron chandeliers. Scattered around, sturdy white candles burned, their wax overflowing onto the wine bottles holding them.

Metal suits of armour stood guard on either side of the doorways leading to the interior of the upscale Arlington Hotel lobby. Behind a long wooden bar, running the length of the room along the east side, lay rows and rows of books and encyclopedias. On the other walls of the pubs were mounted stuffed animal heads, Irish crests, flags, and other medieval artifacts salvaged from old bars and schoolhouses.

Cupples looked around and then made his way to one of the tables just inside the front window. The windows of the pub were open to let in some fresh air from the street. That was something of an illusion due to the frequency of the diesel-fuelled buses that flowed along the quay outside. Air-conditioning was still a novelty in Ireland. At the scarred wooden table sat a frail, white-haired man who appeared to be in his seventies. The skin on his face was almost translucent, and spidery blue veins shone through like homemade tattoos. One hand trembled demoniacally on the surface of the table, the other in his pocket. He wore an open-necked white shirt that had once fitted and a heavy tweed jacket.

Beside him sat a beefy, younger version of himself, probably a son or a close relative. Close-cropped dark hair gave him the look of a Shar Pei, and the ruddy cheeks betrayed a fondness for the drink. He wore a green Arran sweater that consumed a fair amount of real estate, its sleeves pulled up to the elbows. Two meaty fists rested on the table, their knuckles scarred. At one time the man had known violence, up close and personal, but he had gone to seed. Badly.

Two half-empty pints of Guinness sat before them, the old man's resting on a beer mat, the other on the table. The younger man, obviously bored, had picked the decal from the cardboard backing of his beer mat. A tobacco pouch lay on the table, and as Cupples approached, the old man produced a pipe from his jacket.

"And there's the great man," he said, seeing Cupples. Riordan followed Cupples' lead and sat down across from the pair. "How the oul leg? Troublin' you much these days?" A shower of tobacco fell from his fingers as he tried to fill the pipe, tamping it down hard with his thumb and jamming the pipe in the corner of his mouth, unlit.

Cupples nodded. "Some days are good, some are bad. But you'd know all about that."

The old man nodded. Watery eyes looked Riordan up and down. "Not any more, Arthur. The cancer's metastasized, whatever the fuck that means. It's gone into me lymph nodes and spread to the brain."

Cupples didn't sound at all sympathetic. "That's too bad for you, Eamonn. How long did they give you?" From Riordan's perspective, given his knowledge of O'Brien, he hadn't suffered enough.

The old man shrugged. "The doctor says three or four months, if I'm lucky. They wanted to do all that radiation and chemo shite, but why bother. My fucking hand won't stop shaking because there's a tumour the size of a golf ball in my brain. I might as well enjoy the time I've got left, rather than pukin' me guts up in a fucking hospital bed."

Cupples nodded. "I'm with you there. So, will you have a wee one, and we'll drink to the shaky gun hand?"

The old man nodded. When the waitress appeared, Cupples ordered a round of double shots of Paddy and three pints. Riordan asked for a coffee.

"Yank, are ye?" the old man asked upon hearing his accent.

Riordan nodded.

"And what are ye doin' with this gurrier?"

Cupples interjected. "He's doing a job for the service, and that's why we're here. This is David Spence. David, this is Eamonn O'Brien. Used to be called the Wolf of the Border, in the good old days. And this is his son..."

Damien, Riordan thought. *His last remaining son. Fuck me, Arthur, what have you gotten us into?*

"...Damien. Eamonn put the bullet into me in the last days of the Troubles. But that's all water under the bridge now, isn't it, Eamonn? Eamonn here is now what the local cops call an ODC, better known as an ordinary decent criminal, up to robbing banks and the like, isn't that right?"

"So what do ye want, Arthur?" O'Brien asked. "I haven't a lot of time left, and to be perfectly honest, I'd rather not spend it in your company." The drinks arrived, the shots disappearing in rapid order. Riordan sipped his coffee and waited, trying desperately to keep his heartbeat steady. Eamonn O'Brien looked like a shadow of his former self, and Riordan remembered the surveillance photos well enough. He never forgot a face, even after all these years. Damien was a fourteen-year-old boy, a tall drink of water, when Riordan first saw the surveillance photographs of the family, so he had gained about a hundred pounds over the years, rendering him virtually unrecognizable.

The other two brothers, Fergal and Shamus, both IRA volunteers, had managed to blow up a school bus by mistake when their detonator failed to function as the Army Saracen, their designated target, had passed over the culvert bomb that had been planted the previous evening. They were frantically trying to get it to work and not paying attention to what was going on at the target site as the detonator light eventually flashed green. What they failed to notice was that a local school bus had just driven into the killing zone.

The driver of the school bus and six of the children who had been sitting at the front were blown to bits, and many of the others suffered grievous physical as well as mental wounds that would haunt them for the rest of their days. The IRA spin doctors had gone into overdrive, blaming the British Army for detonating the bomb by accident, but Riordan's adopted father had discovered the truth. The terrorists, at the insistence of their father, the frail old man sitting across from him now, went on the run for a while, until everything died down, their mistake buried under a new list of atrocities.

Riordan had found them in the Spanish resort of Palma, on the island of Majorca, sunning themselves and hooking up most nights with a couple of female members of ETA, the Basque Separatist group that collaborated closely with the IRA. He watched and waited for an opportunity, and one evening when they were coming back from the local nightclub, staggering under the weight of alcohol they had drunk, Riordan executed them. His orders were to give them a Belfast six-pack — shots in both elbows, knees, and ankles — so that they might at least suffer some of what they had dealt out. They were both still screaming when he administered the *coup de grâce* — bullets in both eyes, trademark of the Raven. Their father had gone mad trying to find the Raven but had never been successful.

Cupples replied, "I'm here to call in a favour, and then we'll be on our way."

O'Brien didn't look too happy but put on a brave face. Riordan thought it must have been quite the favour that Cupples had done for him. When O'Brien glanced over at his son, Riordan understood. Whatever Cupples had done involved the son, the weak link. Perhaps it was avoiding a jail term, or worse. Riordan knew how these things worked.

"Spit it out, then."

"Sean Dempsey, he was one of yours. I need to find him."

With trembling hands, O'Brien lit up his pipe, blew a cloud of fragrant tobacco smoke into the space between them, and instantly a red beam arced through the cloud. A tiny red dot appeared on Riordan's chest, just above his heart.

Riordan froze.

He knew a laser sight had targeted him. Somewhere, in one of the buildings across the Liffey, a sniper had put him in his crosshairs. It was a profound moment, and even if he had been wearing a ballistic vest, it would afford no protection against a sniper rifle. A caress of a trigger and his heart would be shattered. He calmly looked to Cupples, then to O'Brien.

"What the fuck is this about?" he growled, his voice hard.

"Merely a precaution," coughed O'Brien. "Arthur here is not the most trustworthy of people, so forgive me for making sure we were safe." The smoke dissipated, but the dot remained for a few seconds then disappeared.

"Eamonn," Cupples said, opening his hands on the table. "We didn't come here to cause you any grief. If I wanted you dead, I'd have put a bomb under that old shitbox of a Volvo you drive. This is just about information. Besides, can you do that trick with the smoke again?"

O'Brien grinned, revealing tobacco-stained teeth, then leaned forward and blew another cloud of smoke between them. The tendrils of smoke wrapped themselves around a green beam of laser light, and the green dot moved away from Riordan's chest and landed on Damien's forehead.

"What the fuck?" Damien growled. His father glared across the table at Cupples.

Cupples said, "You see, Eamonn, I don't trust you either, and I imagined you'd pull a stunt like this. I had my guy locate your sniper and take him out. He's merely unconscious at the moment ... if he did what he was told."

"You always were a sneaky cunt, Arthur," O'Brien hissed.

Cupples raised his pint glass. "May ye die in Ireland. Now, about Dempsey?"

"I don't know where he is, Arthur, and that's God's honest truth. He was off doing freelance work somewhere in Spain, and then somebody told me he had surfaced in London, working for some underworld figure."

Riordan watched O'Brien's face like a hawk. The old man was lying but was very good at it. There was some truth wrapped up in the lie, so it would be hard to prove otherwise. But given the advanced deterioration of the old man's health, his microexpressions were impossible to control.

Cupples sighed and leaned back in his seat. He hadn't been taken in either. "You're a fuckin' liar, Arthur, and if you waste any more of my time, those files will make their way into the hands of the local authorities of the local authorities, and yer son here will be spending the next ten to twenty in Portlaoise jail. I already know a great deal about Dempsey, so stop fucking around and tell me where I can find him."

"He works for Max DeLisle, a cunt of the highest order. He's a former para and one of the top gang bosses in London. I've only heard whispers, but Dempsey was living over in Kilburn."

"Well, Arthur, he *was* living there. He crossed DeLisle over a job and has disappeared. We need to find him."

"And what's your interest in all of this, Arthur? Consorting with villains now?"

Cupples sipped his pint. "I've got bigger problems than criminals, Eamonn, and DeLisle controls a good part of what goes on in London. My bailiwick is to keep Muslim fundamentalists from detonating any more bombs over there, just like you fuckers did back in the day, and DeLisle provides me with info. Now and again I have to return the favour. Just like you're doing now. Except you're not being much help."

"What can I tell you, Arthur? I'm not as connected as I once was. I'll make a few phone calls and see what I can turn up, and I'll let you know."

"Fair enough," Cupples replied, "but do it quickly. So will you have another drink?"

O'Brien nodded toward the shot glass. "The doctor says it's bad for me, Arthur, but you know that famous saying, 'The drink and I have been friends for so long, it would be a pity for me to leave without one last kiss.' Another pint and a Paddy."

Cupples ordered another round. Riordan had another coffee, and when it arrived, he took a sip. "Can I asked you a question?" he asked, staring at the older O'Brien, "and this has to do with Dempsey."

"Ask away. I'll no promise ye an answer."

"Who is Elva McCormick?"

The old man's hand started its demonic trembling, despite his fierce attempt to get it under control. It was like something out of an old Hammer Studios movie. There were so many microexpressions revealing themselves on O'Brien's face that Riordan knew he had touched a nerve. It was like worms crawling under his skin. Cupples saw it too.

"Elva..."

"Don't bother," Riordan said, his voice firm. "We know she's with him."

"Well now, you know something I don't," O'Brien spat.

Cupples leaned forward. "This is all news to me too, Arthur, so start talking."

O'Brien shrugged. "What the fuck? She was one of our best, and she's eluded you lot for years. If she's with Dempsey, you'll have a hard time finding them, I promise you that."

"Any family?" Riordan asked.

O'Brien scratched his chin. "As I recall, her brother Frank owns a pub out in Dun Laoghaire. Arthur's, I think it's called, just off the high street there. You might want to ask him if he's heard from her. Her mother is still living in a big house out in Stillorgan."

"Did you run her?" Cupples asked.

O'Brien shook his head. "She was one of the wild cards that only the Army Council knew about. I found out about her after the Troubles were over, and from what I heard she never missed. Wee Martin was her control."

Cupples wrote his phone number on the back of a business card and slid it across the table. "I'll be expecting to hear from you in the next day or so, Eamonn. And when I do, if the info is reliable, I'll ship my files directly to you. Then we are clear." Cupples pushed away from the table and stood up, leaning heavily on his cane. Riordan did the same.

"I don't expect to be seeing you again, Eamonn," Cupples said, "at least not on this side. Enjoy what you've got left."

*

When they left the bar, a light rain had begun to fall, and all around them umbrellas popped open. People here paid attention to the weather forecast. The fields in Ireland were green for a very good reason. Cupples turned up the collar of his jacket and made his way across the street to the outdoor cafe. He ordered a cup of tea and a coffee then sat under one of the patio umbrellas.

"Nothing like baiting a tiger in its lair," he commented.

Riordan took a sip of coffee. It was awful. The Irish were not renowned for their coffee, and times had not changed. "Irish" coffee, now that was a different matter, but now was not the time. "You might have warned me we were meeting O'Brien. That came as a bit of a shock."

Cupples shrugged. "I wasn't sure he'd even be there, so there was no point. He ran Dempsey, so if anyone can find him, he can. And don't let the frail demeanour fool you either. He's one of the most vicious bastards I've ever come across, and when he saw the writing on the wall in the North, he simply moved his activities down here, along with an assortment of ex-IRA terrorists, and set up shop. There's not much that gets past the old bastard, and when some of the villains here in Dublin complained about him muscling in on their territory, they simply vanished. Rumour has it that many of them are encased in concrete barrels at the bottom of the Irish Sea."

"That was quite the stunt with the sniper."

Cupples grinned. "I figured he'd do something like that, just to prove a point. My guy would have spotted him right away and put him out of commission."

"And what did the son do, if I may ask?"

"He got caught at Liverpool docks with a boat full of heroin. Seems it's a lucrative commodity over here at the moment. I saw an opportunity to squeeze O'Brien and did so. As I said, smuggling drugs is the least of my worries presently, as we're more focused on weapons and explosives. The IRA ran a lot of the supply routes into England, and some of these terror groups may attempt to use the same routes. The suppliers don't care who they provide weapons to as long as they have money to pay."

Cupples sipped his tea and made a face. "I think the Liffey would taste better, or maybe that's where yer man gets his water!"

"So why are you planning to send him the files? Don't you want to use him some more?" Riordan asked.

Cupples shook his head. "He's used up, and most of the stuff he's been passing isn't worth my time following up on. No, if he can give you Dempsey, that's as much as I can ask for now."

"Thanks for doing this, Arthur," Riordan said.

"Don't mention it, lad. It was the least I could do."

The rain increased in intensity, the surface of the mighty river, the sweet Anna Liffey of song, dimpling with raindrops, and a wind blew up, driving the rain under their umbrella. "Let's go," Arthur said. "We'll catch a drink at the Temple Bar Hotel and decide on what to do next. Text yer pal over there and tell him to meet us at the bar."

Riordan did so quickly then followed Cupples across O'Connell Bridge, turned right down Aston Quay, and then crossed the road and headed down the slick cobblestones of Prince's Lane, which ended at Fleet Street. The Temple Bar Hotel was just a few steps along from the end of the lane. Cupples grabbed a table, Riordan slid in beside him, and moments later Sean appeared, shaking the rain out of his hair like a wet dog.

"Everything go okay?" he asked.

Riordan nodded. "Got some more info, but not exactly what we hoped for. Maybe in the next day or so."

"What do you want to do now?" Cupples asked. "Me, I've got to get back as I've got an important briefing this evening at the office, so you can come back with me or wait here."

Riordan shook his head. "We'll wait. Call me if you get any further information, and I'll follow it up from here. Other than that, I may head out to Dun Laoghaire and see what the brother has to say."

"Fair enough." Cupples took out his BlackBerry, selected a number, and held the phone to his ear. "Temple Bar Hotel, ten minutes," he said and broke the connection.

"I take it that's our angel," Riordan commented.

Cupples laughed. "I'll tell him you said so. That'll make his day."

"Anyone want a drink?" Sean asked.

Cupples shook his head. "I have to be rather sober for the briefing this evening, so I'll pass."

Riordan thought about it for a moment then realized he was hungry. "Let's get a bite to eat, Sean, before we do anything."

"Fair enough. The Terrace restaurant here in the hotel here serves pretty good grub, and besides, I don't feel like getting soaked again."

A few minutes later, outside the window Riordan saw the Range Rover pull to the curb and honk its horn. "That'll be me," Cupples said. "I'll be in touch, and try to stay out of trouble. I don't have as much influence with the authorities over here as I do elsewhere."

"Meaning?" Riordan asked.

Cupples shot him a dirty look. "Remember the couple of ne'er-do-wells from the Kilburn area who are being held under the prevention of terrorism act. I have more than one angel at my disposal!"

"Okay, Arthur, I get your point," Riordan said. "And thank you again."

*

Behind them, as soon as Cupples and Riordan had left the bar, Eamonn O'Brien opened his cellphone and dialled a number. "Follow them. I want to know every move they make, especially the big guy. No detail is too small, do ye hear me?" He closed the phone. To his son: "Talk to the boys across the way and find out what Dempsey did that has DeLisle on his tail. And find out if

Dempsey has been in touch with any of our people. He probably has enough papers to get around, but he may have been in need of new stuff. Talk to Michael Kiddie over on Mespil Road. He's the best forger around, and he's acquainted with Dempsey, so find out if there's been any contact. There's something big going on, and I want to know what it is."

*

"You've been pretty quiet," Sean said as their appetizers arrived. Riordan had ordered the Dublin Bay prawn cocktail, and it arrived accompanied by a basket of warm wheaten bread and a healthy slab of butter. Riordan could just picture the look on Nancy's face if she could see this. He took out his BlackBerry and snapped a quick photo. He'd send it later.

"Sorry, Sean," he offered. "That wasn't the most pleasant encounter I have ever had, and it stirred up a bit of old business that I'd rather forget. It seems your past really does come back to haunt you from time to time."

Sean made a weird sound, almost indignant, and said, "Isn't that the truth?" Riordan felt a story coming, and he welcomed the distraction. Besides, it would stop Sean from pressing further. Sean took a bite of his chilli shrimp, put down his cutlery, and wiped his mouth with the napkin. "A few years ago, I was going out with this bird called Carol, and her da decided to build a glazed-in porch around the back door of the house to keep the draft down a bit. He did it himself, to save a bit of money, and when it came time to put in the glass, he asked me to help him. What made it tricky was that the porch was at the top of a flight of stairs, so we had to use ladders to lift the last piece into place. So we're up there, hanging on to this huge pane of glass, and he's trying to get it into the frame. Somehow, he's made a mistake with the measurements, and the fit is really tight, so he's bending the glass a bit to get it in place. I'm about to point out that glass doesn't bend well when the fucking pane snaps in half, all the way across the middle, and the top bit slides down over the lower piece like a guillotine and hits my thumb." Sean paused to take a sip of wine.

"Then," he continued, "blood is spurting everywhere, and my bird, who's a trainee nurse, decides that I have to have stitches. Her da takes me to the hospital, a doctor puts three stitches in my thumb — all without anaesthetic I might add — and I'm about to leave when he tells me I need a tetanus shot. He calls for a nurse, the curtain gets drawn back, and there is Alison. You see, Alison and I had gone out for a while, and it did not end well. So, I start rolling up my sleeve, and she shakes her head and points at my trousers. 'Drop them' she says, and I do and lean over the gurney. I think she got the biggest fucking needle she could find, then went to the end of the ward and sprinted, launching it into me arse like a javelin. To this day I think she damaged something. So I know what you're talkin' about."

Riordan laughed so hard, he almost choked on a prawn and coughed and spluttered, his eyes filling with tears. "Jesus, Sean, you always have a story. Even when we were kids, you could always make us laugh."

After they finished, they walked down the street to a taxi stand and grabbed the first in line, the cabbie only too happy to drive them out to Dun Laoghaire. Riordan knew it was a big fare, but the only alternative was the 8A bus, and it stopped frequently. The cabbie, a jovial Dubliner, entertained them along the way. He was a rugby fan and was very much looking forward to the big game coming at Lansdowne Road, part of the Six Nations Cup. The match was against England, which was historically a politically charged rivalry.

Sean and the cabbie got into a detailed and animated discussion about the tournament, and Riordan was surprised at the depth of his knowledge about the team, the players, and the competition. It was a welcome respite. He let them ramble on as they made their way out through the suburbs, through Donnybrook and onto the Stillorgan Road. From there the pace picked up, and they were soon turning off onto Mount Merrion and south toward the coast. As soon as the sea came into view, the cabbie asked where they wanted to be dropped. When Sean mentioned the pub, the cabbie nodded.

"Aye, tis a grand place, and it's been there for years. Do a good pint, they do, and the grub's pretty good as well." Coming unsolicited from a cabbie, Riordan knew the recommendation would be accurate. Given their profession, cabbies were privy to conversations about pubs and food and built their own directory of reviews.

When they stopped outside the pub, Riordan paid the man and gave him a good tip. The rain had stopped, and a stiff breeze blew off the ocean, just a couple of blocks away from the pub. Seagulls swooped and perched precariously on TV antennas attached to the side of chimneys of the houses. Dark clouds, heavy with rain, scudded across the horizon. Adjacent, a ten-storey office building towered over the pub, all of its windows facing out over the bay. Heavy sheets of plywood, painted blue and topped with barbed wire, were mounted across the front entrance of the building, the entrance sealed with a brand-new padlock. The building was an obvious victim of the recent recession. A couple of scooters were parked on the sidewalk, and several small cars, mostly fuel-conscious Renaults and Toyotas, lined the narrow street.

Inside, the room was quiet. Three men sat at the bar, their heads upturned toward a TV screen in the corner of the room, and half-empty pints accompanied shot glasses in front of them. A soccer match was in progress. There were also a few twos and threes sitting at tables scattered around. It was obviously a local bar; heads turned for a closer look at the pair who had just walked in the door. Both hands resting on the bar, the barman's triceps stood out large in profile against his black Guinness t-shirt. He was obviously a fan of pumping iron, and in a bar like this that would probably be a good thing, Riordan thought.

It seemed like most bartenders these days were required to double as bouncers. The local gym had replaced hours of drinking with the locals. The place itself possessed an air of neglect; the wooden floor was scratched and worn, the furniture old and heavy, tired old posters on the wall, their corners curling against the pins that held them in place. Spider veins criss-crossed the surface of the painted walls in places, and a dusty tricolour flag hung on the wall behind the bar.

The only thing that looked out of place were the gleaming brass taps on the bar, polished to a high sheen. Pub owners took pride in the quality of their product. The air was filled with the scent of a deep-fat fryer, but then again, this was Ireland, where the mantra "If it's not fried, it's not food" was repeated over and over. Sean sniffed the air like a hound dog picking up a trail.

The barman pushed himself up from his position and crossed his arms, the bulging biceps now on display. A wild mop of dark, curly hair covered his head, and a gold stud containing a sizeable diamond glinted in the low light cast multi-hued prisms of color across one ear lobe. Riordan could never remember if that was still a gay thing or not. His nose had been broken and reset a couple of times, and there was a bit of scar tissue around his eyes. Maybe he was a boxer, or perhaps an overly enthusiastic bouncer. Dun Laoghaire, despite the boats and the ferry and the tourist trappings, had a reputation of being a tough town.

"What can I get yiz?" came the gruff demand.

Riordan slipped on to a bar stool and Sean did the same. "We've been told you serve a good pint, so I think we'll sample your fare."

On hearing the accent, the barman grinned, revealing nicotine-stained teeth. The bottom two teeth were chipped, the others well in need of a visit to the dentist. He busied himself at the taps, and Riordan took the opportunity to scan the wall behind, where several crinkled photographs had been tacked to a cork noticeboard. The barman was in a few, while others looked like they had been taken from a fishing trip where patrons were holding their catch — maybe a pub trip — and some from a golf outing. The barman had several different females in the photos, standing with his arm around them, and then in one, he had his arms around what looked like sisters, both with mops of wild curly hair. It was an old photo, since in it the barman had dark, curly hair. The three looked like they could all be related.

A few minutes later, two pristine pints sat in front of them. "You'll find no better in the town," the barman said. Riordan tossed a twenty Euro note on the bar.

"Keep the change," he said.

"Tourists, are yiz?" the man asked. "I hear a bit of an accent." The twenty-Euro bill disappeared into his pocket.

"Are you the owner?" Riordan asked, and the man nodded. "That's good," Riordan continued. "You're the man I need to talk to."

A wary look crossed the man's face. "Oh aye?"

Riordan sipped the pint, enjoying the creamy head and the malty nectar underneath. "Now, that's a good pint." He set the pint back on the bar. "To business then..."

The barman eased his neck from side to side slowly, like a boxer about to start the round, the creaks audible. His body tensed, and his arms dropped loosely to his sides. He tried to stare Riordan down, but Riordan just grinned.

"Lose the attitude, pal," Riordan growled. "You're way out of your league. I've got a couple of questions, and then we'll be out of here."

"You'll fuck off now," spat the barman, pointing toward the door. The other locals turned to watch, this little incident more interesting than the soccer match. It was something they had witnessed before. Riordan didn't move. The barman grabbed their pints, emptied them into the sink, then came storming out of the end of the bar and up to face Riordan. He had worked up a good head of steam by that point and was spoiling for a fight. He clenched and unclenched his fists.

Riordan slipped off the bar stool and stood up. At six four, he was a good four or five inches taller than the barman, and at two hundred and forty pounds, most of it was muscle except for the parts that Nancy pulled at from time to time. He gave most combatants pause for thought.

Flecks of spittle erupted from the barman's mouth. "I told yiz to fuck..."

Riordan hit him hard, straight knuckles to the throat, his hand a blur. The barman's eyes widened, and both hands instantly went to his throat, weird, gurgling sounds emanating from his mouth. Riordan grasped him by the elbow, his thumb digging painfully into a nerve cluster located there. The momentary resistance faded, and the barman allowed himself to be directed to a barstool. Drool streamed from his mouth.

Placing his head close to the barman, Riordan said quietly, "I can keep this up all night, so if you're smart, you'll answer my questions."

There was more gagging, but the barman nodded.

"You have a sister called Elva. Correct?"

A nod.

"Elva has hooked up with a very bad person called Sean Dempsey, ex-IRA, who works, or should I say 'worked' for a man called Max DeLisle. Max is a big cheese in the London mob and wants to find Dempsey. He hired me to do the job, and in the course of my search I discover that Dempsey's girlfriend, Elva, has also vanished. So I'm doing everything I can to find this guy, which brings me to you. Where is Elva?"

A shake of the head. Riordan pushed the guy's head up to see eyes that had teared up. "You should be able to speak by now," Riordan said. "I've got it down to a fine science. Just hard enough to stop you in your tracks and give you a moment to contemplate life, or hard enough to crush your larynx, which also gives you a moment or two to contemplate life before you die."

"I don't know where Elva is," the barman whispered, his voice pained. "Last I heard she was living in Chiswick, but that was a few months ago. I get the odd call, but we don't stay in touch."

"Do you have a number for her?"

Another shake of the head. "No. She travels about a lot, so she always calls the pub from a callbox." Riordan stared at the barman as he asked the questions, looking for any microexpressions that might show he was lying. So far, though, the barman was telling the truth. And so far, another dead end.

"Let's go," he said to Sean and went outside.

They walked back up to the main street and waited by the taxi stand until a cab showed up. "Drop us at the Westin Hotel," he ordered, and the cabbie sped off. The drive took less than fifteen minutes, and when they got out, Riordan looked around to get his bearings and then headed off down the street. When he got to College Green he turned left and walked along to Temple Lane, Sean in tow.

"Where are we going?" Sean grumbled. Apparently, he wasn't a big fan of walking anywhere.

"Down to Wellington Key," Riordan replied. "I made reservations at the Clarence, just in case we had to stay over."

Sean grinned. "Brilliant, that's Bono's hotel, and I always wanted to stay there. So why did you get us dropped off at the Westin?"

"Force of habit, I guess. Just in case the barman wanted to report us, and the police did want to get involved, they might trace the cab who picked us up. And he'd tell them..."

"...that he dropped us at the Westin." Sean finished the sentence. "Jesus, isn't it just like a movie? And you do this for a living?"

"Some days are better than others," Riordan said.

As they walked, Sean said, "Did you hear about the U2 concert in Glasgow?"

Riordan shook his head. He hadn't seen anything in the newspapers and usually picked up on articles about the band. He was fan of their music, thought the Edge was a musical genius, but had no time for Bono and his quasipolitical ramblings during their concerts.

"It's a great story. You know the way Bono's always pontificating about world hunger or some such cause during the concerts."

Riordan nodded. Apparently, he wasn't the only one annoyed by such things.

"Anyway," Sean continued, "he stops after one song and starts clapping his hands slowly, once every few seconds. Then he says, 'Every time I clap my hands, a child in Africa dies.' True to form, some Scotsman in the audience yells out, 'Maybe you should stop clappin' yer fucking hands then.' The crowd went wild over that one, and that shut him up for a while."

When they got to the hotel, Riordan went straight to reception and checked them in. He had used one of his "special" credit cards under the name Richard Hede to hold the reservations for himself and Sean. After signing the paperwork and receiving their room keys, Sean headed for the bar to see if he could meet Bono or anybody else famous.

CHAPTER 11

TOFINO

The bald eagle twisted in the air, its massive sixty-six-inch wings beating gracefully as it descended into the nest perched atop the majestic cedar, one in a stand of many that surrounded the Wickaninnish Inn. Located on Chesterman Beach, just outside Tofino, the place was a surfers' paradise hiding on the northern coast of Vancouver Island.

A whole salmon, freshly plucked from the ocean, twisted in its death throes held firm in the mighty talons. Through the open windows of the loft suite, a series of chirping whistles, harsh and shrill, arose from the two young birds in the nest. It was feeding time, and the woman watched through a pair of binoculars as the two chicks that she had named Susan and Desmond tore into the salmon. Picking up her camera, she balanced the lens on the windowsill and then proceeded to snap of series of images of the birds.

They had seemed to grow larger and stronger over the two weeks that she had been staying at the inn, and the feeding times could almost be set by the clock. Then, turning the camera toward the beach, she spotted the solitary runner in the distance, heading back toward the inn. The beach stretched for miles. Each day she walked along its twisted shores, examining tiny relics that had been brought in by the tide with the enthusiasm of a small child. In the rocks that dotted the shore she marvelled at the masses of red and purple starfish stranded by the receding tide. The locals told her that if she was lucky, very lucky, she might just end up with a Japanese glass float. The hand-blown pieces, looking like big glass bubbles, were used by Japanese fisherman to keep their nets afloat. She hadn't found one yet, but she had high hopes, since this was home now. Staying at the inn was a special treat until the real estate person found them a more permanent home.

She had read about the history of the place, and the people, and had been introduced to the Haida culture by her sister's husband, a local artist who made a substantial living selling original oil paintings, all heavily influenced by the images and culture of his people.

Tofino was located in a remote, very remote, geographical region of Vancouver Island called Clayoquot Sound, which suited their purposes perfectly. The Nuu-chah-nulth First Nations had made Clayoquot Sound their home for several thousand years, and one of the villages on a local island was thought to have been continuously inhabited for at least the past five thousand years. She had booked a trip later in the week to visit the place.

The earliest recorded European contact with Vancouver Island's First Nations residents occurred just north of Clayoquot

Sound, between Estevan Point and the Escalante River. In 1774 Captain Juan Pérez was sent north by the viceroy of New Spain to reassert the long-standing Spanish claim on the west coast of North America. After some trading with the Haida people from aboard his ship, the *Santiago*, Pérez turned south and made contact with another first Nations tribe, and the place was named Perez Rocks after him.

Pérez preceded the more celebrated Captain James Cook, who arrived three years later at Nootka Island, in the spring of 1778. As usual, a fact that was not wasted on her, Cook claimed the region for Britain, giving rise to heated verbal and written exchanges between the British and the Spanish. During a later exploration of Vancouver Island by two Spanish captains, Galiano and Valdez, the southernmost area was given the name Tofino Inlet, the name honouring Vincente Tofiño, a Spanish hydrographer who had taught Galiano cartography during the expedition.

Tofino was officially established in 1909 but in the early sixties was a haven for draft dodgers and hippies who then let it be known that the surfing was amazing. It was another of things she intended to try and had made arrangements with the local surf school to give them both lessons. It was booked for two days out, and she was looking forward immensely to riding the waves. Many times she had watched in awe as the black-clad surfers cut in and out of the heavy surf with such grace. Her sister, of all people, was an avid rider and owned her own blue wetsuit and custom board.

Down below, the solitary figure pounded across the last hundred yards toward the villa at a sprint, his feet throwing up tiny wisps of hard-packed sand. The grey t-shirt was dark with sweat, the tightly muscled body flexing as he ran. She smiled, turned on the taps in the large, two-person soaker tub overlooking the beach, and poured in a generous helping of the aromatic oils that she had purchased at the spa. She lit a few candles, slipped off her dressing gown, and appraised herself in the mirror.

At forty-five years old, she was still in good shape, maintained through an intensive daily regimen of Pilates, yoga, and cardio. There were no grey hairs yet, despite the stresses and strains of the past few years, and she cupped her breasts and raised them a little. They were still firm and highly sensitive, but lately she felt that they had started that inexorable sag. Still, Sean adored them, and that was good enough for her. Tying her mad red tresses back with a ribbon, she stepped into the bath and sank blissfully into the warm water.

It had been a long time since she had been so spoiled, if ever. They had booked the Canopy suite, the best the inn had to offer, considered by all who had stayed there previously as the ultimate accommodation. At nine hundred square feet, it was bigger than most of her previous apartments. The thought of the dingy basement apartment in Chiswick, even though it had only been temporary, made her cringe.

The panoramic view of the bay through floor-to-ceiling windows that stretched right across the room took her breath away.

335

The tandem bath was her favourite, but they had had a few romps already in the multi-jet shower that comfortably accommodated two.

The suite came equipped with a chef-designed kitchen, and the first night they arrived, arrangements had been made to have one of the chefs from the inn cook a private dinner for them. For her, a simple lass from the back streets of Belfast, this was as close to heaven as it got.

The room door clicked open, and suddenly there he was, all six feet of him dripping with sweat and panting heavily. She brushed the suds away from her breasts, her nipples full and hard, and he groaned. "Now there's a sight for sore eyes." He laughed.

His clothes fell to the floor as he ripped them off, and she was delighted to see him hardening before her eyes. "I hope you've got some energy left," she said, grasping his cock firmly as he stepped into the bath. She washed him gently, using a small cloth to get rid of the suds, then took him into her mouth, feeling his blood pulse in his veins, his hardness driving her crazy with desire.

"This one's for me," she said, pushing him down and straddling him and sliding his engorged cock all the way inside her.

"Jesus, Elva," he exclaimed, as his hands grasped her hips. "You're trying to kill me."

She laughed and kissed him. "Ah, darlin', me mother always said it's hard to kill a bad thing."

"Well, she's probably right about that," Sean Dempsey replied.

Later, dressed in the plush white robes from the room, they had supper by the fire and then headed off to bed. The eaglets had quieted for the night, sated by the constant feed of salmon. Dempsey wrapped his arms around her, and she fell asleep to the sounds of the winds in the trees outside the window and the gentle rushing of the waves against the shore.

All was at peace.

CHAPTER 12

IRELAND

Riordan threw off his clothes, slipped below the sheets, and expelled a huge breath like a deflating balloon. The feel of the sheets tight around him, combined with the expanse of the huge bed, made him feel relaxed, albeit for a fleeting moment. Closing his eyes, he took a few long, cleansing breaths, and then slipped his hand out of the bed and grabbed his cellphone. It was time to check in with Billy K. He flipped to the call menu and pressed the number.

"Yeah?" came a voice after a couple of rings. A heavy bass beat pounded in the background, and Riordan heard the chatter of excited voices. Closing time at the pub.

"It's me," Riordan said.

"Hold on for a sec," came the reply.

Riordan heard a door slam, and the background chatter ceased instantly.

"Okay, what have you got?"

"There's still no sign of Dempsey, or his girlfriend, but I've managed to track down her brother. He owns a pub out in Dun

Laoghaire called McKenna's. They don't keep in touch frequently, but he heard from her a couple of months ago. I saw him earlier tonight..."

"What the fuck? You're in Ireland?"

"Your grasp of geography is staggering, Billy. I'm trying to find Dempsey, so I'll go wherever I need."

"Watch your lip, you cunt," came the gruff reply. "What's his name?"

Riordan smiled. It was always fun to bait a bully like Billy K. The fact that he had such a short fuse could always be used to Riordan's advantage. Assholes with a bad temper tended to lose control quickly when pressured, and that often led to mistakes in judgement. Jails were full of people who had lost their temper, lashed out in the heat of the moment, and caused a grievous, if not fatal injury. He passed the name on to Billy then agreed to call at the same time the following evening to provide a further update.

*

Billy K closed the connection and stared out across the river at the lights of the O2 Arena. The masses of cars parked outside the arena showed there was some event happening. A garbage scow headed south toward the estuary, rocking on the tide, gulls swooping in like miniature jets on strafing runs. The scows ran mostly at night so as not to ruin the postcard-perfect images for visiting tourists. Billy K had made use of their facilities more than once. Taking out his cigarettes, he lit up and blew a long stream of smoke into the night air. A door opened behind him, and Max DeLisle stepped out.

"What's the word from our boy?" DeLisle asked.

"He's a mouthy cunt," Billy K snorted, "I'll give him that. He's in Dublin..."

"What the fuck?" DeLisle fumed.

"Oh, it gets better." Billy K took a long drag on the cigarette. "I heard a few dickie birds about some guy hammering a few of the locals over in Kilburn the other night. From the sounds of it, it was our guy, but nobody can confirm anything as they're locked up tighter than a Scotsman's wallet. So maybe he's chasing down a lead or two. He says he's found Dempsey's girlfriend's brother running a pub out in Dun Laoghaire. Dempsey and this chick were going at it hot and heavy, keeping it on the quiet, and she disappeared along with Dempsey."

"Fuck me," DeLisle exclaimed, somewhat mollified. "He certainly has got farther than we did, and in only a couple of days. I told you, Billy, it takes one to know one. So what's he going to do next?"

Billy K shrugged. "Fucked if I know. Maybe lean on the brother some more. He said the two kept in touch, although it was infrequent."

DeLisle stared out across the dark waters, silent for a few moments. Then he grinned. "Get the car, Billy, and call ahead to the airport and have the boys get the plane ready. We're taking a trip to the Emerald Isle. I've got a better idea."

DeLisle turned on his heel and went inside, leaving Billy K at the railing, fumbling with his phone. Max tended to be a bit impulsive at times, and sometimes reckless, if the truth were known. Billy K felt the beginnings of an uneasy feeling stirring in his gut, like a seedling of grass pushing up through the soil. It was one thing to take chances on their own manor, but to do something mad in a different country could lead to serious consequences. Still, Max would not tolerate anyone questioning his authority, so Billy scrolled through his contacts and pressed the call button. The pilots were on standby 24/7, so the phone was answered immediately.

"Get the plane ready. Max and me will be there in about thirty minutes. He wants to go to Dublin."

"Dublin?"

"Yes, fucking Dublin," snarled Billy K.

341

CHAPTER 13

NANAIMO

Just after 2:00 a.m. the phone rang. Elva picked it up and heard her sister's voice, almost hysterical, and her world fell apart. It was like one of those dreams when you think you are falling off a tall building.

Rubbing tired eyes, she tried to keep her voice under control. "For fuck's sake, Mairead, I can barely understand a word you're saying. Take a breath and tell it to me again, from the beginning. "She felt Dempsey behind her, one arm encircling her waist.

"What's the matter, love?" he asked.

"I'm putting you on speaker phone so Sean can hear," she said and pressed the speaker button on the cordless phone. Through the static she heard Mairead take a deep breath.

"Mammy just phoned, and she's in bits. The Gards are just after calling round to tell her that Frank is dead. Somebody shot him. They say they found a lot of drugs around his house, and they think it might be related." Elva knew that the Gards, the colloquial name for An Garda Síochána, Ireland's national police force, were fighting a losing battle in the war against drugs, especially in Dublin, which was a major transshipment point for all of Europe. She knew that Frank did make a bit of money dealing on the side, despite the many warnings she had given him. With the influx of Eastern Europeans into Ireland, the trade had become that much more brutal as various gangs battled for control.

She felt Sean's arm tighten around her, his breath warm on her neck. "Are they looking at anybody for this?" she asked. "Does she know?"

"No, no, she's beside herself right now. Her neighbours are in with her, and Uncle Michael is on his way over. We'll get more out of him."

Elva sighed and looked out the window at the distant lights of a passing freighter. *So much for peace*, she thought. "I'll book you and me on the next flight home, so pack a bag. I think there's a regular 9:00 a.m. flight from Vancouver to London, and that'll get us into Heathrow at six tomorrow morning. We can grab the shuttle from there. Sean'll drive us down to Nanaimo, so get your stuff together and we'll be over in ten minutes."

She broke the connection, replaced the phone, turned into his comforting arms, and he held her tightly until the violent paroxysm of tears had ceased. "Ah, Jesus, Sean, my wee brother's dead. Frank's dead. Will it never fucking end? I was so happy here."

"Do you want me to come with you?"

She shook her head. "No, love, you need to find us a house, a home where I can see the ocean and never have to think of things like this again. I'll be back as soon as we get things sorted. Uncle Michael will be dealing with the arrangements for the funeral and all that, and after the funeral I'll be on the next flight back. I love you." She kissed him fiercely, then got up and busied herself with packing, grateful for the momentary distraction of having to deal with practical things. As she did so, Sean was on the phone booking their flights.

CHAPTER 14

LURGAN

Riordan slept fitfully, tossing and turning through the night, and found himself waking up on the right side of the bed, Nancy's usual spot in their own bed at home. As often before, when she was working the night shift, he would unconsciously look for her in the night, seeking the comfort of her body. For him, worries would seem to dissipate, like steam from a kettle, when she was close. Perhaps it was her endless capacity for love or the total devotion that he felt from her that saved his soul from the darkness that from time to time threatened to envelop him in its grasp. He was always reminded of one of his favourite Irish folk songs, "The Rare Ould Times," where the main character referred to himself and his love as a "rogue and a child of Mary, from the rebel Liberties." That certainly fit the bill when it came to describing Nancy and him.

His cellphone vibrated again — he had set it to vibrate during the night so that he might have some peace — but when he picked it up he saw that Cupples had phoned four times in the past hour. There were voice messages, but he pushed the redial button and was immediately connected.

"Arthur, it's me, Daniel," he said. "What's so urgent?"

"Listen, kiddo," came a harsh voice, "what the fuck did you do last night?"

Riordan rolled his feet to the floor, rotating his neck from side to side, hearing the ever-present creaks as he stretched it out.

"What do you mean, Arthur? We got back from Dun Laoghaire around eleven, had a couple of pints, and I came to bed. By the way, I need you to check his phone records for me. He says that Elva calls him from time to time, so there might be something worth following up there."

"Forget that," Cupples snarled. "If she was smart, she'd have used a 'burner,' a throwaway cellphone. But you have got bigger worries. Frank McCormick was shot and killed last night, and the police are all over it. They're treating it as some sort of drug thing, as McCormick has had one or two run-ins with the law already for possession. The bad thing is they are looking for two men who apparently had an altercation with him just before closing time. You fucking two..."

"Listen, Arthur," Riordan interrupted. "He was alive and kicking when we left, and that's the truth. If I whacked him, I would tell you."

Riordan heard the breathing pattern on the other end of the phone change and realized that Cupples had thought that he was

346

responsible for McCormick's death. Given his past history, that wasn't such a long stretch. "Listen, Arthur, what should we do?"

"There's no 'we' anymore," Cupples said. "Send your friend away home. This isn't his world, and he'll only get in your way. You know how to handle yourself, and you've still got to find Dempsey. I'll see what I can find out through my sources, but this is where I need to tread lightly. I'll be in touch when I can."

Riordan looked at the time. Seeing it was almost nine, he rolled out of bed and showered quickly. Pulling on a fresh set of clothes, he called Sean and went downstairs to the restaurant to get some breakfast. He ordered from a harried waitress and quickly scanned the morning newspaper, casting an eye about the room. It was packed, which was a good thing. Sean showed up a few moments later, looking somewhat bleary-eyed.

"I ordered a pot of coffee and a full Irish breakfast for us. You're going to need it."

Sean rubbed his face. "Jesus, you've got a face like a Lurgan spade. What's the matter now?" Just as he did so, the waitress arrived with a plateful of hot food. Riordan was hungry, so he gobbled down a couple of mouthfuls of sausage. There was nothing to compare with a full Irish breakfast.

"You remember our trip to the bar last night?"

Sean nodded.

"Some time after we left, Frank McCormick was shot and killed." Riordan gave him a moment or two to digest that revelation.

Sean's brow furrowed. "Are the cops looking for us?"

Riordan nodded.

"Jesus, I'm a wanted man ... me and Johnny Cash!" Sean grinned.

Riordan shook his head. This was hardly the reaction he expected. "We've got to split up, Sean, as the police will be wanting to question anyone who came in contact with Frank, and they're probably chasing down the cab drivers in the area. Your background is easy to corroborate, but mine, that's another matter."

"So what do you..." Sean looked up past Riordan's shoulder, a puzzled look on his face.

Riordan felt a hand grip his shoulder, and a familiar scent wafted into his nostrils.

"Well, well, look what the cat dragged in, Billy," said Max DeLisle. "Mind if we join you?"

Riordan nodded, his mind racing, as DeLisle and Billy K took the two free seats at the table. Both men were freshly showered and shaved, and Billy K had doused himself in aftershave. Max DeLisle was dressed in a blue button-down Oxford shirt and a pair of khakis, and Billy wore his standard uniform of a soccer jersey and jeans. The waitress appeared, and

DeLisle looked at their plates. "We'll have whatever they're having, love," he said.

DeLisle carefully unfurled the green linen napkin and placed the cutlery on the placemat, lining it up just so. Billy K did the same.

Riordan waited.

He tried to think of how DeLisle could have tracked them to the hotel, since he hadn't noticed a trail, and there was no tracking device. Those were easy to find.

"Don't look so shocked," DeLisle offered. "We're just as surprised as you are. Billy here has wanted to stay at Bono's hotel, so we checked in. We were about to have a bit of nosh when I look across the room, and there you are. Who's your friend?"

"I'm Sean Daly," Sean said, but no hand was offered in greeting.

DeLisle looked at Riordan. "He knows?"

Riordan nodded.

"Fair enough," DeLisle said. "In for a penny..."

"It was you," Riordan said quietly, the thoughts in his head coalescing. "You killed him."

"Sometimes you just have to move things along," DeLisle replied. "You done good, but rather than wait for some more poncing about, I figured that since she's family, she'd come home for the funeral. And if Dempsey and her are an item, as you seem to think, then he'll show as well. A good result all around, don't you think?"

Riordan was immediately reminded of a question that was posed to students at the Behavioral Science Unit at the FBI headquarters in Virginia, where those who wished to become profilers and the track the most evil of predators were trained. The scenario outlined that when two sisters, in their thirties, and both single, attended their mother's funeral, a dark, handsome stranger showed up. One sister was attracted to the man but did not get a chance to meet him. Shortly after the funeral, she kills her sister. Why would she kill? There were many suggestions as to the reason, but the real answer, from the FBI files, was that the woman thought that if the handsome man showed for her mother's funeral, he would show up again for her sister's funeral.

Riordan stilled his breathing. In his world, the underbelly of society, people were often used as pawns. From his early beginnings in Belfast, he well understood that sometimes those pawns had to be sacrificed for the greater good. However, in this case there was no greater good. This was simply DeLisle protecting his turf and his reputation, and on a base level he understood the strategy, but Frank McCormick wasn't an evil person; he was merely a means to an end.

"What happens now?" Riordan asked.

"We watch, we wait," DeLisle said. "The funeral will likely be tomorrow or the day after, so we do a bit of observation, covert style, and hope that Dempsey appears. If not, we grab the woman, and Billy here can have a bit of a chat with her. He's very good at making people talk."

Billy K grinned. "I learned from the master."

"Eat your breakfast, or it'll go cold," DeLisle ordered.

"Nah," Riordan replied. "I've lost my appetite. Let me know when the funeral is going to be and how you want to handle things. Billy's got my number." He got up from the table, and Sean did the same.

"Suit yourself," DeLisle replied, picking up the newspaper and flicking it open. They were dismissed.

In the lobby, Riordan quickly took out his cellphone, scrolled through his contacts, and dialled a number.

"Featherstone here."

"Feather, it's me, Daniel. Listen, things have gone pear-shaped over here."

"Over where?"

"I'm in Dublin. DeLisle and Billy K are here. I tracked down Dempsey's girlfriend, Elva McCormick, and she has a brother living just outside Dublin. Or had ... we went to see him last night, had a bit of a row, and then I reported in to DeLisle. Following our conversation, he got the brilliant idea that if he offed the brother, Elva and perhaps Dempsey would show for the funeral, so that's what he did. DeLisle and Billy K are staying at the Clarence Hotel."

"Shit. The guy's a psycho!"

"And then some ... however, since he's here, his place in London will be empty and will be for a few days. That should give you some uninterrupted time."

"I see," came the reply. "I've got a couple of guys lined up, so they'll have a look around inside the place today and see what they can find. I'll keep you posted." Featherstone broke the connection.

"Nasty piece of work," Sean commented. "And the bastard kept me from my breakfast."

Riordan laughed. "Jesus, Sean, if it's not eating, it's drinking..."

"And don't forget the sexing!"

"Alright, alright. Let's get out of here and go and get you some breakfast. I've got a couple of days to kill before there will be any movement here, so I can at least feed you before you head home."

Sean nodded, a sad look crossing his face like a cloud passing in front of the sun on a summer's day. "Funny thing, isn't it. I haven't had as much fun in a long time as I've had in the last few days. Pretty sad comment about my life, isn't it?"

"I'd hardly call it fun," Riordan replied. "It's the element of danger that gets everyone excited. Except here the conflicts are real — this isn't a movie where the actors get up after they've been shot. These people are dangerous, and as you just heard, they kill, like feral animals. The thing that worries me most is that DeLisle has you on his radar, and that's not a good place to be. You are a witness to one of the top crime bosses in London admitting to complicity in a murder, and witnesses don't seem to survive long around DeLisle. He uses people, just like he's doing to me, exploits their weaknesses, and then puts the screws to them. If he didn't have this thing hanging over me, I'd fucking gut him."

"Remind me to stay on your good side." Sean laughed.

They had breakfast at a small cafe on the quay, and then Sean suggested taking the train to Belfast for the night. His house was not far from the Central Station, or they could get a room at the Europa, "for old time's sake." Thinking it wasn't such a bad idea to get out of Dublin, Riordan agreed, and they checked out of their hotel and caught the 1:00 p.m. Enterprise express to Belfast. Riordan bought tickets in the first-class coach, as Sean suggested, because they served drinks all the way to Belfast.

Several beers later, they arrived at just after 3:00 p.m. at Central Station, the rain lashing against the windows with an intimidating ferocity. Heavy rain clouds hung low out over the lough, the buildings almost invisible under the onslaught. The covered platform offered little respite as the rain was blowing in almost horizontal, soaking everyone who stepped down, and umbrellas were ineffectual against the wind. Some brave souls attempted to open large golf-type umbrellas, only to have them snatched from their hands and hurled away into the distance. Riordan turned up the collar of his jacket and smiled.

A summer's day in Belfast.

353

The Raven was home.

Outside, they caught one of the infamous Belfast black taxis for the short ride to the Europa. Riordan had made reservations using the free Wi-Fi in first class for his iPad browser, and also checked on the status of the murder investigation in Dublin by scanning the local newspapers. It was one of many incidents in the *Irish Independent* relating to the drug trade, which had become so prolific that drug-related homicides were commonplace. The police had no leads and offered the pat "pursuing many lines of inquiry" to the reporter.

At the Europa, Riordan checked in while Sean headed across the road to the Crown Bar to try to "catch a bit of the match" and get a couple of pints in. There was always that momentary shiver when he walked through the glassed doors. The Europa had the distinction of being the most bombed hotel in Europe, having survived some twenty-eight attacks during the Troubles. During Riordan's time in Belfast, the hotel bar, called the Whip and Saddle, was a notorious gay hangout, which in his mind probably contributed to some of the attacks. The IRA were not fond of gay bars, or perhaps the fact that they tended not to pay their protection money.

He chose one of the new, air-conditioned rooms built in the new wing at the back of the hotel, and after getting to his room, changed into his other pair of jeans and hung the damp pair over the shower rail in the washroom. He smelled like a wet dog.

Back downstairs, he watched through the glass and waited until the traffic lights turned green, then sprinted across the road to the Crown. The rain stung his face like a hundred tiny needles. During the Troubles he had frequented the place, and some of the most barbarous acts of violence had been launched from this place, so it was little wonder that he found himself facing the doors, unable to go in. Taking a few deep breaths, he admonished himself quietly and went in.

The interior had not changed one iota, and for him it was truly like stepping back in time. Above him was the burnished primrose yellow, red, and gold ceiling, and in front of him the well-polished floor, laid in a myriad of mosaic tiles. Throughout the pub were many wood carvings, ornate mirrors, and wooden columns with Corinthian capitals and feathered gold motifs.

The long, red granite-topped bar, divided by columns, was faced with brightly coloured tiles and a heated footrest that came in handy on a day like today. The distinctive feature of the Crown, however, was the ten differently shaped, cosy, and elaborately carved wooden booths, better known as "snugs." Given their privacy, it was no wonder that much revolutionary conspiracy and many clandestine meetings took place in these little snugs. The place was crowded, most people focused on the soccer, and the air was full of the scent of beer and damp clothing.

Sean was not at the bar, so Riordan walked along the row of snugs until he found his friend, happily ensconced in one of the smaller booths, sipping a pint and watching the match. Several packets of Walker's Beef and Onion potato chips lay in front of him on the table. Riordan slipped into the booth and sat down then took a sip from the pint of Guinness. Above the door he saw a camera, pointing into the room.

"What's that?" he asked.

"That's the famous Crown Bar webcam," Sean replied, not taking his eyes off the TV.

"Really? Is it live streaming video?"

"Yep."

Riordan pulled out his cellphone and texted Nancy, who would probably just be getting up. There was an eight-hour time difference between local and Vancouver time, and a few times he had unfortunately woken her up in the middle of the night. So now he always did the mental math to calculate the time. The place was too noisy to have a conversation, so he texted her the web link for the webcam at crownbar.com and waited.

A few minutes later, he received a text back saying, *you could at least wave,* so he did, grinning like an idiot, and made Sean wave as well. He texted her a cryptic message, *will talk latr,* and received a happy face in return.

"Is that the wife?" Sean asked over his shoulder, barely taking his eyes off the screen.

"Yeah," Riordan replied, sighing. "She's a real trooper, that one. She got shot during one of my assignments, but she stays around."

"Shot, you say..." Sean turned around to face Riordan. "Maybe my life isn't so bad."

Riordan nodded. "The guy I was chasing grabbed her. The only way to slow me down was to put a bullet in her, not to kill but to maim, so that he could get away. He shot her in the lung, and when I got to her I thought she was going to die. That was the second-worst moment of my life."

Sean sipped his Guinness. "I can't imagine anything worse, so you might as well tell me. We'll be friends for a long time now."

"I was married once before," Riordan said, the memories flooding back. "And I had a little girl called Annie. I was living in Toronto at the time, and her mum and Annie had come back to England to visit Susan's parents. There was no way I could travel at the time 'cos there were too many people looking for me, so I happily packed them off and settled in for a couple of weeks of playing the bachelor." He paused and blew out a long stream of breath. "I was at work one day, waiting for them to arrive home, when my boss told me I should check with the airport. Turns out they were on the plane that had been hijacked by a bunch of Palestinian terrorists, and it was shot down by our own government just off the coast."

"I remember that," Sean said. "There was a whole thing about the prime minister and a cover-up and ... I saw it on the news. Someone had taken him hostage and..."

Riordan nodded. "That was me."

"But they said the kidnapper was killed..."

"That was the Old Man. He came to help me. When we got jammed up, he sacrificed himself to get me another chance."

"Wow," Sean said. "I don't know what to say to that. Except I am doubly glad I have a quiet life. We should probably have a 'wee one' to celebrate life, pal. I know how fragile it can be."

Several hours later, having consumed vast quantities of beer, followed by a porterhouse steak, dauphinoise potatoes, and onion rings for dinner in the restaurant, Riordan staggered across the road to the hotel, Sean in tow, and they both collapsed on the beds. Riordan was asleep in minutes.

*

In the Knightsbridge pub, just after closing time, Eamonn O'Brien's cellphone buzzed. He picked it up, flipped open the screen, and pressed the answer button. As he did so, he felt the cough start in his throat, a precursor to the spasms that were occurring much more frequently these days.

"Hold on."

He spat, grabbing a damp handkerchief from his pocket. The paroxysm started, and huge, wracking coughs bent him in two.

By the time it ended, the handkerchief was soaked in bloody phlegm. Those at the table with him, his closest friends, looked at him then at the bloody rag, knowing, as he did, that the end was not far off.

He stuffed the stained rag into his coat pocket then downed his shot of whiskey to help clear his throat. He motioned to his son. "Get another round in."

Picking up the phone, he said, "Talk to me."

"They're in Belfast."

O'Brien thought for a moment, processing this information. "Belfast?"

"Aye. They took the train to Belfast this afternoon and spent most of the night in the Crown acting like a couple of tourists. They're staying at the Europa. What do you want me to do?"

O'Brien sighed. *Fuck you, Arthur*, he thought to himself, and smiled. "They'd probably like to have a scenic tour of Lough Neagh. It's nice at this time of the year. None of those nosy tourists to bother anybody" He closed the phone just as the waitress brought the round. The others raised their glasses, knowing well what a "scenic tour" involved.

"To Ireland," he roared, and they clinked glasses.

CHAPTER 15

PATIENT

Elva and her sister sat quietly in their mother's living room, each balancing a cup of tea on their lap. The room was dark with the drapes pulled down, as was the tradition when there was a death in the family. The flight had been long but uneventful, and she had even managed to catch a few hours' sleep. When they landed in Heathrow, she had taken some melatonin to help ward off the effects of jet lag prior to catching the shuttle to Dublin.

In the kitchen, her Uncle Michael was on the phone again, this time making arrangements for the body to be released to the funeral home. He had taken care of most things already and had put the death notice in the daily newspapers. In lieu of flowers, her mother wanted people to donate to the Society of St. Vincent de Paul, a charitable organization that she had supported all her life. However, despite her religious leanings, her mother was an incredibly superstitious woman, and Elva had just listened to a litany of tasks that were to be undertaken when her brother's body arrived home. He was to be buried tomorrow, which meant the family would sit with the body during the night.

Her mother had repeated, several times, that in Ireland the dead are carried out of the house feet first in order to prevent the spirit from looking back into the house and beckoning another member of the family to follow him. Her mother had pointedly looked at both girls when she said she was happy that Martin had stayed at home in Ireland and not left. She reiterated her belief that the souls of the dead who die abroad all wished to be buried in Ireland and that the dead would not rest peaceably unless buried with their forefathers and people of their own kind. Which was her mother's roundabout way of saying the girls never should have left.

Elva could not stand it anymore, the heaping of the guilt, and so got up and went into the kitchen. Her uncle was sitting at the kitchen table, nursing a glass of whiskey. A retired homebuilder, now in his sixties, he still had a full head of dark wavy hair, and he kept his trim body in shape by running almost every day. He competed in the Dublin marathon each year, finishing in a time that would put much younger men to shame. A half full bottle of Jameson's whiskey sat on the table in front of him, and beside it his cellphone. She took a seat beside him.

"She's off on a tear, that one," he commented, nodding toward the living room. "I cannot imagine how she feels, nor you or your sister, but that oul shite she keeps telling me would try the patience of Job. It's all I've heard for the past couple of days, and some of this stuff she must have heard when she was growing up in the country. She told me that a dead hand is believed to be a cure for all diseases, and when she was a girl many times sick people were brought to a house where a corpse was laid out so that the hand of the dead might be laid on them. Feck me, I hope she doesn't start any of this when Frank comes home."

Elva smiled. "It's okay, Uncle Michael, we'll take care of her. I think she's still in shock, so we'll have to be patient."

"Right enough," he growled, taking a stiff swig of his whiskey. "If she keeps it up, I'm going to be a fecking patient!"

"When's the funeral home bringing him here?" she asked, pouring a splash of whiskey into her teacup.

"Probably this afternoon," he replied. "We'll put him in the front room, and I've warned them, under threat of violence, to bring him in head first and take him out feet first. They agreed as if it wasn't the first time they had heard such a thing. Gives me the fucking heebie-jeebies!"

Elva laughed and then caught herself. Her mother wouldn't approve.

Her uncle continued his rant. "I hope to Jasus that no more flies get in the house, or she'll be goin' on about the spirits of the dead watching over the body. I've been running about here for the last couple of days like an eejit with a rolled-up newspaper, killing every fucking fly I see when she isn't looking. Anyway, we'll sit with him tonight, and then the service will be tomorrow. We'll put him with your father down in Glasnevin."

"We better get some booze in," she said. "I know what the family are like."

"It's taken care of," he replied. "The fellow that supplies the pub will be dropping a few cases off here shortly, and I've ordered trays of sandwiches as well, and that might slow down the effects of the booze."

"Thank you," she said, and laid her hand on his.

"It's an awful world we live in at times," he commented, his eyes moist.

"Isn't that the truth," she said, blinking furiously to stave off the tears.

CHAPTER 16

SPECOPS

Arthur Cupples hung up the phone and leaned back in his chair.
For Max DeLisle to have acted so rashly, there would have to be a
great deal at stake, so Dempsey must have done something of
significance. He ruminated for a moment, thinking about where he
might find more information, then grabbed his old school Rolodex
and flipped through a bunch of cards. He knew exactly whom to
call.

The phone rang and was answered immediately. Cupples
had a direct line to most people to avoid the laborious screening by
secretarial staff.

"Miller here. What can I do for you, Arthur?"

Cupples said, "La Bottega, twenty minutes."

"Done."

Cupples grabbed his jacket, told his assistant he was
heading out, and went downstairs and grabbed a taxi. The ride took
about ten minutes over to the swanky area of London known as
Belgravia, where sheiks and footballers and movie stars knocked
elbows. It was home to some of the most expensive properties in

the world. Cupples kept tabs on such things, since much of the wealth had been created through criminal enterprise. The Russian businessman Roman Abramovich bought two stucco houses in Lowndes Square in 2008, and once completed, the merged house with a total of eight bedrooms was expected to be worth £150 million, exceeding the value of the previous most expensive house in England.

This was also home to the headquarters of the Serious Organized Crime Agency, or SOCA as it was better known, located not far from the headquarters of New Scotland Yard. The SOCA team were not police officers but given their role they needed to be an elite, highly secretive team. Their targets were people in the highest echelon of organized crime and as such required a high level of dedication, a vast array of expertise, and a team of officers who were multi-skilled and highly devoted to their task.

Cupples knew that Max DeLisle would certainly be on their target list. He expected Ben Miller, head of the Intelligence Unit, would have the latest street news about Max DeLisle and his crew. Cupples and the SOCA team often collaborated on assignments, since the SOCA purvey did extend to Northern Ireland. Since the establishment of the peace process and eventual disarmament of the terrorist groups, the latter had used their smuggling routes to transport drugs instead of weapons.

The place was relatively quiet when Cupples arrived, and he ordered two cappuccinos, arguably the best in London, and took a table by the front door. He saw Miller appear a few moments later across the street, dressed in a dark suit and wearing a black polo neck sweater. In his early forties, Miller was ex-SAS and as hard as they come.

Miller walked in, saw Cupples, but scanned the cafe anyway, a force of habit for specops members. They were always looking for threats and exits. Cupples smiled. No matter how many times they met, Miller always behaved the same. Cupples absentmindedly wondered if Miller was armed, but the loose-fitting jacket gave nothing away.

"Hello, Arthur," Miller said, sliding into his seat. "Thanks for the coffee." He dunked the home-made biscotti, his blue eyes focused like lasers on Cupples, which always made him uncomfortable.

Cupples said, "I need info on Max DeLisle and some of the team that work for him."

"Will you tell me why, Arthur, or is this a 'need-to-know?'"

Cupples shrugged.

"Okay, it's like that," Miller said, taking a bite of the biscotti. "Our dear friend Max is a psychopath. He runs the criminal enterprise in the east end of London with an iron fist and is reputed to be worth tens of millions, if not more. He also has several legitimate businesses, which we believe he is using to launder money from his less-than-legal enterprises. I could give you chapter and verse on the companies, but it might help if you could narrow the focus for me, Arthur."

"He had a guy working for him, name of Sean Dempsey. He's ex-IRA, which is why I'm interested in him."

"Ah yes," Miller said, sipping his coffee. "Dempsey's a nasty piece of work for you. Given his training, he was a valuable asset for Max when it came to knocking over armoured cars, banks, jewellery stores, etc. From what I hear, Dempsey and team were responsible for the robbery at Lloyd's bank in Feltham a few weeks ago. They got a lot of cash, but they also cleared out most of the security deposit boxes. As it happens, either by misfortune or design, and knowing DeLisle probably the latter, some of these were used by a bunch of villains. At the last official count, they got away with at least five million quid. The villains don't want to share what they lost, so you might imagine that the actual haul will be far higher. After the job, Dempsey disappeared, and DeLisle has been turning the place upside down trying to find him."

Cupples leaned back in his seat. It was no wonder DeLisle was taking chances trying to find Dempsey. That was quite the job that Dempsey pulled. "Thanks, Ben," he said. "That explains a few things I've been hearing."

"Quid pro quo, Arthur? You now are in the debtor's position. I expect this is off the books, since you decided not to use regular channels of communication."

"Thanks, Ben, I owe you a big one, so call it in whenever you need."

Miller finished munching the biscotti, wiped his mouth with a napkin, and got up from the table. "Thanks again for the coffee, Arthur. Talk soon."

Cupples ordered another cappuccino after Miller left and sat contemplating the information he had just received. He had to admit that DeLisle's move to pressure Daniel Riordan into doing his dirty work had the hallmarks of genius, albeit a very warped genius.

CHAPTER 17

DOLLAGHAN

Shortly after 4:30 a.m., a white panel van with a sign saying "O'Kane's Chicken" drove up to the security barrier outside the loading area of the Europa. An envelope full of cash changed hands, two hotel access cards were passed over, the barrier lifted, and the van reversed up to the loading area. Four men got out, all dressed in white overalls with the O'Kane's emblem on the chest, and went inside. They took the service elevator to the eighth floor of the new wing and made their way along the corridor to room 827. Two of them pushed the oversized laundry cart that had been conveniently left beside the elevator along the corridor. They paused briefly outside the door, drew their weapons, and using the keycard, opened the door and rushed inside. They did not use the traditional balaclavas — this was a one-way journey, so there was no need to conceal identities.

In a deep sleep, Riordan's reptilian brain registered the "click" of the door. He had passed out on the bed, still fully clothed on returning from the pub just slightly the worse for wear. Or perhaps more than slightly. He knew instinctively that something was wrong and was swimming back to consciousness when something hard slammed into the side of his head, stunning him. He had just time to register the shadowy figures filling the room before the second blow sent him into blackness.

The team drove out of the hotel, wended their way on to the M1 motorway, and headed north toward Antrim. The driver took the exit for Antrim town centre at the Templepatrick roundabout and passed down through the town on the Belfast Road until they reached the Antrim Marina near the Six Mile Water campgrounds. The driver knew his way — it was a trip he had made many times before.

At the marina, he pulled up to the dock, switched off the ignition, and tossed the butt of his cigarette on to the ground. Their destination, the hundred-passenger cruise ship named the *Maid of Antrim* rocked gently at her moorings. The boat had been built on the Clyde in Scotland in 1963 and was the oldest working boat on the Lough. It had fallen into disrepair but had been recently restored and now carried visitors to the various places of interest on the Lough. The Lough itself, the largest freshwater lake in the British Isles, was renowned for its commercial eel fishery and was home to a unique species of brown trout called the Dollaghan.

Two of the men pulled the laundry cart out of the back of the van and rolled it along the dock to the gangplank. Behind them, the van turned and drove away. To any curious eyes, if there were any, they looked like they were loading supplies. The captain of the ship, a stocky, white-haired individual, met the men on the deck as they heaved their burden aboard. He had already been notified about a "special" cruise and had made ready. Dawn was breaking, and the entire area was bathed in shades of grey. They had had several days of rain, followed by thick fog, and today looked to be more of the same.

"Morning, lads, where are we headed?"

"Let's drop them out by Coney Island, in that deep spot," suggested one of the men as he shrugged out of his white uniform. The other kidnapper did the same.

The captain nodded. The lough was shallow, compared to others, mostly about thirty feet deep, but around some of the islands were deep areas that went down over eighty feet. It was also much favoured by fishermen, and many fishing clubs had sprouted up along its banks. There were eight small islands in the lough, some of which had been inhabited since the Bronze Age and a favourite haunt of archaeologists due to the rich deposits of artifacts that could be found. Their destination, Coney Island, made famous in song by Van Morrison, was connected to the mainland by a submerged ridge, which could be seen in the summer months when it was under less than two feet of water.

The causeway was known locally as Saint Patrick's Road, as the saint was said to have used the island as a place of retreat. The captain himself often said, in times of melancholy, that Patrick would be spinning in his grave if he knew how many bodies lay adjacent to his former home. At least remnants of bodies — the eels would have made sure of that.

"Alright, then," the captain said. "One of yiz go and cast off the lines and we'll be away. I want to get there before the fisherman get out and get nosy."

*

Inside the laundry hamper, Riordan listened to the conversation, his heading throbbing from the blows he had received. Lying tangled underneath him, Sean was still unconscious, which was probably a good thing. Riordan had come around just before the van stopped, but he recognized the discordant rattling of mast lines and the sounds of other boats tied to a jetty. There was no salt tang to the air, so they were not at the coast. He expected they were at one of the many loughs that dotted the province. *A good place for dumping bodies*, he thought.

His hands and feet were tightly bound with the ubiquitous plasticuffs, those much favoured by law enforcement, but they had secured his hands in front of his body, not behind, as was normal practice. A large strip of duct tape covered his mouth. As the cart rocked back and forth over the ground, he felt something digging into his upper thigh and realized, to his great relief, that his knife was still in his jean's pockets. They would have given him a quick pat-down to see if there was a gun and then checked for a cellphone, but he had left his BlackBerry charging in the night table. He managed to get the knife out of his pocket and thumbed the gravity release blade open. It took less than a minute for the razor-sharp blade to get through the toughened plastic at his wrists, and even faster to slice the restraints at his ankles. Massaging his wrists, he waited for the tingling to subside as the blood flowed freely into his fingers, then quietly took stock of his situation.

Cigarette smoke wafted into his nostrils, and he heard three distinct voices. One he knew belonged to the captain of the boat, for he had overheard the earlier conversation. The other two were much more guttural, the rasp of the back streets of Belfast. His mind wandered to the who, what, where, why, of the situation, but the intense pain in his head brought him quickly back to focus. He tentatively touched his fingers to the side of his head, and they came away sticky, probably with congealed blood, having discovered a lump the size of a duck egg. Sensation having returned to his fingers, he gripped the duct tape at the corner and peeled it slowly off his mouth. His eyes watered as he felt his skin tear slightly.

The two men were mostly likely armed. Given the speed and efficiency that they had used in subduing himself and Sean, these were likely seasoned terrorists. *So much for the peace process*, he thought. Moving slowly, he reached upward and pressed gently on the top of the laundry cart. It was one of those that had a hinged surface that fell down on both sides when it was in use, and then joined in the middle to seal the contents. A thin line of grey light showed above him as he exerted more pressure.

That was a good thing. It meant the top was not secured in any way. He could just pop up like a jack-in-the-box. However, given the two men were carrying weapons, that move would be great target practice for them. So he could either wait until they tried to open the cart, which meant they would be on high alert, or try to take them now. And it would be nice if he could manage to take one of them alive to ask a few questions, although that was a much lower priority than actually surviving the encounter. He smiled as he remembered one of the Marine Corps rules for a gunfight: never bring a knife to a gunfight. The knife, one of the finest constructed by SOG, felt solid in his hand. He moved slowly in the confined space so he could get into a convenient position for escaping the cart. He needed to get on firm footing.

A tap opened, and the adrenaline flowed as his breathing stilled. This was the moment where the instinctive fight-or-flight reflex engaged, and for Riordan the latter did not exist. It never had. The feral creature known as the Raven, his alter ego, or dark passenger, crouched over, its back touching the top of the cart. Riordan pushed upward, releasing like coiled spring, leapt over the side of the cart, and rushed the two men standing at the side of the boat, their backs to him, smoking cigarettes. The scenario could not have been better for him.

He roared, expelling air from his lungs, and the bloodcurdling scream did what it was supposed to do: it startled their reflexes just enough to allow him to get close. They were both similarly built, in their thirties, neck tattoos, close cropped

374

hair and wearing jeans and sweatshirts. He slammed into them as they were turning, all two hundred and forty pounds of airborne anger. He elbowed the guy on the right hard in the face, hearing the gratifying crunch of cartilage shattering, then stabbed forward with the knife, sinking the blade all the way to the hilt in the other kidnapper's eye. A warm wetness poured over his fingers as he twisted the blade, pulled it free, and then did a reverse elbow strike up into the other kidnapper's nose, driving shards of cartilage up into his brain. Both men dropped to the deck, dead before they made contact.

Without pausing, he grabbed a handgun from the back of one of the kidnapper's jeans then raced for the cockpit of the boat. As he did so, the captain stepped out to see what was causing the commotion and found the barrel of a pistol jammed into the side of his head.

"Answer my questions, and you live," Riordan hissed.

The man nodded, and suddenly the air was filled with an astringent aroma. Riordan looked down to see the spreading stain on the front of the man's jeans. "Real tough guy," Riordan muttered and pushed the captain back into the cockpit. "Sit — on your hands."

The captain collapsed down onto a small bench and did as he was told. "Who are you?" Riordan asked.

"My name's Damien, Damien Law."

"Is this your boat?"

The captain nodded.

"When did you get the call?"

"About half eleven last night." Riordan thought back. They would have just left the Crown bar and gone back to the hotel at that time, which meant that they had a tail. And given the Belfast trip was spur of the moment, the tail must have been on them all the way from Dublin. Someone must have been in the bar or watching the bar. Christ! He realized then who was behind the attack.

"How well do you know Eamonn O'Brien?" Riordan asked.

"Who?" came the reply, but the momentary microexpression betrayed him.

Riordan jammed the pistol into the captain's chest, just over his heart, growled at him, and pulled the trigger. The sound was somewhat muffled. The captain's eyes went wide in surprise, he blinked a couple of times, and then slumped over.

One time, Featherstone had brought a knife-fighting instructor to work with the team. Riordan remembered the man telling them that when killing an opponent with a knife or a gun in close quarters, you should never look them in the eye. "They are about to die," the man had said, "and if yours is the last face they see, you will become the face of death." And for most people that would be a heavy burden to bear.

The Raven had no such qualms.

He went back outside, leaned into the laundry cart, and sliced through Sean's bonds. His first attempt to get Sean out proved to be awkward, so he pushed the cart on its side and then pulled his friend out on to the deck. Pressing his fingers to Sean's neck, he felt for a pulse, relieved to find it strong. A large, purplish bruise had risen on the side of Sean's head. He had obviously been knocked unconscious as well. Grasping the duct tape, he ripped it off quickly, sparing Sean some additional pain. Riordan then went back into the cockpit, where he had seen a bottle of water, grabbed it, and poured some of the contents over Sean's head.

Nothing happened for a moment, and then Sean coughed and spluttered, his eyes slamming open. "What the fuck?" he moaned, his hand immediately touching the side of his head. "Jesus, what a night! I'm never drinking..."

As his eyes focused, he saw the two bodies lying on the desk. Blood had formed dark pools around their heads. "What the fuck?"

Riordan grabbed his friend by the arm and pulled him to his feet. "Look at me, Sean. Look at me."

Sean swivelled his head from side to side, blinking furiously, as if trying to make the images of the bodies go away. Then he saw the blood on Riordan's hands.

"Sean, we got lifted last night after we got back to the hotel. That's why you've got that lump on your head. I've got the match of it on mine."

Sean winced as a spasm of pain shot through his head. Riordan could relate.

"What happened?"

"I managed to free myself and took care of them."

"And where the fuck are we? We're on a boat!" There was disbelief in his voice.

Riordan grasped him firmly by the shoulder. Sean shook his head and rubbed his eyes. "So what happens now?"

Riordan shrugged. "We've got to get back to the marina, and then you go home and stay home. They still don't know who you are, and the only reason you got lifted was because you were with me. We can take the captain's car, I'll drop you back to Belfast and after that I've got to get down to Dublin quickly. As for this bunch, the police will have a field day. It will probably be put down to rival paramilitary factions fighting over something or other. These two were pros, so it's likely they will be known to the authorities."

"That makes sense," Sean replied. "But who's driving the boat?"

"No one at the moment," Riordan said. "We're kinda going in a straight line. I'll get us turned around in a minute."

"I can help you there," Sean replied and headed for the wheelhouse.

"Fingerprints," Riordan yelled, and Sean slipped off his jacket. After tossing the laundry cart over the side, Riordan felt the boat turn around. Sean draped his jacket over the wheel and took over the helm while Riordan dragged the bodies out of sight. Apparently Sean owned a part share in a cruiser with his two friends the "Ginger Whinger" and the "Aga Khan," and was quite adept at handling the vessel. Riordan was too tired to ask. He found a set of car keys for a Toyota in the captain's jeans, slipped them into his pocket, and then joined Sean in the wheelhouse.

As they neared the marina, the first golden rays of the sun crept up over the horizon, blazing a path across the now still waters. Riordan was astonished to see a flotilla of white swans emerge from the misty docks and set out along the shore. "The children of Lir," he commented.

"Aye, and then some," Sean replied. "Ferocious bastards, they are."

Riordan just looked at him.

"Ach, long story. Involved a lovely wee bird and a picnic that went horribly wrong ... another time!"

Sean guided the vessel into the dock, reversing the engines at the last moment to slow their momentum, then turned the boat gracefully and backed into the moorings. As soon as they neared the dock, Riordan leapt off and secured the front mooring.

"Listen. Give me a minute and then cast off the line," Sean called from the wheelhouse. Riordan paused for a moment, then lifted off the rope, keeping the tension to hold the vessel in place. The boat started to move forward slowly again. Sean appeared a moment later and leapt onto the dock. "Let it go," he shouted, and Riordan dropped the line as the boat set off slowly again into the lough. "I tied up the wheel," Sean offered, "so it'll head all the way to the end of the lough. It's twenty miles long and pretty deserted at the lower end, so it may be a while before the bodies are found."

Riordan grinned. "Not bad, pal, not bad for a newbie. Now let's get out of here." There was only one Toyota Corolla parked near the docks, so Riordan opened it and climbed inside. It had seen better days, judging from the state of the bodywork, but would serve their purpose. The interior reeked of smoke, comingled with a fading pine scent from an air freshener in the shape of a pine tree hanging from the rear-view mirror. Fast food wrappers littered the floor and burned out cigarette stubs filled the ashtray. It was a stick shift, so they traded places quickly. Riordan was out of practice, and they did not want to attract any further attention such as the teeth-grating grinding of gears that usually accompanied a first timer in a stick shift.

They drove back toward Belfast at a fast clip in silence, content to stew in their own thoughts until the city came into view. Sean spoke first. "Thank you for saving me," he said. "If you hadn't managed to stop them, we would both have been at the bottom of the lough. Scary thought."

Riordan replied, "In my line of work we try to avoid the 'might've, could've, should've' questions, 'cos they're irrelevant, and you can consume a lot of energy if you start to dwell on the past and how things might have turned out differently. I've been shot, stabbed, and blown up more times than I can to remember, but what I do know is I'm here and the bad guys are not. I try not to lose too much sleep over it."

Sean's brow furrowed. "I've been angry a few times, but I don't think I've ever got to the point where I could just kill someone, like these evil cunts."

Riordan nodded. "That's what criminals do, Sean. Some are the ODC variety — ordinary decent criminals — but some, like this crew, have been blooded during the Troubles, so taking a life isn't a big deal for them. They simply follow orders, and if they don't, they end up on the bottom of the lough. It's just a matter of survival. Thankfully, you didn't seem to have too much of an issue with dead bodies. Most people freak out at the sight of blood."

Sean sighed. "You forget that I stayed here when you disappeared. I started my business here and made it through the worst of the shite that happened. I've lost a lot of friends along the way, so these weren't my first. I was there you know, when the car bomb went off in Omagh."

Riordan expelled a lungful of air. The bomb blast in Omagh, in 1998, one of the most devastating acts of violence during the Troubles, killed twenty-nine people and injured two hundred and twenty. It had been carried out by a splinter group of the IRA, the so-called Real IRA, who were totally opposed to the signing of the peace accord with Great Britain. Riordan had followed the events closely but had no idea his friend was there.

"We had a debrief in the office just after that one," he offered. "The team are constantly training, and we analyze the tactics, incident response, and communications to see if there were areas of improvement that we could learn from when there are any significant terrorist attacks anywhere in the world. How the hell did you survive?"

Sean took a deep breath. "I haven't told another soul about that day. Maybe staring death in the face tends to open you up at bit."

"Tell it in your own time, and only if you're up to it," Riordan replied. "It's our great Irish heritage to keep things bottled up until we fucking well choke on them. Nancy has been great in that respect, pulling that old shite out of me, even though she gets mad at me at times for clamming up about stuff."

Sean laughed. "I was installing some computer hardware in a boutique on the main street, about three doors away from where the car bomb was parked. I remember a tour bus full of pensioners pulled up outside the shop, and they had an argument with the driver. They wanted to go shopping, but he was supposed to take them to Belleek, to the factory shop, and told them they would be late. So they all crowded back onto the bus, and it pulled away. Shortly afterwards, a lady came into the shop, and she was at the counter paying the salesgirl for a dress when the printer jammed. I was on my knees behind the counter, when the bomb exploded."

Sean's eyes teared over and he paused for a moment, collecting himself. He knuckled back a tear.

"When I came around, the first thing I saw was the head of the wee girl lying in front of me. Her face was covered in dust, but her eyes were staring straight at me. A piece of the plate glass window had cut her head clean off. The woman who was buying the dress was blown to pieces. There were bits of her everywhere, and the blood... I got up and staggered out into the street, and there was blood literally flowing in streams, and bits of people — arms, legs, insides, scattered in all directions. It looked like the inside of a slaughterhouse. If that printer hadn't jammed, we wouldn't be having this conversation."

"It wasn't your time, Sean, so be grateful," Riordan replied, as a tear ran down Sean's face while he relived the nightmare. "Given what I do," Riordan continued, "I've rolled the dice once or twice and walked away, while others have not."

Sean nodded, listening intently.

"Now I drink the good wine first," Riordan said. "And sometimes I make new friends, or reacquaint myself with old friends."

Sean brightened. "Isn't that the truth. Anyway, before we ditch this car, can you do me a favour?"

"Sure?"

"Can you wipe that blood off your hands? It's giving me the creeps."

CHAPTER 18

OSCAR

At the chapel, the service had been dreary. Just like the day outside, dark, rain-laden clouds scudding over the horizon, the air thick with moisture. As the crowds filed out of the chapel to watch the coffin being placed into the hearse, Elva stood beside her mother, her sister Mairead on the other side, providing an emotional and physical prop for the distraught woman whose ornate lace handkerchief was never far from her eyes.

During the previous evening, as Elva sat with her brother's coffin at the house, there were moments of sadness as she focused from time to time on the array of family photographs displayed in the living room. There were many pictures of herself and Mairead and Frank on a beach when they were teenagers. It looked like the strand at Portstewart where they went every year for their holidays to the same little guesthouse on the pier. From there, they would take the bus over to Portrush to spend their allowance on the bumper cars at Barry's amusements, or the slot machines, or the tiny, rickety roller coaster that Frank loved.

Then there was the tower where you climbed to the top and sat on a canvas mat that acted as a slide. No matter that it was only a few feet. For children it seemed to touch the sky. For a treat there was the delicious pink and blue candy floss that stuck to everything and you spent ages licking it off your fingers. Those were gentler days, before the innocence was stripped away, like tearing a Band-Aid off a fresh wound. The Troubles came, and nothing was ever the same again.

As the door closed on the hearse, she was about to move back to the family limousine when her uncle touched her on the arm. The cortege would be heading off to Deansgrange cemetery, where Frank would be interred in the family plot beside his father. It was one of the largest cemeteries in Dublin, covering almost seventy acres, and many years ago her father had purchased a family plot in the shade of a pine tree, where he wanted the family to rest for all eternity.

Barry Fitzgerald, one of her father's favourite actors, was interred not far from the family plot. Her father always remarked that when he passed, he would be in good company. Her father had celebrated like mad when Fitzgerald won an Oscar for Best Supporting Actor for his role as Father Fitzgibbon in the movie "Going my way." He loved telling the story about Fitzgerald, who, being an avid golfer, accidentally broke the head off his Oscar statue while practicing his golf swing. During World War II, Oscar statues were made of plaster instead of gold, owing to wartime metal shortages. She remembered the family gathered around the television to watch *The Quiet Man*, starring John Wayne, Maureen O'Hara, and Fitzgerald, and one of her father's favourite films.

"You can ride with me," he said, steering her away from the limo, "but first there's a fellow here I want you to meet. He was in the pub the other night — one of the locals, a lorry driver — but he had to make a run over to Liverpool, and he just got back."

Elva allowed herself to be guided back to her uncle's car, where a scruffy individual stood waiting nervously, wearing an anorak over a white shirt and a black tie, the standard uniform for mourners. Both hands were stuffed in the anorak pockets. The shirt strained against the buttons around his middle, producing tiny elliptical openings through which black wiry hair protruded. He had thick, curly hair and a day's worth of stubble. His eyes were red and puffy, although whether it was from tears or lack of sleep or something chemical, she couldn't decide. She had heard stories about long-distance drivers and the lengths to which they would go to stay awake as long as possible.

"This is Malachy, a friend of Frank's who was in the pub the other night. I thought you might like to hear what he has to say."

"Sorry for your troubles," Malachy said, extending a hand from his anorak. Elva shook it and sized the man up immediately. The hand was warm and clammy, the grip weak, and the skin soft and pliable. His breath reeked of cigarettes. His skin wore a greasy sheen.

"What happened?" Elva asked, wrapping her shawl around her shoulders. The wind had brought a chill to the onlookers, and the boughs of the surrounding willow trees swung languidly back and forth, the wind whispering like voices of spirits through the leaves.

"I was der," Malachy started in a thick Dublin accent, "having a quick pint, when these two lads come in. One was a big fucker — pardon the language — well over six feet and built like a shit house door. The other fellah was a bit smaller, had a beard and a bit of a gut. The big fella had an accent for a while, then it changed and then it changed back."

Elva frowned. "What do you mean it changed?"

Malachy thought for a moment. "He sounded like a Yank when he first spoke to Frank, and then Frank got upset with the guy for some reason, and the next time he spoke it sounded like Belfast to me. And then it changed back. Frank was a tough wee man, but this guy took him apart like he was a child."

"What did they want with Frank?"

"I don't know, but I think they were looking for you." Elva felt a chill as she looked over to her uncle. A frown creased his brow at this tidbit of knowledge.

"Me? What makes you think that?" Her mind raced furiously to come up with a reason why anyone would be trying to find her.

387

"I heard the name Dempsey, and then I think I heard the big guy say something like Lilly or Billy or…"

Elva sighed.

Her heart sank, but she knew. "Was it DeLisle?" she asked.

Malachy's face brightened. "Aye, that was it, that was what I heard."

"Who's DeLisle?"

"Thank you, Malachy," she said, ignoring his request. "We'll be holding the wake in the pub, so come by and I'll make sure you'll be looked after. And not a word of this to the Gards." She wanted to ask him why he hadn't stepped in to help Frank, but she knew. Malachy didn't have it in him.

"What's that all about?" her uncle asked after they had climbed into his car.

"Old ghosts," she replied. "I'll tell you all about it later."

*

After leaving Belfast, the high-speed Enterprise train raced for the border, stopping only in Newry to take on new passengers. In the distance lay the brooding dark hills where British Army observation and listening posts once stood, monitoring traffic running across the border during the Troubles. Riordan had driven the roads many times. This area, known as South Armagh, became the most heavily militarized area in Northern Ireland. In an area with a population of 23,000, the army had stationed around 3,000 troops in support of the RUC to contain an unknown number of paramilitaries. So successful were the IRA in their attacks that the army resorted to using choppers to carry personnel back and forth between bases — the roads were simply too dangerous.

The train moved on, and Riordan watched the patchwork countryside fly past, then they were over the river and into the republic, heading for Dundalk and Drogheda. As he nursed a double shot of Bushmills, his BlackBerry buzzed. Sliding it from the holster, he saw the incoming call was from Billy K.

There were no niceties. "Where the fuck are you?" Billy demanded.

"On my way back from Belfast," Riordan replied. "I'll be arriving in Connolly Station in about twenty minutes."

"We'll pick you up outside," Billy said and closed the connection.

Riordan walked out of the station in a throng of people, past long lines of travellers who were heading back up north on the evening Enterprise run. He went down the stairs and out to the street. He paused for a moment at a long, low railing that had numerous bicycles chained along its bars and scanned his surroundings. The streets were slick with rain, but for a moment at least, it was dry. Across from the station, outside Grainger's bar, sat a Blue Range Rover, its tinted windows protecting the identities of the passengers inside. That would be Billy K.

Riordan crossed the street, and as he approached the vehicle, he heard the locks pop. He climbed into the back seat, his nostrils immediately assailed by the overpowering scent of Billy K's aftershave. Max DeLisle sat in the passenger seat.

"Fuck me, Billy," Riordan spat, no longer able to contain himself. "Do you bathe in that shite? You smell like a fucking peeler!"

"See, Billy." DeLisle laughed. "I'm not the only one!"

"Fuck off," Billy snorted and pulled out into the flow of traffic.

"So what were you doing in Belfast?" DeLisle asked, half-turning in his seat.

"As it happens, trying to get myself killed," Riordan replied. "You wouldn't by any chance have some Tylenol? Some bastard cracked me over the head and tried to feed me to the eels."

Much to Riordan's surprise, DeLisle looked in the front glovebox and came out with a full bottle of painkillers. "Take a handful," he ordered. "We need you fresh when we go to lift this chick."

"Chick?"

"Yeah, the one called Elva. Our girl showed up for the funeral, without Dempsey, which is a bit of a shame, along with her sister, and the wake is tonight at the pub. We'll lift her from there."

Riordan nodded. He hadn't expected anything less from DeLisle. "And then?"

Billy K grinned. "She's a bit of a looker is Elva. Fiery red hair, masses of curls. I love redheads, and especially, I love red muff. We'll take her for a drive along the coast, ask her a few questions, I'll have a bit of fun with her, and then she'll be off for a swim."

"And then we'll go and get that cunt Dempsey," DeLisle continued. "Wherever he is, and then you can go back to your lovely little wife and kiddies. Everybody's happy."

"And I get the files," Riordan interrupted. "That was the deal."

"And you get the files." DeLisle laughed. "I'm nothing if not a man of my word. Isn't that right, Billy?"

Billy K grinned. "Too true, boss. Too true."

Riordan settled back in his seat. He didn't trust DeLisle, not even for a moment. He dry-swallowed a handful of the painkillers, hoping the throbbing in his head would soon subside. The heavy bass from the sound system — apparently Billy was fond of the current rage in Britain called dubstep, which was a kind of reggae, punk, electro fusion combined with a heavy, heavy beat — pulsated through Riordan's head like a minor earth tremor.

Rush hour traffic slowed them to a crawl, and it seemed to take forever to get out onto the motorway. Riordan closed his eyes and dozed, feeling the pain slowly drain away. He was vaguely aware of voices in the car, and then DeLisle was prodding him awake.

"Wakey, wakey," DeLisle crowed, and Riordan opened his eyes to see the barrel of a Glock 22 poking into his ribs.

He rubbed his eyes, grateful for the momentary catnap, and peered around. Billy K had parked on the pier at Dun Laoghaire near a fish and chip truck, and the scent sent Riordan's hunger pangs into overdrive.

"Could do with something to eat," he commented.

DeLisle looked at his watch and then out toward the horizon. "It's still too light," he commented. "C'mon, let's grab a bite to eat, but I'm not having greasy fucking chips. There's a good restaurant down the road a bit called Hartley's. We'll go there."

Billy dropped them off outside the restaurant and headed down the street to find parking. Hartley's turned out to be a good find. Constructed from cut stone blocks, it had originally been a railway station. A massive patio umbrella, measuring about forty feet square, provided patrons with shelter from the rain. It had cleared up nicely, the dark clouds moving out toward the Irish sea, and they were presented with a magnificent view of the harbour. Despite being packed and having a line of people waiting, DeLisle had a quiet word with the hostess, a large bill changed hands, and she guided them to a table directly under the umbrella, "just in case it rains again." A waitress arrived promptly and handed them menus. Apparently, word had been passed along about a generous tipper. The clientele was mostly upscale, from what Riordan could see, and so were the prices.

Billy arrived a few minutes later, dressed in a black Hugo Boss suit and wearing a white shirt and a black tie. Riordan hadn't noticed as he had been sitting directly behind him. DeLisle wore a black leather jacket over a black polo neck, jeans and black, tasselled loafers. Very dapper. Riordan refrained from commenting about Billy's suit. If you were going to try to kidnap someone from an Irish wake, you needed to look the part.

DeLisle scrutinized the wine list with an air of sophistication. "I fancy a nice Chardonnay," he commented. "Billy here isn't a wine man, but I suspect you are." Riordan nodded. "Then we'll have a nice bottle." He raised a hand, and the waitress appeared in a flash. "We'll have the Meursault premier Cru Les Perrières, Dom Yves Boyer-Martenot," he said in a passable French accent. The waitress was impressed. "And a bottle of your best beer for my friend here." Billy K grinned.

The waitress recited the specials from memory, and they all ordered then sat in awkward silence for a few moments until the drinks came. Riordan ordered the Dublin Bay prawns, mostly to put something in his stomach, for there was no knowing when he would get a chance to eat again. DeLisle and Billy K both ordered the steak Diane, medium rare with all the trimmings. DeLisle made a huge fuss of sampling the wine, swirling and sniffing, as if trying to impress his company. Riordan wasn't impressed.

DeLisle turned to Billy K. "Who do you fancy this weekend, Coventry or Hull?"

Billy K shrugged. "I fancy the Blaze, Max. Put a few quid on them, I did."

"They've been on quite the streak this season, so I reckon you're on a sure thing. Maybe I'll try a little flutter myself." To Riordan, "Watch much hockey, do you? It being the national pastime and all..."

Riordan was about to correct him and tell him that the national sport was lacrosse but thought it wisest not to provoke him just now. He said, "I watch the Canucks from time to time."

"Brilliant," DeLisle replied. "I love a game where they encourage a good scrap, and those guys from Coventry aren't afraid to drop the gloves. Just like gladiators, they are." He took a long sip of his wine. Pebbles of condensation spotted the glass. "The major's notes say you work for a security firm," DeLisle commented, abruptly changing the conversation.

Riordan was immediately on edge, wonder what else could possibly be in the files. "Mostly freelance stuff," he replied. "Insurance investigations, surveillance and the like." He didn't want DeLisle to delve any further into his employment, since several of his workmates were back in London, covertly entering DeLisle's apartment.

"My, my, how the mighty have fallen," DeLisle commented. "Peering through bushes at unfaithful spouses. Still, you got us this far."

The waitress arrived with their salads, a thankful respite to the questioning. Riordan started in and silence descended. He hoped he would make it through dinner as he kept eyeing the well-honed steak knives that the waitress had brought for his dining companions. His training instincts were firing on all cylinders, and he knew the two would be down in seconds, if he so desired. Taking a deep breath, he calmed the dark beast.

There would be time later.

*

The bar, in true Irish tradition, was thronged for the wake. The Pogues blasted out from the speakers, and the place had devolved into a raucous mass of hard-drinking friends and relations and a few hangers-on who had heard that there was a free bar. A large black and white photograph of Frank had been placed behind the bar, and many toasts were raised in his honour as the night progressed. Elva and her sister had slipped behind the bar to assist the harried waitstaff, such was the size of the crowd. Frank, and the extended family, had many friends. She had gone home and changed into a black top and jeans, despite the disapproving looks from her mother. She was obviously breaking some other ancient tradition, but at this point she couldn't care less.

A long line of pints of Guinness ran the length of the bar, an honour guard for the photograph, and Elva replaced them as fast as they were picked up. Powers was the whisky of choice, and she had placed the bottles on the bar. It took too much time trying to fill glasses from the optics, so she gave up and let the crowd fuel themselves. Her cellphone buzzed in her back pocket. She pulled it out and saw it was from Sean, and she smiled, but the roar was deafening and there was no way she had time to answer it. She clicked it off, promising herself to get in touch later.

When she looked up, her uncle was at the bar, sipping a pint, his eyes roving across the crowd.

"Are ye all right there, girl?" he asked, his blue eyes crinkled in mirth.

"Run off me feet, I am," she responded.

"The wee fellow would have appreciated this," he said, raising his glass to the photograph.

She felt her eyes go hot, and she fought back the tears. Swallowing hard, she nodded, not trusting herself to speak for fear floods of tears would come, and that would bring more unwanted attention. Taking a deep breath, she paused in the eye of the storm and took a sip from the bottle of sparkling water that she kept under the bar. There would be time for her later to have a few drinks. Flushed faces laughed and chatted, a myriad of conversations all occurring at the same time.

Politics, soccer, Gaelic, the economy — it was always a hot topic now that Ireland had to be bailed out by the European Union, and the young ones were heading abroad looking for work. They had always been referred to as "the wild geese," those who left to find fame and fortune in foreign lands. For a few glorious years, while the economy aptly named the Irish tiger roared, the young folks had decided to stay and find employment. But like most things, it was too good to last. The economy tanked, sinking faster than the famed *Titanic* built in her very own shipyards, and with it the hopes and dreams of many sorrowful families who saw their young depart.

She heard and absorbed snippets of all these and was comforted, very much at peace. During a lull in the conversations, the bottom door of the pub opened, and a tall figure stepped inside, pressing his way into the throng. He was dressed in black, like many of the others, but his tie was still in place. The suit was high end — she recognized the hallmarks of expensive tailoring. He was in his thirties, well-built, his hair thinning a bit, but attractive nonetheless. As he moved toward the bar, she saw several of the other females in the bar size him up. Even the happily married Mairead winked at her and nodded toward the stranger.

He approached the bar, easing his way into the spot where her uncle had been, and then seemed to flex himself and expand into the space. Patrons on either side grumbled, turned to look at the intruder, and immediately shifted. Despite the heavy fog of alcohol and smoke, his aftershave touched her nostrils. He smiled and reached out his hand.

"I'm Daniel," he said, but she could barely hear him. His grip was firm and hard, and she had to lean forward to hear him. "I'm sorry for your loss." The Cockney accent came to her ear.

"What can I get you?" she asked. "Pints are on the house, and so is the whisky."

His eyes scanned the shelves. "I'll have a shot of Jack," he said.

"Double?"

"Why not." He grinned.

She poured him a healthy shot. He lifted the glass in a toast and knocked it back, slamming the glass on the bar. He looked her straight in the eyes.

"Another?" she asked.

"It's a wake, isn't it? We're supposed to drink until we fall down."

She strained to hear. "How did you know my brother?" she asked.

"What?" He put a finger to his ear then pointed to the door.

She nodded. This wasn't the normal type of person her brother would hang around with, and her curiosity got the better of her. Untying her apron, she handed it to Mairead. Leaning close, she said, "I'm going to have a word with this guy outside. I'll be back in a minute."

Mairead laughed. "See if he'd like a threesome."

Elva shot her a look and then burst out laughing. She hugged her sister fiercely. "God, we're going to have so much fun together."

She stepped out in the street, standing under the single light bulb that illuminated the back door of the pub. The guy was leaning against a Range Rover, just a few steps away, sipping on the Jack Daniels.

"That's better," he said. "Couldn't hear a dicky bird in there."

"Aye," she replied, walking over, enjoying the cool night air on her skin. With all the bodies crammed into the pub, the atmosphere was stifling. "It's always the way. The more they drink, the louder it gets. So how did you know Frank?"

"I'm in hospital supplies," he said, nodding toward Saint Michael's hospital that was just a block away. As she recalled, their emergency room did a fair amount of trade on the weekend, especially after closing time. It was a shame to admit it, but a lot of their business came from her brother's pub. "I'm here about once a month and always go in the pub for lunches and dinners. The food is always great, and Frank enjoyed a chat."

Elva nodded. "That he did. It was one of those things that make a great barman. The ability to relate to people. God, he was great..." The blow came out of nowhere. He punched her hard on the side of the head, so fast that his fist moved in a blur. Her legs buckled, but he grasped her arm, holding her erect. Lightning flashed behind her eyelids, and he punched her again. Everything went dark.

*

When she came to, she panicked for a moment then realized that a canvas bag of some kind had been pulled over her head. Settling back, she calmed herself, as she had been taught, then took an inventory. A gentle tug of the wrists, and she felt the plasticuffs dig into her wrists. She slowly moved her lower jaw back and forth, making sure it hadn't been broken. Her cheek throbbed where the guy had punched her. It was painful, but pain was a good thing. During her training, she had been sent to work with an ex-Navy SEAL who owned a hunting camp in the Everglades. She spent a year there under his tutelage and sometimes under him in the literal sense. He had worked her to the point of exhaustion on the fitness level, but also in the black art of covert killing.

Every time she had complained, his response was always the same. "Pain is your friend. It will tell you when you're seriously injured. It will keep you awake, and angry, and remind you to finish the job and get the hell home. But you know the best thing about pain? It lets you know you're not dead yet."

She was in the back seat of a car, probably the Range Rover that the guy had been leaning against. The guy was driving — the aftershave helped pinpoint his location — and she sensed there were others in the car, but there was no communication between them. So she waited, her ears pricked for any sound or clue where they were heading. Assess the situation, formulate a response, and act. One against three was not the greatest odds, but then again, they had no idea what they were up against.

After driving for several more minutes, a voice from the passenger seat in front said, "This is the place. Turn in here." The "here" was pronounced with a distinctive Cockney accent — not the one she had heard from "Daniel" — and sounded like 'ear." If the information she had gleaned earlier at the funeral was correct, these were probably some of DeLisle's boys, trying to locate Sean. That meant they knew about her relationship with Sean, a relationship they had tried very hard to keep quiet.

She realized then, suddenly, why Frank had been killed. It was not because he wouldn't tell them about where she was living — he really didn't know — but to get her to come to his funeral. It was fucking diabolical, something she would attribute to DeLisle. Anger flared within her, blossomed, and then sharpened into a point that was directed at those in the car. These were very likely the men that had killed Frank.

She felt the car turn off the main road and move slowly down a bumpy track, jostling her back and forth. She had not been strapped in with a seatbelt, so, keeping her body slack as if she was still unconscious, she let herself fall all the way across the seat. Immediately, two strong hands grasped her shoulders and pushed her upright, leaning her back against the doorframe. Under the hood she grimaced, now having confirmation there were three people in the car.

The car crunched to a stop on gravel, so they were in some sort of parking lot. Doors opened, and immediately the rhythmic pounding of waves came to her ears, followed by the sharp tang of sea air seeping through the bag. Her door opened, and she fell out, her reflexes blocking her fall at the last moment.

"The bitch is back," the driver commented, grabbing her arm and pulling her roughly to her feet. She brushed against him as she did so, feeling the hard lump in the inside of his jacket. He was carrying.

"Let's go," said another voice, this of the passenger, and the driver propelled her forward, all the while grasping her elbow. They were walking on sandy soil, and the scent of pine was also in the air, so she figured they were outside of Bray, in one of the many parks that dotted the coastline. The pounding of the waves grew to a crescendo, and she sensed that they were far above the waves, perhaps near a cliff. That could mean only one thing. For her, they had planned a one-way trip.

"This'll do," said the passenger.

She felt herself pushed backward and slammed into a tree trunk, slightly winding her. Then the bag was ripped from her head and a massive hand grabbed her by the throat. It was a dark, moonless night, and she could barely make out the other two standing across from her. The driver was right in her face, his aftershave overwhelming. One of the other figures moved toward her.

"So, love," the man said. "We're looking for Sean Dempsey, and our friend back here thinks you know where we can find him." This was the front-seat passenger speaking. So the shadowy figure standing in the background must have been with her in the back seat. She squinted but could not focus. He was tall, well built, and the sense of power that she had felt when he pushed her upright, shocked her. It was the same sensation she had felt when training in the everglades. The ex-SEAL possessed massive grip strength, the death grip, as he called it.

"Are you fucking listening to me, love?" the passenger growled.

"Yes, yes, I am," she whispered, her eyes filling with tears. "Please don't hurt me, please?"

"Where's Sean Dempsey?" the passenger asked.

"I ... I don't know," she cried. "One day the bastard's bringing me roses, the next day he's gone. I thought he might have gone back to Amsterdam, so I went looking for him. That's..."

The passenger punched her in the stomach, hard, striking her solar plexus, the dense cluster of nerve cells just below her diaphragm. Pain flooded her senses. She gasped like a fish out of water, struggling to get air. Bile rose in her throat, but she fought it back. Her legs buckled.

"Don't fuck with me," the passenger snarled. "Hold her still, Billy."

She recognized the name. Billy meant Billy K, one of DeLisle's enforcers. Sean had mentioned him once or twice. And if Billy K was here, that meant the passenger was likely DeLisle himself.

"DeLisle?" she whispered. "Are you Max DeLisle?"

DeLisle grinned. "That I am, love. I see you made the connection, so that means you've got a brain. All I want is Dempsey. So tell me where he is, or maybe we'll have to see if he'll come home for your funeral."

"Did you kill Frank?" she asked.

"Nope, but Billy here did," DeLisle replied. "However, it was my idea. I figured if you two lovebirds had fucked off somewhere with my money, I needed to lay my hands on one of you. And since Dempsey doesn't have any family left, you fit the bill."

"But I don't know..."

DeLisle slammed her hard again in stomach, driving the air out of her lungs and making her double over like a rag doll. No longer able to control her bodily functions, she threw up and collapsed on the ground.

DeLisle stepped back into the shadows. "Okay, Billy," he said. "Time to cut on her a bit."

Billy K dragged her to her feet and slammed her against the tree trunk. She heard the click of the switchblade and felt the tip touch her cheek. "Last chance, bitch," Billy K said.

Taking a deep breath, she focused her energy.

It was now or never.

She exploded her knee up into Billy K's testicles. It was a solid, rewarding strike. A long moan escaped his lips, and nature's reflexes took control. He immediately released his grip from her throat, dropped the knife, and leaned over, cupping his shattered balls to prevent further trauma. The moment he did so, she slammed her knee into his face. He staggered back a couple of steps. Tears trickled down his cheeks.

Then his head exploded.

"Run, Elva," came a voice from toward the car park, and suddenly gunfire raked the entire area.

She ran.

*

Across from her, Riordan watched in awe as Elva dismantled Billy K. Talk about David and Goliath. DeLisle was about to rush her, as was Riordan, when he heard the distinctive metallic sound of a cocking lever being pulled back. DeLisle recognized it too. Riordan immediately dived for cover, just as the first round blew through Billy K's skull. It was a fine shot, especially in the darkness, so the shooter must have been wearing PNVs — night vision goggles of some form — either that or he had a night scope mounted on the gun. Riordan recognized the weapon's report immediately. It was the ugly report from an AK-47, and he knew what was coming next.

As soon as he had eliminated the threat to Elva, the shooter switched to full auto and sprayed the entire area with covering fire. The thirty rounds spewed from the barrel, tearing up trees and ricocheting off rocks, sparks flying everywhere. There was a momentary lull as the shooter changed mags, and Riordan sprinted across the ground, past Billy K's body, and concealed himself behind the tree. At least it was solid enough to withstand a round from the AK.

The firing came now in selective bursts. Riordan could see the muzzle flash from farther up the hill. As soon as there was a pause, DeLisle opened up with his handgun, trying to drive the shooter back. Riordan leaned back against the tree and waited. On the ground beside him he saw a cellphone and picked it up. The body of the phone was warm to the touch, so it must have fallen from Elva's jeans. He quickly flipped it open and scrolled through the last few calls, committing them to memory.

The bursts of firing were getting closer now as the shooter was attempting to drive them out into the open. A bullet blasted away a chunk of the tree near Riordan's head, and he immediately dropped the phone and crawled behind a cluster of rocks. DeLisle had opted to run the other way, the reports from his handgun fading. Riordan kept crawling and crawling, moving from cover to cover, anything to get away from the shooter, bullets dancing after his heels.

He heard footsteps crunching over the ground near the tree where he had first taken cover, then they disappeared off in the direction Elva had run. A few minutes later, he heard a car start up and roar away. Silence enveloped the area once more, but he remained concealed until he was certain the threat had gone. Rising to his feet, he brushed off his jeans and made his way back to the clearing. Several whitish gouges in the pine tree showed how close the shooter had come. He scrabbled about on the ground, but the cellphone had disappeared. The shooter must have picked it up. Hearing footsteps approaching, he dived behind the tree.

"Riordan," a voice hissed.

It was DeLisle.

He got up and moved around the tree. DeLisle knelt beside the remains of Billy K, removing all identification from him. "Grab this," DeLisle growled, holding up a wallet and a BlackBerry. Riordan took the items while DeLisle searched Billy K's other pockets. Satisfied there was nothing more to find, DeLisle stood. "Let's go," he said and walked away without a backward glance.

In the car park, the Range Rover sat completely disabled, all four tires completely flat. "Fuck me," growled DeLisle. "Who the hell was that?"

Riordan shrugged. "Not a fucking clue. But whoever it was certainly knew his stuff. It's lucky for us we recognized the sound of the cocking handle, otherwise we'd be lying there with Billy.

"Shame about Billy," DeLisle commented. "He was a good lad."

Riordan said nothing. Billy K was a foot soldier and consequently expendable, as were most of the people with whom DeLisle associated.

"Think it was Dempsey?" DeLisle asked.

Riordan shook his head. "Nope. But I think I know where he is."

"Oh yeah?"

"Elva's cellphone fell out of her jeans when Billy was tuning her up. I had a quick look at it but dropped it when the shooter made me move. It looks like he came by and picked it up. There were a few calls from area code 250, which covers most of British Columbia, where I live. Then I remembered seeing a bunch of postcards in Elva's flat. They looked like they were all from Spain, but now the 250 area code triggered me that one of the postcards was from Tofino, which is a pretty remote community on the east side of Vancouver Island. I missed that earlier. It's a surfer's paradise and frequented by a bunch of old hippies. You've got to give it to Dempsey, 'cos that's the last place on Earth anyone would think to look."

"Fucking brilliant, mate, fucking brilliant."

"Now what?" Riordan asked.

"What else? I've got the plane here waiting so they can take us over to Heathrow and we can catch the next flight to Vancouver. I do a bit of business with the folks there so we can get tooled up and then go find Dempsey."

Riordan nodded.

"Let's go nick a car and get back to Dublin," DeLisle said. "We passed a pub about a mile back, so we can get one there. The rental company can sort this one out."

CHAPTER 19

KALEIDOSCOPE

"Who the fuck was that," asked her uncle, his hands steady on the wheel as he drove them back to Dun Laoghaire. The reek of cordite hung heavy in the car, seeping from the AK nestled on the floor between her feet. The barrel was still warm to the touch. "It's a good thing I stepped out for a smoke when I did, as I saw them heading away and put two and two together."

Elva smiled, clenching her fists together to stop them from trembling. He saw what she was doing and put his hand on top of hers. "It's over, now," he said. "Oh, and by the way, you dropped your phone."

Elva replied, "That was Max DeLisle, the guy that Sean robbed. He's a big name in the London mob. The bastard you shot was the one who killed Frank. They..." She burst into tears and pounded her legs with her fists in frustration. "They killed Frank just to make me show up for the funeral. Apparently DeLisle found out somehow that Sean and me were an item and decided to use me to get at him." She sobbed. "I got him killed."

Her uncle patted her leg. "Well, at least that didn't work, and you'll soon be away back to your new home," he said, handing over her cellphone. "I found it on the ground beside the tree. Jasus, I haven't had this much fun in ages."

She looked at the satisfied look on his face and leaned over and kissed his cheek. "Thanks for saving me," she said. She rubbed her wrists where the plasticuffs had chafed the skin.

"Looked to me like they were the ones needing saving," he replied, and she laughed, then groaned as her stomach muscles clenched. "Gave you a couple of good shots there, he did. Sorry about that, but I had to wait to get a clear shot."

"That's okay." She smiled. "Pain is our friend."

"And who was the other guy?" he asked. "The big fellow standing in the back. I've never seen anyone move so fast. He knew the sound of the cocking handle, that's for sure, and was diving for cover before I fired. DeLisle was the only one armed, and he was shooting back at me, trying to keep me pinned down. The big guy just moved from cover to cover like a cat."

Elva shook her head. "I don't know. Probably another of DeLisle's goons. I never really got a good look at him but just had a sense of something powerful when he was beside me in the back seat."

Her uncle nodded thoughtfully. "Maybe a wild card, just like you." As former district commander for the South Armagh wing of the IRA, he had known that she was involved in the

411

struggle, but her role was a well-kept secret, and only a select few of those on the army council knew she existed. His own exploits, leading well-planned, well-coordinated guerrilla attacks against the British Army, were the stuff of legend, and the assaults had been dissected, analyzed, and finally taught to new army recruits as examples of what they could face. He had planned and participated in the notorious Warrenpoint ambush, or massacre, depending on your point of view.

During the early eighties, when the conflict was in full swing, an army convoy consisting of a single Land Rover and two four-ton trucks was driving past Narrow Water Castle near Warrenpoint. As it passed, a five-hundred-pound fertilizer bomb, hidden in a lorry loaded with bales of straw and parked close to the castle, was detonated by remote control. The explosion caught the rear truck in the convoy, killing six members of the 2nd Battalion, the Parachute Regiment.

After the first explosion, the soldiers, believing that they had come under attack from the IRA, began firing across the narrow maritime border with the republic, which was about two hundred feet away. A civilian was killed as a result and another wounded. Later reports suggested a sniper also opened fire on the soldiers after the first bomb ripped through the truck.

On hearing the first explosion, a Royal Marine unit alerted the army of an explosion on the road, and reinforcements from other units of the Parachute Regiment were immediately dispatched to the scene in Saracen units. A rapid reaction unit, consisting of medical staff and a senior commander of the Queen's Own Highlanders, together with a signaller, were sent by Gazelle helicopter; another helicopter, a Wessex, landed to pick up the wounded. The senior commander assumed control once at the site.

Then, thirty-two minutes after the first explosion, a second device concealed in milk churns exploded against the gate lodge on the opposite side of the road, destroying it. Elva's uncle and others from the IRA army council had been closely studying how the army acted after a bombing. He had correctly assessed the soldiers would set up an incident command point (ICP) in the nearby gatehouse.

The second explosion, caused by an eight-hundred-pound fertilizer bomb, killed twelve soldiers, ten from the Parachute Regiment and the two from the Queen's Own Highlanders. The attack was so precise and so brutally effective that many people considered it to be one of the turning points in the conflict in Ulster.

"Somebody gave me up to DeLisle, or gave Frank up," she said, gritting her teeth. "There's not too many people on that list."

"Fuckin' touts," he spat, using the colloquial term for informers. "Bane of our existence during the troubles. MI5 turned so many of ours that it was hard to know who to trust. And then we turned on ourselves, like a pack of rats. It didn't matter what we did to the ones we found out about. However vicious we were, there was always some other fool ready to sell us out for money or safety. That fucker McGartland did us a lot of damage."

413

Elva nodded. She had seen the movie *Fifty Dead Men Walking,* allegedly based on his life story. McGartland, a working class Belfast boy during the Troubles, became both a respected member of the IRA and an informer for the British secret service. When he was uncovered, McGartland went on the run and had been living in hiding ever since, during which time he had been tracked down and shot twice.

Once by Elva herself.

They drove on in silence for a few minutes, giving her time to mull over the events of the evening and to ruminate about who might have given her up. She looked at the problem from a myriad of angles, rejecting one thought, replacing it with another, until things became a blur, like looking at a single object through a kaleidoscope. And then that single object came into sharp focus, no matter what angle she approached it from. She felt the heavy hand of the grave settle about her, and she physically sagged under its weight. There was nothing worse in this world than being betrayed, not by an informer, but by someone she considered to be a friend, a mentor. She sighed.

"God, that was a heavy sigh," her uncle commented.

"I think I know who shopped me," she said. "I've been going over the list in my mind. There's only one name who keeps coming up."

"Can you tell me who's on the list?"

"It's probably better you don't know," she answered honestly, even though she knew she could trust him to the grave. "But I need a piece — something small."

"Don't you want to take my baby?" He laughed, pointing toward the AK on the floor.

"It's a bit big to put in my panties," she said, and he blushed.

As they arrived on the outskirts of Dun Laoghaire, and he turned off Queen's Road onto Marine Drive to go back to the pub, she placed her hand on his arm. "Take me back to the house. I've got to deal with this tonight and then get out of here tomorrow. Mairead's the only one who knows where we are, and she knows to keep her mouth shut. DeLisle will never find us, never in a month of Sundays."

He replied, "Just to be on the safe side, I'll drive you up to Larne tomorrow, and you can take the boat over to Stranraer. There's not much of a paper trail for the boat. You can take the train to Glasgow and then catch a flight over to Frankfurt or Amsterdam. After that you can make your connection..."

"Teaching your grandmother to suck eggs, are ye?" She laughed.

He looked a bit sheepish. "Sorry, love. Forgot you were an old hand at this."

He pulled up outside the house and cut the engine. "Go and change. I'll wait for you."

"Are you sure?" she asked, looking him straight in the eye. "I don't want this to come back on you."

"You're the only family I have, love. Besides, someone's got to look after you." He nodded to her wrists, at the angry red welts that had risen on her fair skin. She got out of the car, ran into the house, and grabbed her leather jacket. She hurriedly threw her things in her case — there wasn't much to begin with — scribbled a quick note for Mairead, and ran back out. She put the case in the back seat then climbed into the front.

"How's this?" her uncle asked, handing her a small pistol. "Think that'll fit?"

She looked at the weapon and smiled. It was a stainless steel, .25 calibre Bersa Firestorm automatic that fit in the palm of her hand. The suppressor was about the same length as the gun. It was a nice piece, well kept, and a model she had used before. It held ten rounds, which was more than enough for her purposes, yet she took the extra mag when he offered.

"All right, love, where to?"

"Verbena Avenue, out near the Leopardstown golf course."

"Foxrock?"

She nodded.

His jaw set in a hard line, and she could see the muscles working in his cheeks. "O'Brien?"

"The one and only."

"Fuck! So much for not being involved!" He stretched over and opened the glove compartment. Inside sat two large automatic pistols, both Glocks. "I don't think that little pea shooter will cut it. Times have changed. He's got cancer and is not long for this life — it'll be even shorter now — but he's a big name in the criminal enterprise in Dublin. He runs most of the south side. Guns, drugs, sex trade, slaves, anything to make a Euro, and he's into it. His son's next in line to the throne, and they're using the old routes to smuggle in their gear."

"So…"

"He still lives in the old house with his son, but there are bodyguards everywhere. It's a rough business these days, what with all the Eastern Europeans flowing in here and wanting a piece of the pie. Fucking drugs have ruined us. Our once fair city has the highest incidence of AIDS per capita than anywhere else in the world, and it's all down to gurriers like O'Brien. No one will lose a minute of sleep over that old bastard. But it won't be easy…"

"Well, to paraphrase a Navy Seal I once knew," she laughed, "'No one said it was going to be easy…'"

They parked two streets away then crossed through the golf course, approaching the stately home from the rear. The north side of the building almost touched the dense growth of trees, the ground underfoot soft and spongy. The air was full of the scent of freshly mown grass. "Fuck me, that's quite the place," her uncle offered, peering out through the leaves, the faithful AK-47 cradled in his arms. He had a Glock in each pocket.

417

"His bedroom is up on the second floor, the one facing us with the lights on. The room beside he uses as an office." As she spoke, there was movement on the ground floor, and two men walked into the kitchen and over to the fridge.

Her uncle whispered, "The one on the right is his son. The guy on the left is one of the resident bodyguards. A thoroughly nasty piece of work and not to be underestimated."

"That's okay," she replied. "I've no intention of meeting them." Silently, she pushed past him and ran across the grass, crouching low until she reached the back wall. The grass was soggy after all the rain, the moisture creeping into her shoes. It was chilly, but she ignored the sensation. Thick boughs of ivy coated the walls, and she moved along until she found the drainpipe running to the top gutter. Using a combination of the ivy and the drainpipe, she quickly climbed up to the window of the second-floor office then paused to check the inside of the frame using a tiny Maglite.

There were no magnetic breakers or wires running around the window. She eased a thin credit card between the acrylic edges of the frame and jiggled the lock until it popped free. She eased the frame upward a fraction at a time, listening intently for noises from inside the house. The faint sounds of a soccer match drifted up from downstairs, interspersed with the occasional curse as a favourite player did something stupid or an attempt on goal was stymied. The windows had recently been replaced, a blessing in itself as old frames were often painted over and virtually

418

impossible to open. They required a glass cutter and a lot more time and patience than she currently had at her disposal.

She moved the frame all the way up and clambered over the sill, leaving the window open behind her. A silent exit would be required. Pausing for a moment, she attached the suppressor to the barrel of the Firestorm. As it turned out, her uncle's car was a rolling arsenal of weapons, each one concealed well enough to pass a cursory glance at a traffic stop.

The office carpet had heavy underpad that nicely absorbed her footsteps, allowing her to cross silently to the door. Cracking open the door a fraction, she peered out on to the landing. Across from the office was O'Brien's bedroom. A thin sliver of light peeked out from under his door, and as she waited, she heard a muffled, phlegmy cough. It sounded painful. Slipping out of the office, she put her ear to the bedroom door then eased down the handle. It opened without a sound.

She opened it far enough to get inside, slipped in, then closed it behind her. The room was in darkness, save for a bedside lamp that was turned low. O'Brien lay in the bed, his emaciated body propped up against a heavy set of pillows. On the sheets in front of him a book lay cracked open. He had fallen asleep while reading. A snifter beside the bed held what looked like a healthy shot of brandy. A wide selection of pill bottles of various sizes sat arrayed beside the snifter.

O'Brien's eyes were closed, his breathing raspy. A discoloured washcloth lay beside him on the other pillow. She

419

walked across the room and sat on the bed, staring at the man she had once trusted with her life. He was a mere shadow of the once vigorous warrior that she had known, the cancer having rotted him away to nothing. The once strong hands now looked like talons, their veins outlined against the translucent skin.

She tapped his hand with the barrel of the pistol.

He swallowed hard, and from the expression on his face, it pained him to do so. His eyes popped open, blinked a few times as he tried to focus, then widened in surprise.

"Elva," he croaked. Then he saw the pistol.

She said, "Max DeLisle tried to kill me tonight. He admitted to killing Frank, all to get to me, to get to Sean. You're the only person who could have provided that info."

She watched his eyes, the cunning intelligence that flickered there. Even though he only had a little time left, she knew he wanted to go on his terms. Everyone wants one more day.

He nodded. "MI5 blackmailed me. They caught my boy running drugs over from England and made me a deal to keep him out of jail. They're mostly interested in raghead terrorists these days, but then the other day they show up and ask me questions about Sean Dempsey. I didn't have anything to give them on Sean, but just as they were leaving, they asked me about you. Sounded like they knew and wanted to know how they could get in touch with you. Frank came to mind, but as God's my witness, I had no idea they would pass the information on to DeLisle or that Frank would be in any danger. I'm sorry for what happened."

MI5.

DeLisle.

She frowned, trying to make sense of what she was hearing. "What the fuck has MI5 got to do with DeLisle?" she asked.

He shrugged, the movement causing a spasm of coughing. He held the washcloth to his lips, and when he brought it away, she saw it was stained with blood. His breathing was shallow, a liquid sound emanating from his chest. "The war on terror has brought together some strange bedfellows," he replied. "DeLisle's a hoodlum of the highest order, so maybe he's trading information as well."

"Who from MI5 came to see you?"

"I only recognized Arthur Cupples. There was one other, but I didn't recognize him, and no introductions were made. Built like a shithouse door, and he had a funny accent..."

"It changed from a Yank accent to a Belfast accent," she interrupted.

O'Brien nodded. "That's right. He's the one who asked about you."

She sighed. MI5 and Max DeLisle.

And now a wild card.

"Thanks for the info," she said and shot him in the face. The tiny weapon made a quiet cough, and a tiny brass shell landed on the bed. The round did not have the power to exit the skull, instead tumbling around inside and shredding brain matter to pulp. She emptied the entire clip into his head, the ejected shells falling in a neat pile on the centre of the bed. She then laid the gun on the sheets, tiptoed across the room, crossed back into the office, and made her way back down the drainpipe after closing the window behind her. Pausing for a moment when she reached the ground, she checked the kitchen windows, saw they were clear, and raced across the garden. After getting back into cover beside her uncle, she peeled off the surgical gloves and stuck them in her jeans. They would be discarded along the road.

"Let's go," she said.

They slipped back into the darkness of the trees and were soon swallowed up by the shadows.

Her uncle dropped her back to the pub, where she went inside quickly, grabbed her sister, and took her into the office. Mairead's face darkened.

"Where did you disappear to?" Mairead demanded. "You left us all here to look after things. Mam went off home a while ago..."

Elva grabbed her sister by the arm. "Mairead. Shut the fuck up and listen. That guy earlier was one of Max DeLisle's mob. DeLisle is here in Dun Laoghaire, and they grabbed me outside. Fortunately, Uncle Mick was having a fag and saw what happened. One of them is dead, so I've got to leave, and leave now. Please tell Mam I'll call her as soon as I get landed. Make up something to explain why I had to run."

Mairead sagged, and Elva hugged her fiercely. "I'll see you shortly."

She quickly went back out through the well-inebriated crowd, slid in beside her uncle, and said, "Let's go."

He patted her knee in a paternal fashion, switched on the ignition, and drove off. They headed back into Dublin, along the quays, and up O'Connell Street for what would be, for her, the last time. Despite the late hour, the streets were bustling with locals and tourists enjoying the abundant nightlife that the city had to offer. Dublin buses creaked and groaned, belching noxious fumes as they carried partygoers off to the suburbs. The massive stainless-steel needle gleamed, its base thronged with photographers. The centre median of the street was cluttered with bicycles of every shape and size, a mecca for thieves.

She felt a gentle tug at her heartstrings; she loved Dublin, loved the craic; a pint in the Abbey Mooney, coffee at Bewley's, a stroll through Stephen's Green on a sunny day — yet the prospect of starting life anew filled her with hope. Despite the fact they had only been in Tofino for a few days, she had fallen in love with the place. Besides, Mairead was there, and they had shopped and laughed and spent time going in and out of the local galleries and art shops, and hanging out and drinking coffee, something they had not done in many years. They had met up each day at Breakers, a local coffee shop, and it had become their "local," creating the roots of a tiny tradition. The connection had been re-established, and now she was looking for a house. She could hardly believe it herself.

A house.

Normalcy was something she had only dreamed about.

The big car provided an extremely smooth ride, and by the time they had passed out of Dublin and were heading north toward the border, she was fast asleep. She came awake when she felt her uncle shaking her gently. Opening her eyes, she found herself parked outside a massive building that had a blue and red logo on top that proclaimed, "Stena Lines."

"We're here," he said.

Looking about, she noticed that everything was new; buildings, fences, even the marking on the roadway. "Where's here?" She rubbed her eyes.

"This is the new Stena Line ferry to Stranraer. We're just outside Belfast, and the city airport is over on the other side of the inlet."

Glancing at the clock on the dashboard, she noticed it was just after 2:00 a.m., and she was surprised to see the lot filling up. "Busy place," she commented.

Her uncle nodded. "We're booked on the 3:30 a.m. sailing, which gets into Stranraer at just after six. It's a popular route with businesspeople, as they can be pretty much anywhere in Scotland by about nine o'clock for meetings. I've used it a few times as the crossing from Dublin to Holyhead in Wales can be a real bastard at times, especially if a storm blows up. It's a pukefest when that happens."

She laughed. Then, realizing they were in the lane to board the ferry, she asked, "Are you driving over? I thought you were just going to drop me!"

"Ach, I thought I'd drive you to the airport in Glasgow. It'll be faster that way, and at least I can keep you out of trouble until then."

She punched him on the arm. "Thanks. For everything."

"They've got a great wee cafe on board, so we can get a bite to eat. All this excitement has got me ravenous. We'll be boarding in about twenty minutes."

*

At Glasgow Airport, after her uncle dropped her off, she booked the first EasyJet flight she could find to Amsterdam, and then while waiting for her flight, she went online and booked a direct Air France flight from Amsterdam to Vancouver. She knew the seaplane shuttle to Tofino ran regularly from the Harbour Air terminal, so she would reserve a seat when she arrived in Vancouver, just in case there were any delays in the connecting flights. At the same time, she sent off an email to Sean, letting him know the travel details.

With the travel now all being sorted, she headed for the duty-free area, picked up a backpack, some clothes, fresh underwear, and makeup, and made a beeline for the washrooms to freshen up. Her dirty clothes went into the backpack, and she felt much better having washed up and dressed in the new outfit. That being done, she grabbed a newspaper and headed for the nearest Starbucks to get a decent coffee. If all went according to plan, she would be back at the Wick with Sean in just under ten hours.

CHAPTER 20

WHIPLASH

At Dublin Airport, the jet was waiting for them, fuelled and ready. Following a perfunctory check of their credentials, they took off on time, the first part of the journey somewhat turbulent, as announced by the captain, heavy offshore winds buffeting the tiny jet. Riordan grasped the armrest firmly, mostly to keep his balance. Flying never bothered him — he had done so much he never gave it a second thought — but this level of turbulence was slightly unnerving. It sounded for a moment like the galley was going to come apart. In a huge jet it would be barely noticeable, but in this small vessel, every motion was magnified significantly. At one point he thought he might get whiplash.

But then the pilot climbed above the incoming storm, and the violent buffeting ceased. Riordan breathed a sigh of relief. DeLisle got up and fixed himself a drink, ignoring Riordan completely. Which was fine by him. The less he spoke to the man, the less likely he was to kill him. DeLisle pounded back several belts of whisky and spent the remainder of the trip staring out the window. Maybe he was more affected by Billy K's death than he let on. Or maybe, psycho that he was, he was figuring out which one of his team could step into Billy K's shoes. Just like large corporations, even criminals had to do some sort of succession planning. But that was always a risky business, since once you announced you were grooming someone to be your successor, they might just decide they didn't want to wait for years to take the reins. Some sort of accident could be arranged to hasten the demise of the incumbent. After all, they were criminals.

The flight to London passed quickly and he felt, then heard the note of the engines change as the pilot started their descent into London City Airport. It was raining in London, so the landing was less than smooth, but they were soon deplaning and handing over their passports to the immigration officer who greeted them at the VIP terminal. The interaction was brief, the examination of documents so cursory that Riordan was convinced the officer was in DeLisle's pocket.

They walked outside to the curb, where a Range Rover sat idling, and DeLisle climbed into the back seat. "Need a ride?" DeLisle asked, slipping his cellphone out of his pocket. No doubt it was time to make a few calls about Billy K's demise.

Riordan shook his head. "I'll take a cab out to Heathrow and get a room for the night," he replied, grateful to be away from DeLisle. "I'll check the flight times to Vancouver and give you a call to confirm if you still want to make the trip."

DeLisle nodded. "I've got business to take care of tonight, so check in later." Riordan pushed the door shut, and the big vehicle eased away into the stream of traffic. He waved over a waiting cab, climbed inside, and asked the driver to take him out to a decent, upscale hotel close to Heathrow. The driver nodded enthusiastically; it would be a hefty fare. They settled on the Hilton, based on the driver's glowing recommendation and what he felt would be their ability to find a room. The more expensive the hotel, the more likely they would have rooms available.

The cabbie turned out to be right, and after he was dropped at the front door, Riordan gave him a handsome tip. He grabbed his backpack and headed inside. After checking in, he was about to make his way to the room when he noticed the hotel bar was fairly busy. *Why not*, he thought, detouring his way to the bar. He found himself a comfy seat and ordered a large Bushmills. He filled his nose with the peaty aroma before knocking it back. The fiery liquid burned, an old, familiar feeling, and he nodded for the barman to hit him again.

Taking out his iPad, he connected to the hotel's Wi-Fi network, opened up the browser, and checked out the times of direct flights from Heathrow to Vancouver. Surprisingly, the Lufthansa flight was the earliest and most direct, so he booked a ticket online and had the confirmation emailed to him. His cellphone buzzed as the mail arrived, and he checked to make sure the 2D barcode was available on the screen. He fired off a couple of quick emails as well.

That being done, he took a long sip of the whiskey and perused the late-night snack menu. He decided to have an order of wings — good old comfort food — and then ordered a Guinness at the same time. Putting away the iPad, he picked up his cellphone and called Featherstone.

"Daniel, how goes the battle?" When in pursuit mode, Featherstone liked details.

Riordan complied and filled him in on the events of the evening. The big man listened intently, gently probing from time to time to get clarity around a specific incident. He was particularly interested in the call log on the phone. When Riordan finished, he asked, "Do you think it was Dempsey with the AK?"

"No, it was someone else who followed us from the bar. Dempsey was a no-show, which is why they lifted the girl in the first place."

"Where are you now?"

"Out at Heathrow at the moment. I've booked the 10:25 a.m. Lufthansa flight to Vancouver, and that will get me in around noon local time. I'll head over to the Beaver and get the shuttle to Tofino."

The Flying Beaver was one of the haunts for the team. It served good beer, good food, and was in close proximity to the international airport. The fact that the waitresses were all attractive and friendly also helped. The owner knew the team all by name and treated Featherstone like royalty, given that Feather's crew had helped him out of a serious bind a few years earlier. Situated on the middle arm of the Fraser River, patrons of the Beaver were able to watch seaplanes depart and land from the dock. Harbour Air, a local airline, was located in the adjacent building. With over twenty-five years in business and more than thirty aircraft, Harbour Air had made several strategic acquisitions to allow it to become the largest all-seaplane company in the world. Riordan and team used them all the time. They provided frequent flights connecting Vancouver to various destinations on Vancouver Island, as well as the Gulf Islands, along with a wide selection of scenic adventure tours and private charters.

Featherstone had a standing account with Harbour Air, and Riordan had emailed them to let them know he needed a seat. It was the fastest way to get in and out of Tofino. A motorcycle would also be waiting for him in Tofino, since a car rental might draw too much attention.

"Zo, you are flying with ze Germains," Featherstone said, quoting from *Snatch*, another of his favourite movies. Riordan believed Featherstone could recite the entire dialogue, word for word.

"Yep."

"Need some help at that end? I can put one of the lads on standby."

"Thanks, but just a suitcase."

"Small or large?"

"I better go with the large," Riordan replied. "Large" was a euphemism for a long gun such as the type a sniper would use. The box would also contain a handgun, plus various assorted weapons and munitions.

"So you really think that's where Dempsey's gone to ground? It's a long way if it turns out to be a wild goose chase!"

"I know," Riordan replied. "But if you wanted to disappear, what better place than Tofino?"

"You have a point."

"What's been going on at your end?" Riordan asked.

"The good news is we've been in and out of DeLisle's place a couple of times. I've got one of the best safecrackers in the business, and he managed to break into DeLisle's safe. The bad news is the documents are not there. He's obviously stored them somewhere else. We've got eyes on his place, and the phone is bugged, as well as the rooms, so maybe we'll pick up something when he gets home. I'm afraid you'll have to keep up this charade until we get more intel."

Riordan sighed. Frustration built at the recognition he was still in a bind, with no end in sight. DeLisle was still calling the shots, and Riordan was dancing around like an organ grinder's monkey. After breaking the connection, he called DeLisle.

"Riordan here," he said when DeLisle answered. "I've booked the morning Lufthansa flight to Vancouver."

"You'll have to make this run solo," DeLisle replied, his voice strained. "I've got a couple of things I have to get sorted, so go and get me my money, kill the cunt, and get back here. You know what's at stake."

DeLisle hung up.

Riordan ground his teeth, seething in anger. It took every ounce of restraint he possessed not to head over to the restaurant and empty a full clip into DeLisle. He caught himself just before hurling the cellphone across the room. Turning off the lights, he buried his face in the pillow, anxious to get some sleep before his flight. Tracking down Dempsey required him to be on top of his game, and a good night's rest was badly needed to recharge his batteries.

*

The flight passed without incident. Riordan was much relieved that he managed to doze a little in between meals and movies. First-class in Lufthansa was exceptional, much better than the Air Canada and British Airways treatment to which he was accustomed.

After an initial futile attempt to sleep at the hotel, he had given up and taken a brief few minutes to connect with Nancy and to hear the frenetic voices of his boys stampeding around the house in the background. They came dutifully to the phone when asked, and he choked up when he tried to speak. When Nancy came back on, he could hear the strain in her voice, no matter how cheery she

433

attempted to be. She well understood the threat hanging over their heads like the sword of Damocles.

Their lives stood in the balance, held there by DeLisle. Ever the pragmatic person, during the conversation Nancy had asked, "Do I need to pack our stuff?" meaning would they, as a family, have to disappear. That was the trigger. The black fury resurfaced, and he held it at bay, at least until the phone conversation was over. He had no illusions as to the type of person DeLisle was and what the outcome of the assignment might be. DeLisle held all the cards at the moment, and Riordan desperately needed to swing the balance back in his favour. However, doing that was not going to be easy.

The call finished, he rolled over, and much to his surprise, went straight to sleep.

It was just after 10:00 a.m. when the plane started its descent into Vancouver. Looking out the window, Riordan was heartened to see the ocean and the wondrous views of the surrounding mountains. It was good to be home. After an interminable wait at immigration — there were only two officers on duty to handle the entire aircraft — and since there appeared to be many foreign visitors, the analysis of documents and passports and questions seemed to take forever.

He went straight outside and grabbed a taxi over to the Beaver. It was just a short drive from the airport, and the cabbie was grumpy that he had received such a short fare. When they pulled up outside the pub, Riordan climbed out and gave the man the exact fare, which elicited another frown. The car tried to roar off, a hard thing to do in a Prius hybrid, and Riordan gave the man the finger. He went into the pub, deciding to have a bite to eat before heading off to Tofino.

It was just after opening time, and the waitress recognized him immediately. "Hi Daniel, there's a case in the storeroom for you," she offered. "Buster dropped it off earlier." Buster, an ex-Navy SEAL who loved to blow things up, was the latest addition to Featherstone's team. His rugged good looks made him an "absolute chick magnet," according to Nancy. All the waitresses loved Buster, and Buster loved them all back — frequently.

He went out on the patio, which was empty save for one table. The glass-enclosed patio protected patrons from strong breezes coming in off the river and had a combination of tables and chairs, as well as comfortable sofas scattered around. A man sat at one of the tables overlooking the water, an almost full pint on the table, his newspaper splayed open and a large dog lying on the ground beside him. The dog stirred when Riordan walked out, and climbed to his feet.

Riordan held out his hand, and the dog sniffed it. "Hello, Otis," Riordan said, patting the dog on the head. It, like its owner, were permanent fixtures at the pub. "Hello, John."

The man put down the paper and pulled off his shades. The morning sun glistened off his bald pate. "Daniel," he said, "haven't seen you around here for a while." They shook hands.

435

"Looting and shooting, John," he replied.

"Well, someone's got to do it," John replied, slipped on his shades, and went back to his paper. Otis, satisfied there was no threat to his master, lay down.

Riordan grabbed a corner table and sat down, closing his eyes and letting the sun seep into his pores. He heard a rustle by his side, and a voice said, "What can I get for you?" His eyes slammed open, a wide grin splitting his face. Nancy stood there, the sun casting golden aura around her, a menu in her hand. She wore a simple white cotton dress that showed off her tanned arms and legs. She laughed.

Tossing the menu aside, she eased herself into his lap, wrapped her arms around him, and kissed him fiercely. Otis looked away. It was several moments before they broke the embrace. "I ordered the eggs Benedict for you," she said. "I know it's your favourite, and they don't make them as good as this in England." He felt a momentary pang of guilt and made a mental note to delete the incriminating photographs on his cellphone.

He hugged her again, holding her close, burying his face in her neck and savouring her scent. "Miss me?" she asked, and he kissed her again.

"Thank you for coming over," he said, his soul lightened. He couldn't stop grinning.

"Feather called and told me you'd be here," she replied. "Said you might need some TLC."

"And Feather knows best."

"So?" She cocked an eye.

"What?" he said, puzzled.

"Do you really want me to draw you a picture?"

The light came on. "Nope," he replied.

She led him downstairs to the washrooms, giggled, looked around and then pushed him into the ladies' room. There were three large stainless-steel stalls, two regular and one extra-large for wheelchair access at the end. Dragging him inside the largest, she pushed the door shut, locked it, and kissed him savagely, tugging at his belt.

"We have to be a bit more careful!" Riordan whispered.

"Fuck that," she growled, tiny beads of sweat erupting on her forehead. Pushing him down onto the toilet seat, she lifted one foot and rested it on his leg, then pulled back the sundress tantalizingly slowly. Her well-tanned thighs gleamed. Leaning forward, he kissed the inside of her knee then ran his tongue along her inner thigh. She groaned, grasping a handful of his hair and pulling his face hard against her pussy. She wore no panties, and she had had the fresh wax that she had been threatening before he had left. The musty scent attacked his nostrils, and he dipped his tongue into her moist cleft. Her body shuddered.

His hard-on ached. Running his hands up under her dress, he cupped her firm breasts, rubbing his thumb over the taut nipples. Leaning over, she kissed him deeply, his tongue playing and dancing over hers. She started to moan loudly into his mouth as he sucked her tongue, playing with her breasts while she slipped one hand between her legs, her toes curling on his leg as she rubbed herself.

He broke away, kissing down her neck, all over her collarbone and down between her breasts. He breathed across her left breast, then started to nuzzle her beautiful pink nipple, drawing it into his mouth and biting ever so softly, then flicking it with his tongue. Kissing her stomach, he tasted the sweat on her body. Stopping at her belly button, he tugged on her gold stud just as she pulled her fingers from her pussy, glistening with her juices. He grabbed her hand and licked the sweetness from her fingers, and she bent over. She took his cock head inside her mouth and ran her tongue all over it, circling and flicking. He gasped. She took more of his cock into her mouth, bobbing her head up and down, letting her teeth graze just a little, so that they gave just enough pressure for it to feel amazing. She slid it in and out of her mouth, pausing at the tip sometimes to suck on it or to circle it with her tongue.

She grasped him in her hand, her mouth working just the tip of his cock, her hand stroking the base of his cock slowly so as not to drive him over the edge. After a few moments, she let his cock pop out of her mouth.

"Fuck me, Daniel. Fuck me now!" She straddled him, pushing his cock deep inside her pussy, all the way in, the whole length slipping into her in one smooth, slow motion. The feeling was like a surge of electricity. Riordan gasped. She pulled the sundress over her head, tossing it one side, then locked her fingers around the back of his head. There was not much movement to start, the way she always did, tantalizingly slowly, holding his cock deep inside her. With every thrust he came out a bit farther, sliding more back in, just slowly enough to build toward the inevitable.

Pulling her head toward him, he kissed her deeply. Almost breathless and sweaty in the confined space, he grasped her hips and pounded into her, completely soaked in her juices. Nancy started moaning beneath her breath, her eyes tightly shut, her muscles clenching on his cock as she shuddered in a powerful orgasm. He pushed in and out of her one more time before erupting in vigorous, glorious thrusts. She slumped against him, her chest heaving, and he wrapped his arms tightly about her.

"Okay, you're hurting me now," she whispered in his ear. "Sometimes you just don't know your own strength." She stood up. "Time to switch, big boy."

After cleaning up a little in the washroom, they headed back outside. Her cheeks glowed, and as they sat down, the waitress appeared with his meal.

"Perfect timing," Nancy said, and the waitress winked at her.

"Can I get you something, Nancy?" the waitress asked, her accent betraying her Irish roots. Not that the red hair and freckled skin didn't give a hint. "We've got some lovely sausages in fresh from the market."

Nancy couldn't help herself. "No thanks, Tina." She giggled. "But maybe a glass of white wine."

Tina laughed and wandered off.

Riordan shook his head. The two had obviously been in collusion. He noticed such things. The eggs were poached to perfection, as always, the hollandaise freshly made, and the peameal bacon cooked just right. Around them, the patio had started to fill with the afternoon crowd, in for a quick pint, thirsty after a long walk along the dike. The buzz of conversation stepped up a notch.

"How long before you'll know?" Nancy asked, sipping her wine.

He shrugged. "To be honest, a lot depends what I find over on the island. I think I'm in the endgame, so maybe a few more days."

"Will you have to go back to London?"

"I think so."

She placed her hand on his, a simple gesture that conveyed so much. "Be safe. And remember, our home is wherever we all are together. I'd miss this place, but it's not like I grew up here. Do whatever you need to do, just come back to us."

He smiled.

"And no more bullet holes!"

After he finished his meal, he ordered a cappuccino, and they spent the next while chatting about her work: the latest crisis at the hospital, potential cutbacks in healthcare funding, and which doctor was leading the pool in the "asshole of the week" category. Riordan knew most of the doctors by sight, if not by name, and shook his head often at some of the stories that Nancy shared. To him it was incredulous how some of these so-called well-educated, dedicated to care people behaved, especially to nursing staff. There were many evenings when Nancy came home, tossed her stuff on the counter, and said, "I need a martini." Which was his cue that she had had a run-in with a doctor and that he better get his ass off the sofa and get the fixings out.

There were also some evenings that he wanted to get in his car, head over to the hospital, find one of these "special people," and give him a five-knuckle sandwich. The doctors had their reserved parking spots at the hospital, conveniently bearing name plates, so there had been occasion when he found himself late at night with a slim-jim, popping the lock on a particular car and then taking a few minutes to urinate inside. He knew it was childish, but when he confessed his extracurricular activity to Featherstone one night over a beer, the big man actually downed a couple more pints and accompanied him on the next "raid."

The flight departure was announced over the tinny PA system, and he paid the bill, got up, and wandered over to the check-in desk. The long, hard-plastic case was sitting by the desk. Nancy lifted one eye. She knew what was inside.

441

"Remember what I said about the bullet holes," she whispered. Kissing him fiercely, she looked him in the eye. "I love you," she said and walked away.

"Love you too," he replied.

CHAPTER 21

BRAVEHEART

The flight to Tofino took only forty minutes, the seaplane heading out across the Straits of Georgia, passing over Nanaimo, and then crossing Clayoquot Plateau Provincial Park before descending into the bay outside Tofino. The sky was unusually clear, turbulence free, and Riordan enjoyed the glorious view of the park as they made their descent. He and Nancy loved Tofino, and they had visited on many occasions. The Wickaninnish Inn, better known as the "Wick," was one of their favourite places to stay, and the next time they visited they had promised each other to take surfing lessons.

It was only a few months ago that they had been to the Wick for the wedding of one of Featherstone's team, a small but mighty Scotsman named Jock Findlay, an ex-Royal Marine with an accent so thick that he required a translator. For fun, they had all rented kilts — an additional bonus, as Nancy loved men in kilts. Just before the ceremony on the beach, the lads had all painted their faces blue and charged down the beach like extras from *Braveheart*, roaring, "They can take our land, but they can never take our freedom!"

Findlay loved that part.

As with most things Scottish, everything done to the nth degree possible, the party had gone into the wee hours, with toasts and drams and dancing that bore some resemblance to its Celtic roots, until many just passed out. Findlay's accent got thicker and thicker until they eventually gave up trying to understand him. Riordan often joked that they didn't need to encrypt their phones as long as they had Findlay around.

A majestic bald eagle soared in the thermals as they approached, searching the waters for food. Salmon were plentiful in the area, and the eagles could swoop down and hoist a thirty-pound salmon effortlessly. As a result, the locals kept close watch on their pets. The tiny craft was rocked heavily by the waves as they landed. Unless the waves were low, there was no such thing as a smooth landing in a seaplane. The pilot cut back on the throttle, the vibrations ceased, and they cruised slowly to the docks, where the local airline representative tied the pontoons to cleats. The pilot finally cut the engines, and the small group deplaned onto the long wooden dock where the crew were busily extracting the luggage from the interior of the spacious pontoons.

Riordan picked up the long, plastic case, walked along the weathered planking, then climbed the steps to the office of Harbour Air. Outside sat a brand new Husqvarna TC 449 motocross bike, its new tires gleaming. Given the remoteness of the area, there was always a chance that he might have to leave a paved road and head into trails, so the robust motocross tires would give him the purchase he would need on uneven ground, even rocky terrain. Strapping the case to his back, he climbed on, took the keys from inside the helmet — crime was not a big issue in Tofino — pulled it on, and thumbed the electric starter. The engine roared to life, a gratifying visceral sensation, and he revved it a couple of times before engaging the clutch and tearing off down the street. He headed out of town, along the Pacific Rim Highway, passing stands of majestic pines and cedars until he saw the turnoff for Osprey Lane, where the Wick was located.

As he drove, he noticed the signs that had been placed along the road, bold arrows pointing toward high ground. The sign said, "Tsunami escape route," which he always found to be more than a little disconcerting. At the fork in the road, he turned away from the Wick and headed into the heavily forested area that lined the beach. Pulling into the trees, he parked, covered the bike, with some pine boughs, and headed toward the shore, the heavy case still on his back.

Trying to put himself in Dempsey's shoes, he felt that having come into a shitload of money, Dempsey would splurge for a few weeks, given he felt he was safe. There were two places to "splurge" in Tofino: the Wickaninnish Inn or the Clayoquot Wilderness resort, the latter being known as the location of Ryan Reynolds and Scarlett Johannson's wedding, even though, like most Hollywood marriages it had not lasted.

The Clayoquot was located a shortish boat ride from Tofino and advertised the perfect pairing of soft adventure and soft beds.

445

"Yuppies camping" was how Riordan described the place. It was situated at the mouth of the Bedwell River, where it spilled into a nine-mile-long fjord. Riordan had been there once. The resort boasted an enclave of twenty white canvas guest tents, massage and treatment tents, dining tents, lounge tents, and a massive timber cookhouse, all nestled in dense bush. For the well-to-do, it offered the ultimate experience in individual pampering and remote, untamed wilderness.

Riordan hated pretension in any form, and one morning, following a sumptuous breakfast, he announced that he was going in search of the young virgins who rose before the dawn each morning to hand churn the butter that was served at their table. That got him a slap. Nancy loved the place, but for Riordan, whose life consisted of a series of safe entrances and exits, it was the ultimate trap. So he figured Dempsey, given his background, would be thinking the same.

That left the Wick, and hence the decision to set up an observation post to put eyes on the people staying at the inn. If that didn't work, he would spend some time in the town, watching and waiting.

Dempsey was here.

He could feel it.

At the edge of the tree line, he paused, opened the case, and took out a pair of high-power Zeiss binoculars. A soft breeze blew off the ocean, carrying with it the invigorating salt air to his nostrils. He breathed deeply, reminded as always of the wonderful Irish ballad called Fiddler's Green, and the line: "as I walked by the dockside one evening so fair, to view the salt waters and take the sea air."

The Wick sat perched on a rocky promontory, about four hundred yards away, and he had a clear view of both the old building and the new suites that had been built facing the beach. Putting the binos to his eyes, he focused on the small outdoor patio where several patrons sat drinking coffee and reading newspapers. The new building had a little cafe on the ground floor, which produced the most delicious chocolate croissants, and a splendid cappuccino. Riordan had enjoyed the croissants on more than one occasion. The completely fearless, abundant red squirrels loved croissant flakes. Ignoring the couples, he focused on each face in turn, looking for his target, but Dempsey was not one of them.

Squatting down, he then turned the binos on some of the figures strolling down the long beach. Again, his search proved fruitless, but he was not discouraged. That was the thing about surveillance — many, many hours of boredom followed by moments of intense activity when a target was sighted. Or sometimes, the surveillance failed to turn up a target. But that was the name of the game. He had learned a long time ago the value of patience and could lie for hours, unmoving, totally focused on the task at hand.

His memory flew back over the years, as it often did during periods of quiet contemplation, to the times spent by his father's

447

side on the banks of the Braid River, watching and waiting for the trout to strike. They had their favourite spots along the river, all the way from the "carry" and up past the ancient iron bridge to deep eddies along the curving bank where their quarry could be found. There they would stand in silent communion, heads bowed, intently focused. The circumstances were perfect; line hauled tight through the eyes of the rod, the tip slightly bowed against the drag of the current and the sun hidden behind ever-present clouds. In the distance would come the occasional crack of gunfire from the nearby army barracks as the young squaddies commenced their morning routine.

A tiny twitch at the end of the rod, and then another, slightly harder this time, and his heart would race. As his hands would stretch toward his rod, his father would rest a hand gently on his shoulder and say, "Not yet, he's just playing with the bait." He knew his father was right — there had been many times where in his excitement he had grabbed the rod and hauled back, only to find nothing on the hook. The tiny twitch would grow to a frantic blur of movement, and his father would take a long drag of his cigarette and nod. Gently lifting the rod, he would wait for the final tug and then pull back to sink the barb. There was nothing like that feeling, knowing the quarry was on the line.

A flurry of movement from the trees near the Wick caught his eye. He turned the binos to see a massive bald eagle sink into its expansive nest atop a solitary pine tree perched on the edge of the beach. He settled down at the bottom of a cedar, nestling into its exposed roots, and lay back, enjoying the feel of the sun's rays on his face and hoping that the rain would hold off. Outdoor surveillance was only tolerable when the weather cooperated.

The next couple of hours proved to be fruitless. Then a few more people appeared on the beach, dressed in wetsuits and carrying surfboards. They plunged eagerly into the charging surf, many of them expertly riding the churning waves all the way to the beach. Whoops of joy and excitement reached his ears. But there was no sign of Dempsey. A thought came to him as he was staring at the inlet behind the hotel, where they had all stood in their kilts as Findlay and his bride took his vows. Taking out his cellphone, he searched for the image of Dempsey that Cupples had provided, and when he verified the picture, he emailed the image to Findlay, gave him a few minutes, then dialled his number.

"Findlay here," came the prompt response in a heavy Scots burr. Featherstone's team carried their devices at all times, and unless they found themselves in dire circumstances, they were required to answer immediately, no matter the hour. Their smartphones ran a special paging software that brought the device to life, even if it was shut off. The GPS tracking feature was always on, a safety precaution for the team. One of the more interesting features of the device was their ability to remotely activate the phone, so that they could surreptitiously listen in to what the participants thought was a private conversation. It had proved useful many times during meetings, when the BlackBerry had "accidentally" been left behind.

"Why do Scotsmen wear kilts?"

"Daniel, my wee friend, have you got a new one?" Riordan could picture Findlay's face splitting in a wide grin as he replied, "Because sheep don't like the sound of zippers?"

Riordan laughed. "Nope. To keep the back of the sheep dry when it rains!"

Findlay roared with laughter at the end of the phone. "Now that's a good one, Daniel. I must share that with the lads. Anyway, you didn't call me up just to tell me a sheep joke. What can I do for you?"

"What's your workload like at the moment?"

"It's no bad," Findlay replied, the soft burr pronounced. "I can spare a wee bit of time. Have you got something interesting for me?"

"It's not exactly hardship — a bit of surveillance — and you can bring the wife."

"On a job? You must be joking."

"No, no," Riordan quickly replied. "It's not dangerous. I just emailed you a photograph of a guy I think is staying at the Wick with his girlfriend. I don't have a photo of her, but she's about five six or seven, about a hundred and twenty pounds, and has a mass of red, curly hair just like your good lady wife."

"Is this something to do with the gig in London? I know Feather and couple of the boys legged it out of here pretty quickly." Word spread quickly around the office.

"Yes. But all you have to do is show up at the Wick for two or three days and let me know if and when he appears. I'd be too conspicuous on my own, so I'll take a room at the motel just down the road and keep my OP during the day. I'm lying in the bushes, even as we speak."

"No bother, lad. I take it this is urgent."

Riordan glanced at the time display on his cellphone. "There's a flight from the Beaver in an hour. That means you'll be here in time for dinner. I know there's an office Jeep on standby at the harbour in case you want to do a bit of sightseeing after, and bring the usual supplies. And best of all, it's on me."

"Even the wine?"

Riordan sighed. Findlay loved his wine, especially the rare and expensive Côte du Rhône varietal. Riordan had introduced Findlay to his own favourite, wines from the Côte-Rôtie region, a small growing area just to the north of Lyon in France. He knew that on the Wick's superb wine list there were at least three or four selections from that region, each progressively more expensive.

"Yep, the wine's on me."

"Deal."

Just over two hours later, as night was falling gently around him, Riordan heard the drone of the seaplane coming in to land at Tofino harbour. Then, about twenty minutes later, the Jeep pulled up beside the hotel. Putting the binos to his eyes, he saw Findlay and his wife climb out of the Jeep and head into the reception area.

451

A few minutes later they re-emerged, followed by a bellman pushing a brass luggage carrier, and headed down the path toward the new part of the hotel. They stopped by the Jeep, and the bellman heaved three suitcases on the carrier. Riordan shook his head in amazement. It was like traveling with Nancy — there was no such thing as packing light for a few days.

Focusing on the building, he saw a light come on in one of the second-floor units, and then Findlay appeared in the window, looking out at the beach. He had a large glass of red wine in his hand. Each of the units had a tandem soaker tub set in the window so the occupants could have a luxurious bath with candles and a glass while gazing out at the spectacular view. Riordan grinned as he saw Findlay's wife start to run the tub.

Picking up his cellphone, he dialled Findlay.

"Findlay speaking."

"I'm still out here, should you be contemplating a shag with the curtains open."

"Fuck off. I thought you were heading to the motel."

"I am now, pal. Wouldn't want to spoil me pizza dinner."

"Enjoy yourself, Daniel, I know I will. And I'll call if I see or hear anything. Oh, and by the way, the wine is spectacular."

"You didn't let it breathe long," he commented sarcastically. Findlay was a wine snob.

"I'm only here for a couple of days, so I'm making the best of it," Findlay laughed.

Riordan broke the connection and eased himself out of concealment. He stood upright, then went through a series of elaborate, slow, yoga-like stretches to relieve his aching muscles. Covert surveillance was a game for young, flexible guys. Every time he moved, some joint cracked. It sounded like popcorn popping.

He made his way carefully back through the trees until he found the bike then gunned the engine and headed down to the Sea Star Beach retreat, where earlier he had booked a cabin. After picking up the keys, he went to his cabin, a studio unit. It turned out to be an open-concept design, with rustic pine floors, a vaulted cedar ceiling, and a modern kitchenette. The walls were decorated with West Coast prints from Tofino's finest artists. He recognized some of the paintings because he owned similar work by the same artists. It had a queen-size bed, which was great for him, and off in one corner was a Jacuzzi tub/shower. It was outfitted with rudimentary supplies, so he stripped off his clothes and tossed them in the washing machine. They were getting a bit gamey, even for him.

Wrapping himself in one of the large bath towels, he climbed onto the bed and called Tony's Pizza, the only place in Tofino that actually delivered. His stomach growled, so he ordered the meat lover's special, some Buffalo chicken wings, a Caesar salad, and a few cans of Coke, then switched on the TV and lay back to watch some mindless entertainment. Everything was in play. Now all he had to do was wait.

Shortly after 9:00 p.m., his cellphone rang, and he set the remains of the pizza aside and picked it up. Findlay was calling.

"I hope you've got good news," Riordan said.

"That would be affirmative."

Riordan was instantly alert. "Go," he said.

"Yer man is here. He finished dinner about ten minutes ago. I heard the waiter asking if he was on his own tonight, and he responded that his wife had gone away for a few days on business but would be back shortly. He charged the meal to his room, and I found out he's in one of the suites at the top of the new building. The waiter loves to gossip, and apparently your target is pretty ripped, as he sees him on the beach when he goes for a five-mile run every morning, just before breakfast. The waiter works mornings in the cafe, so after his run, the target then sits and reads the newspaper on the patio outside the cafe. His wife joins him most days as well."

Riordan smiled. The little Scotsman had a knack for engaging people in conversation and was so casual about it that they didn't know they were being interrogated. Wait staff loved nothing more than to gossip about guests.

"Thanks, pal," he said. "I hope you enjoyed the dinner."

"We have another bottle of Guigal La Turque Côte-Rôtie 2006," Findlay replied. "I didn't want to switch from the one I ordered in the room." Riordan winced, knowing it cost five hundred dollars per bottle. "It was, as you are fond of saying, 'like an angel crying on me tongue.' It was so good, as a matter of fact, that another sits breathing on the table, even as we speak. I have raised a toast to you, my friend, for this wonderful meal. By the way, how was the pizza?"

"Fuck off," Riordan replied.

"But how shall I fuck off, oh master?" came the snarky response, courtesy of Monty Python's *The Life of Brian*. Findlay was renowned in the team for his accurate mimicry of accents and was often called upon to perform during an operation. Rumour had it that during the Falklands War, Findlay had impersonated an Argentinian officer and sent squads of soldiers running all over the place, causing mass confusion and providing significant delays in the deployment of Argentinian troops.

*

The next morning Riordan rose early, showered, and pulled on his freshly washed clothes. He munched on a cold slice of pizza and drank the remnants of a can of Coke. There was a coffee maker in the room, but no supplies, so his beloved morning brew would have to wait. He drove over to the Wick, parked out front of the main building, and walked past the enormous wooden Haida carvings that lined the entrance to reception. He grabbed a newspaper, made his way to the dining room, and asked to be seated by the window that overlooked Denman Beach, the long, sandy bay in front of the buildings.

When the waiter arrived, he ordered the eggs Benedict, something of a work of art at the Wick, and a pot of coffee, his mouth watering in anticipation. The coffee, as always, was hot and strong, and two man-sized cups disappeared in rapid succession. The dining room was almost empty, save for another elderly couple getting prepared for a walk on the beach. Findlay was nowhere in sight, nor did Riordan expect him to be. After two bottles of Côte-Rôtie and God only knew how much Armagnac, he was probably sleeping it off in preparation for a morning shag.

His eggs arrived, and as he took his first bite, he saw Dempsey step out on to the patio near the cafe. Dressed in a pair of running shorts and a sleeveless running vest, he looked pretty fit, his muscles toned. Both arms were heavily tattooed. Riordan grinned. "Got you, you bastard," he hissed, watching as Dempsey went through a long set of calisthenics before starting off down the beach. He ran toward the water's edge, where the sand was hard packed, and then headed off down the long, curving expanse, his footprints visible in the wet sand.

Riordan finished the eggs quickly, almost an act of sacrilege, paid the bill, and headed out to the new building. The cleaner's cart was parked outside one of the rooms, and Riordan grabbed the master key as he walked past. Robbery was never a big issue at the Wick. He ran quickly upstairs to the third floor, made his way to Dempsey's suite, and used the key to open the door. When it opened, he used the security bar to hold the door open, then ran back downstairs and replaced the key on the cart. When he returned, he closed the door behind him and took a moment to absorb the room. The bed was already made up, and everything looked — he struggled for the word — and then it struck him. The place looked orderly. Newspapers were neatly stacked on a coffee table and a couple of hardback novels sat on the night table. Clothes must have been put away, since there were none lying on the floor.

The guy must be a neat freak, Riordan thought. When he and Nancy had a hotel room to themselves, the aftermath looked like a Motley Crüe concert afterparty: empty bottles of wine scattered everywhere, candy wrappers, and newspapers strewn on every conceivable piece of floor, not to mention clothes.

He quickly examined the closet, opening each suitcase, looking for some clue as to what Dempsey had done with the money. The bags, high-end Louis Vuitton travel cases, were empty. Searching the rest of the room, he found only a cellphone. There was no laptop or any sort of computing device. That meant the money was in a bank somewhere, possibly the Caymans or the Bahamas, or maybe even Switzerland, but the Swiss were becoming much more cooperative with security forces, and it was no longer the haven for illicit funds that reputation once dictated. Which meant Dempsey knew the codes.

Concealing himself in the washroom, he waited until he heard Dempsey return. Dempsey was pulling his sodden running

457

shirt over his head when Riordan stepped into the main room, his pistol raised. Riordan took in the muscled arms and the rippling pecs. Dempsey hit the gym pretty hard. Close up the tattoos were comprised of ornate Celtic script and knotwork.

"Who the fuck are you?" Dempsey asked, and already Riordan saw him sizing up his circumstances, measuring the distance between him and the pistol. In Dempsey's place, Riordan would be doing exactly the same.

"DeLisle," Riordan said, and Dempsey's face fell, his body almost deflating like air leaking out of a balloon. He must have thought he was untouchable.

"How the fuck did you find me?"

"It's what I do," Riordan replied.

"So what now?" Dempsey asked.

"You give me the codes, DeLisle gets his money back, and you get to live," Riordan replied. When he had mentioned codes, a fleeting microexpression on Dempsey's face showed him he had hit a nerve.

Dempsey snorted derisively. "What do you take me for? DeLisle doesn't do mercy. If I know good old Max, his last words were likely 'shoot the cunt.'" Balling the red running shirt in his hands, Dempsey tossed it angrily to one side, where it hit a tall vase full of flowers, toppling it sideways. The glass shattered on the hearth, a momentary distraction.

Riordan's eyes turned for a fraction of a second, a reactive response, but that was all Dempsey needed to close the distance. Dempsey grabbed the inside of his wrist and squeezed hard on the pressure point, which caused Riordan's fingers to flex and drop the gun. In the same fluid motion, Dempsey struck him with his elbow, and Riordan felt and heard the rib snap. Before he could get a grip on him, Dempsey spun away out of Riordan's reach, pivoted on his heel, and launched another blistering attack.

Riordan felt himself being driven back by the flurry of kicks and punches, and it was all he could do to prevent another damaging blow from landing. Dempsey kept targeting the broken rib, and Riordan was forced to drop his guard to protect the vulnerable area. Cursing under his breath for underestimating his prey, Riordan parried each blow and tried to respond, but Dempsey flitted out of reach. He certainly was fast on his feet.

"Come on, big man," Dempsey taunted him. "Is this the best Max could do?"

Riordan winced at the stabbing pain in his side, cupping the broken rib with one hand. Forcing himself to take shallow breaths, he turned sideways to Dempsey in a desperate attempt to shield his side from any more blows.

Dempsey had started shadowboxing now, weaving back and forth like a professional boxer. From his posture and the almost balletic movement, Riordan realized that Dempsey, at one time in his life, had been in the ring. Dempsey moved like a snake, and before Riordan knew it he had landed a flurry of powerful

459

punches on Riordan's chest. They hurt, and Riordan staggered back. He felt blood trickle down the side of his face and touched his fingertips to his temple. They came away bloody.

At the sight of blood, Dempsey sprang forward once more, driving his fist directly at Riordan's face. Riordan waited to the last possible moment, then moved his head slightly to one side, allowing the punch to graze his cheek but not do any serious damage. He grabbed Dempsey's wrist fiercely with his left hand, pulling it away, twisting at the same time. When he felt the tension in the arm peak, he slammed his other fist down hard on Dempsey's elbow, breaking the joint. The bones shattered loudly, and Dempsey screamed as Riordan continued twisting until Dempsey was almost doubled over. Then he brought his knee hard up into Dempsey's face, and the screaming stopped abruptly. Dempsey collapsed to the floor.

"Take that, you bastard," Riordan groaned, his rib on fire. Panting heavily, he retrieved his pistol and went over to the closet. There was only one way now to make Dempsey talk, and he needed to improvise.

The broken rib made it difficult to manhandle Dempsey's prone form, and he had to stop several times when the pain became unbearable. What he wouldn't have given for a fistful of Tylenol. He eventually managed to drape Dempsey over the ironing board that he had positioned across the bathtub and then proceeded to use duct tape to securely bind Dempsey to the board so that there was no possible way for him to move any of his extremities. It took almost the entire roll, but he wanted to make certain Dempsey could not escape. He had been lucky once, but even a one-armed Dempsey would be a formidable opponent.

The many scars on Dempsey's body told the story of his life: bullet wounds, knife wounds, shrapnel wounds, some properly treated, others fixed by amateurs or maybe even himself.

Grabbing an ice bucket, he filled it with cold water and tossed it over Dempsey's face. He spluttered for a few seconds, and then his eyes blinked open. Dempsey tried to struggle, but the tape held him firmly. Even his head was totally immobile, so all he could do was move his eyes.

"Welcome back," Riordan said. "Not so tough now, are ye, boyo? We're going to have another chat, you and I, and I want you to give me the codes."

"Fuck you," Dempsey snarled, trying to spit out of the side of his mouth. Riordan punched the shattered elbow, and Dempsey groaned, his eyes rolling back in his skull.

Riordan smiled. "Let me explain to you exactly what is going to happen. Waterboarding is a form of torture in which water is poured over the face of an immobilized captive, meaning you, causing the individual to experience the sensation of drowning. Are you with me yet?"

Leaning over, he stared in Dempsey's eyes. "Although a variety of specific techniques are used in waterboarding, the captive's face is usually covered with cloth or some other thin material, and the subject is immobilized on his or her back. That's where the ironing board came in handy. Water is then poured onto the face over the breathing passages, causing an almost immediate gag reflex and creating the sensation that the captive is drowning. Waterboarding can cause extreme pain, or even what known as dry drowning, when a person's lungs become unable to extract oxygen from the air.

"There is also damage to lungs, brain damage from oxygen deprivation, and other physical injuries. These can include broken bones due to struggling against restraints, but I think I've taken care of that scenario. There is also lasting psychological damage, and, if uninterrupted, death, which of course I don't want right at this moment. Horrible physical consequences can manifest themselves months after the event, while psychological effects can last for years." Riordan paused for a moment to let Dempsey absorb that information and construct the experience in his mind. Many people had heard of the CIA's rendition flights where terrorist suspects were flown surreptitiously to countries whose interrogation methods fell into the category of "torture," waterboarding being their ultimate interrogation technique.

"Now, I hoped I've summed it up correctly, as I imagine you have never experienced anything like this. I would like to try the easy route. Being from Belfast, you probably have witnessed some punishment beatings or maybe even some interrogations. You think you're a hard man, but I can promise you this. You will talk — everybody talks. It's just a matter of how much you want to suffer."

Riordan slipped one of the clean white towels from the rail, draped it over Dempsey's face, and then got up and refilled the ice bucket, whistling to himself. The psychological impact of Dempsey hearing the bucket being filled would be significant.

He took the bucket and slowly poured the water over Dempsey's mouth and nose. Nothing happened for a moment, but then Dempsey started to choke, his body trembling under the duct tape. Riordan continued to pour the water slowly, listening to Dempsey choking and spluttering. Dempsey's chest heaved as his lungs desperately tried to get air. By the time the bucket was empty, all of Dempsey's muscles were twitching furiously, as if he was on the receiving end of multiple electric shocks. His body sagged as for the first time in several seconds he was able to take a breath.

Riordan calmly refilled the bucket then repeated the process. This time, Dempsey's physical response was much weaker. The five-mile run had fatigued his muscles. He filled the bucket once more then leaned and whispered in Dempsey's ear. "I can keep this up for hours, if you want. I've done this many times, and I can tell you're pretty close to your breaking point. Just give me the codes."

He felt his cellphone vibrate but ignored the call. He was close now to getting the information he needed to get DeLisle off his back and didn't want to be interrupted. Tearing the damp cloth off Dempsey's face, he peered into his eyes. Dempsey had a faraway look, his eyes barely focused. His chest heaved. Then he blinked once or twice, his eyes focused on a spot just over Riordan's shoulder.

"Okay," he whispered, "I'll tell."

"Go," Riordan commanded.

"Cayman Islands, Bank of Bermuda. Twelve zero seven sixteen ninety, password GLORIOUS."

Riordan laughed. Dempsey had a sense of humour. The code was the date, July 12th, of the annual Orangemen parade celebrations in Northern Ireland, where the Protestants celebrated the victory by William of Orange over the Catholics at the battle of the Boyne in 1690. It was known as the "glorious" twelfth.

Just at that moment, Riordan felt the air shift in the room and turned. A heartbeat before the heavy piece of Inuit soapstone slammed into the side of his head, he caught a glimpse of a mass of red curls. Then everything went black.

CHAPTER 22

STITCHES

"Daniel! Daniel!"

Riordan cracked open one eye and inhaled deeply. There was an Oakley Special Forces boot in front of his face, which was pressed hard against a dusty, worn plank floor. Green mossy stuff covered the toe of the boot. The scent of ancient timbers filled his nostrils. He blinked a few times and then winced as a wave of pain shot through his head. His side was on fire, the broken rib sending jagged spurts of pain shooting through his body.

"Fuck!" he exclaimed.

Flexing his fingers next, he was relieved to discover he was not bound.

"Slowly, big lad," came the voice, the Scots burr pronounced.

Findlay.

He did a half push up to get to his knees and saw Findlay kneeling beside him, a pump action Remington in one hand. A deep gash ran down one side of Findlay's face, blood seeping from the wound like a red curtain down his cheek. Ignoring the fire in his side, he filled his lungs with air, several deep, cleansing breaths, and then got to his feet, assisted by Findlay. His vision shimmered like waves coming off tarmac on a hot day. Findlay held on to him until he managed to stabilize his bearings.

They were in a small hunting cabin: four timber frame walls, two windows, and a door. Iron-framed bunk beds sat in one corner of the room and in the other an ancient cast iron, pot-belly stove. A dry sink was located under one window. Beside the stove sat a sturdy table. There was a fair amount of dust on the floor, so it had not recently been used. Cabins like this dotted the wilderness across the remote areas of the island. This one, although apparently unused, was in better condition than most. Chained to the leg of the bunk beds and lying prone on the floor was Elva, a large bruise forming on one cheek. She appeared to be unconscious.

Findlay looked over in her direction. He touched his cheek gingerly. "Fucking bitch. She's got more knives on her than you do, and that's saying something. She nearly got my jugular. Fortunately, she hit the barrel of the shotgun, and that deflected the blow, but she managed to open up my cheek pretty well. She got the butt right in her face for her trouble. I took out lover boy over there first, thinking he'd be the biggest threat, but man was I wrong!" Riordan looked over in the other corner. Dempsey sat slumped over, both hands firmly handcuffed to a solid-looking wooden chair.

"Here," Findlay said, pressing the shotgun into his hands. "Look after this for a moment while I get the first-aid kit from the

Jeep. I need to get a couple of butterflies on this to stop the bleeding." Riordan took the shotgun and then carefully probed the back of his head, where a large bruise was forming. The tips of his fingers came away clean, so the skin hadn't been broken. *Small mercies*, he thought. It was fortunate that he possessed such a thick skull.

Findlay returned a few minutes later carrying a yellow plastic box. It was standard for all the operatives on Featherstone's team and held an abundance of medical supplies for every possible contingency. He set it on the table, flipped open the catches, and extracted several small packets. Above the dry sink was a dusty mirror, so he wiped it off quickly and began to clean his wound with steri-wipes.

"That's going tae need stitches," he commented as he expertly applied several butterfly dressings to the wound. "Jesus, the wife's gonna shoot me for ruining me good looks." Findlay pressed one last dressing across the wound.

Riordan grinned. "If you ask me, it's a bit of an improvement … like a German duelling scar!" He rummaged in the pack and found a bottle of Tylenol 3s. Flipping the cap off with his thumb, he dry-swallowed a couple then put the bottle in his pocket. He would be needing more shortly.

"Yawohl," Findlay replied, "zee Germains."

"So what happened?" Riordan asked.

"I was just heading down for breakfast when I saw yer woman here coming back to the room. I remembered her description, so I called to warn you." Riordan remembered the BlackBerry buzzing in Dempsey's washroom.

Findlay continued, "When I didn't hear back, I waited for a while, and shortly they both appeared, pushing a laundry cart out to a Range Rover. When I saw them bundling you into the back, I followed at a distance. It's a good thing your BlackBerry was powered on, so I followed your GPS coordinates. When they turned off on to the unmarked road, I parked and followed them on foot. They were planning to have a little session with you, similar to what you did with Dempsey here, to find out exactly who you were and how much DeLisle knew about them. Then I imagine you were headed for the bottom of the lake. Fortunately enough, I interrupted their plans and got my souvenir here as a reward for my trouble."

"You'll get your reward in Heaven." Riordan laughed.

"Perhaps in the pub would be better," Findlay replied. "Hopefully those pearly gates will be a long way away."

"For you and me both, pal," Riordan joked.

Findlay nodded. "After I got these two under control, I went and got the car, just in case, so it's parked outside. I'll go have a seat and give you a few minutes with these two."

Findlay looked him straight in the eyes, and Riordan nodded.

Findlay knew what was coming.

Riordan hefted the shotgun and waited until Findlay had closed the door before walking over to Dempsey. The broken arm had turned a dark, bluish purple at the elbow, where blood was seeping under the skin from shattered ligaments and ruptured blood vessels. A piece of bone had pierced the skin, poking up through like a submerged branch on a lake. Findlay had used handcuffs on both Elva and Dempsey.

Laying the shotgun on the table, he grabbed a fistful of hair and dragged Dempsey's head back. His eyes were closed, but there was a steady pulse in the vein at his neck. Riordan slapped him hard across the face a couple of times, leaving angry red welts on his cheeks. Eventually Dempsey stirred. He blinked hard, trying to focus, and then saw Riordan. His eyes filled with rage.

"Nice to see you too," Riordan replied.

Dempsey looked around him, his face dropping, until Riordan stepped back and allowed him to get a good look at Elva, lying prone on the floor.

"Is she?" Dempsey croaked.

"Not yet," Riordan replied. "Soon. You know how these things are."

Racking a shell into the breech, he stepped across the cabin to where Elva lay. Her fingers twitched slightly as she returned to consciousness. Riordan placed the barrel of the shotgun against her head.

"Please, don't," Dempsey pleaded. "Please?"

He couldn't let them live.

DeLisle would have his money, and that would get him off Riordan's case, if only for a short while. If he did let them live, he would be constantly looking over his shoulder, for he knew they would relentlessly try to track him down. He knew this as a certainty, for he would do exactly the same thing if he were in their shoes. The big Remington had a heavy pull, and he turned his head away to avoid any back splatter. It was one of those things you learned quickly.

As he did so, Elva's free hand moved down across her stomach and softly, almost tentatively fluttered cross her abdomen. Riordan paused. It was a motion he had seen Nancy make a thousand times when she was pregnant with the twins, as if she was communing with the growing children inside. "Please," begged Dempsey from behind. "Please, mister, please don't ... I can help you with DeLisle ... I know all about him, all his stuff."

Riordan paused, taking the pressure off the trigger. Executing Elva wouldn't have given him a moment's concern, and there were enough wild animals around that there would be little left of her body. However, she was carrying a child, and that changed the game completely. Elva's eyes popped open then widened in shock as she stared at the black 'O' pointing directly at her face. Riordan stared at her, his face hard, then turned back to Dempsey.

Riordan pulled up a chair, rested the shotgun on the table, its barrel pointing directly at Dempsey's chest, and said, "So talk."

"Thank you," Dempsey said, tears streaking his face. He sniffed.

Riordan said, "I need to know about DeLisle's organization, any associates he has, and anywhere he might run and ride. He'll have to take my word for it that you're dead, but at least he'll have his money back."

Dempsey nodded, eager to speak. "He's got a little bolt hole down by the river in Richmond, near St. Margaret's. It's on Old Palace Lane, down beside the White Swan pub — number 26, it is. Nobody knows about it, and he takes the occasional bird there for a bit of strange. He's got a fiancée, but he plays the field. I followed him there one night, just for fun."

Dempsey paused, as if trying to organize his thoughts. He was putting himself in Riordan's shoes and so was focused on any bit of Intel that would provide an edge. "There's a woman, Natalya, who runs one of his clubs over in Mayfair. She's Romanian and has a spider tattoo on the back of her right hand. Quite the looker, she is, but she's a mean a bitch as I've ever come across. I've seen the results of her handiwork on some of the girls who refused to service her customers. Worked on them so hard with a straight razor that even their own mothers wouldn't recognize them. The clubs are a nice front for running girls out of the Eastern Bloc — white slaves, if you think about it."

Riordan took out his cellphone and initiated the microphone as Dempsey was in full flow, and so rather than interrupt the data dump, Riordan recorded everything instead. After about thirty minutes, and with the assistance of a few probing questions, Riordan had everything he needed to deal with DeLisle.

Picking up the shotgun, he walked over and opened Elva's handcuffs, keeping her well at bay with the shotgun. She massaged her wrist then went over to the table. She kissed Dempsey tenderly on the forehead then sat down beside him. "What now?" she asked.

"I've got to take care of DeLisle." He tossed the handcuff key on the table. Nodding to Dempsey, he said, "He needs medical help, and fast, otherwise it's gangrene and that arm'll be off. Your car is still outside. Give me five minutes, and then you're free to go. If I see either of you again I'll kill you."

Elva stared at him. "DeLisle killed my brother, so put an extra bullet in him from me!"

Riordan nodded. "And you should tell Dempsey you're pregnant. It's the only thing that saved you."

"What?" Dempsey exclaimed. His eyes welled up again. Elva wrapped her arms around him and held him tightly.

She held Riordan's eyes for a brief moment then looked away. She well knew the gift she had been given.

*

Outside, Findlay sat patiently waiting behind the wheel. Mumford and Sons were playing on the CD player, and Findlay hummed along. Riordan got in, set the shotgun in the back seat, and strapped on his seatbelt.

"Don't smell burning cordite," Findlay commented.

"Couldn't do it," Riordan replied.

"That's no like you," Findlay commented, switching on the ignition.

"She is pregnant."

"Ah, that makes a difference. But you're still taking a risk, you know."

Riordan sighed. "I know where to find them, so I'll keep an eye out. Besides, they have no idea who I am, or where I'm based."

"You're a good man, Daniel, despite what people say," Findlay laughed, reversing back down the rutted track.

"You're wrong there, pal. I'm a bad man, but I do have good intentions!"

Findlay drove down through the mountains, the jeep slewing round the rained-slicked corners as Riordan sat in the passenger seat, carefully typing on his iPad. They had stopped at the motel while he picked up his supplies, and then Findlay set off across the island to Nanaimo to get the ferry.

The signal was spotty, and he kept having to reset the browser and reconnect. He cursed Telus, the local service provider.

473

He had logged into the Caymans website using Dempsey's username and password, and instead of transferring the funds to a different account, he simply changed the account password. That seemed to be the most prudent way of handing the money back to DeLisle.

Taking out his cellphone he called the office, identified himself, and asked to be directed to the tech area. Featherstone employed a number of computer gurus in the tech area. This team specialized in technological eavesdropping, hacking, and information mining from the web. A ragtag bunch, they were probably one of the finest groups of techies that Riordan had ever worked with in his career and they treated him as one of their own due to his fondness and capabilities with hardware and software. Coffee with them always deteriorated into a session of who possessed the greatest bragging rights for their latest hack. They were very fond of putting local politicians' heads on the bodies of porn stars and then posting the results on the pol's website. The other team members, the ex-military folk, were treated with disdain. "Knuckle draggers" was one of their more colourful descriptors for the commandos.

"Simon here," came the response.

"Hey, Brains, it's Daniel," Riordan said. "I need some help." Brains was the informal leader of the group because he possessed some form of social skills. He had received the nickname because his high forehead and thick, dark-rimmed glasses made him a dead ringer for one of the puppets on the show

Thunderbirds. It was rumoured that Featherstone had intervened to prevent Brains from spending a lengthy stint in the penitentiary for hacking a politician's private email account and reading intimate correspondence from his mistress. The hacking might have been tolerated, but Brains decided to share the aforementioned correspondence on a Facebook account. The politician's fall from grace was spectacular, and the subsequent divorce and massive settlement to his wife provided fodder for the tabloids for weeks. Having very little to lose, he went after the person who had exposed him.

"Hi there, Daniel, what can I do for you?"

"I need you to write a piece of code for me."

"Oh, yes?" Riordan could hear the curiosity in the man's voice. Code junkies lived to write code. That was their crack.

"I need an automated keylogger for the iPad, a piece of code that will send me an email with every keystroke made from the virtual keypad. The user must never know what is happening, so all of this has to take place as a background task, and the email must be encrypted and untraceable. Do you think you can handle that?"

"Is the pope a Catholic?" came the sarcastic reply.

"Great. I've got a flight out this afternoon, so send the code to my email address with a self-installer package. I'll test it out in the airport before I go, and I'll get back to you if there are any problems. I have another iPad that's running on the Orange network in London, so I'll need to install the code on it as well. It is the target device."

"Okay, Daniel, I'll fire it off to you in a couple of minutes!"

Riordan laughed and broke the connection.

"All sorted?" Findlay asked.

Riordan nodded. "Just about. I need to book a flight to London as well." He did the mental calculations about drive time to Nanaimo, which usually took three hours, but given Findlay's impression of an Italian racing car driver, they would shave about thirty minutes or so off that run. He would catch the Harbour Air flight over to the terminal in Richmond at the Beaver then grab a taxi over to the International airport. They had decided that it would be better for Findlay to take the ferry back, given the number of weapons they were carrying.

After checking the flight schedule, he selected the 6:15 p.m. Air Canada evening flight that would get him to Heathrow just before noon the following day. That gave him a few hours to strategize about how to handle DeLisle.

A small grin creased his face.

He was in the endgame.

CHAPTER 23

SPOOKS

On the flight to Heathrow, Riordan spent most of the journey listening to Dempsey's recording over and over, making notes and detailing the addresses that were provided. He was astounded at Dempsey's eye for detail, like the colour of the door on DeLisle's bolthole in Richmond and the exact location of the spare key, hidden behind a loose brick on the back wall. He dozed a bit, avoiding coffee, watched a couple of movies and felt somewhat refreshed when they landed. After deplaning, he wound his way along the interminable corridors that led to the immigration waiting area. It seemed like Air Canada had somehow pissed off the powers that be, for their aircraft were always parked at the furthest point from where he needed to be.

He followed the first class express line to customs and immigration, a small blessing when he saw the volume of weary, sweaty, travellers herded into the adjoining general area. Behind the agent stations, heavily armed police officers roved constantly, keeping a watchful eye on the crowd. This, he knew, was merely an act of intimidation to cause duress in any potential terrorist or criminal trying to get into the UK. The agents were trained to look for the giveaways: perspiration, rapid respiration, avoidance of eye contact, nervous twitches, and then direct the traveller into a separate waiting room.

When called, Riordan presented his passport to a bored-looking, pimple-faced youth whose uniform was about two sizes too big. The routine questions were asked and answered, and then the youth swiped his passport through the electronic scanner. Something strange must have appeared on the screen, because the youth was too inexperienced not to react. It was the slight widening of the eyes, the transformation from lethargy to alertness that gave him away, like flipping a switch. Riordan lifted his eyes and peered at the two-way mirrored wall behind the youth, wondering what was happening in there. He half-expected to see an armed response team come charging out, but then again, that was what he always expected.

Instead, the youth handed him back his passport, wished him a nice vacation, and waved to the next person in line. Riordan hefted his backpack, slipped the passport into the pouch, and headed out through the "Nothing to Declare" exit. Again, nothing happened. In the arrivals area, he went directly to the Air Canada arrivals lounge, a luxury reserved for executive travellers, where he took the opportunity to have a long, refreshing shower.

Following the shower, he called Featherstone and updated him on his progress. Then he had a quick breakfast and spent the next thirty minutes downloading the software patch onto the iPad that Sean had purchased. Then, calling up a browser, he logged into his personal bank accounts, transferred some funds between the two, and logged off. Seconds after he closed the browser, his BlackBerry buzzed. Opening the incoming email, he reviewed the details of the transaction he had just completed to make sure all accounts and passwords were what he expected. Satisfied that it was working correctly, he went outside and stood in the long line waiting for taxis. He gave the address of the hotel to the driver then settled back for the slow ride into the heart of London.

A few minutes after they left Heathrow and moved out on to the M4 motorway, Riordan's cellphone buzzed again. Picking it up, he saw it was Featherstone calling.

"What's up, Feather?"

"You've got a tail. Three cars back, a blue Ford Fiesta, reg DRG0211. Two guys inside."

"Thanks," Riordan replied with a wide smile. Featherstone and some of the team had been following him since he arrived. He had not noticed, even though he was on high alert from the encounter at immigration. Someone had flagged his passport, and that was what had triggered the response from the young immigration officer. So either DeLisle had connections at the airport, or it would have been Arthur Cupples. They were the only people who were aware of his presence.

At the hotel, he paid the driver and went directly to his room. It had been booked for several days, so there was no reason for it to be compromised. Tossing his backpack on the bed, he lay back and waited. When the BlackBerry buzzed again he picked it up.

"Yes, Feather?"

"Looks like you've got a couple of spooks on your tail."

Riordan smiled, relieved somewhat at the news. "Yep. That would be Arthur Cupples, keeping an eye on my back."

"Okay," Featherstone replied. "In bar, ten minutes."

"Done."

He paused for a moment then scrolled through the list of phone numbers on his BlackBerry. Calming his heartbeat, he connected the number and waited.

"Well, if it isn't a little birdie," came DeLisle's voice. "I hope you've got good news for me, my son!" He sounded a lot more cheerful than the last time they had spoken.

"There's been a couple of deaths in the family," Riordan replied. "A tragic accident by all accounts. But the good news is there's quite the inheritance coming your way."

"Oh, really?" The note of DeLisle's voice changed. "Any numbers you could share?"

"Looks like about four point eight million, give or take."

"Fucking brilliant, that is," DeLisle exclaimed. "I knew you could do it."

"There is some paperwork involved," Riordan replied. "When will you be available to take care of that detail?"

There was a pause on the end of the line. "Come to the Gun tonight after last bell. Use the side door, and one of the lads will let you in. I presume it's an electronic transfer."

"Yep," Riordan replied, looking at the iPad lying on the bed. "I'll bring a tablet with all the relevant stuff on it."

After breaking the connection, he rolled off the bed, picked up his backpack, and took out the brown envelope that Cupples had given him back at the inn. Opening it, he slid out the white envelope, still tough and weathered with age, this one sealed with a hard wax insignia. A warm smile crossed his face at the image of the old man burning the red seal and dripping it across the envelope before pressing the top of his ring into the molten liquid. Riordan had watched him repeat the performance several times while he lived in Belfast and was always in awe of the process. It seemed somewhat medieval, but the gesture in itself spoke of trust, of a secret contained within.

It seemed almost a shame to break it, so he took out his knife and cut carefully around it, preserving the round seal. There were three sheets of high-quality paper, all typed double-spaced, the final signed by the Old Man.

Riordan looked at the date. It was two days before the Old Man had arrived in Canada to help him when his life was falling apart. A lump rose in his throat. It looked like the Old Man had known that for him it might be a one-way journey and had put his affairs in order before leaving. No surprise there. The Old Man was a meticulous planner. As he read the words, Riordan felt the

Old Man's presence, as if he was in the room, reading the letter aloud.

After he had run away from Belfast to escape the Troubles, Riordan had always believed that no one could possibly have tracked him down. The movement had harsh rules: once in, never out. The only way out was by forfeiting your life for the cause. Those who ran, for whatever reason, were hunted down and executed in some public manner as a warning to others.

As the years passed and his new life seemed impenetrable, violence in the form of Palestinian terrorists came calling and left him without a wife and a young daughter, who perished in the plane crash. The Old Man had come to help him track down those responsible and in doing so lost his life.

Until now, Riordan had not realized that the Old Man had been keeping a watchful eye on him from afar. The last page contained two account numbers and a key, taped below the signature. The key was to a safety deposit box held at Barclay's Bank, located at 2 Victoria Street, London. Riordan shook his head. The bank was literally just down the street. The other was for an account with a brokerage firm called Redmayne Bently, based in Finsbury House, near Finsbury Circus. It also had a codeword required, but instead of having the codeword written down, it simply said *you will know the code when prompted.*

Riordan took out his cellphone, took a photograph of the page, and checked to make sure the image was readable. He then folded the sheet of paper and slipped it into his jeans. There would be time later to check the details. Just like the Old Man, Riordan had a family to look after, and should things go sideways tonight, he wanted to make sure that Nancy and the boys were well looked after. From his operations over the years, Riordan had quietly amassed a small fortune, to the extent that he and Nancy would never have to work again. But they loved their jobs, and so they kept working. Retirement was a future conversation.

The momentary reflection spurred him to check the time and do the mental arithmetic to deduct eight hours from local time. It was just after 1:00 p.m., which meant it would be about 5:00 a.m. Vancouver time. Nancy was an early riser, especially when she was on the early shift, so he took a chance and called the house. The phone rang once and was instantly picked up.

"Sweetheart, it's me."

"Look, Jose, I've told you not to call the house. One of these days Daniel will pick up the phone and then what will we do..."

Riordan roared with laughter. "Good one, love, good one."

"So where are you?" she asked. "Any progress in getting things sorted?"

"All being well, I should be home in a couple of days," he replied. He was being realistic, since the coming night's events would put the matter to rest.

DeLisle would try to kill him.

He would try to kill DeLisle.

One of them would succeed, and he intended to come out on top. He had the upper hand: DeLisle thought he was working solo, so Featherstone and the team would sway the scales in his favour.

"That good to hear, love. I miss you, and so do the boys."

They chatted about nothing for a few more minutes, the easy conversation that married couples fall into. Mostly it was about what devilment the boys had gotten into or what scandal was happening at the hospital. It seemed like every other day some politician was taking bribes from a health official, or vice versa, to the point where the local folks were growing tired of their elected officials. In the background, Nancy's alarm went off, putting an end to the conversation and marking the beginning of her day. He broke the connection, feeling a lot more grounded than he had for a while.

And then he realized he hadn't mentioned the inheritance to her. "Fuck," he swore. It would have to keep.

Featherstone was downstairs in the bar, nursing a cappuccino, when Riordan entered. He slid onto a stool beside the big man and nodded to the barman. "I'll have what's he's having."

The barman looked none too happy. It wasn't going to be a profitable bar tab for him. The place was pretty quiet for lunchtime, but then again, with the exorbitant prices, locals wouldn't be dropping by for a quick drink.

"I hear you had a bit of excitement in Tofino," Featherstone said. A master of understatement was Featherstone.

Riordan nodded. "I got what I needed from Dempsey, and I'm meeting up with DeLisle at the Gun this evening around eleven to make the exchange."

"Hmmm. A very public place," Featherstone commented. "He'll likely try to kill you afterward."

"That's what I was thinking," Riordan replied. "The place is always busy, even around closing time. But I do have you lot to run interference, should he try anything, and as soon as he gets his money and I get the papers, I'll be out of there. If you still have eyes on his apartment, you can verify if he takes the papers or not. That might give us some idea of what he's planning. I'm not giving him anything until I see those documents."

"There is one other possibility." Featherstone frowned. The barman arrived with Riordan's cappuccino, accompanied by a large biscotti. Then he returned to the end of the bar, out of earshot, and started polishing a beer glass, the usual activity for bored bartenders.

Riordan sipped the cappuccino. It was delicious, the caffeine giving him the kick he sorely needed. He saw Featherstone eyeing his biscotti. He knew what was coming.

"Are you going to have that?" Featherstone asked.

"Knock yourself out," Riordan replied. "And the other possibility is..."

Featherstone chewed happily. "He knows you have got the information he needs. What's to stop him from extracting the information and reneging on the deal? You and I both know how to make people talk, and I imagine DeLisle does too. That means he gets his money and he still has you in his pocket."

Riordan sighed. He had missed the obvious. He thought hard for a moment. "That means one or two of you guys will have to be nearby, and if things go sideways, come and get me."

Featherstone slid a small box across the bar. "Comms net earpiece. Test it just before you go into the bar tonight. We'll be able to hear everything that's going down, so we'll create a codeword. If we hear it we'll come in, guns blazing, so to speak."

"Sounds almost like a plan." Riordan laughed.

"Best we got."

"Any idea where Finsbury Circus is?" Riordan asked.

Featherstone thought for a moment. "Nah, can't remember." To the barman he said, "Have you any idea where Finsbury Circus is?"

"Sure, guv," came the reply. "It's over near the Liverpool Street station. You can take the Tube from Victoria and then change, or take a cab. It's about twenty minutes or so from here."

Feather tossed a twenty-pound note on the bar. "That's for the coffee and the info." The man's face brightened, and the entire twenty disappeared into his pocket instead of the register.

"What's at Finsbury Circus?" Featherstone asked. "Or do I not want to know."

"When we were at the wedding, Arthur Cupples gave me a letter from the Old Man. He had prepared it for me just before he died, but failed to let Cupples know where I was living. So it's been in his possession ever since. I opened it this afternoon, and there's an account with a brokerage firm and a safety deposit box in Barclay's Bank, just down the street here. I thought I'd check them out this afternoon."

Featherstone gave him a strange look. "Putting your affairs in order, are you?"

"Fuck off," Riordan snorted. "Just being prudent. You know how these things can go."

"I suppose so," Featherstone reluctantly agreed. "We're not exactly accountants!"

"Anyway, I was wondering. It never dawned on me before, but there seem to be a lot of these 'circuses' in London: Piccadilly, Oxford, and now this one. What does circus mean?"

"Ah, grasshopper, this I do know. In this context, a circus is from the Latin word meaning 'circle.' So all of these places are a round open space near a street junction."

"Brilliant. You never cease to amaze me."

Featherstone grinned. "That's why I'm the boss."

*

487

The offices of Redmayne Bently reeked of old money. The weathered sandstone exterior was in the midst of an upgrade to remove years of accumulated grime. A huge portico framed the entranceway to the building, and all around the circle, window boxes teemed with bright flowers. Newly painted wrought iron railings guarded the lower floors, with offices clearly visible from the street. Inside, Riordan took the stairs to the second floor and entered the office. The building had retained the original oak doors and brass fittings. Opening the door took quite a bit of effort.

The inner walls were dark mahogany, the expansive panels filled with copies of old masters. The room had a decidedly Victorian feel, almost like stepping back in time. The only thing not ancient in the room was the receptionist, an attractive brunette dressed in high-end clothes and showing an appreciable amount of thigh when she stood to greet them.

"Good afternoon," she said, showing a set of pearly white teeth. "Do you have an appointment?" Very proper, upper-crust accent.

Riordan shook his head. "I'm afraid not. I only received this letter yesterday, and I'm flying out of the country tomorrow, so I was hoping someone could explain this to me. It appears that my father opened an account here in my name several years ago. He is now deceased, and this was given to me by his guardian."

The receptionist took the sheet of paper and perused it for a moment. "If you'll take a seat, I'll see if one of our senior partners can assist you in this matter." She disappeared through another door, and Riordan and Featherstone sat.

"Nice bottom," Featherstone commented in a posh British accent.

"Yep," Riordan replied.

"Panties?"

"Hard to tell."

The door opened a few minutes later, and the receptionist returned, followed by a man wearing a three-piece suit with creases that looked sharp enough to cut wood. A white shirt, button-down collar, and red tie completed the ensemble. He appeared to be in his early thirties. Tall and gangly, his handshake nevertheless was firm.

"Mr. Spence, I'm Nigel Hawkes, one of the senior partners in our firm. Can you come into my office please, and we'll have a chat? My assistant is pulling the file for you now."

Riordan followed the man through the door and into a long corridor with offices that faced the front of the building. Brass nameplates adorned each of the doors, with the occupant's name and title underneath in ornate script. Hawkes paused outside his door, pushed it open, and stood to the side to allow Riordan to pass. The office was small, sparsely furnished, and had a desk that faced away from the window. The only modern objects in the room were a large Mac, a phone console with more buttons than the Starship *Enterprise,* and what looked to be a printer/fax combination. On one corner of the desk sat a two-level tray stamped with IN and OUT.

Riordan grinned at the tray. "Very old-school. I like that."

Hawkes went behind his desk and picked up a manila folder that had been placed there. A neatly typed label at the top said "David Spence." He ruffled through the folder for a moment, his face tight.

"According to this, a brokerage account was opened for you back in 1986 and a purchase of one thousand shares of Microsoft deposited there. All you have to do is provide me with the codeword and I am instructed to provide you access. The security phrase is 'where did you go most often to fish with your father?'"

Riordan smiled. As a boy they had fished every stretch of the river outside his house and then up and down the coast. But the place they had returned most often was the little fishing village of Cushendall. For some reason they also seemed to have the most success on the little outcropping, hauling out cod and plaice, the odd crab, and one time a dogfish.

"Cushendall," he said. "I can spell it if you like."

Hawkes nodded. "No, that is sufficient." He tapped a few keys, pursed his lips, and turned the screen around so that Riordan could see the account details. Riordan knew a bit about the stock

490

market, having dabbled a few times with technology stocks for companies that he expected to make it big. As it turned out, he was rarely wrong, and he earned a significant return on his investments.

Nothing, however, could have prepared him for the numbers on the screen. The Microsoft stock had split many times since 1986, and the accumulated value of the shares was now over ten million dollars.

He stared at the screen in disbelief. He shook his head. "Holy shit!" he exclaimed.

Hawkes nodded. "That's quite the portfolio," he commented. "The question is, what do you want to do with it?"

That was the question. Riordan thought for a moment. "I can access the account online now, I take it," he asked.

"That is correct. Do you want to sell the shares or any part thereof?"

"Not at the moment," Riordan replied, knowing that Hawkes would get a hefty commission should he decide to sell. "This is all a bit overwhelming, if you must know. I'd like to update the information and provide access to my wife as well."

Hawkes slid the keyboard across to Riordan. "No time like the present. Can I get you a coffee, or tea perhaps?"

Riordan asked for a coffee, black, then settled down to make the necessary changes to the demographic information on the system. He had just completed the information when Hawkes returned, carrying two cups of coffee. Riordan signed out.

"Here you go," Hawkes said, sliding back into his seat with his back to the window. Outside, workers continued sandblasting the stonework, sending huge plumes of spray into the air. The generators droned loudly through the ancient windows.

"How long has this been going on?" Riordan asked, making small talk.

"Far too bloody long, if you ask me," Hawkes snorted. "I don't know why they can't do the work at night, instead of disrupting everyone in the building. It gets to be terribly annoying."

"I can see that," Riordan replied.

"Are you here on vacation?" Hawkes asked.

Riordan nodded. "Over for a wedding." When he didn't volunteer any more information, Hawkes took the hint. Riordan finished his coffee, stood, and shook hands again. "Thank you for your help." He took the business card from Hawkes, slipped it into his wallet, and followed the man back to the reception area.

Featherstone was deep in conversation with the receptionist, who seemed to be hanging on his every word. He did have that effect on women. Hawkes disappeared, and Featherstone stood up and followed Riordan out the door.

"So?" Featherstone asked.

"Ten mil."

"Come again?"

"The old man bought me a thousand shares of Microsoft stock back in '86. Sort of an inheritance. That's the current value of the stock after all the splits."

"Nice inheritance." Featherstone laughed. "If we didn't have such an eventful evening planned, we'd be painting the town several shades of red."

"Maybe after the fireworks," Riordan suggested. "We've got one more stop to make, and then I want to get back to the hotel and have a nap for a while."

More surprises lay in store in the security vault at Barclay's bank. The safety deposit box contained five hundred thousand pounds in used bills, a Beretta .22 with two clips of hollow points, a silencer, and four leather pouches, all containing twenty four gold Krugerrand coins. For someone on the run, it provided an easy way to get cash. Riordan emptied the box, leaving behind the weapons. The gun was of little use. Now, if anything happened, Nancy and the boys would certainly never have to worry about money.

*

Back at the hotel, he called room service and ordered a decent-sized steak to get a blast of protein, forcing himself to eat because he was anticipating some sort of physical activity in the coming hours. The steak was really delicious, a perfectly sautéed bacon-wrapped filet mignon and frites. Following dinner, he watched TV for a few minutes to catch up on world news then pulled the drapes, stripped off, and crawled between the sheets. With all the excitement of the past couple of hours, he felt somewhat drained. He was asleep in minutes.

His phone alarm woke him a few hours later, and he showered quickly and pulled on his jeans, feeling refreshed and invigorated. He looked sadly at the gun and put it away in the wall safe. It was pointless to take a gun — it would be easily discovered — but he popped open his knife and strapped the blade to his forearm. He took two rolled bandages from his pack, gritting his teeth as he strapped them tightly around his chest, and then pounded back a couple of Tylenol 3s. It was not his first broken rib, and he knew it was simply a matter of waiting for it to heal. It was always annoying that he was unable to play squash or attempt any sort of physical activity. Then, throwing on a t-shirt and his jacket, he headed down to the lobby.

Following a quick call to Featherstone, Riordan grabbed a cab over to the Gun. Jittery with nerves, he forced himself to breathe slowly, trying desperately to drive away the knots of anxiety. The Tylenol dulled the ache in his ribs. Before he knew it, the taxi was pulling up outside the Gun, which surprisingly still bustled with energy even after closing time. Patrons who had managed to get in a last call before midnight continued their revelry. Smokers congregated outside near a potted plant that had been turned into an improvised ashtray. He paid the driver, gave him a good tip, and stepped inside.

The reek of stale alcohol hung heavy in the air. Faces, flushed with too much alcohol, swayed gently in the bar, and beyond, on the crowded patio loud voices crackled in debate. All around were staccato bursts of uncontrollable, alcohol-fuelled laughter. At the end of the bar sat Jean-Marc, pretty much in the same place as he had been before, sipping on a glass of red wine and carrying on a conversation with a brunette who seemed entranced by every word. He was paying close attention to her ample bosom. The dress was so low-cut, Riordan could hardly blame him.

Riordan strode past him, trying desperately to keep the butterflies in check. Comforted by the fact there were so many people around, he was well aware of what DeLisle would attempt at some point during the coming hours. That simply honed the senses to a fine edge, the fight-or-flight reflex preparing itself for trouble. But for him, the latter was never an option.

The entrance to the back room was blocked by a massive black man who would have trouble getting through the door. His shoulders fit the entrance nicely, and the bulging biceps and shaved head were sufficient to warn off anyone who came near. Riordan stopped in front of him.

"I'm here to see Max," he said.

The bodyguard nodded and unfolded his meaty arms. "You know the drill, mate."

Riordan shrugged and stood motionless as the man frisked him professionally. He checked his front, back, both legs, inside and out, and arms. The jewels got a good grope as well. What he missed, and what most people missed, was the knife strapped to Riordan's inner forearm. It was not much of a defense, but for Riordan it was comforting just to know he had some means of protecting himself. He could certainly create havoc with a knife, but there was always the one about "don't bring a knife to a gunfight!"

After checking his backpack, the giant stepped aside, allowing Riordan into the room. DeLisle sat in a curved leather booth with two other men, both of whom looked like they had been struck from the same mold. *A motley collection of villains*, Riordan thought. Interspersed with the men were four young women, all scantily dressed and all sipping glasses of champagne. Two silver ice buckets sat on the table, with champagne bottles protruding from their necks. Condensation ran down the sides and pooled on the table. From the size of the accumulation, Riordan figured the party had been going on for some time. Several plates lay scattered on the table, mostly with empty oyster shells stacked on top.

DeLisle looked up and grinned. "Well, here's the man of the hour. Ladies, please excuse us, as we have a bit of business to discuss. But don't go far. This won't take long."

The girls, glassy-eyed and full of giggles, slunk out, pouting. All four had to constantly wriggle their tight dresses down over their thighs. There were no visible panty lines. "Have a seat, mate," ordered DeLisle. "Let's have a look."

"You must be joking," Riordan replied. "You first."

DeLisle's eyes narrowed for a heartbeat. His face darkened. Then he nodded and hefted a briefcase on to the table. "Okay, I think you've earned it." Opening the briefcase, he extracted a set of manila folders stamped with the words "Top Secret" and handed them over. It took a childish tug to get them from DeLisle's grip, an overt reminder of who was the top dog. Riordan set his backpack on the table and flipped through the folders quickly, his heart sinking when he saw the damning amount of intelligence the major had managed to collect. Exhaling, he closed the folders, placed them on the table, and took the iPad out of his backpack. Powering it up, he waited until a web browser appeared and then selected the website for the Cayman Islands bank that he had previously bookmarked. He keyed in the account number, saved it when prompted, and then entered the password.

"The password is DeLisle1," he offered. After a moment, the screen filled with deposit and withdrawal information. Turning the screen around, he handed the device to DeLisle. The others moved in to look, but DeLisle growled and waved them off. As DeLisle focused on the account, Riordan slipped a tiny listening device off the back of the backpack and stuck it under the arm of his chair.

497

"You can transfer the funds wherever you want," Riordan said. "The account and password are already defaulted for you."

"Fuck you very much," DeLisle, snorted, taking a huge swig of whisky. "I think we're done here." He nodded to the bodyguard, who immediately stood to one side of the door. Riordan stood.

He was being dismissed. Slipping the folders into his backpack, he stepped outside and walked over to the black iron railings running along the embankment. Lights of the city glittered on the surface of the Thames. In places the dark waters roiled, as if a giant creature was passing just under the surface. The currents and eddies were treacherous, even for seasoned swimmers, and many a life had been lost in these waters. He paused for a moment then hurled the backpack as far as he could into the dark waters. It floated for a moment then slipped beneath the surface. The water would destroy the contents. It was a fitting end to such a dangerous trove of information.

Nerves jangling, he joined the line of happy punters who were waiting for a taxi. He slipped in front of a drunken couple who were necking furiously and hadn't noticed the line had moved. He was trying to randomize his movements to reduce the chances of one of DeLisle's goons surprising him. A line of taxis stretched far into the distance, so the chances of every one of the drivers being in DeLisle's pocket was fairly remote.

When his turn came, he climbed into the back seat and told the driver to drop him off at Buckingham Palace. He would walk to the hotel from there. Just in case. In his earpiece, he heard Featherstone's voice.

"All clear from this end. There's no tail on you. Jean-Marc is watching from the bridge." There was a momentary pause, and he heard a loud click. "I've just got something off the bug. Listen to this."

Riordan put one hand over his ear. He heard DeLisle say, "Do it at the hotel when things are quiet." There was a pause. Riordan heard muted voices. The next statement made him shiver. DeLisle said, "What about his family?" as if repeating a question he had been asked. "You know the drill — no loose ends. Right, ladies, who wants more bubbly?"

Featherstone clicked the recorder off. "We picked that up a few minutes ago. I've already put a team on Nancy and the kids — around the clock, so no one will get near her. You're the priority for now. We'll be along presently and stake out the hotel. I took a room down the corridor from you, so I'll keep an eye from the lobby. The bar's open twenty-four hours."

"Thanks, Feather," Riordan replied. "Off net." Extracting the tiny earpiece, he slipped it into his pocket. Any further communication would be via cellphone.

The cabbie dropped him at the intersection of Birdcage Walk and Buckingham Gate. Traffic was still heavy, even at the late hour. The palace itself was lit up, majestic in the muted glow. Many tourists stood outside, taking photographs of the massive structure. Riordan noted a heavy police presence on the ground. He knew from past experience that it was a prime terrorist target, not so much from a tactical perspective, but from a political standpoint. This was the heart of the monarchy, the beating heart of Great Britain, where the queen and her family actually lived and worked. The fallout from a strike at the heart of the monarchy would reverberate around the world.

He strolled down the street and into the hotel, still on high alert. At least back in his room he had the pistol that Billy K had provided him. It had been stored in the room safe, away from the prying eyes of chambermaids.

For a moment, he contemplated waiting in the bar for Featherstone but decided against it. It would be better to be out of sight. He rode the elevator to the second floor, stepped cautiously out into the corridor, and walked briskly to his room. Looking both ways before he moved, he slipped the card into the lock. The mental loop tape of DeLisle's voice had been playing in his head, and there was something nagging at him about the conversation. It seemed one-sided, almost as if DeLisle was talking to someone on the phone, not one of the thugs in the bar. From a logical standpoint it made sense. DeLisle, after reading the files about Riordan's background, would have called in a professional hitter or hit team to do the nasty.

Pressing down on the handle, he stepped into the room and reached for the light switch. The chambermaids were in the habit of pulling the massive drapes completely closed, which had the effect of plunging the room into complete darkness, something he normally wouldn't mind because he liked to sleep in absolute blackness.

The faint scent of Old Spice touched his nostrils. Adrenaline flowed into his veins like opening a tap. Before he could react to the threat in the room, a lamp at the far end of the room flicked on. He understood the situation in the blink of an eye. The closet doors were open, as was the room safe, which was empty.

At the far end of the room sat Arthur Cupples, elegantly dressed as ever, the walking stick in one hand, resting against one knee. In the other hand he held the gun from the room safe. A big, ugly silencer was pointed directly at his chest. Riordan shook his head sadly. DeLisle had been making a phone call after all.

In front of Cupples sat a single chair. Cupples motioned with the gun. "Come and sit down."

Riordan let the door slide shut and reached down slowly and pushed against the side of his jeans, as if drying his hands. Stepping forward with exaggerated, deliberate steps, he raised his hands and sat down on the chair. Mentally, he was calculating angles and distances.

A tiny grin crossed Cupples's face. "You're a chip off the old block. I know what you're doing, but let me tell you, you can't outrun a bullet." Riordan was well aware of how Cupples had been with a gun. On the table beside Cupples sat a tumbler with about a finger of whisky, light glinting off the ice cubes. Two miniature bottles from the mini bar stood empty. The outside of the glass was dry, so Cupples had not been in the room long enough for condensation to form. Beside the glass sat two of the stacks of bills Riordan had taken from the safety deposit box.

"Where's the rest?" Cupples asked, nodding to the bills.

Riordan shrugged. The pistol moved down until it was pointing at Riordan's knee. He fought to suppress the black rage building inside. *Take slow, deep breaths,* he thought. *As long as you're breathing, there's hope.* Yet it took a supreme effort. In Riordan's mind there was nothing worse than a traitor, and to be betrayed by someone you trusted went beyond the pale.

"Money, Arthur?" he said. "You gave me up for money?"

Cupples shrugged. "I had a bit of a problem with the ponies, which grew to be a big problem. When my tab got to be about two hundred grand, I was offered a 'look the other way' deal regarding a smuggling operation, and by the time I found out about who was behind it, for me it was too late. I was in Max DeLisle's pocket, in deep with no way out. So I learned to live with it. I do the occasional job for him, and he pays me handsomely for it."

"I hope he's paying you well for this one," Riordan growled. "I never knew you did women and children, though."

Cupples's face tightened. "You heard, didn't you?"

Riordan nodded.

"Here's the one-time deal," Cupples said. "You give me the contents of the safety deposit box, and it all ends here. Your ticket gets punched, quick and clean, but your family get a pass."

Riordan swallowed hard but recognized it was the only option. Cupples was always a hard man. Back in the day he remembered Cupples and the Old Man frequently arguing about strategy and tactics, especially in the late seventies when Belfast looked like something out of Dante's Inferno on a regular basis. Night after night the city was ablaze, the piercing wail of sirens a constant reminder that peace was nowhere in sight. Cupples was pushing for increasingly violent attacks against suspected IRA members, to the extent that he wanted to car bomb their houses, even those with families. The Old Man preferred surgical strikes, precise attacks.

His mouth went dry. In his line of work, longevity was something you hoped for, but not too many ex-warriors got to die in their beds. Without a moment's hesitation he said, "Deal. The rest of the money is down in the hotel safe. I didn't want to leave it all in one place in case I got robbed. You can never be too careful these days."

"Isn't that the truth." Cupples took out his phone, dialled a number, and said, "51 Buckingham Gate, room 232, one pickup, one hour. Card will be behind 'do not disturb sign.'" To Riordan, "Clean-up crew for off the books stuff."

Riordan understood. Cupples was sending his body for disposal. It would either be a garbage dump, far out at sea, or a crematorium. No trace of him would ever exist. Not a pleasant thought, but not something to dwell on at the moment. As the Old Man had often reminded him, "Where there's life, there's hope."

"Let's go then," he said, standing.

"Just so you know," Cupples said, "any attempt to warn anyone, or any funny stuff, and I'll shoot everyone in sight."

They took the stairs, Riordan in front, Cupples three steps behind. There was no way Cupples was getting into the confines of an elevator. At the ground floor, they walked across the lobby, Cupples nearby but just out of reach. Riordan still had the knife strapped to his forearm, but it might as well have been back in the room for all the good it would do him. The night assistant, a young, attractive woman in her mid-twenties, was still on duty. Riordan had said hello to her when he arrived earlier. Her badge said, "Marlea."

"Hi there, Marlea," Riordan said. "I'm back to disturb you again."

She smiled. "Not at all, sir, what I can do for you?"

"I need to get my backpack out of the hotel safe," he said. "I stored it there earlier today."

"Certainly. Can I see your passport?" Riordan handed it over. "And your room?" Riordan gave her the room number and his key card.

She disappeared into the back room and came out a few moments later, a little red-faced from hefting the bag. "My goodness, that's heavy," she commented, struggling to get it on the counter.

Riordan grinned. Slinging the bag over his shoulder, he walked back toward the stairs. As soon as they were out of earshot, Cupples asked, "What's in the bag?"

"The rest of the money that was in the box, about four hundred grand. And a whole bunch of Krugerrands." Cupples gave a low whistle. He made Riordan wait while he ascended the stairs, then motioned for him to come up. The pistol never left the centre of Riordan's chest. They walked along the corridor to the room, then Riordan slid the card in and pushed the door open. Cupples wedged his cane at the edge of the door, preventing Riordan from diving into the room and kicking the door shut. He knew his time was running out fast. Once Cupples had him back in the room and checked the contents of the bag, that was it.

Heart pounding, he took another step along the narrow entranceway. As Cupples moved behind him, the huge door slammed into Cupples, knocking the gun from his grip. He hit the far wall hard, his head rebounding off the concrete, and dropped to the floor. Riordan spun around, turning into the grinning face of Featherstone, who had concealed himself behind the door.

"Cutting it a little fine?" Riordan said, looking down at the prone figure. He expelled a huge breath.

"Good job your pants called me again," Featherstone replied, nodding to Riordan's jeans. He bent down, picked up the gun, and handed it to Riordan.

Riordan said, "I had high hopes it might work. I'm always calling people back accidentally, so this time I figured if I touched it enough and pressed on it enough, it might actually dial out. You were the last person I called, so it redialled."

"What now?" Featherstone asked.

Riordan raised the pistol and shot Cupples twice in the back of the head. Featherstone's only reaction was a slight raise of one eyebrow. After picking up the shell cases, Riordan slipped them in his pocket, along with the gun, then went through Cupples's pockets and removed his wallet and secure BlackBerry. He quickly reset the device password. There was no other identification. Satisfied, he went into the washroom, stripped the shower curtain from its rings, and then spread it on the floor beside the body. "Give me a hand here," he said.

Between them, they rolled Cupples's body tightly in the shower curtain. Riordan then pulled away a couple of the heavily braided gold cords used tied back the drapes and secured the package. Given the small calibre of the pistol, the rounds had merely ricocheted around inside Cupples's skull, pulverizing his brain, so there was no blood left on the floor.

"What now?" Featherstone asked.

"Cupples ordered a disposal team to come here in an hour. They are to pick up the keycard from behind the 'do not disturb' sign. Instead of me, they'll be picking up dear old Arthur. These guys are contractors, and the probability of them actually knowing Cupples is pretty slim, so they'll dispose of whatever is wrapped up."

"Fucking brilliant!" Featherstone exclaimed. "And then what?'

Riordan quickly packed up his sparse belongings, handed the heavy pack to Featherstone, and then said, "The only downside to this is that I've got to spend the night in your room, and I know you snore like a fucking banshee."

Featherstone laughed.

Riordan found a piece of tape in the drawer, attached the key card to the back of the "do not disturb" sign, and hung it on the outer door handle.

"Let's go," he said.

CHAPTER 24

WANKER

When he got to Featherstone's room, he went straight to the laptop sitting on the workstation, powered it up, and opened a web browser. He signed into his office email account and smiled when he saw the email from Brains, sent less than an hour ago. A loud hiss behind him indicated Featherstone was sampling a beer. "Make that two," he said.

Featherstone muttered something about a "slave dying" but plonked a can of cold Corona on the desk beside him. "What's this about?" he asked. "You seem to be in a mighty hurry to check your email, and you're the one who's always giving me shit about checking my BlackBerry."

"Have a look," Riordan replied, leaning back to allow Featherstone to have a look at the stream of data contained in the email.

Featherstone peered at it for a moment. "Is this one of those things where you've got to squint your eyes and suddenly you see a zebra?"

Riordan laughed. He did a cut and paste on the mass of text, opening a word document, and then slowly began to punctuate the stream, inserting a line break after what he believed to be the data. The first screen showed a transfer request, then an account number, followed by the total amount of money that had been in Dempsey's account.

"Ah-ha," Featherstone said as he watched the mass of data start to take on meaning.

Riordan moved the "confirm transaction" on to the next line, followed by the logout request. The next request was the all-important data. He had hoped that Dempsey would continue to use the iPad that he had left behind. From the stream of data that Brains had intercepted, he obviously done just that. "Yes!" he exclaimed, pounding the desk. The Trojan horse had worked.

He broke the next string down quickly, seeing that there was a new web link, an account number, and three different levels of password access. The first was a ten-digit password, obviously mandated by the bank as having to be a "strong" password. It contained a combination of numbers, upper- and lower-case letters, and some special characters. The second level was a phrase, easy recognizable, as it said, "Billy K is a wanker." Any hacker would have trouble coming up with that as a code phrase. After that was another series of ten digits, similar to the first string.

Riordan arranged the character strings on separate lines of the document so that they would be easy to cut and paste then launched the browser with the new website address. The home

509

page for a Swiss bank appeared, and Riordan went directly to the customer login section. Beside him, Featherstone virtually inhaled a jar of incredibly expensive Planter's peanuts.

At each of the prompts, he cut and pasted the appropriate string from the word document, and presently he was allowed access to the main account page for a Maxwell Charles DeLisle.

Featherstone spluttered. "Is that..."

"The one and only," Riordan replied. "I had Brains help me out with a piece of code that I loaded on to the iPad just before I gave it to DeLisle. I used it to show him the money in Dempsey's account and then left it with him. Since he's a greedy bastard, I figured he'd want to do the transfer right away. Which he did. Then he logged into his own account to make sure the money was safely deposited. And there it is, all 4.8 million of it." He pointed to the list of active transactions, the most recent being the transfer from Dempsey's account. Riordan scanned the list, nodding appreciatively at the size of some of the deposits. There were at least three or four each month, ranging from between two and six hundred thousand pounds.

"And they say crime doesn't pay." Featherstone snorted, looking at the overall balance, which just topped seventeen million pounds.

"Well, it used to pay," Riordan laughed, opening up the electronic transfer page and moving fifteen million out of

Dempsey's account to his own private account in the Cayman Islands.

"Why don't you take it all?" Featherstone asked.

"Nah," Riordan replied. "If I take it all, that would prompt a phone call or two from the bank to DeLisle to check out the reason he was leaving the bank. This is just another transaction, and the fact that the remaining balance is over two million will keep them quiet."

"Nice little nest egg," Featherstone commented. "You've had a most profitable day, my boy, so I think I'll have some more stuff out of the mini-bar." Opening the mini-bar door, he perused the high-priced items. Having come to some internal decision, he slammed the door shut and picked up the wine list from the top of the unit. The hotel had a very fine cellar, as would be expected from such an establishment, so after a few minutes' deliberation he called down to room service, ordered a platter of artisanal cheeses, and two bottles of Châteauneuf-du-Pape, Chateau de Beaucastel 2006.

Riordan smiled. He knew the wine. "I take it I'm paying."

"Oh, that you are, rich boy," Featherstone commented. "That you are. As you always say, 'drink the good wine first!'"

CHAPTER 25

BLESSING

He rose early the next morning, having spent a good part of the night with his head buried under a pillow in an attempt to muffle the roars coming from the next bed. Featherstone was just stirring as he stepped out of the shower.

"I think I've eaten a squirrel," Featherstone commented, sticking out his tongue. "That was a lot of wine." He climbed out of bed, completely naked, and gave his balls a good scratch.

"Jeez, Feather, do you mind? I was looking forward to my breakfast!"

Featherstone sighed and pushed past him toward the shower. "Be just a jiffy," he said, sliding the shower curtain shut.

Ten minutes later they were comfortably seated in the restaurant.

"I'll have a full English breakfast, and he'll have the same," Featherstone said as the waiter returned to their table with a silver carafe of coffee. He filled the two fine bone china cups then proceeded to drink the coffee, holding the cup with his pinky finger extended delicately.

"Fuck me," Riordan snorted. "What's with these Barbie doll cups? Couldn't they produce a mug from somewhere? Two sips and the fucking thing is empty!"

"This is British dining, dear boy," Featherstone replied in a very droll, upper-class accent. "Mugs are vulgar, for the riff-raff, who can't manage to hold their pinkies like this..." He demonstrated again, this time accentuating the motion. Riordan burst out laughing. Heads turned.

"I suppose it's vulgar to laugh as well," he commented.

"Of course, you cannot guffaw in an establishment like this, braying like a donkey. No, you have to titter, like a proper gentleman."

Riordan grinned. "Thanks, Feather, I needed a laugh."

Featherstone refilled their cups again. "Maybe there's a Starbucks nearby," he commented. "We could go there after."

"I need to pick up a change of clothes," Riordan said. "I've been wearing the same stuff for days now."

Never one to let an opportunity pass, Featherstone said, "I did mean to tell you that you were getting a bit ripe. Last night I couldn't tell if it was you or the cheese that was giving off such a pong."

Among the cheeses that they had sampled last evening was an Époisses, an incredibly pungent raw cow's-milk cheese that reportedly had been one of Napoleon's favourites and was often referred to as the "king of all cheeses."

"I'll head out to the high street after breakfast," Riordan said, just as their breakfast arrived, delivered on hot plates covered by silver domes. The waiter whisked the domes off with a flourish, checked if there was anything else they needed, and then disappeared.

"Would you look at that," Featherstone commented, admiring the plate of food. "It's almost too pretty to eat. Almost..."

"I was expecting him to go 'ta da'," Riordan said.

They both tucked in, Riordan amazed at how hungry he was, and they passed the time chatting aimlessly about everything and nothing, planning a squash game for the weekend and arranging to go for dinner. Ever since Featherstone had completely given up his bachelor ways and settled into a comfortable relationship with Jennifer Lee, the four of them tended to socialize on a regular basis. It was idle chit-chat, but the bigger discussion would come later.

Featherstone recognized that DeLisle would have to be dealt with, but he was leaving it to Riordan to come up with a plan. Riordan knew it would have to be done quickly, and he had been running some tactics through in his head. But nothing had landed as yet.

In his head he heard the words, "Look to the shadows. On a dark street, on a dark night, I will come for you."

After breakfast, he took a leisurely stroll down Victoria Street to a small boutique recommended by the concierge and purchased a pair of jeans, a couple of shirts, and some underwear. The prices were staggering. He had agreed to touch base every hour with Feather, who had gone to the apartment where the remainder of the team was keeping an eye on DeLisle's place. If anything out of the ordinary happened, they would call him directly. He also checked Cupples's phone regularly as well. His disappearance would not likely be cause for concern for a couple of days — that was par for the course for clandestine services — but any longer and the alarms would go off.

Taking the clothes back to the hotel, he changed quickly and then went outside to the garden to have a quiet think. The cloud had disappeared, and the sun shone brightly, warming his face. "May the sun shine warm upon your face" was a line from an old Irish blessing, and he basked in the glory of the day. DeLisle's guard would be down now that he thought Riordan had been "disappeared" by Cupples, but he never went anywhere without his bodyguards. The underworld was fraught with peril, and never more so for those at the top.

Riordan could, of course, take a shot from the observation post, but there were too many complicating factors, and if it went wrong and DeLisle felt under attack, it would be difficult to reach him. As each permutation of a plot came up, he twisted it in his mind like a three-dimensional model, examining it from every angle, probing like a surgeon for weaknesses. The longer he sat, the more he was convinced that it would have to be up close and personal. That was fine by him. And to do that, DeLisle would have to be off balance.

People came and went from the garden. The rich scents from the myriad brightly coloured flowers filled the air, and tiny sparrows came hunting for morsels of food. He ordered another cappuccino, only for the fact that they at least came in cups the size of large bowls. Crumbling a few pieces of the biscotti, he tossed them on the ground, where they were frenziedly set upon in a flurry of feathers.

Dipping the remainder in the bowl, he relished each bite. It was like sitting in a tiny oasis, shielded from the city. Closing his eyes, he cleared his mind, listening to the gentle splashing of the water in the fountain and to the flutters and chirps of the tiny birds.

Riordan smiled.

The model he had constructed held firm.

*

Later, Riordan sat in the shadows of the tiny yet tastefully decorated row house. It had certainly felt a woman's touch. The antique leather wingback chair creaked like old flooring when he moved, yet there was something comforting in the sound. Featherstone's ancient leather jacket made the same sound. Occasionally the room would be slightly illuminated as a passing car's headlights cast their beam through the narrow crack in the drapes. He looked at his BlackBerry. It showed twenty minutes past eleven, just beyond the last bell at the White Swan, three doors down.

Not long now.

Loud voices, fuelled by alcohol, carried through the window as groups of punters left the pub. Locals would hang on until their drinks, ordered at one minute to closing, ran dry. He stilled his breathing. The cellphone screen still showed the last text message he had sent from Cupples's device at just after 7:00 p.m... The message simply read, *Am wounded. He got away. He knows...* There were several calls after that, all from DeLisle's cell, but Riordan ignored them.

Following the disturbing text message he delivered, as Riordan had predicted, DeLisle rallied the troops, and within twenty minutes two taxis arrived at DeLisle's building and several hard cases got out, all carrying sports bags. Looking on from the observation point using high-powered binos, Riordan thought the bags looked heavy, to which Featherstone replied sarcastically, "Do you think?" It was probably true, as their contents were not likely to be used for sport. In the apartment, DeLisle held court over the crew, and then the guns came out. According to Featherstone's estimation, they were all well armed with mostly UZIs or shotguns.

They settled in, and Featherstone let them be for a while.

When it looked like they were starting to loosen up, Riordan had Jean-Marc put two rounds through the massive glass windows fronting the Thames River. The panes, sturdy as they appeared, were constantly under stress in the large frames. As a result, putting a round through the centre of the window produced spectacular results. The entire span of both windows fragmented and blasted inward, showering the bodyguards with tiny glittering fragments of glass, deadly miniature razors. They all went diving for cover, coming back up with their weapons at the ready, searching for the source of the attack. Riordan recognized the movements, the lethal ballet, that exposed most of the bodyguards as ex-soldiers. He knew there was nothing that soldiers and ex-soldiers feared more than a sniper.

When one of them popped his head up for a fraction of a second longer than necessary, Jean-Marc sent a round through his skull, spraying a fine red mist across the room. A few minutes later, a Black Kawasaki Ninja motorcycle sped out of the underground parking lot and disappeared into the maze of streets behind DeLisle's building.

"You called that one right," Featherstone commented, holding out his fist. "Mind how ye go!" Riordan matched it, pulled on his jacket, and ran downstairs to catch a taxi.

That same motorcycle was now parked two doors down, outside the White Swan. Dempsey's information, all the way down to the location of the key, had been spot-on. DeLisle had gone to ground in a place where he felt safe.

Riordan's ears, finely attuned now to any sound, heard footsteps approach. There was some fumbling in the doorway as the key slid into the lock. Adrenaline rushed into his veins. Riordan raised the pistol.

End game.

The door burst open. He heard a giggle, and two bodies, tightly entwined, entered the room. There was a lot of groping going on in the entranceway. The door slammed shut, propelled by a heel. Something fell on the floor.

"Shit," Riordan cursed under his breath.

"Fuck," DeLisle exclaimed. "You're wrecking the place." Another giggle.

The lights flicked on.

DeLisle stood with his arms around a dark-haired woman, nuzzling her neck. She wore a light summer dress, and one strap was completely off her shoulder, one breast exposed. A pert nipple was held firmly between DeLisle's thumb and index finger. She saw Riordan first and screamed.

DeLisle looked up, astonishment on his face, as he faced his nemesis.

Riordan raised the pistol, but DeLisle used the woman as a shield. In a flash, a switchblade clicked open, and DeLisle had the blade at her throat.

"Shut the fuck up," he growled, and the woman whimpered, both hands struggling against the arm blocking her throat. The knife pricked her neck, sending tiny globules of blood streaming down her pale skin. Her eyes widened in fright.

"Please?" she whispered.

"Put the gun down," DeLisle hissed, "or I'll cut the bitch's throat."

Tears streamed down the woman's face, smearing her mascara. Riordan knew there were always innocent bystanders getting hurt or maimed or worse during times of conflict. But not tonight. Shaking his head, he eased back the trigger so that DeLisle could see the threat was diminished. Riordan lowered the pistol as DeLisle backed up to the door, dragging the woman. One side of her dress was stained with droplets of blood.

DeLisle moved the knife away for a moment to open the lock. As he did so, his grip on the woman's throat eased, and she twisted her hand to get better leverage on his elbow. Riordan sighed, raised the pistol, and blew off the top of her head. Blood and brains splattered DeLisle as he flicked off the light switch, plunging the house into darkness. Pushing the lifeless body aside, he slammed the door shut and was gone.

Riordan rushed over, careful in the darkness so as not to trip, and dragged the woman's corpse out of the way. She had fallen backward against the door. The tiled entranceway was now slick with her blood, so he flipped on the light and stepped over her. As he did so, he saw the spider tattoo clearly. It was a black widow spider. That he knew from the red hourglass shape in the centre of the body. In the form of a female, their bite was most dangerous to humans due to the unnaturally large venom glands.

Pulling open the door, he slipped the pistol inside his jacket and stepped out onto the street. The sound of running footsteps echoed in the distance, and he turned toward the river and raced after DeLisle. If he got away ... well, that would be unthinkable. Riordan had spent the afternoon poring over pictures of the area, familiarizing himself with the streets using Google Earth and Street View. DeLisle was headed for the path that ran along the Thames.

There were two choices open to him at that point. Left would take him away from populated areas, into the undergrowth at the side of the river. Right would take him to the stairs leading to the road bridge that spanned the river.

Riordan headed in the direction of the footsteps. As he approached the Thames, he saw that DeLisle had run through a puddle, which fortunately for him showed the glistening tread in the direction his quarry had run. The vast expanse under the bridge was in complete darkness, the lights along that part of the path having been smashed and not repaired. Riordan slowed as he approached the bridge, relieved to see that the footsteps led away from the stairs leading up to the main road. If DeLisle had made it up there and managed to stop a car ... Riordan shuddered at the thought. However, he realized that DeLisle was being prudent. From his military training, he knew that heading up the stairs would have silhouetted him against the lights of the bridge, providing an easy target for Riordan.

Riordan approached the pool of darkness slowly. The footfalls had gone quiet, and beyond the bridge he noticed a dense patch of hedgerow shimmer. Maybe it was the wind, or maybe DeLisle had just plunged recklessly through the bushes. He stepped into the stygian darkness, squinting into the dark recesses where rusting iron trestles embedded themselves in ancient, crumbling concrete. The scent of urine hung in the air.

DeLisle could be hiding anywhere.

And he had a knife.

Riordan knew well how to use a knife, but it was not one of the forms of combat he relished. When you came up against someone who knew how to use a knife, you always got cut. It was never a matter of if you got cut, just where you got cut. Featherstone and team practiced regularly with dummy knives, faking and feinting and trying hard to gain the upper edge in the adrenaline-fuelled hand-to-hand combat. Their instructor, a martial arts expert who specialized in bladed weapons, showed them how to stand correctly and which parts of the body could withstand a knife slash without completely disabling the combatant. The outer forearm was the block. It could withstand a slashing cut. Riordan had the scars to prove it.

The inner forearm guided all the major veins and arteries to the hand, so any form of cut there would likely end in a fatality. He moved slowly along the path, the pistol tracking across each beam. A truck rumbled overhead, saturating the expanse with sound as the heavy tires rolled across metal expansion plates in the road. The hedgerow at the other side of the bridge rustled once more, momentarily distracting him. His aim wavered. A few tiny flakes of rust from the beams overhead landed on his cheek. Almost without thinking, a completely reflex action, he dived to one side but was too late to escape the trap completely. DeLisle had managed to climb out along one of the spans, waiting to pounce. If he had not moved, DeLisle would have crushed him completely. Pain blossomed in his chest as the broken rib grated under the skin. He gasped but knew he had to move.

Move or die.

Rolling back to his feet, Riordan spun as DeLisle landed a massive blow to his right arm, sending the pistol skittering off into the darkness. His arm went numb. Riordan scrambled away as DeLisle pressed his attack, the knife flashing in the faint light.

"I'm going to gut you, you cunt," hissed DeLisle, slashing through the air with the blade. He was wary enough not to get too close to allow Riordan to grasp his arm. They circled one another, Riordan flexing his right arm, desperately trying to shake some feeling into his muscles. His fingers tingled.

"I just want you to know I stole all of your money," Riordan said, grinning, goading DeLisle. Angry people made mistakes.

"Cunt," DeLisle hissed, jabbing forward with the knife.

Mindful of the lessons from the instructor, he kept his body side-on to DeLisle, holding one arm as a block. With the other, he slipped his hand into the back of his jeans and grasped the Benchmade knife. Thankful that the blade was gravity-opening — it was the primary reason he had purchased the weapon — he depressed the button and felt the satisfying click as the blade swung down and locked into place. He gritted his teeth. Each movement sent waves of pain rolling down his side. Taking a full breath hurt like hell.

DeLisle, thinking that Riordan's arm was still numb and that he had the advantage, rushed straight at him, using the concept of overwhelming force to overpower your opponent. It was a derivation of the Israeli army's Krav Maga fighting style. Riordan pretended to be caught off-guard, but in that moment, the confrontation slipped into fine focus, every second feeling like three. DeLisle's knife came slashing upward. Riordan could see the frenzied spittle on DeLisle's lips, his teeth bared in anticipation of victory.

Riordan used the man's momentum to parry the blow, pushing DeLisle's knife arm harmlessly across his chest. After that it was simple mechanics. DeLisle's body followed the turning motion, exposing his left side completely. Riordan thrust his knife into DeLisle's side, just under his ribcage, twisting upward, then removed the blade and stabbed again, repeating the motion several times in quick succession. DeLisle gasped at each thrust, as if unable to comprehend what had just happened. He staggered forward, mortally wounded. Riordan tossed the bloody knife into the river as dark streams of blood pulsed through the fingers of the hand that DeLisle pressed to his side.

Riordan calmly walked back and retrieved his pistol. Then, stepping forward, he fired two shots in rapid succession. DeLisle's body pitched backward and tumbled over the embankment, falling ten feet into the river, the splash easily drowned out by traffic overhead. Riordan watched the swirling current drag the body down into the murky waters then hurled the pistol as far as he could into the middle of the river.

CHAPTER 26

ROSHEEN

One year later…

It was one of those rare summer days in Vancouver where the temperature was in the high twenties, not a cloud in the sky, and English Bay was filled to overflowing with tourists and locals, relaxing and enjoying the day. Out on the bay, a virtual flotilla of summer craft hurtled across the waves, their sails bulging to capacity, filled by the stiff offshore breezes. Vancouver Island shimmered in the distance. Passing freighters hooted loudly as they passed. The tide was out, exposing a large swath of sandy beach where children scampered about with tiny buckets and spades, shrieking and yelling. Seagulls preyed upon any unwary beachgoer who took their eyes off any exposed morsel of food for even a second.

Riordan sat on the grass, leaning back against one of the many trees that lined the beach. Roller-bladers and cyclists whizzed by on the path behind him. Beside him sat a red cooler full of juice boxes and sandwiches for the boys, and a couple of Bacardi Breezers for dad, to keep his thirst quenched in the hot sun. Nancy had the early shift at the ER but had promised to join them when her rotation finished. Michael and David were absolutely fearless about the water and would go tearing off into the sea, splashing each other and anyone near them with reckless abandon. Protesting, as he witnessed, only served to encourage them further.

They were both lathered head to toe in sunscreen — Nancy was very particular about that — and Riordan too. His fair Irish pallor would turn to a crispy red in the blink of an eye, so he kept himself well covered. He wore his new pair of Oakley wraparound shades, a gift from Nancy, and a white canvas fedora to keep the sun off his face. Periodically, he would go down to the water's edge and paddle around with the boys, a means of keeping cool in the heat.

Someone shouted "Rosheen." Normally he wouldn't have paid any attention — parents were always shouting out kids' names when the little darlings strayed too far — but Rosheen was a very typical Irish girl's name, and his subconscious tuned in on that fact. As he turned slightly, a tiny girl about one year old, with the red hair and freckles of an Irish Tourist Board poster, came racing across the grass in his general direction, chuckling like mad. In one hand was the typical half-melted ice-cream cone and in the other a bag of potato chips. She wore a simple little sundress with some ornate Celtic script in the front. Her feet were bare.

The little girl grinned mischievously, and his heart just melted. She turned to look at her pursuer, and in that fraction of a

527

second her toe caught a tuft of grass. She went flying, the cold ice cream landing on his chest. He caught her before she did any major damage and planted her firmly on the ground. Behind her, he saw the boys come racing out of the water.

"You little minx," came the exasperated voice of a parent who was at her wit's end. The little girl's face dropped as her mother caught up to her. Then her lip dropped as she knew what was coming. Riordan stared up into the sun, seeing only the outline of the little girl's mother.

"She's okay," he said, and the woman knelt down to examine the child.

"I'm really sorry about your shirt," the woman said, and he heard the accent. Pulling off his sunglasses, he looked at the woman's profile as she tried to wipe some of the ice cream from the little girl's face.

It was Elva.

"She's a beautiful child," he offered, just as the boys arrived to check out the scene. They didn't like anyone getting too much attention from their dad.

"Who is she?" asked Michael.

"Her name's Rosheen," he replied.

"That's a funny name," David said.

"And that's her mummy. Her name is Elva." He saw the muscles on her back tense, and he watched her hands carefully.

528

She wore tight denim shorts, so there was no concealed weapon anywhere in sight.

She turned, and their eyes met.

Recognition dawned.

"I'm not looking for trouble," she said quietly.

"Me neither."

She seemed to relax, but he was sure she was remembering the shotgun barrel against the side of her head. "Are these your boys?"

Riordan nodded. "These are the best of me. That's why I had to do what I did."

"I hear DeLisle got whacked," she offered.

He nodded and took a sip of his cooler. "I seem to recall hearing the same."

"One bullet in each eye."

"Seems like history caught up with him."

She was quiet for a moment, processing those bits of information. After a moment, she sat back, the little girl cuddled in her arms. She kissed the mass of curls.

"Would you like a juice box?" Riordan asked the little girl, and she nodded, now going all shy. A reddish curl was now entwined around her finger. "Okay, boys, break out the juice boxes."

They did as requested, pulled out a bottle of Daddy's juice as well, and offered it to Elva. She smiled, her face lighting up, the hard edge he remembered gone in a heartbeat. She had put on a few pounds from the last time he had seen her, yet that had only served to eliminate that gaunt look that people got when they were on the run. She wore a nice-sized diamond on her finger, and her purse looked like a real Louis Vuitton. He suspected Dempsey had put some of the money he stole from DeLisle into another account. He took a sip from his bottle then held it toward Elva.

"To better days," he said, and she touched the neck of his bottle in a toast.

"To the Raven..."

About the Author

For more about Roy French please visit his website <u>Roy French</u> or follow Roy French Author on <u>Facebook</u> or <u>Instagram</u>.

Roy French is a screenplay writer and novelist, well known for writing thrillers that are best described as "a wild ride".

His first published novel A SENSE OF HONOR, now RAVEN'S HONOR, was the 1992 Arthur Ellis Award Runner up for Best First Novel.

His first independently produced film TWISTED PIECES is being released in 2020. Fans of Roy French will be excited to know that the film is based on his novel RAVEN'S BLOOD.

An Irish lad, Roy has lived in Canada for 30 years and visits "home" often.

Born in Ballymena, Northern Ireland, Roy attended high school (notably with the famous actor Liam Neeson!) at Ballymena Technical College.

An accomplished musician, Roy played lead guitar in a rock band (Scrudriver) and never misses a chance to pick up and play whenever he can.

Made in the USA
Middletown, DE
09 July 2020